RISE OF THE RAVENISHA

P. GRACE LAWSON

P. GRACE LAWSON
pgracelawson@gmail.com

Printed in the United States of America
First Printing 2021
First Edition 2021

10 9 8 7 6 5 4 3 2 1

In memory of Margaret Nell Cass Lawson, and her mother, my grandmother, Ceola Pointer Cass. The original Ravenisha.

I don't think that monsters are all bad or evil, actually. I think what they have is a story.

—Saffron A. Kent, Gods and Monsters

You can't do wrong and get by.

—Lethal A. Ellis

Foreword

I never thought I would write a novel at age 55. I have watched horror movies, read scary books, and have had an overactive imagination ever since I can remember. I'm sure I must have been a weird, creepy child to people in the rural community where I grew up in Talladega, Alabama. I remember asking the funeral director about the embalming process at my father's funeral. He looked at my eleven-year-old bespectacled face and took a breath—unsure what to say. He then carefully explained the procedure and probably prayed he wasn't talking to a future serial killer. I've known that I wanted to be a forensic pathologist from a young age. I was that child who stopped to examine roadkill during my daily walk to and from school to see how the carcass had changed since the day before. I read "The Medicolegal Investigation of Death" and other forensic pathology books when I was in high school. I was a weird Black girl before the phrase was coined.

UC Berkeley, however, put an end to my dream. I discovered I didn't like *any* of the sciences (biology, chemistry, physics) and hated math even more. Yet, it was here that I had my first hint that maybe I should be a writer. I took a medical anthropology course during my senior year. I wasn't thrilled with the assignment: to write a story of how AIDS had changed the world. I decided my story would have no happy ending. Instead, I wrote how scientists kidnapped homeless people and deliberately injected them with an AIDS-laden virus, which caused the lab subjects to mutate into hideous creatures. Imagine my surprise when I got the paper back and an A was written on the front, along with a note saying I should consider writing movie scripts, books, etc. Of course, I did nothing because I was still hell-bent on entering the forensics field in some capacity. Years passed and I worked a series of drab jobs, barely making enough to pay for my horse riding lessons.

I have always been a horse crazy girl. One of my earliest memories of my paternal grandfather is of him astride his white horse, Sandy. My maternal grandfather bought me a Shetland pony. Unfortunately, my father gave him to a family with ten children because he repeatedly bucked me off. I began riding as an adult, and was hooked. I started with hunter/jumper lessons, and eventually settled into dressage. I would constantly tell my instructor I should write a book about an African American detective who rode dressage. Of course, I did nothing.

Enter 2019—the year my family's reunion was held in the Poconos. I had a bad fall. Seriously, I have never been so hurt in my life. As I lay in bed at the hotel, writhing and moaning in pain, I began formulating a story in my head. *What if there were these warrior women? What if they shapeshifted into werepanthers and ate humans?* And, so, the genesis for Rise of the Ravenisha was born. I returned to California and wrote the novel in three months. Of course, it was a hot mess.

Chapter 1

Present-day Southern United States, Ravenswood, Alabama

Honeycutt Highway (formerly Eutaw Crossroads)

To outsiders, the three women picking poke salat, a southern delicacy that can be fatal if not prepared correctly, and wild onions along the side of the country road looked like relics from bygone days. The women, who were now always cold due to their loss of body fat, wore long cotton dresses. Large straw hats protected their heads from the unrelenting Alabama sun that was just rising on the horizon, painting the sky a beautiful smorgasbord of mauves, oranges, corals, and yellows. Dew sprinkled the grass and foliage and the air smelled of the unlikely mixture of pine cones and honeysuckles. Now and then, a woodpecker tapping on bark or the call of a wren or sparrow broke the peaceful silence. A motor growled in the distance, polluting the air with its sound. The women looked up, did a collective eye roll and resumed the task at hand.

"What does he want now?" one woman mumbled under her breath, stabbing her hoe into the ground with extra vigor.

They had to pay attention to what they were doing, for poke salat looked like any other weed. Mature poke salat weeds were distinctive.

The stalks were tall and purple with likewise violet berries. This was when the plant was at its most toxic. Therefore, the women focused on harvesting the immature tender shoots, whose stalks were green and berries white. They used their hoes to avoid the root, which was poisonous.

All three Black women were striking. Their skin tones ranged from honey to chocolate to ebony. Their features were as diverse as their skin color—a sharp blend of Caucasian, African and Asian elements. All had beautiful high cheekbones, though some appeared razor-sharp because of the drastic weight loss. Their movements were sinewy, cat-like, and at odds with the clunky, baggy clothes they were wearing. While they looked like old women, there was something about them that belied their age.

Ceola Lulabelle Eudora Furie wasn't the tallest of the group. In fact, she was rather petite, but still, she clearly was the group's leader. While she wasn't as fierce-looking as the one called Matilda, a quiet menace radiated off of her, and humans instinctively avoided her before they even got the full blast of her stormy green eyes.

Matilda "Tildy" Arvelle Arceneaux, was an intimidating presence. Even though she had a buzz cut, there was no mistaking her gender. Her high cheekbones and full, sensual lips were all female, while her alert green eyes constantly surveilled her surroundings.

The third woman, Elizabeth "Lizzie" Sarah Gadsden, was distinguishable from the others by her mane of long, dreadlocked hair. Her kind, and clear green eyes often lulled people into trusting her with their deepest secrets and her Ph.D. in psychology had come in handy on many occasions over the years.

A black SUV pulled to a halt on the road's shoulder, kicking up gusts of red dust that blew everywhere. The back door opened, and a tall, late-middle-aged, cadaverously thin man stepped out. The women's captor, torturer, rapist, and arch nemesis had arrived.

~ ~ ~

To say the Ravenisha regretted the day they allowed their capture would be an understatement. They had known they were in trouble as soon as the slavers packed them on the slave ship and hunger began to eat away at their insides with an intensity they couldn't recall having ever experienced. To exacerbate the torture, there was food all around them. The steady beatings of healthy hearts inundated their souls and thoughts day in and day out. They could hear the blood coursing through veins in their delirium. It would have been effortless to break the manacles that bound them and feed to the point of bursting. Instead, they had to appease themselves with the slop the slave catchers haphazardly fed them.

When they finally docked and were on the auction block, it shocked them that they were all bought together. Apparently, Idia wasn't a completely cold-hearted bitch and had bribed the slave catchers handsomely to ensure the friends' joint sale. Thankfully, the slave catchers honored their part of the bargain because they could have taken the money and sold them separately and Idia would have been none the wiser. That one minor act of kindness was the only thing that kept them going nearly four hundred years later.

The plantation's owner and their first master in 1650, Montrose Norland Honeycutt, had been a cruel taskmaster. The women spent those miserable years acclimating to being slaves and learning English. After the mysterious disappearance of his father, Balfour Wilkie Honeycutt inherited the plantation during the heyday when cotton was king and worked the women mercilessly. Overseers noticed the women were far outpacing the others and brought it to Balfour's attention. Balfour, who was more interested in being a scientist than a plantation owner, observed the women and made notes in a diary. The War of Northern Aggression came, and the women experienced four brief years of happiness at the plantation. They surreptitiously fed without arousing suspicion as people disappeared all the time throughout those chaotic years. They faced a hard decision at the end of the war: should they stay or should they go?

It had been shockingly easy to remain on the plantation all those years. They had kept low profiles, and only a select number of humans knew about them. They took care of the ones they felt would be problematic. The same dilemma plagued them every time they tried to discuss leaving. How would Idia find them if they moved? The plan had been for them to establish a base in the new land and build a new Ravenisha army. Idia would unite with them when she felt the moment was right—after she had conquered the African continent. Surely, Black people would find freedom at some point in history and the Ravenisha would be ready. So, they stayed on as sharecroppers after the war, although they might as well have still been slaves. Rufus's father, Zebulon Leverette Honeycutt was born and like his father before him, he was more interested in science than running a modern plantation. He was the first Honeycutt to get his doctorate in biology since molecular biology wasn't a field then. He pored over the diaries left by Montrose and Balfour and set about learning everything he could about the women who never seemed to age and possessed superhuman strength.

Rufus was an only child for many years. His younger brother, Beauregard, was born when his parents were middle-aged and thought they couldn't have more children. Whereas the other men had dabbled in science as a hobby, Zebulon quickly recognized that his son was a scientific genius and had what was, at the time, a cutting-edge lab built for them both. Unfortunately, Zebulon learned about the women's abilities firsthand, up close and personal, and this was the start of their modern imprisonment.

Rufus had been a young adult, home from college for Christmas break when it happened. He had surprised everyone by arriving early. Exiting his cherry red roadster, he had skipped up the antebellum mansion's steps, flung open the door, and entered a bustle of activity. The three fierce-looking women he remembered his father studying were cooking and cleaning and, most curiously of all, they weren't under armed guard. By then, he and his father knew their secret, having witnessed them changing and feeding several times over the years. Why were they allowed to be around his mother with no armed guards present? Something wasn't right. He kept a wary eye on them as he called his parents' names. His mother, Isabelle, answered from the kitchen where she had been supervising Ceola, who was cooking the Christmas meal. Normally, he would have let his gaze linger on Ceola. He found her honey-red color, curvy body, emerald green eyes, and curly hair worn in two long braids intoxicating. Upon seeing his mother, he gave her an enormous hug, sweeping her into his arms and out of the house. Once outside, he put her in the roadster and drove off. He asked his mother where his father was. She replied he was at the lab and asked what on Earth was wrong with him?

They drove to the lab and asked for Dr. Honeycutt. He wasn't in the building or on the grounds. They returned to the house, along with some guards. This time, the women were sitting on the porch with leers on their faces, and Rufus could see murder in their eyes. Before he could stop her, Rufus's mother jumped out of the car and ran into the house.

"Zeb! Zeb!" Rufus's mother called, running up the stairs to their bedroom.

"If his body is up there, so help me God," Rufus snarled.

The women rolled their eyes, and the darkest and tallest one—the others called her Tildy—smiled her wicked, intimidating smile. Her doe-like green eyes pierced into him as her full, sensual lips curled. "Don't worry. It's not."

His mother's screams pierced the air.

"Detain them!" he ordered the guards, running upstairs. "Mother, what is it?" Rufus found his mother in the bathroom, throwing up in the toilet.

"Those bitches," she sobbed. "Look what they left of him."

Rufus turned to where his mother pointed, and on the vanity were a blue eyeball and a severed penis. Garnet-red blood had dripped down the vanity's edges and congealed on the floor in a macabre Rorschach pattern. Taking a deep breath and grabbing some tissue, Rufus picked up the organs, threw them into the toilet, and pulled the lever.

"Why did you do that?" his mother screamed in hysterics.

"Don't worry, Mother," Rufus replied in a voice laced with ice and iron. "Trust me, I know what I'm doing. I'll make them pay, and they will wish they had never been born."

"Promise me," Isabelle simpered, staring up into Rufus's glacial blue eyes.

"I swear on Papa's soul."

Rufus, who would earn his doctorate in molecular biology, was true to his word. Lizzie—the calmest of the women—protested that even though Zebulon had raped her in that very room hours earlier, she and the others hadn't killed him. Deaf to her entreaties, Rufus had the women shackled and beaten almost to death. Isabelle, always fragile, never recovered from the shock of her husband's death and died a year later, leaving Rufus and

Beauregard orphans. Very rich orphans, but orphans nevertheless. Thankfully, Beau was visiting a friend that fateful day and missed the horrific event. Rufus knew he couldn't take care of his much younger brother, so he had the eight-year-old shipped off to various military boarding schools until he graduated and went on to attend a military college.

The women's lives changed very little. Rufus purchased the property that would later become the town of Ravenswood and the site for the Ravenisha's current home, Ravenswood Farm. Seemingly, there were no locked gates, and the women were free to move about, but Rufus had made the consequences of trying to escape very clear. Rather than keeping their powers secret, Rufus gambled and informed local law enforcement and the army, assuring them he had the women securely contained and that he could harvest their remarkable abilities to benefit the American government. So, Rufus finished all of his schooling and continued the experiments, now sanctioned by those in power. He constantly goaded the women about their situation. Let them try to escape. He promised to hunt and shoot them down like the animals they were. He even seemed to have a "special" relationship with Ceola. Somewhere along the line, the women grew complacent, so when Rufus brutally seized their beloved daughters, they didn't see it coming.

"What about the prophecy?" they cried.

How could a new breed of Ravenisha arise in an unknown world if their daughters were taken from them? The women didn't understand. They had followed La Panthère Noire's and Idia's orders. Would they ever be free?

As the women shrank in on themselves and became ghosts of their former spirits, Rufus celebrated gleefully. One afternoon, on the 30th anniversary of his mother's death, he dressed in his finest suit and left work as dusk fell in the beautifully maintained roadster he'd driven home those tragic years ago. Rufus drove to the once segregated cemetery where rich white families such as his buried their dead until the mid-1980s in a peaceful garden-like setting. Rufus entered through the grand columned gates and drove slowly under the arches. He shook his head as he passed the huge fenced marble mausoleum that had caused so much heartache and anger amongst the genteel southern aristocracy. They just don't get it, *he thought. Despite the cemetery being desegregated in the 1970s, people had somehow kept the Blacks out until the mid-1980's when a prominent Black family had forced the city to allow the burial of the family's patriarch in that gaudy mausoleum. Granted, the mausoleum was probably the most expensive monument in the cemetery, but that wasn't the point. White folks just didn't want those people in their cemetery.*

Rufus reached the Honeycutt family plot. He pulled to the side, got out and removed his mother's favorite liquor, a fine cognac from the brown bag on the passenger seat. He walked over to her grave and gazed at her headstone. Isabelle Fredericka Honeycutt, Loving Wife and Mother. Gone too soon. Rufus murmured a requiescat for his mother.

"I made them pay, Mother, just like I promised I would. May you rest in peace." Rufus poured an appreciable amount from the bottle onto the grave and took a sip. "You hated drinking alone." He tilted the bottle to the headstone. "To revenge. Although, I'm not sure how successful the revenge was, considering you have a mixed-race granddaughter, Cleodora," he muttered, leaving.

Chapter 2

Rufus stepped from the SUV, well aware of how striking he looked. His immaculately coiffed pale blond locks glowed white as a cotton ball in the morning sun. Piercing Husky ice-blue eyes coldly took in the tableau before him. He had a sensual mouth, or so he had been told, with lips neither plump nor thin. He hadn't always been gaunt like he was now, which was why it was imperative that he somehow appropriated the women's powers. Rufus remembered the day he had found his grandfathers' diaries. He'd read with disbelief as the old men described the women's mystical and wondrous abilities, recounting their attempts to harvest the magic for themselves. Obviously, they had failed to gain those powers or they wouldn't be dead. Rufus read how the women wouldn't cooperate even back then, sabotaging his ancestors' experiments. They polluted blood samples, burned down labs, and destroyed formulas. Rufus vowed to succeed where the old men had failed. If benevolence wouldn't work, and it looked like it hadn't worked one iota, then he would do whatever he had to do and to whomever he had to do it to. He wasn't ready to die. He had more money to make, more things to discover, more life to live, period. With that thought, Rufus steeled himself as he walked toward the women for what was about to be a taxing and acrimonious encounter. It always was.

Rufus surveyed his surrounding land—the tree-covered rolling hills shrouded in mist, the mountains in the distance, and Alabama's famous red dirt. He mulled that if men weren't searching for money and power, then it was for the elusive fountain of youth—a way to live forever. The clock was ticking for Rufus. He recognized he couldn't continue to survive by just harvesting the women's platelets: he had to discover their secret to immortality or he would be dead soon. *Damn them,* Rufus thought, as a multitude of emotions flitted across his eyes. His mouth turned down at the thought of the coming confrontation, but he forged on. The women's hatred and disdain for him was apparent in the way they curled their lips, raking their eyes up and down his body like he was trash and they couldn't wait to be out of his presence. They would probably find a way to rid themselves of the lethal collars he had placed on them and kill him one day. He'd felt the hold he had on them gradually slipping away through the years. He'd had a complicated relationship with the women, fraught with heated passions, battles, and threats. His immediate survival was at stake, though, and if he needed to whip, starve, tase, or otherwise coerce them, then so be it. Rufus hadn't gotten where he was in the world by being soft-hearted.

If only he'd never accepted Idia's proposal and gotten involved in creating the serum. Then, he never would have gotten sick. He could have freed these women. He could have tried to pursue Ceola and perhaps she'd even be able to accept his love. But love wasn't going to get him his cure. He was stuck in this battle now.

Although they were technically prisoners, they had every creature comfort. He even allowed them to attend the local historically Black universities after they proved they wouldn't try to run away or pull another stunt as they had with his father. Granted, he had mistakenly thought educating them would benefit him. They were obviously smart, and he had hoped to use them as lab assistants. However, their defiant attitudes, supreme intelligence, and his ego had quickly squashed that notion. *Why won't they just cooperate with me?* he fumed. Hell, he even had that expensive equestrian center built to please Theodora, because it would please her nana, Ceola. Those women lived better than most white people in the area—hell, even the state—except for him. And had that buttered those haughty bitches up any and stopped them from looking down on him? Of course not. Well, he was done placating them. If they didn't voluntarily give him what he wanted, he'd take it, just like he had taken their daughters. He had an ace up his sleeve today, and he was sure the women would finally capitulate.

Chapter 3

Ceola watched as a diminutive woman came around from the other side of the SUV. A laminated identification card affixed to a lanyard around her neck identified her as Dr. Mariposa Vasquez, a scientist employed by Honeycutt Laboratories, Ravenswood, Alabama. There was something familiar about her, but Ceola couldn't put her finger on it. The woman held firmly onto a coltish young tween, who was taller than her by a good four inches. The scientist's veins stood out in her muscled arms, showing how much force she was really using to contain the writhing tween. The air filled with a zephyr of aromas as dueling scents wafted over the area. Among the sweet pungent aroma of ripe guava mingled in with the Ravenisha's and the pine-scented air, the musky odor of panther was undeniable.

Dr. Mariposa Vasquez appeared to be in her twenties because of her mohawk, tattoos, piercings, jeans, and Doc Martens, but on closer inspection, was older than first presumed. There was a world-weariness in her bright jade eyes, which stood out in sharp contrast to her rich, copper skin and Aztecan features. Her turquoise and jade jewelry looked to be old and authentic.

The tween's eyes roamed everywhere, greedily taking everything in. Her nostrils flared as she breathed in the myriad musks enveloping her. It was as though she had never been outside before. She was desperately trying to break free of the scientist, but Dr. Vasquez held firm. She was preternaturally still as she watched the emotions flit across Rufus and the women's faces. Ceola couldn't help noticing the all-too-familiar collar circling the tween's neck.

For a moment, everyone stood still, scenting each other. Ceola's inner alarm sounded on high alert as she and the other Ravenisha caught a whiff of La Panthère Noire and some other unidentifiable scent on the still, humid Alabama air. She thought this woman wasn't what she seemed, but she appeared to be somewhat kindred, not a threat. Ceola's brows knitted in confusion. When she inhaled the woman's scent, her nasal passages detected no whiff of La Panthère Noire on her. She had smelled her pleasant overripe fruit-like scent before, but for the life of her, Ceola couldn't remember where. Whatever the case, she would have to monitor the woman, though, because there was something odd about her. Something otherworldly. That only left the young one. Yes, the familiar pheromones were emanating from her, but before she could investigate further or even fully examine the girl, her body fell to the ground, racked with pain. Ceola had been so intent on studying the newcomers, she hadn't even noticed Rufus advancing on her and the other Ravenisha.

Suddenly, Elizabeth and Matilda also doubled over in pain and dropped to the ground, spasming. *Damn that man*, seethed Ceola. Why was he torturing them before they'd even done anything to him? Damn him to Hell! That explained why he had enfeebled them. He knew they couldn't fight or change in their current weakened state and the strangers would distract them. *The snake*, she raged inwardly.

"Y'all, I can't bear this pain much longer," Lizzie gasped in a voice so low and shaky they barely heard her even with their heightened hearing.

"Be strong, Lizzie," Matilda croaked. "Don't let him break you."

"I can't, Tildy. Our bodies have gone too long without the change...without fresh meat. We're aging faster and faster and—"

Ceola screamed. The caterwaul that tore from her throat gave way to a deep growl, as her voice got lower and seemed to be coming from a place deep down inside her. She and the other women clutched their stomachs and rolled around in pain. As they mewled and writhed about on the ground, their hands morphed into clenched claws, hair grew over their bodies, and their eyes became cat-like. As their canines grew, spasms made them bite their tongues and blood poured from their mouths. Just as quickly as the pain came, though, it ended, and the women lay impotently on the ground, soaked in sweat, blood, and tears. Their features reverted to normal, except their worn faces seemed to show even more wrinkles. Ceola slowly got up and faced Rufus, lips in a thin line, nostrils flaring as she struggled for breath. Rage overtook the pain.

"Rufus, you low-down sonofabitch, why can't you just greet people like a normal person? Done having fun with us?" Ceola began advancing toward Rufus.

"Ceola," Rufus sighed, "you know I abhor harsh language. It's so uncivilized and uncouth coming from such beautiful women's mouths. Besides, is that any way to talk when a minor is present? I see I'll have to teach you a lesson, as usual." Rufus used the remote in his hand to shock Ceola again. She fell to the ground, nothing but the whites of her eyes showing as blood-flecked spittle ran from her mouth. Her body shook and trembled and then went still, the heaving of her chest the only indication she was still alive.

Rufus turned to the horrified girl and sneered. "Look at her. There's your nana, gal. The magnificent warrior. Go say hello." Rufus shoved the girl forward. Ceola's eyes fluttered open, and she appeared dazed as she tried to sit up.

The tween rushed over to Ceola crying, "Miss Ceola, are you all right?" but not before glaring at Rufus. Something passed between them when the girl touched Ceola, and in the blink of an eye, she flicked out her tongue and licked the blood from Ceola's mouth.

Ceola's vision gradually sharpened and focused. "Cleo?" Ceola moaned, but no, this girl had piercing light blue eyes and white-blond frizzy curly hair—not to mention her being lighter. Otherwise, she could have been a doppelgänger of her daughter, Cleo, or even her granddaughter, Theodora. Ceola's eyes widened as understanding slowly dawned.

"You twisted, sick sonofabitch," she snarled at Rufus while she slowly rose to her feet. "You imbecile. You could cause all kinds of mutations."

Rufus merely looked through Ceola and the others, only the coldness emanating from his eyes betraying his genuine feelings. "I can't be too stupid. I'm not the one in bondage on what is basically a large preserve, now am I? You *Negresses* have been on this property since after The War of Northern Aggression and yet you've never escaped."

The women looked at each other, faces scrunched in confusion at the mention of the word Negresses.

"I'm not the one experiencing a hunger so deep, it's gnawing at me from the inside out, am I? I'm not the one standing here picking weeds to eat from the side of the road like old nigger women used to do, am I?" He shocked Ceola again. This time, she crumpled to the ground and didn't move, her dress falling in limp folds around her.

Having had enough, Matilda stood up to her full six feet two inches and got in Rufus's face. To his credit, he didn't back up.

"Cut the bullshit, Rufus. I know you didn't just call us niggers. You know damn well we're not stupid. You also know we could leave if we wanted. But we made a promise centuries ago, and unlike some people, we keep our word."

By now, Tildy's neck was rolling and her spit flecked Rufus's face. "I'm tired of your bullshit. So stop." She stabbed him in the chest with her finger, her nose mere inches from his nose.

Rufus shook his head and sneered right back. He flourished his remote in Tildy's face and she slapped his hand away.

"Fool, we could have gotten these collars off and you'd be none the wiser a long time ago," Tildy snarled, rolling her eyes, just before Rufus shocked them all again. Ceola didn't even move a muscle, still stunned from the last jolt.

"No, I don't think so, or you would have removed them," Rufus responded slowly, a smile spreading across his face. "You still haven't figured out how to remove the collars without activating them to kill you, and you still haven't a clue where your daughters are located."

After the women recovered from the latest shock, they glared at Rufus, canines bared, the hatred emanating off of them so thick, the air seemed heavier and harder to breathe. The tween and Dr. Vasquez stood uneasily, frozen, with their backs to the SUV.

Ceola finally stirred and stood up. She seemed none the worse for the wear, except for wet sweat areas on her dress and spots of blood speckling it. She was, however, pissed. A fearsome vibe radiated from her thin body, and she seemed on the verge of exploding. Massive canines filled her mouth, and her eyes had contracted down to slits.

"You're getting on my last, last nerve, Rufus Beckett Theodis Honeycutt," Ceola rasped in a bass alien voice. "Shock us again and see what happens. You should be afraid, Rufus, very afraid. Do you really want to release the she-beasts in us, and I mean *all* of us? We may have the energy to change. We may not, but do you really want to find out? I dare you, you little punk-assed bitch. You're only alive now because you have our daughters. And these collars may or may not kill us in our beast forms." Ceola growled sinisterly and held Rufus's gaze until he looked away first. Wrath roiled off of her in waves. She wanted to eat Rufus so badly.

Rufus looked around and realized if the women did muster up the energy to change, he'd never make it back to the SUV in time. "F-Fine, it's not worth my time arguing with your foul-mouthed butts, anyway. I came here to tell y'all the time has come for the young generation to break the bonds from y'all old crones and make their contribution to the prosperity of science." Rufus's icy gaze settled on the tween, Fredi. "My new vessel here is ready, and it's time y'all done finally earned your keep. Your old blood just isn't doing it for me anymore."

Lizzie scented the air, spitefully taunting, "I don't know, oh great pale one. You smell even sicker to me. You must be desperate to heal yourself and prolong your miserable life. Why should we care if you're dying?"

"You better care if you ever want to see your daughters again."

The tween looked at Rufus as if truly seeing him for the first time. Her mouth formed an *O*, and she put her hands on her non-existent hips.

"Vessel?" the young girl snarled, feeling empowered through the sheer proximity of her kin as she watched the shameful exchange. "Fuck you." A scream tore from her throat as Rufus calmly shocked her with the remote for the collar attached to her neck. He did it again, just to be evil, as it was clear he had incapacitated her with the first shock. The tween's eyes rolled up in her head, and she dropped to the ground, unconscious.

When her arms flopped on the ground, an IV port attached to a vein came into full view. The flesh around this port was purple, black, and dark red. Tears filled the women's eyes and they gasped. They had to use all of their self-control not to rush forward, tear Rufus to pieces and finish him once and for all. Perhaps Rufus sensed it was time to take his leave, for he nodded to the SUV's driver, who had been standing outside his door with his gun drawn. He walked over, picked up the tween and unceremoniously threw her into the back of the SUV.

Dr. Vasquez opened her mouth as if to say something but closed it. Her jade green eyes flashed with lurking menace, and if Rufus had bothered to look at her, he would have seen her eyes' pupils narrow into cat slits. She climbed into the back of the SUV and comforted the incapacitated girl, but not before a look passed between her and the other women.

Rufus opened his door and paused before he stepped inside. "Call in Theodora and the others. And don't try to lie to me. Ozzie told me about their birthmarks. You understand me, Ceola? I will tell you one time only, and to prove to you I'm not the heartless bastard you think I am, I'll give you a week with your she-bitch grandchildren to get your affairs in order. Not that you have any affairs to get in order," Rufus snickered as he sat down and closed the door. The back window silently rolled down. "Never forget. I own everything around here, and I mean everything. And, I have your daughters. Just remember their lives are in my hands."

"Whatever Idia is having you do to that poor chile isn't going to work, Rufus," Ceola voiced. "Your only hope of developing your magical elixir is to work *with* us."

Rufus scoffed, "How touching and magnanimous of you. I tried working with you once. Remember? You just let me worry about things and do as I say."

Ceola swallowed her pride and tried one more time. "You know, Rufus, you don't have to treat us this way, like—"

"Like animals?" Rufus chortled. "Oh, the irony. But that's what you are in every sense of the word—animals. Is that not the truth? Goodbye, Ceola."

"Then why do you want to be like us so badly?"

"I don't have to explain anything to you, Ceola." He nodded at Elizabeth and Matilda. "The same goes for y'all, too. It's not my fault your own people sold you to America. One week." Whistling, he pressed the button, and as the window slid silently up, he motioned for the driver to leave. Ceola raced after the SUV, watching her grandchild's tear-streaked face turn around and stare at her, her arms reaching out to her as she ran after the vehicle.

"Whew, chile, I tried," Ceola panted. They gathered their things and began walking up the windy road back to their home. "My God, I didn't know Cleo had given birth to another child. I don't even know my granddaughter's name. Did you see the way she reached out her little arms to me?" Ceola sobbed before collapsing on the road, which was already hot as an oven under the scorching Alabama sun. Her sister-friends helped her up, and they continued walking.

"We've got one week to get those girls ready. Lord, we are truly doomed," lamented Elizabeth.

"At least I've taught them everything I know about fighting and battle strategy," Matilda said. They walked on in companionable silence.

"Did we really spend all these years in bondage for nothing?" Matilda pondered. "Waiting, waiting, waiting for the rise of the Ravenisha. Were we wrong to pin our hopes on the shoulders of this New-Generation?"

The women stopped for a moment to rest and then continued walking. When Ceola broke the silence, it was with a timbre of determination.

"I don't know about y'all, but I'll be damned if I'm going to allow that evil man to defeat us. He is right about one thing, though. The time to break these bonds is here. That bitch Idia promised us we'd be free. Instead, she's taken our children. Now she wants our grandbabies? This means war! And what's with him talking in that old white southern vernacular? Ugh! When we get back to the house, Tildy, please ask Leona to summon Lieutenant Allensworth. We need him and his men here yesterday. Also, notify the sheriff to prepare because the shit is about to hit the fan. Lord, I just hope that baby girl licked up enough of my blood just now. There may be hope for us yet, sistahs. We'll get back at Idia. And once we do, we can carry on what La Panthère Noire has always wanted from us. We can rule this land, and all others, as Ravenisha. Rufus and Idia done picked the wrong women to fuck with. We are warriors! We are queens! We are Ravenisha!"

They raised their fists in the air and gave the Ravenisha war cheer, their ululations and roars singing on the still air.

Chapter 4

As the Ravenisha crested the hill, their spacious contemporary Craftsman, constructed of stone, glass, and wood, was a welcome sight. Horse paddocks, whose structure shared the same wood from which they constructed the house, lined the paved driveway. Their Tennessee Walking Horses excitedly neighed as they recognized their riders' scents and footsteps. The women could see a jumping lesson ongoing in one of the outdoor rings, and after feeding their horses the treats they had put in their pockets earlier, they made their way up the drive to the only home they had known since their forced stay in America besides the old plantation homestead where Rufus still lived. They had remodeled the house over the years. Theodora's vision and Rufus's funds contributed to the current look.

Ceola and Lizzie sighed as they spied the shadows of their estranged husbands in the big picture front window. Ceola's husband, Oziegbe, came out onto the vast wrap-around porch while Lizzie's husband, Caesar, slunk behind him and hovered in the background. Ceola removed her big floppy hat as she reluctantly walked up the steps, her wet dress clinging to her drenched body. She used the bottom of her dress to wipe away sweat from her hair and face.

Ozzie stopped in front of Ceola so quickly, she reared back. His chest was pressed against hers to the point he barely had room to point his finger in her face. "Ceola, something has to be done about that girl. Do you know what she's done now? Sarge, over at the base, told me she done got suspended from the Paranormal Reserves and she done got these women's grandbabies suspended, too, for fighting. She just about darned near killed those men the night before last. She's gettin' too wild. She's too much like her mama and you. If you don't watch out, the guv'ment go take her just like they did our Cleo and..." Ozzie noticed the frowns on the women's faces and fell silent for a moment.before plowing on. "Baby, what's happened? What's wrong?"

Ceola glared up at Ozzie, her lips curled in contempt. Her jaw jutted and her face was immobile as stone. The only thing alive was her emerald eyes, which radiated danger. When Ozzie, who was no little man, saw the rage in Ceola's eyes, he took a step back, feeling a chill wind blow through him. The hairs on his arms prickled from static electricity in the now heavy air. Ozzie, who couldn't take his eyes off of Ceola, felt rather than saw the other women join ranks with her.

Ozzie had known Ceola all of his life and knew she was about to explode on his ass. Trembling, he began backing up. "N-n-n-now look here, Ceola. She was my daughter, too. I loved her just as much as you did. It would only follow that I would love my grandbaby, too. Believe it or not, I care about us."

Ceola held up her hand. "Stop, Ozzie. Don't say another word. Save your foul breath. I know you and Caesar done betrayed me." Lizzie's husband Caesar stepped back, wilting from Ceola's piercing glare and bared canines. "Betrayed all of us," she hissed. "I know what you did. You sold out your own daughter, Oziegbe," Ceola cried, her voice rising. "We have to fight not only that fucking Rufus but our partners, too? Where's the right in that? You vowed to love and protect us, not backstab us. It hurts me to say it, but Malcolm X was so right when he said 'the most disrespected, unprotected and neglected woman in America is the Black woman.' "

"Baby..." Ozzie tried to touch Ceola's cheek, but the vehemence in her eyes made him drop his hand instantly. Also, it didn't help that the noise she made at him was between a hiss and a growl.

Ozzie took a deep breath, stood straight and tall, and looked Ceola in her eyes. "Everything I did, I did for us. Rufus and the guv'ment knew. They *knew*. There was no way we could fight them. Rufus promised me he wouldn't hurt Cleo and the others. He said he and the guv'ment just wanted to study them, and he would only keep them for a week. You know our bodies would have mysteriously disappeared if I hadn't done as they said. It was only supposed to be a week. One week of our lives. I didn't know I was trading their whole lives away and twenty-five years would pass without us seeing hide nor hair of our daughters again. I was doing what I thought was best. Trying to make the best life I could out of a no-win situation. I saved y'all from living a life of being locked up and experimented on. I put food on our table, a roof over our heads. I thought we were safe when it seemed that Theodora wasn't like you and our baby, but now, I'm not so sure," Ozzie wailed, tears coursing down his dark cheeks. "Ceola, what have I done?"

"You've been a fool like you always have," Ceola replied, her voice as dead as her eyes. "Some *Asoro* warrior you've been. I should have kicked you out after that devil impregnated me and you didn't do a damn thing about it. If you weren't already old and your days numbered, I'd kill you right here and now." Ozzie tried to speak. "Shut up!" Ceola commanded, eyes flashing fire, nostrils blazing, and lips drawn back over her teeth. "And don't worry about Theodora. She's not your concern. Just like Cleodora wasn't your concern. She's not hurting or killing anyone who doesn't need hurting or killing."

Ozzie swallowed and looked like he was about to muster up the courage to say something to Ceola, but decided not to at the last minute. He hung his head in defeat.

For the love of God, Ceola grimaced, watching Ozzie struggle to stand up to her. What had happened to the tall, strapping, masculine man she had married? He looked so pitiful.

"If you have something to say, say it, Oziegbe," Ceola relented, going back on her earlier command for him to shut up. Ozzie just continued looking at her with his arms at his sides, shaking his head. "And that right there is part of your problem. You're a spineless coward, Ozzie. You can never say I didn't love you enough. I didn't support you enough. I didn't let you be the man. Do you think I want to stand here and berate you, Ozzie? I truly don't. I get tired of having to be a strong Black woman all the damn time."

"I'm going to go take a nap," Ozzie responded dejectedly, walking away.

"That's all you've got to say? Motherfucker." Ceola sighed, and her shoulders fell. "Ozzie, wait."

Ozzie stopped walking and turned around, tears in his eyes.

"I'm sorry, Ozzie. I'm sure you did the best you could," Ceola said in a conciliatory tone. "We'll get through this."

Lizzie sighed heavily. "The same goes for you too, Caesar. We'll take care of this like we take care of everything else around here. You two go on back to your cottages and chill."

Ozzie, who had already started walking back to his quiet abode like the devil was nipping at his heels, stopped and waited for Caesar to catch up to him. The men walked off, their steps heavy, shoulders stooped and heads bowed in defeat.

"I could just spit!" Ceola fumed to Elizabeth and Matilda after the men had wisely scurried away. "You know they're probably calling us man-hating bitches at this very moment," Ceola said, mouth tight. "What I wouldn't do for a strong Black man."

"Girl, don't even waste your breath or get your blood pressure up. It's a wonder they didn't threaten to leave us for other women," Lizzie added.

"Chile, I'd pay Ozzie to leave me—and the woman too. I'd be sure to add a no return clause. I knew we should have gotten rid of them when they betrayed us, but their service and loyalty as Asoro over the years saved them. I need a damn drink! I'll tell you this one thing, though. I'm done. I'm not mad or upset anymore. I'm just done."

"Amen!" Tildy and Lizzie agreed.

Chapter 5

Earlier that morning, Ravenswood Farm

"I hate everybody and everything!" Teddy espied her favorite mug on the bedside table. She grabbed it and threw the mug against the far wall, where it shattered into tiny fragments.

Immediately, the household came alive as four irate voices yelled in unison. "Teddy!"

She heard one person grumble, "What's wrong with that girl now?"

Teddy stalked into her bathroom, pointedly ignoring the mess she had just made. She was so tired of this shit. Take what happened two nights ago. Men were always underestimating her because she was a curvy, petite, and lightly muscled woman, almost feline in appearance and movement. They learned soon enough when they got their asses kicked. It wasn't like she was required to tell them she'd been trained by warrior women since she could walk and she was far stronger and faster than she looked. Still, she'd fucked things up to Hell and back this time. She hadn't even met her new boss, and she was already in trouble. And it would gut her to tell Nana Ceola she'd messed up yet again. It's not that Nana would berate her. It was the sigh and the way she'd look at Teddy with sorrow in her tired green eyes. Her mouth would turn down, and she'd slowly shake her head from side to side before looking away and down at the ground that made Teddy feel so bad. Why, oh why, couldn't she control her emotions better? What was wrong with her? Lord knew she had listened to her therapist drone on and on about using techniques like picturing herself as a rock floating to the bottom of a lake, or journaling her feelings over the years to have handled the situation better. With a sob of despair, she wished she could crawl into a dark hole and never come out.

Teddy groaned and clutched her abdomen. Her stomach was cutting up today. As a violent cramp rolled over her, she rushed to the toilet and barely made it. Once her guts had stopped churning, and it seemed she could evacuate no more, she wiped and wobbled over the cool white marble tiled floor on unsteady legs. She undressed, turned on her giant rainfall shower head and stepped into the huge stall where scalding water from the jets on the stall's walls massaged her tired and aching muscles. While her body didn't deal well with her near-constant state of anger, frustration, and sadness, Teddy wasn't a fool. Something else was going on. She and her crew had been experiencing unbearable hunger lately. No matter how much they ate, it was never enough to sate them. Teddy imagined she could see her stomach's insides, red and inflamed, where acidic bile had undoubtedly worn a hole through the lining. The change was upon them, and their bodies were preparing them for the occurrence.

Teddy soaped her loofah with her favorite lavender and eucalyptus shower gel, spending extra time massaging the shoulder she'd used to block one man's sloppy punch as hot water massaged her aching muscles. She remembered the sorry events as if the fight had just occurred instead of two days ago.

~ ~ ~

Being an ass-kicking warrior, albeit one still in training, wasn't always what it's cracked up to be. That and freeing The Ravenisha were the foremost thoughts occupying Theodora Lulu K'Abella Furie's mind. It was Friday night and the Ravenswood Bar was packed with base personnel and townsfolk. The joint, as the saying goes, was jumping. A live band was setting up and Big Ray's hickory-smoked barbecued ribs, chicken, brisket, and hot links, along with the hops and ryes, emitted a tantalizing aroma that permeated the cavernous former warehouse.

Teddy swiveled around and scanned the crowd as she took a long pull on her lager and immediately wished she hadn't made eye contact with a group of soldiers across the room. Teddy knew the men were trouble as soon as her ex-cop instincts warned her they were taking an unnatural interest in her. All she wanted was a quiet evening drinking a great hoppy IPA at the local bar with her crew. But no, it wasn't to be. Men were always challenging her.

"Damn, they're still staring at us. This can't be good," she noted, swirling back around on her bar stool to address her girlfriends, Celeste and Naima. Sure enough, the four men dressed in fatigues made a beeline straight for them.

"Evening sweet thangs. Can we buy you gals a drink?" The group's leader was a tall, muscular man with tanned skin and great teeth. His buddies weren't hard on the eyes, either, the women noted, looking them up and down. Especially the Latinx one, his curls still visible even though his hair was close-cropped.

Celeste quickly shut them down. "No thanks. We're good." That should have been the end of the confrontation, but it wasn't. If anything, the burly men crowded the women's space even more, their alcohol-tinged sweat and testosterone causing a sensory overload to the women's newly enhanced sense of smell.

The lead soldier finally asked Teddy the question she knew they had been dying to ask all along. "Hey, aren't you Quick Draw McGraw?"

"I hear you're supposed to be hot stuff handling a gun," chuckled a blond, the smile on his face as fake as one of those "designer bags" you buy off the street.

"Look guys, we're just here trying to have a nice quiet Friday night with no drama," Celeste snarled.

"We ain't looking for no drama, sweet thang." His eyes returned to Teddy. "We just want to know if you're as good as the rumors say you are. Why don't we have a little gun drawing contest? I'm not so bad at handling pistols myself. We can unload the guns if that'll make you feel better."

Immediately, the clamor fell quiet, and then the din resumed as patrons began making bets on who was the fastest gun drawer.

Naima and Celeste rolled their eyes and ignored the soldiers. "Damn, Teddy. When is this going to stop? Can't we ever have a normal evening out with you?" Naima sighed loud and long.

"Well, you can't be more tired of buffoons challenging me than I am. Damn that newspaper article! I know the reporter was just trying to highlight a Black female Atlanta police officer, but did she have to call me a Black Annie Oakley and highlight every single marksmanship tournament I've won? And it was so long ago. I rarely draw my guns now."

"That's what you get for being such a show-off," Naima sniffed.

Teddy thought, I'm going to just ignore these idiots instead of punching their lights out. She coached herself: breathe in, breathe out. And she continued ignoring them for five full minutes, the fumes from their alcohol saturated bodies and breaths swirling like a miasma around her. Finally, she whirled around, her trusty Glock 27 40-caliber semiautomatic in her hand so fast they didn't even see her take it out of the holster. She placed the gun's barrel in the center of the challenger's forehead and put pressure on the trigger.

"No, Teddy, don't do it!" Her friends pulled Teddy away from the challenger, who still hadn't even drawn his gun and was staring at Teddy with gaped eyes and mouth.

"That's impossible. Nobody's that fast," he repeated several times. And damned if that woman didn't have freaky eyes. He could have sworn that one eye was blue and the other one green.

"Okay, you've made your point. Now holster your weapon," the bartender ordered Teddy. "I don't care if Alabama is an open carry state and practically everybody in here is armed; you know better than to draw your weapon in a bar. I'm going to look the other way since it was just a stupid weapon-drawing contest, though."

Teddy sighed, swirled her gun around her finger like old-time gunfighters used to do, and replaced it to its holster.

It should have been over then for real, but it wasn't. The yahoos continued to heckle her and her girls once the bartender returned to his station. Again, what was she supposed to do? Then, when one of them called her, Celeste, and Naima uppity Black bitches, that was the last straw. It was on and cracking. All three women jumped from their bar stools and stood facing the soldiers.

"What, you mad because we called you uppity Black bitches," the shortest soldier leered. "At least we didn't call you uppity nigger bitches."

All of the air went out of the cavernous space. You could have heard a pin drop. The only sounds were music and people's feet shuffling as they moved away from the group. Even the musicians stopped playing when they noted the tense situation.

Teddy's fist slammed into the offending soldier's mouth so quick and hard his head snapped back and forth like one of those bobblehead dolls. Teddy made sure she knocked multiple teeth out of the man who called them out of their names. She watched in satisfaction as they fell out of his mouth onto the sawdust-covered floor. It was like watching a bowling ball knocking down pins. The ensuing beatdown may have been a little excessive, but that wasn't her problem. Teddy and her crew had recently noticed their bodies becoming stronger, more muscular and faster during their gym workouts and training, and they were confident in their abilities to beat the much larger men.

Teddy, Celeste, and Naima had the men cornered when the sound of guns being cocked brought them out of their rage. Someone had called the police. The base's military police had answered the call due to the bar's close proximity and patronage by army personnel. They were taken into custody and transported to the base while the men were transported to Ravenswood General Hospital.

"You broke my fucking hand!" the lead soldier had screamed, holding his already swollen hand to his body. Another had whimpered that his ribs were broken as he glared up at the women encircling him.

It didn't take long for the base's boss to chew them out and slap them with a six weeks' suspension, plus a night in jail for Teddy. Teddy had been shocked at how quickly the top brass of the Paranormal Division's headquarters had handed the order down. She and her girls had been tried and sentenced before they could even defend themselves. Teddy was fit to be tied. She hugged Celeste and Naima and they went home, while Teddy allowed herself to be escorted to spend a night in the military jail.

Teddy prayed, Please Lord, don't let me discover the name of the toady in the bar who called the base's head before I could even tell my side of the story. She couldn't help it if the shitbags were demolition experts and the Paranormal Division of the army base would sorely miss them while they recuperated.

~ ~ ~

Teddy thought about Great Auntie Tildy training her and wondered how she was still alive. Forget play-sparring. Auntie Tildy had given zero fucks about hitting children. She taught Teddy and her sister-cousins to fight through the pain. Teddy couldn't count the number of black eyes, broken bones, and bruises her aunt had inflicted on her throughout the years. That made the men's tears even more pathetic.

What was even more ridiculous were the empty apologies from the soldiers over Zoom at an ungodly hour this morning. *We're not racist.* Well, Kumbaya. *We had too much to drink.* No shit, Sherlock. The soldiers' commanding officer had done nothing to punish them. Not a damn thing. Teddy punched the shower's wall and instantly regretted it as fresh pain shot through her already sore knuckles.

At least the Ravenswood Bar and Grill had banned the shitheads for six months—longer if they couldn't abide by the rules.

"Banned?" the man she'd punched had lisped incredulously from his spot on the floor.

"You can't abide REOO, you're banned. Easy as that," the manager had replied.

"You're going to cite Respect for Each Other? Those bitches—" began the third soldier, who probably had a broken leg, before the manager cut him off.

"Nope, I don't want to hear it. You made your bed, now you have to lie in it. You boys drank too much. There were other women in the bar, yet you chose the three African American women to talk shit to. Take your beatdown like men, and learn from it or don't learn from it."

Teddy scrubbed her body so hard, red streaks trailed in the loofah's wake. She was so tired of having to prove herself and always being embroiled in some conflict. What was that James Baldwin quote? *To be a Negro in this country and to be relatively conscious is to be in a rage almost all the time.*

She reflected while it was great and all townspeople had agreed to make the world a better place, people were still people. To make matters worse, this was the Deep South, where she received looks of shock and grudging admiration over her prowess with a gun and knife at the gun range. She still bristled about the unnatural curiosity displayed when she pulled her Microtech Combat Trodon knife from her specially made ankle sheath. Then the lookie-loos had really lost their shit when she removed her SOG Fixation Bowie knife attached to her other ankle and stabbed the target with extra vigor.

One yokel had approached her and said, "Damn girl, what's up with all the heavy-duty weapons? You a drug dealer or something?" He and his buddies had stopped laughing when Teddy fixed them with her unsettling stare and whipped out the sword that was in a sheath under her shirt.

She'd coldly replied, "It pays to be armed, especially when encountering assholes at a gun range."

The man had quietly muttered, "Freak" under his breath as he and his buddies had slunk off to watch her surreptitiously from a distance.

Like they couldn't believe a woman, especially a Black woman, should be allowed to consistently nail her targets from various distances using multiple guns and in different simulated situations. Well, fuck them! They could suck her balls.

And so could all the Black men she threatened. Teddy couldn't remember the last time she had been on a date. Hell, she couldn't remember the last time she had even been catcalled. It wasn't her imagination, either, that people wouldn't treat her so abysmally if she were blonde and blue-eyed. Even though Nana was always telling her everyone had a purpose in this life, she still wished she excelled at something other than beating people up. Why, oh why, couldn't she have gone to law or medical school? She had long ago dismissed Nana and the great aunties' proclamations that she was destined to lead the Ravenisha as idle talk. Did she really have what it took to be a warrior? Was leading the Ravenisha her true purpose? As the once scalding water became lukewarm, she knew she needed to get her butt dressed, stop comparing herself to others, and quit feeling sorry for herself.

Teddy snarled, turned off the water, and stepped out of the shower. All she needed was for the other great aunties to be mad at her because she used up all the hot water.

Teddy looked at the young woman staring back at her from the mirror while drying off. Her eyes were puffy, and her mouth was turned down in the frown that seemed glued to her face these days. She gingerly wiped the towel over her bruises and blew her breath out. She thought part of the reason she was so ill-tempered was she was short. Well, 5 feet, 4 ¾ inches didn't make her a little person, but she wished she was tall, like Celeste, Naima, and Auntie Matilda. At least people admired and thought of tall Black women as Amazons. Many modeled or played sports. They definitely seemed to have more boyfriends, in her opinion.

Why didn't men think she was cute, she wondered for the umpteenth time? *What's the point in being receptive to love when men ignored you?* she thought, still unable to get off of the pity train she was on. She could see where she was curvy like Nana Ceola, but whose hair did she have? The only picture she had of her mother, Cleo, showed Cleo with a big afro. Teddy's hair was curly but not as curly as Nana's, and it had that awful bright white narrow stripe that resisted all dyes and was planted right smack in the center of her head. It started at her forehead and ran all the way to the end of her waist-length hair. People always said she had Indian hair, but that didn't seem to be in her favor, either. Everyone had weaves these days, so what difference did it make if her hair was real? She wished she remembered her mother, Cleo, more and that Nana and Gramps had taken more pictures of her so she could see if she had her mother's eyes.

Teddy sighed. "I know why I'm alone, and I'm not willing to do anything about it at the moment." She mimicked Ceola as she muttered, "Smile sometimes, and maybe a man won't be afraid to approach you; go out more; ask a man out; don't be so stand-offish; get out of your shell…blah, blah, blah. Forget that! Besides, I just want a man for sex, not for him to be in my space and raising my blood pressure everyday."

Teddy walked into her vast closet, admiring its layout and realizing she'd never fill it with clothes in her lifetime, which is why she had her own private arsenal stowed here, as well. Humming, she began rummaging through the built-in drawers and racks. She pulled on a pair of navy full seat riding breeches, a no-bounce bra for her full breasts, and a navy moisture-wicking sun-block technical shirt with arm vents, which she tucked into the breeches. A belt, compression socks, and paddock boots rounded out the outfit. She would put on her tall, stiff boots just before she got on the horse.

Whenever she needed relief from the pressures of the everyday world, she could always be found in one of two places: somewhere curled up with a book or riding one of her horses, be it a trail ride or a lesson in an arena. The best thing about riding was that she had to focus all of her energy and emotion on riding her horse; otherwise, she'd find herself on the ground. When she was around horses, nothing else mattered at that moment. While dressage and jumping a course fulfilled her need for order and exactness, being on the back of a horse fulfilled a hole in her soul. It was a time when she didn't have to think about racial tensions, or whatever was plaguing her that day. Her mind could just be free of whatever was bothering her. She even loved the smell of horse poop and the sawdust shavings that filled the horses' stalls. Teddy smiled thinking about the sheer joy cantering gave her, especially over a jump. If she closed her eyes, the feeling was akin to flying.

Teddy knew she was lucky to have an equestrian center to call her own. She had always been one of those horse-crazy little girls, and old man Moses, their nearest neighbor, had gladly let her ride his Tennessee Walking Horses. Even the aunties had taken up trail riding Tennessee Walkers.

Teddy discovered dressage serendipitously. She had been on a trip overseas and had been driving in the English countryside when out of nowhere, she saw the most amazing sight of her life. A woman was riding this magnificent horse in a field. The horse looked like it was dancing, seeming to defy gravity by skipping and high-stepping its legs like it was marching. Teddy had been so enrapt. She stopped the car, got out, and flagged the woman down. She learned the woman rode dressage, and to advance to her level of riding would take many years. Teddy vowed she would do whatever she had to do to ride like the elegant woman she met that day. Oh, to be young and naïve. Teddy hadn't understood the expense involved when she returned home and announced to Nana she wanted to build an equestrian center. She'd all but given up hope once she had tallied the costs—a multimillion-dollar undertaking when she'd wanted the full 120 acres of Nana's land to include a barn for dozens of horses, multiple arenas, and the necessary paddocks, covered round pen, and manicured trails for lessons and riding—but Nana had produced the money like she was writing a check to pay for a utility bill.

She'd brushed off Teddy's protestations, saying, "Rufus and I can't take the money to the grave with us. I've always loved horses myself. Please don't deny this old woman the pleasure of seeing you ride."

Now, the equestrian center housed not only her dressage horses but the TWHs like her neighbor's she and the others rode for fun. They also trained them in dressage, since every horse benefited from some dressage training. Rufus. What a complicated relationship that seemed to be. But who was she to question it?

And now, she could look ahead to her riding lesson. At least she would have a little joy today.

Chapter 6

Teddy gulped down some yogurt and coffee. She cleaned up the mess she'd made earlier and was sorry she'd lost her temper and broken her favorite mug. As she walked down the sloping driveway and made the turn to the main barn, she decided to ride Rachmaninoff Z, affectionately known around the barn as Rocky. Rocky neighed and whinnied as soon as he saw Teddy. A wide grin broke on Teddy's face as she walked toward the 16.2 hands, black Hanoverian gelding's stall.

"Hi, cute boy." Teddy fed Rocky a carrot and rubbed his white blaze. "Ready for our lesson today?"

Teddy quietly entered the European-styled stall, the shavings' aroma reminding her of pine and cedar trees. She placed Rocky's halter on him and led him to a cross tie for grooming. As she went over the grooming checklist in her head, she knew she was fortunate to have a schoolmaster like Rocky. Not only was he beautiful with his white blaze and four white socks, but his temperament was also to die for. His previous owner trained him to FEI Intermediare; just short of Grand Prix.

Rocky was that elusive unicorn all riders sought, and he'd had no problem adjusting to Teddy's lower level of riding. His previous owner, Barbara Gluck, had sold him to Teddy after Teddy saved her life when she was with the Atlanta PD, and she had learned of Teddy's burgeoning interest in dressage. It also helped that while Rocky was a total saint in the arena and out on the trail, he absolutely hated the show environment—to the point where he was actually dangerous. Barbara recounted to Teddy how a groom would often drag him into the arena, nostrils flaring, prancing and bucking. The smallest thing, such as the clicking of a camera shutter, loudspeakers, or hands clapping, would set him off. He would rear, crow hop and take off. She was too old to deal with him and needed another competition horse to complete her Gold Medal on. Teddy assured Barbara she was nowhere near showing and that she had the means to purchase other horses on which to show when she was ready for that stage.

Grooms bolstered Rocky's diet each day with a special supplement given to all the horses. Teddy knew this supplement contained pheromones and other ingredients so the horses wouldn't freak out from the Ravenisha's scents. Nana was a brilliant scientist and had come up with the formula herself. Teddy knew she was extremely blessed to have a horse of Rocky's caliber and Barbara had a standing invitation to visit and ride him anytime she wanted.

Teddy donned her helmet and tall boots. As she made her way to the huge wood and stone sky-lighted indoor arena, she noted several people were already riding. It looked like the jumping lesson was ending and other riders had entered the arena, warming up for the next lesson. Even though it was only 10 a.m., the scorching Alabama sun was making its power known. *Thank goodness for Big Ass Fans,* she mused, while inhaling the citrus scent of Rocky's fly spray.

"Oh my God, my eyes must be deceiving me. I know that's not Teddy and Rocky," boomed the German-accented voice of Christian Metternich, the facility's resident trainer.

A cacophony of "Hi Teddy's" and "Good Mornings," and "Long time, no sees," rang out in the arena while Teddy led Rocky to the three-step mounting block. He stood still and she placed her left foot in the stirrup and swung her right leg up and over Rocky's back.

"Good Morning, y'all. Some of us have to work, ladies. We ride when we can." Teddy smiled, already feeling the love of her fellow riders as she and Rocky walked away from the mounting block.

"Mm-hmm," Christian said, rolling his blue eyes. "Go ahead and warm up Rocky while I finish this lesson. I hope you ate your Wheaties this morning."

"Ooh, Teddy, your butt is about to get whipped today, girl. Let me hurry and untack Fleur because I wouldn't miss this lesson for the world," said one rider.

"Great," muttered Teddy under her breath. "I'll be damned if I'm going to be today's entertainment. Come on, Rocky. Let's have a good warm-up."

Teddy didn't provide much entertainment for the railbirds watching her lesson today, but there were some close moments. Rocky saw ghosts in the corners twice, but fortunately, he scooted forward each time and easily came back to Teddy. It always amused Teddy when people believed all you had to do was sit on a horse and the horse did all the work. Obviously, they had never ridden a horse, much less a dressage horse. You engaged core muscles and muscles you didn't know you had when you're an active rider. And let's not talk about the precision and finesse involved.

To the outside eye, Teddy knew dressage just seemed like a sport where people guided their horses around in circles and patterns. People didn't realize you had to learn the dimensions of the arena and the geometry of circles in meters! Judges expected your horse to have brilliant movement one moment and come to a complete halt the next. There was a reason so many Type A people chose dressage. As frustrating as it was, Teddy loved dressage with a passion. It took many, many years to make a dressage horse and rider.

Christian worked her and Rocky to the point of exhaustion. When the lesson ended, both she and Rocky were dripping buckets of sweat. Christian had them working on shoulder-in in both directions, leg yielding, sitting the trot, trot canter transitions, canter trot transitions, counter cantering, cantering in a straight line away from the rail, halting in various places in the arena, and perfecting their ten-meter circles. Teddy slumped in her saddle, and her legs felt wobbly like jelly. Her breathing was almost as loud as Rocky's.

"Good job today, Teddy." Christian gave Rocky a horse cookie. "I keep telling you if you'd take lessons more consistently, you'd advance much quicker. Your seat is much better, and you're sitting less crooked in the saddle. Physical therapy has really helped correct your body's crookedness. You're making inroads with your geometry, but I don't want just okay circles; I want perfect circles. Don't give away points during a test because you rode a nineteen-meter circle instead of a twenty-meter circle."

"Thank you, Christian. I'm trying to be more mindful of my position and hey, now that I've been fired from just about every job I've ever had, I'll actually have more time to ride." Teddy grimaced. She hurt like hell, but she was secretly proud of herself and Rocky. They had done some good work today. "Man, you kicked my butt to Hell and back, but I feel good. I had several aha moments. Plus, I could truly feel Rocky stepping under himself. Thank you so much, Christian. I know I must torture a big-name trainer such as yourself, but I appreciate you. And I'll work harder on my geometry. I'm inspired after today."

"It's my pleasure teaching you, Teddy." Christian smiled. "You're a piece of cake compared to my true torture," he whispered as his next lesson, a group lesson comprising girls aged ten to twelve, arrived in the arena exuberantly talking and laughing.

"I feel your pain," Teddy whispered back. She waved to the girls and walked Rocky out of the arena to enjoy a cooling down walk on the track she had built around the property.

She and Rocky walked over to the gate that led to the trail. As they ambled down the hill from the equestrian center, the area became more wooded. Some of the old-growth pine trees had stood for hundreds of years. As Teddy and Rocky meandered along the path, the wind made a gentle susurration, rustling the leaves. Water gurgled from the creek that ran through the property. Teddy took a deep breath and exhaled. The pine-scented air acted as a balm for her soul.

Teddy couldn't wipe the grin off of her face as she walked around the property. She loved this piece of land so much. It was heavenly here in the mountains. The air was clean and crisp and birds were always filling the air with their songs. Fall was fast approaching; leaves were turning as the last vestiges of the Indian summer struggled to stay. Teddy couldn't envision living in a better location than this unincorporated area near the Monte Sano Mountain near Huntsville. She wondered how Nana and the other aunties had found it...or had Rufus discovered it and ensconced her people on the land? She decided she didn't care who found the land. It was so beautiful and she felt beyond blessed to be on it now.

She loved the feeling of being up high when she was on the back of a horse, especially warmbloods, a breed of horse normally used for dressage and show jumping equestrian activities. They often towered over their quarter horse kin and weren't as stocky.

No anxiety or nail-biting plagued her whenever she was in the saddle. As she ruefully thought about her fingernails, she envisioned how she had bitten them to the quick and how the skin around the nail bed looked like ground-up hamburger meat. The underlying skin sometimes bled from where she had picked and nibbled the top layer away.

"Shit!" Teddy had been so engrossed in her thoughts, she failed to see the deer on the path until it was too late. Startled, both the deer and Rocky leaped into the air. Teddy squealed but stayed on. The deer bounded off, and before Rocky could fully spook and take off with her, she had bent him away from the deer and kicked him forward, effectively telling him nothing to see here. Move along. Teddy exhaled and grinned when Rocky followed her prompts and gave him copious pats and "good boys." There was a time when she would have tensed up, curled into a fetal position, and definitely would have fallen when Rocky leaped sideways. Riding had boosted her confidence tremendously. She felt not only badass and free but also at one with nature.

Teddy dropped the reins and raised her arms in the air. She threw her head back and laughed and laughed and laughed.

Chapter 7

Teddy made her way around the property and back to the barn, which was now bustling with activity, as more people had arrived for their lessons or just to hack. It was gratifying having outside boarders. The women, especially Auntie Matilda, were apprehensive at first about inviting strangers into their environment but so far, everything had worked out better than fine. The boarders, of whom the majority were women of all ages and ethnicities; although most were white because of the nature of the equestrian world, had quickly formed a tight bond because of their love for horses, and they were like a family. Even grouchy pro-Black Tildy talked to the women and shared a cackle with them sometimes. Teddy awakened from her reverie when she saw Nana and the other women sitting on the porch.

She yelled, "Y'all could take lessons, you know. If Queen Elizabeth still rides, you can, too."

"It looks like such fun! We just might do that, Lulu," Lizzie replied, using Teddy's middle name as a term of endearment.

"Shiit, if some of these women are still riding, we can, too," Leona said, with a sniff. "Some of them look like they have to be in their seventies and they ride several horses a day."

"Girl, hush yo' mouth," Lizzie chuckled.

“But am I lying, though?” laughed Leona.

“I’m fine riding my Walker, thank you very much.” Then, Tildy shocked them all to their core by saying, “Although, I wouldn’t mind taking a lesson on one of those big boys one day. Just for a little variety, you know?” Mouths dropped open. Was this the same Tildy who eschewed all things she perceived as white and frivolous? “What? Can’t a woman learn fresh things? Damn, y’all so old-fashioned and stuck in your damn ways!” She stalked off in fake indignation.

Lizzie shook her head, dreadlocks swaying, but Leona held up a hand. “Girl, don’t even try…although I better go see if my baby is sick or something. I wonder what awakened this willingness to try something new? Whatever it is, yaaassss, I’m here for it! I’m liking this new Tildy.”

Lizzie giggled. “I think the new boarder, what’s her name? Cinnamon? Nutmeg? Saffron—that’s it. Showing you a little extra attention is what’s changing Tildy’s ways and all I will say is, Hallelujah!”

“Amen!” shouted Ceola as she and Lizzie fist-bumped.

Teddy laughed and walked away to put Rocky up.

The women’s smiles faded, and they resumed the conversation they’d been having before Teddy greeted them. Leona and Tildy returned and sat down. The others explained the morning’s events to Leona, who was still processing the startling revelation of the unknown granddaughter. The bones hadn’t revealed this news to her.

“The change will be stressful enough, and she will need to focus all of her attention and energy on it. Then, we can focus on freeing that little pumpkin from Rufus’s clutches.”

“I agree, Leona. Besides Rufus’s damn visit today, La Panthère Noire has been calling my beast and issuing some kind of warning. I just hate to burst the girls’ bubbles, but they have to grow up sometimes. Twenty-eight can be a rough age. It's when you're introspective and always in a crisis because thirty is just around the corner. Teddy looked so happy after her lesson today," Ceola said wistfully. "I know she's been going through some kind of emotional turmoil, but she won't tell me what's wrong. At any rate, we notified all the girls, and they should be home today."

"The spirits have been contacting me, too," sighed Leona. "Raven has been trying to reach me. I just don't know if it's because of the infusion of Tildy's blood or through the spiritual realm. Raven seems almost...I don't know...desperate? Something isn't right. Something momentous beyond our control is about to happen, and it's ominous. We may not survive what's coming." Leona shivered even while beads of sweat rolled down her face on the sweltering summer day. She left the women rocking and went into the house.

Leona poked her head out of the door a little bit later. "I have just the thing to calm you ladies down. The banana pudding I baked last night should be delicious with a nice cup of coffee."

Without a word, the women stopped rocking, got up, and filed past the full-figured Leona who held the door open, and into the spacious kitchen where they sat at an enormous granite island while Leona served them banana pudding and coffee. Ceola took a bite and closed her eyes. She looked at Leona, taking in her light complexion, now flushed from the heat, and her frizzy hair, which was arranged in a tight ball. She had that fluffy yet hour glass-shaped figure that so many celebrities paid for these days. She could see why Matilda had fallen so hard for her.

"Thank you, Leona, I needed this. Girl, you're getting there. This pudding tastes almost as good as mine." Ceola moaned as she licked her spoon clean.

The others nodded their agreement and ate in silence, letting the early morning's unpleasant events wash over them as Leona beamed from the compliments.

The women returned to their spots on the porch after their snack. "Boy, I look back on those dark days and wonder how we made it," Lizzie said, gazing off into the distance, rocking. "While that Devil didn't impregnate me, it felt like he was somehow behind Caesar, ejaculating into me at the same time. Remember, our men were being used as guinea pigs, too? Especially when Rufus was injecting our men with that mysterious shit. Now he's doing who knows what to our children. No doubt studying what his serum has accomplished."

Matilda stopped rocking and narrowed her eyes. "There's some fuckery going on here. Those two are up to something again." Tildy nodded in the direction Ozzie and Caesar had walked. "Rufus is plotting something, and you can bet that heffa Idia is driving all of this."

Ceola shivered and slowly stopped rocking. "Ugh, that wasn't a pleasant feeling. Instead of feeling like someone was walking over my grave, Idia filled my thoughts. We're about to be in for a world of hurt."

"Oh no, y'all not!" The women looked up startled. They hadn't noticed Leona standing in the doorway listening to them. "Y'all go get up off yo' assess and fight back. It's time."

"But the prophecy…" began Lizzie.

"Fuck the prophecy!" Leona shouted. "Now get in here. We've got work to do."

Chapter 8

Present-day Cotonou, Benin, Africa

In downtown Cotonou, a smartly dressed man nodded at the security guards and walked up to the front desk in a modern building with a big "Laboratoires des Honeycutt" embossed on the outside. "I'm here to see the queen."

"Yessir." The receptionist drank in his tall, dark chocolate muscular physique openly. "She's expecting you. Go right in, Mr. Legba."

As Abaku Legba strode into the modern, airy room, the woman he had come to see had her back turned away from him. Hearing Abaku's almost silent footsteps, the queen turned around and gave him a long kiss. The centuries had been as kind to Idia, now known as Idia Adechi, as they had been cruel to her former friends. Idia hadn't suffered during a single century. She had never been enslaved. She'd never felt the sharp sting of the lash on her back, the degradation and pain of being violated, being made to toil from sunup to sundown, or other indignities the Ravenisha sent to America had been forced to endure. Idia had always positioned herself where she'd been sure to live a life of luxury and remain in a position of power. The day had finally come to branch into America, but her once best friends occupied no place in her plans. They were now liabilities rather than assets. No problem, she'd clean up the shit like she had from every asshole who'd gotten in her way.

"What brings my bae to see me in the middle of the day?"

"Business, I'm afraid, baby. There's been activity noted in the United States at one of Honeycutt's smaller labs. We think Rufus is making his move to genetically modify the strain, using the last two girls he created. I've received word that he plans to start experimenting on the New-Generation of Ravenisha."

"That was never part of the plan," Idia said, spitting. "Who does he think he is to interfere? If he threatens the New-Generation, the Old-Generation will retaliate. I know how this goes. I've been following Rufus's family for generations. I'm the one who invested in his lab. Damn him! I didn't do all of this work and put up with his contempt for me just to have him fuck up my plans. Prepare the plane and the soldiers. We leave in a week's time. Oh, and you know I have your juice ready for you, baby."

"Yes, my queen." Abaku bowed. "Any other way I can be of service?" The queen purred in response and rubbed herself against Abaku while backing him up against her desk.

Later, Idia sat in her chair, closed her eyes and thought about her journey to where she was today. After keeping an eye on the Honeycutts throughout the years, she finally met Rufus and persuaded him to build the lab in Cotonou. She had tried to sway Rufus's father, Zebulon, but hadn't succeeded. Zebulon's murder had worked in her favor, though. That was a stroke of brilliance on her part, she gloated. Rufus thought the Ravenisha killed him and made them pay. Idia remembered the shocked disbelief on his face when she told him she would invest half in the lab as a silent partner. *Arrogant prick*, she thought, still remembering the sting of his contempt for her. Idia had been positive greed would prevail, and she had been correct. But she hadn't forgotten nor forgiven the disdain he had shown her on that day. Idia chuckled as she gloated about the fact that Rufus still didn't know she was the one pulling the strings or that she had murdered his father.

Abaku interrupted her reverie. "My queen, I thought the American scientists are working on the serum since they have the materials there and the Cotonou scientists' job is to refine and mass-produce the serum."

"And that's what we're doing. We're just a little ahead of them, that's all. It was only during a daily meeting last year one of my scientists suggested it was time to test the formula out on live subjects. You know the Americans would have never authorized such a thing even though their president thought we would be developing a serum to create super soldiers. Let's just say I've taken matters into my own hands."

"Ah yes, you sent me and others to villages near and far to recruit single women and men. Offering an irresistibly high fee was genius," Abaku crowed.

"Even I was amazed at how quickly the waiting list formed...and the sheer volume of participants." Idia had paid the participants upfront and told them to meet at the Laboratoires des Honeycutt reception area two days from then at 9 a.m. Idia and her scientists clarified that if the participant accepted the money and signed the consent form, they were expect to be at the laboratory at 9 sharp.

I remember the day that was the impetus to turning my dream of ruling the African continent into reality like it was yesterday."

"As do I. You were resplendent in that African print Ray Darten Misan pencil skirt with the matching peplum top that hugged your curves in all the right places."

"Sweet talking me will get you everywhere. And look at you, using peplum to describe a top. I've trained you well."

"Yes, and having a clothes crazy sister also taught me a lot."

Idia smiled, a faraway expression in her eyes.

Abaku continued. "Most of them even missed the part where you thanked them for the sacrifice they were about to make, they were so smitten with you. They just meekly followed instructions."

Idia and Abaku sank into a companionable silence, both reflecting on the day Idia's dream of creating her own werepanthers almost became a reality.

~ ~ ~

Idia remembered how she had chosen one female and one male subject the next day. They were excellent specimens, strongly muscled and healthy. A guard woke them from their beds in the test subjects' wing and told them to leave their clothes and other personal belongings and to follow the scientist waiting outside the sleeping area to a room at the end of the hall. They were given thin hospital gowns to don. It didn't go unnoticed by the young man and woman how the guard studiously avoided eye contact with them. They crept into the room cautiously and huddled together. Their eyes bulged like animals being led to slaughter—animals who finally realized the fate awaiting them as they eyed the concrete floor, which had a large draining hole in the center. This was a far cry from the wood-like floor of their guest quarters. The test subjects began to doubt their decision for the first time.

The room was bustling with medical personnel, all of whom avoided eye contact with the guinea pigs. Scientists and nurses who had appeared so friendly yesterday while taking their vitals now wore protective clothing. When words were spoken, they were short and brusque.

A tall, stooped, bespectacled scientist, who looked like a praying mantis, nodded toward the two hospital beds set up in the room. "Get undressed and lie down," he ordered, his magnified bug eyes steadfastly glued to his clipboard.

The freezing room made the test subjects rub their arms and shiver. Armed guards blocked the door, discouraging them from even thinking about escaping. Idia and the personnel who worked on the project sat behind an enormous one-way glass window.

A nurse noticed the young man and woman were still glued to their spot in the middle of the room. "It's all right. We're going to inject you with the serum today. The clothes we have on are standard protective lab wear."

"A-a-a-and why the draining hole?" stuttered the spooked man, ready to bolt the lab's coldly ominous environs. Sweat broke out on his brow even though the inside of the room was freezing.

"Oh that," the nurse replied dismissively. "What if you have a reaction and vomit? It will be easier to clean up. We can just spray the area with a power hose, and the mess will go down the drain. Now, come. Lie down on the beds here and let's get you hooked up to the equipment."

The scientist nodded for the nurses to attach the various probes and wires. Without preamble, the scientist released air from the syringe and inserted the serum first into the young man's arm and then repeated the procedure for the young woman. They started timers after the injection of each serum. After forty seconds, the subjects' skin began twitching.

The skittish young adult's back arched off of the bed, his arms and legs flailing. His skin undulated, as though living beings were moving beneath it. The man's deep mocha skin turned jet black and began splitting. Strands of hair appeared here and there. Cat-like eyes rolled back in his head. He dropped to his hands and knees and began writhing around on the floor. Blood poured from every orifice and the tips of his fingers and toes. He tried to scream, but only a high-pitched mewl came out. His labored hiccupping breathing slowed. He exhaled through a tortured gurgle, and his body stilled. No one tried to perform CPR. They noted the time of death and turned all of their attention to the female.

Excitement built in the room. At sixty-five seconds, a copious amount of hair began growing from the female's body. Suddenly, her screams filled the room as her hands impotently scraped her stomach. She then grabbed her head and raked her claws down her hairy face. Her screams became more guttural, her voice an unnaturally low bass rumble. Her skin undulated like the male's; however, her features slowly morphed, or rather tried to morph. While her eyes had become cat-like, her nose was a mangled mess—not human, not feline. She dropped to the floor on all fours and the scientists held their breaths, their hope-filled anticipation palpable in the air. This was the moment they'd been waiting for. With a great popping sound, the woman's body exploded. Lab workers noted canines, and copious amounts of coarse short, black hair in the detritus.

"So close," muttered the praying mantis-like scientist who injected the serum. "So close."

Idia spoke over an intercom. "Incinerate the remains, and dump the waste with the rest in the biohazard container. I'm pleased. We're almost there."

A team of workers clad in Hazmat suits entered and scooped up the body parts that could be scooped, and unceremoniously dumped the mess into red Hazmat bags. The room was hosed down, disinfected, and made ready for the next test subjects.

~ ~ ~

"Those were heady days," Idia sighed. "We were on the verge of success. We ended up going through every volunteer in the lab and everyone on the waiting list."

They learned the hard way that subjects had to have the genes and hormones to shift. A virus had to introduce the gene. The process wasn't perfect, though, and still needed work. Instead of turning into the magnificent, lethal big cats she and the other Ravenisha morphed into, humans injected with the serum morphed into these drab, washed-out black scrawny mutants. Sure, the mutants could kill, but their strength was minuscule compared to the Ravenisha's. Also, they had to inject humans with the serum before they could morph.

"My men even had to resort to kidnapping unwilling participants."

"Which brings me to my warning for you. You must be careful, Queen. Astute citizens have been noticing that people go into this great building but they don't return home. You must also watch Rufus's progress a bit more covertly. Benin law enforcement is on to you."

"I fear no one." Idia dismissively waved her hand. "I do have some protection from someone high up in the government."

While Idia couldn't have cared less whether the serum would also work on men, in her quest to become president of the Republic of Benin, and eventually all of Africa, the one person in a position of power who would help her implied he would only do so if the serum also worked on men. So, she had to go back to the scientists and push them to work out a way to enable men to shapeshift, too, hence Abaku coming to her for his juice. He would be a sacrifice if things went to hell in a handbasket, but she'd just have to put on her big girl panties and deal with whatever happened.

Through sheer perseverance, the genius of her scientists, and a high body count, they had succeeded at enabling men to shapeshift. She smiled while gazing at Abaku, and that fool Rufus was none the wiser. Oh, he was aware the experimentations had begun, but he hadn't been told of the successes. There were still a few things she'd like to tweak, she reflected. The shapeshifted panthers were a little on the slight side. No, that's not true, she corrected herself. They were the size of average panthers. They just weren't pony-sized like the Ravenisha. Also, they couldn't change at will. They needed to improve the serum. Something in it deformed the male and female participants, but no matter what they tried, the bumps wouldn't recede. The virus also affected their panther form: limbs uneven, eyes crossed, teeth misshapen and unevenly spaced. She didn't know what was up with that, and her scientists couldn't explain it either.

For now, eighty mutant werepanthers served as her army, who despite their mangy appearance was adequate. Idia schemed how they would sneak up on men at night with their excellent night vision and climbing skills, and silently strike Benin's human army before they realized what hit them while she and her Ravenisha warriors struck the debilitating blow. She would eat the current president live on national TV and change back into her human body for all to see. People were always afraid of that which they didn't understand, she mused, and even that would work in her favor. She would leverage the people's fear of her and her warriors into reverence. No doubt, she would have to dispel superstitions about them; however, some would have to remain, Idia reasoned. It wouldn't do for the hoi polloi to think of her and her warriors as cuddly pussycats either. She knew she would have to strike just the right balance between fear and reverence. Idia felt her transition to head of state wouldn't be too traumatic for the people of Benin, and she could already see little girls and teens wanting to be like her when they grew up. If she wasn't a marvelous example of "Black Girl Magic", well then, she didn't know what was.

Abaku sensed Idia was off in her own world. He rose, kissed her proffered cheek and left. Idia stood and walked over to her window. People below scurried around like busy bees, unaware of their future if Idia had her way. Everything was coming together. She couldn't have planned it better, she thought. Rufus had gotten in line and was playing his part in her quest to rule the African continent and eventually the world. Once she eliminated the American Ravenisha, her power would be absolute. No new Ravenisha would be replacing her, no matter what the prophecy presaged. Not now. Not ever.

Idia needed to remember one thing, though. She wasn't just one entity. Lurking within Idia's soul, La Panthère Noire stirred, her anger mounting and escalating into a rage.

Chapter 9

Rufus and Dr. Vasquez were engaged in a tense discussion in the lab. They had just left the tween's room. She had been understandably near hysterics when they returned to the lab, crying out for her grandmother inconsolably. Rufus had lost his temper and threatened to tase her again.

"*Dios mío*, Rufus, what is wrong with you?" Dr. Vasquez had finally exploded. "Can't you see she's beyond upset? Leave us! Go get a sedative, if you want to do something useful."

Rufus hesitated. No one bossed him around in his lab.

"I said leave!" Dr. Vasquez growled. Rufus turned on his heel and left. While he was gone, Dr. Vasquez did what she could to comfort her charge, rubbing her back and helping her into bed. Rufus returned with the sedative and inserted it into the IV port. Soon the tween drifted off into a restless sleep.

Dr. Vasquez made sure the girl was sleeping before she nodded for Rufus to follow her out of the room.

"Rufus, I have watched you do many unethical things over the years and I've sanctioned them by my inaction and silence. But I won't allow you to torture that child or her kin any longer. What I witnessed today was disgraceful."

"And just what do you think you can do to stop me, Mariposa? This is my lab—my town. I could have you deported just like that." He snapped his fingers.

Dr. Vasquez looked up at Rufus, and just as her eyes began changing and a growl began emanating from her mouth, a scream sounded from the tween's room. She pushed Rufus away with such force, he crashed into the opposite wall, stunned. Dr. Vasquez rushed into the room.

The young girl lay on her hospital bed, tangled in her sheets. Her eyes were open but unseeing. Her thin arms flailed in the air as she witnessed some horror only she could see.

"It's okay, Fredi," Dr. Vasquez whispered, taking Fredi in her arms. "It's okay."

"No, no, no," Fredi cried as tears poured from her eyes and she gained awareness. "Nana Ceola's blood revealed everything," she whispered in Dr. Vasquez's ear. "I saw everything, and it was awful. How they became Ravenisha, when they left Africa, slavery, beatings, rape, and when they took Mama away. Oh, Nana..."

"Shhh," Dr. Vasquez comforted the wailing girl. Sensing another presence, they turned around, and an eerie quiet settled over the room.

Rufus stood in the doorway; his eyes narrowed. He couldn't hear what they were whispering but he sensed the intense hatred directed toward him.

"I don't know what's going on or what's gotten into you two, but I suggest you both get over it. I'm going to call it a day, and I suggest y'all do the same. We'll discuss this tomorrow when everyone's calmer. I realize this morning may have been a bit stressful for you and has led to this unfortunate moment. We'll talk tomorrow. Good night."

Dr. Vasquez and Fredi said nothing. They looked at each other and listened to Rufus's footsteps fade as he walked out of the building.

Dr. Vasquez put a comforting hand on Fredi's arm as she moved to get out of bed and follow Rufus. She shook her head and whispered, "Now is not the time, Citlalli. You must be patient."

Chapter 10

1600

West African region known as The Dahomey Kingdom, the country known today as the Republic of Benin

The all-female warring party had been gone for months to neutralize one of the village's enemies once and for all. It had been a protracted and arduous battle, but Idia, which means "warrior queen", and her remaining fighters were glad to see the familiar sight of their village's huts on the horizon. She was thinking about expanding her power and enlarging her depleted army of women warriors when something in her line of vision jolted her out of her revelry. What was this? Who was this running toward them? Idia and the others were immediately on high alert, despite their exhaustion. Idia raised her spear, but soon lowered it as she realized it was only Aasira, one of the village's teenage girls coming to meet them.

"Hello, Aasira, how considerate of you to welcome us back." Idia smiled. "You need to approach a war party more carefully, though, young one. You could have easily been mistaken for an enemy and killed."

Aasira's deep brown eyes were red, and there were dark circles underneath. Idia could now see what she had taken as a greeting smile was instead a face of horror.

The war party gathered loosely in formation, eyes wandering constantly, their weapons at the ready.

"Turn around now before they see you," Aasira hissed. "Hurry, hurry! Don't ask questions. Just run. I'll explain on the way. Your warrior trainees, Omolara and Isoke are already there. They fled the village as soon as they could."

Idia and her warriors followed Aasira without further ado. Aasira explained their destination was the Mont Sokbaro Twin Falls of the Atacora Mountains. Several women began to protest, insisting the trip was too far. Their stomachs ached from being empty for days and their battle worn bodies needed rest. They were running on empty. Plus, they missed their men and families. What was so urgent that barred them from going home, eating and resting for a bit?

Aasira explained how some men had overtaken their once-peaceful matriarchal society. Two brothers showed up with an army one day and announced the village now belonged to their new kingdom. She said it was as though they deliberately waited until the war party had left before they came in and claimed the village—one of the area's most prosperous ones. People's lives were now hell. The interlopers stripped them of their weapons, food, and anything of value. The warriors shouted cries of dismay as Aasira told them how these men and their army killed those who opposed them as if they were squashing bugs beneath their feet.

"Queen, they knew all about you and the rest of the warriors, but they didn't seem to care if you returned to the village. In fact, they brought their own female warriors with them, who obediently followed their orders and

killed with brutality I haven't even seen men display." Aasira spoke as if she couldn't believe she was uttering such words.

The warriors looked to Idia, wondering why she hadn't given the order for them to storm the village and rescue their people. Idia was silent. Even though her eyes were sorrowful, they pinged back and forth, back and forth. Aasira stood by, her gangly legs hopping in place so strong was her desire to get as far away from the village as possible.

"What are you thinking, Queen?" Cheola, one of Idia's closest friends, asked her.

"Maybe this is for the best," Idia responded slowly, turning and finally walking away from the village. "We can practice our religion and live the life we choose. I know it will hurt all of us deeply to leave our loved ones, but it will only be a temporary separation until I figure something out. How dare they drive us from our home!"

Soon, the quick walking pace turned into a jog as the women made haste to separate themselves from the unknown danger. They traveled for many miles, alternately walking and jogging. Idia halted the group when she noticed some were falling farther and farther behind.

She turned to the weary group of women around her and shouted, "Warriors, we will rest here for the night and resume traveling in the morning."

Women gratefully laid down their weapons and began setting up camp for the night. The bivouac was silent as the stricken warriors prepared their physically and mentally weary bodies to resume the journey the next day. At daybreak the next morning, there was a cry of alarm from one woman as she crouched over a warrior who lay still on the ground. She had succumbed to her injuries during the night. The mournful unit gathered around their fallen comrade and said a brief prayer. They made quick work of digging a shallow grave in which to bury her, for time was short. Then, the usually buoyant, confident women set out for the foreboding mountain. They fell into an uneasy pace, each woman lost in her thoughts. Some were leaving husbands, children, siblings, and other relatives. Not being able to say goodbye or see them one last time weighed heavily on their hearts. Their world had changed. An ill wind had blown their way.

The trip to the Mont Sokbaro Twin Falls took many days and pushed the women beyond their endurance. They battled harsh terrain, mosquitoes, tsetse flies, snakes, and other predators. The exhausted women weren't as sharp as usual and consequently had several close encounters with nature that bonded them even more. They had long depleted their water supply, and their thirst had reached a critical point. Many were so parched, they had no spit to moisten their split lips. With the scorching African sun already blazing down on them unmercifully, they had to find water soon. They could, at last, see the mountain in the distance, but knew it would take another day, minimum, to reach it. Without water, they would die in a day. Luck was with them, as they found and followed animal tracks to a sliver of a river. To their dismay, hippos and crocodiles had made their way to the water as well. They decided two women would make a horrible racket and draw the animals in their direction while others quickly filled water sacks with the tepid muddy water.

The women could feel dirt particles swirling in their mouths as they greedily gulped great draughts, but still, it was the sweetest-tasting water they had had in a long time. Later, they encountered a herd of gnu and had already made their kill when a sudden stampede of the animals almost ran them over. Unfortunately, a pride of lionesses had chosen that same herd to serve as their dinner. The women quickly gathered up their dead gnu and got the hell out of there.

Then, a storm of monsoon proportions occurred when they finally made it to the base of the mountain. While they were thankful to drink clean water, the rivers cascading down from the mountain almost washed them away. They would made headway up the mountainside several times, only to be washed down several hundred feet by water, sand, and mud. It all felt very Sisyphean. The bone-tired women persevered, though, and after they fought the elements and the mountain for over three days, they finally reached the falls. Omolara and Isoke were waiting for them and they happily reunited.

Because of the rains, the falls had never been fuller and the thundering sound they made was deafening. The women, who had never seen such a sight in their lives, stared in awe. This unfamiliar world enveloped all of their senses. Upon further exploration, the beauty, seclusion, and abundance of wildlife and flora amazed them. Cascading crisp, icy water tasted like honey. They could smell the trees and exotic flowers. Their eyes were drawn to multiple sights at once. It was difficult to take in everything. Varying gradations of green painted the jungle's foliage, and even the sky seemed to appear bluer. Bird song and animal calls sounded like sweet music to their ears. They all agreed it was paradise and settled into their newfound lives without incident.

Months passed. A year, two years. The tribe grew incrementally. Several babies were born to those warriors who were with child before going on that fateful war party, and stray women somehow found the camp now and then and asked for permission to join the tribe. The tribe turned no one away, and the population swelled.

They didn't forget their families in their old village and continued to sneak and meet their loved ones. Over the years, their footsteps forged a path leading from the mountain to the village. The brothers even turned a blind eye once it was apparent the warrior women would not contest them. Both factions had what they wanted.

One day, after Idia had been out hunting, she came back with a bundle of black fur nestled in her arms. The women crowded around her, and everyone immediately cooed over the baby black she-panther Idia had rescued from certain death from being a python's meal. Everyone except the elder Nahwi, who looked at the cub with fear and loathing.

"Don't start Nahwi. Let me guess. She's a terrible omen because she's black. We're going to die. She's an evil spirit or some other such nonsense." Cheola took the cub from Idia and gazed lovingly into her emerald-green eyes.

"A black cat is the sign of a terrible omen. Mock me all you want, you witches. Some of us are not so arrogant as to invite evil spirits into our lives. Some of us revere Mawu-Lisa and Gbadu. I know what your wicked self has done, and you will reap what you have sown, Idia. You will regret inviting such harm into your life." She gazed pointedly at Idia.

Later, Queen Idia and three of her closest friends, Cheola, Zamandla, and Eklezabela met that night and tiptoed to the site they had set up as their altar. The moon was full, and they needed no other light. The falls provided a musical backdrop and bats and other nocturnal animals joined them to form a melodic symphony, instead of the expected cacophony. Raven growled and her fur stood up straight.

"It's okay, Raven," Cheola soothed the cub. As Cheola petted her, Idia eyed the silent warriors who had formed a circle around the four women. It didn't surprise her to see them gathered around her. Theirs was a small world, and secrets were hard to keep.

Idia recounted the vision she experienced while wrestling with the python and why she brought the cub back with her. She took a deep breath and explained the sacrifice each warrior was about to make to ensure the rise, survival, and power of the Ravenisha, the name they were to be known as from then on. She explained the series of events shown to her in her vision—starting from the mixing of their blood with Raven's to Raven consuming a piece of their hearts. Idia informed them that hereafter, they would be the progeny of the spirit La Panthère Noire, walking the Earth as werecats and shapeshifters, consuming human flesh once a month to stay alive. In exchange for their allegiance, they would live long lives and be almost indestructible. Neither gunshots, poisons, falls from high places nor stabbings would kill them. They could try to kill themselves, but La Panthère Noire's essence would revive and rejuvenate them. They could, however, be killed by other preternatural beasts and eaten. Each woman would thereafter bear the mark of La Panthère Noire, a hyperpigmented area shaped like a paw print on her left buttock. Idia explained the bloodline would only pass to the female young and that they were not to interfere in in-house battles, especially if two pantheresses were fighting for control. Idia asked each warrior if she was sure she wanted to embrace the beast and its powers. Every woman replied yes. And so it was done.

Chapter 11

Cheola felt a frisson in her heart. Something told her that Idia was holding information back from them, and she could tell from the looks Zamandla was giving her that she felt the same way. She figured whatever it was would be revealed to them eventually and maybe Idia didn't want everyone to know what she wasn't revealing. Such was Cheola's trust in Idia, she persuaded Zamandla to not press Idia and to let Idia tell them in her own time what it was she was holding back.

Everything had gone according to La Panthère Noire's plans, for she was a Baka, evil and powerful, having the ability to exist in the form of an animal. She had been watching these warrior women for years, moving silently, often within mere inches of them, but never being seen or felt. People often referred to panthers as "ghosts of the jungle" for a reason. After many observations, La Pathère Noire captured a black pantheress cub in which to house her animal spirit. She knew these fierce women's spirits and bodies would be strong enough to contain her soul and endure the change. They would spread her power. Her seed. The world would again experience the rule of La Panthère Noire through the Ravenisha and La Panthère Noire would reclaim her crown from Talonius, Lord of the Legion of the Dead. Okay, he was really called Talonius of the Taloned Dimension, but she had spread rumors of the other name, knowing it would irritate him. She badly wanted to quickly raise her army to topple

Talonius, but prudence reigned. She had waited all this time. She could wait a little longer. Ultimately, what were a few hundred years on the universe's timeline when you had an eternity to carry out your plans?

The next morning, the invigorated women awoke to a fierce racket. Raven was growling in a frenzy while Nahwi screamed, "You're all an abomination! Gbadu is not pleased! This demoness tried to bite me!" Of course, she omitted the the fact that the cub had tried to bite her because she hit it with her walking stick. She pointed her shaking finger at the baffled group of women warriors. "She-beasts! You have gone against everything pure and natural. You think I don't know what you did last night? What you have become?"

"Quiet! You don't know whether the gods are pleased or displeased," Idia roared. "At least I did something. What have you ever done, Nahwi, besides cower? And when those immoral men sell us to the land across the big water, you will thank me for what I have done. All of you. I cast you out of this tribe, Nahwi. I can never trust you. Just go."

"But I'm old and feeble," Nahwi groveled. "I'll never make it back to the people by myself." She mewled, hoping Idia would at least send someone to accompany her.

"That's not my problem." Queen Idia's beady eyes bored holes into Nahwi and from her emanated an aura that was so icy, Nahwi shivered. "Pray to your gods Mawu-Lisa and Gbadu. They'll help you."

"I feel sorry for you, Idia," Nahwi said, gathering up her meager belongings. "You're sadly mistaken if you think you will get what you want by cavorting with black forces. Your end will not be quick or peaceful. May the gods help the rest of you, especially you Cheola. If you think she's your friend, you can think again. Your mother was my best friend, may the gods

rest her soul, but I can't abide by this. I can't watch over you any longer. Beware of this fork-tongued bitch. She will betray you."

Queen Idia slapped the old woman and flung her to the ground as the crowd of women gasped and put their hands to their mouths. It was beyond disrespectful to treat an elder in such a way. Several women rushed forward to help Nahwi up, but Cheola waved them away and helped the old woman up herself.

"Remember what I said, Cheola," Nahwi whispered. "Be wary. She will betray you." She turned to the rest and voiced an African proverb. "Just remember, the axe forgets, but the tree remembers."

As Nahwi slowly made her way back down the winding mountain, almost no one watched or cared about her departure, except the pantheress, its eyes narrowed. The women later learned Nahwi never made it back to the village. Good, Idia gloated. Maybe she got eaten by a lion, or who knows, a black pantheress.

The years passed, and the Fon, as the people in the region came to be known, and the Ravenisha managed to co-exist. They learned it was easier to fight their common enemy, the Yoruba, together than separately. The Fon noticed the warrior women never seemed to age, were abnormally strong, and only bore and raised female children through couplings with Fon men. There were tales of skinwalkers killing and devouring humans throughout Africa, but the Fon weren't afraid, as nothing ever happened to them or their neighboring villages' residents. Also, the Ravenisha seemed to be under the various kings' aegises, as they were excellent role models for the kings' own female fighters, the ahosi or mino. It also wasn't lost on the villagers that each king had a "special" relationship with Idia. Then, something changed with the last Dahomey king and his relationship with Queen Idia. It was said that he asked Queen Idia to help him repel the French, whom he feared would one day take over the Dahomey, and she refused. This was a grave miscalculation on Idia's part. Perhaps Idia didn't have the king under her thumb as much as she thought she did. He had also heard rumors of the Ravenisha's substantial wealth hidden in the mountains, and he plotted a way to get rid of them and simultaneously take possession of their riches.

Idia had observed that this monarch seemed different from his brothers. Whereas his brothers kowtowed before her werecat and pantheress forms, this last brother's reaction had been one of entitlement. It was as though since he owned the Kingdom of Dahomey, that ownership also extended to the Ravenisha. The times she had tried to disabuse him of the notion he owned her or the Ravenisha, he had intimated that the Ravenisha wouldn't like for the king to withdraw his protection of them. Oh, the arrogance, Idia thought. The man was nefarious, but if she could hold on, she would take care of him soon.

Idia discovered the king was right in his belief the French were a threat. She and the other Ravenisha had come upon great numbers of French army troops in their forays in search of human flesh. If the French were successful, the Dahomey Kingdom and its mighty Amazon female warriors were about to be no more. As much as Idia was growing to dislike and distrust this current ruler, she'd still rather see him and her beloved people free than under French rule. Even as powerful as she and the Ravenisha were in their pantheress forms, she knew they were no match for the French: they would be vastly outnumbered and out-armed.

A great melancholy settled over the female warriors' village, for the time had come for the foretold separation. Idia had been acting shifty and aloof for months, but her behavior had been attributed to this upcoming moment. As the sun rose, Cheola, Eklezabela, and Zamandla embraced Idia one last time. They had romped with Raven the night before and killed and eaten their fill in a faraway village. Despite knowing this day would come, it still filled them with sorrow. As the warriors kissed and waved goodbye to their friends, the queen and her remaining cadre moved off at a fast pace deeper into the jungle's canopy only to find a surprise of their own awaiting them. An ambush.

The king thought he would get the drop on Idia and her warriors. He followed his advisors' warnings not to trust her and had ordered his army to take care of Idia and the rest. But Idia had not only been alive for far longer than he had, she had also been in more wars. Idia and her warriors quickly squashed the king's Amazons. After Queen Idia and the other Ravenisha made quick work of the king's guard in their pantheress forms, they consumed the bodies. Rejuvenated, they continued on their trek to their new home, which they hoped would remain undiscovered for centuries to come. Idia knew with certainty the fall of the Dahomey Kingdom was imminent, but it wasn't her fault, she thought. The king had rebuffed all of her offers to share the kingdom. Now she would have her own kingdom and all the spoils. She knew she had probably made a mistake leaving the king alive, but it wasn't her time to rule.

She thought about how easy it had been to get rid of the greatest threats to her ascension to power. Chuckling, she spoke into the air, "Yes. You will bear children. You will bear a second generation of Ravenisha. And once I've taken them from you, I will find a way for them and their progeny to be my key to creating my true army and ruling this land."

Meanwhile, Cheola, Eklezabela, and Zamandla settled in and waited to be caught by the king's slave catchers so they could be sold to America, where they would become known as Ceola, Elizabeth, and Matilda.

Chapter 12

Teddy sat frozen, processing the unthinkable. Nana and the others had dropped a bomb. *OMG, I have a sister. I. Have. A. Sister! I'm not alone in this world. I have people.* Her eyes watered and tears threatened to escape from them.

The sun faded from the horizon and the air cooled as they sat outside on the porch. They watched an SUV wind its way up the mountainside with gleeful anticipation. Since Naima and Celeste lived in Atlanta when they weren't at the home base of Ravenswood, it was easier for them to drive to Alabama in the same car. They'd driven back to Atlanta after the fracas, unaware Rufus would order them back to Ravenswood so soon. Rufus had put up a fuss to them living in another city and state, of course, but after the trial separation went so smoothly with the girls agreeing to be on the radar and let him know when they wanted to travel, he decided to take the approach it was better to lose the battle than the war. Besides, he knew where they lived and they hadn't been of any use to him until this moment.

The Old-Generation Ravenisha had raised the tight-knit posse together since they were babies and regaled them with stories of the Ravenisha many, many times. The young women were well aware of their otherworldly status and what was expected of them.

There were hugs and kisses all around before the girls put their bags in their rooms. Celeste and Naima had been as shocked as Teddy to learn of Fredi's existence. After a meal of fried catfish, candied yams, turnip greens, and hushpuppies, the women remained seated around the huge dining table, finishing the last of the banana pudding and drinking coffee. The mood was pensive and a little tense, as it was time to discuss why they were all gathered together so urgently. Ceola tapped on a cup, and the conversation quieted as everyone gave her all of their attention. The young bevy turned toward her and they sharply inhaled. A myriad of emotions played across their faces. They couldn't remember the last time they had seen Nana cry.

"I'm fine," Ceola smiled through her sniffles. "Just thinking about Cleo and the others and how I wish they were here. They would be so proud to call you girls daughters." Ceola took in a deep breath and wiped her eyes. "Ladies, we have much work to do and not much time to do it."

The elders noted it soon became apparent once they were in America as slaves, and after Rufus had taken their babies, Idia had deceived them.

"I know, I know," Tildy shut Teddy down before she could get started. "We were fools to agree to do such a thing."

Idia abandoned them, and it was left up to them to build a new group on their own. They did everything they could to make it easy for Idia to find them. That's partly why they persuaded the Honeycutts to name the town Ravenswood. They had no idea Idia had been keeping tabs on them over the years and knew their exact location. They had been whipped, raped, and worked from sunup until sundown for so long. They lived through lynching, segregation, and the Civil Rights Movement.

A sullen quiet had permeated the room by now. The New-Generation was largely somber, but some looked as though you wouldn't want to be alone with them in a dark alley as the Old-Gen recounted their journey to this moment.

"B-b-b-but I still don't understand. Why didn't you just eat the slave masters and try to go back to Africa?" Celeste wondered, her light-skinned freckled face flushed.

"Why didn't slaves just kill the masters and take over the plantations? We were fools and still believed Idia would keep her promise," Ceola answered while curling her lips like she smelled something sour, and with her eyes flashing daggers. "Deep down, we knew she wouldn't rescue us. It's tremendously difficult to accept the fact that someone you thought of as a sister, someone you would have given your life for, someone you would cut off your little finger for...that...that person would betray you and throw your friendship away like someone throws away trash. Intellectually, you know all the whys, but in here" —Ceola thumped her chest—"in here, it hurts. Also, a part of us wondered why should we go back to Africa when we helped build this place?"

"I get you don't want to leave your daughters, but why would you think Idia is the only one who was supposed to rescue you? What hold does she have on y'all?" Teddy asked.

"Idia told us that La Panthère Noire had appointed her queen over us and had bestowed her with special powers. Supposedly, if we ever hurt Idia in any way, we would also hurt ourselves. We've been such fools," Ceola said. Matilda growled, hands balled up into fists.

They told the girls how the Honeycutt family members noticed they were different and the men who became scientists started studying them like they were lab rats. They tolerated the poking and prodding in the beginning. Resentment really set in when the men began forcefully taking their blood and tissue samples.

"Hold up," Teddy interjected. "This makes no sense. You could have easily changed and overpowered them. That's different from trying to incite a slave rebellion."

Ceola looked at her and shook her head. "And then do what, Teddy? Eke out an existence by hiding, eating whenever we could, constantly living in fear? The US Army would have hunted us forever. We may be difficult to kill, but it is possible. By the time we felt better and not so beaten and worn down, Rufus and his minions had kept us imprisoned on this piece of land for ages. Idia and Rufus took your mothers away and we haven't seen them since. We know we're here for a higher purpose. It may not be the reason Idia led us to believe, but we are here for a reason. The world is changing. We're not the only preternatural beings in existence. Also, we will *never* leave our babies."

"Nope, that still wouldn't be me," insisted Teddy, who never knew her mother, Cleo. "I would have fought back. Now, I may be dead but a bunch of other people would be dead, too."

"And what would that have accomplished, Teddy Nat Turner?" Matilda gently chided. "You're smarter than that. Hell, I've taught you better war strategies than that. As a smart man once said, *The wise warrior avoids the battle.* Besides,"—Matilda smiled wickedly—"we got our revenge many times. Y'all remember that time that scrawny overseer thought he was going to rape me?"

"Girl, what overseer was this? There were so many," Ceola said, rolling her eyes.

"This was the one with the chicken legs, the little potbelly and he always smelled like pickles and an outhouse," Matilda replied, wrinkling her nose.

"Oh yeah, I remember him now." Ceola kept her eyes fixed on the tabletop and softly shook her head from side to side. "He's the one who beat me until blood ran down my legs and then he literally rubbed salt in the wounds. Then, he raped me." A torrent of tears rolled down her cheeks, and her shoulders shook. "Sorry, guys…for being such a crybaby lately," she sniffled, trying to stop crying, but failing. The silent tears gave way to a keening wail as Ceola finally released the pent-up emotions she had valiantly hidden all the centuries since their capture.

Matilda went over, crouched in front of her, and took her hand. "Look at me. Look at me, Ceola." Ceola reluctantly raised her head and looked into Tildy's eyes. "I got him, baby girl. I got him good, for all the wrongs that cocksucker inflicted on us, but especially for beating you to shreds and violating you."

Teddy, Celeste, and Naima looked at Ceola, never having heard the story before and not used to seeing the matriarch in such a vulnerable state.

"As I said, his little scrawny ass thought he was going to rape me one night. We had just finished an interminable day working our asses off in the field picking cotton, and he had the nerve to pull me aside. I knew what he wanted as soon as he smiled, showing those ugly little brown stumps masquerading as teeth. Y'all know I poked my lips out. I decided then and there what I was going to do. Somehow, I masked the hatred I felt and beckoned for him to follow me into the woods on the edge of the property. Whoo, he thought he was about to get some," Matilda chortled. "I led him as deep into the woods as I could before I took my dress off. That fool actually thought I was undressing for him.

Naw, I was undressing because that was my only dress and I couldn't afford to ruin it. I changed as soon as that dress was off and ate his ass. When I finished, I just threw that dress back on and crept back to our shack like nothing had ever happened." She smiled through her tears; then, her eyes lit up, skin wrinkling at the corners. "Y'all must have done the same thing because that plantation went through multiple overseers."

"You right, guilty as charged," Ceola trilled, holding up her hand.

Lizzie looked around furtively and whispered, "I got me one, too."

Tildy said, "What's strange is the Honeycutt men never said a word. You know they had to suspect something, but I guess the absence of bodies made it difficult to accuse us."

"Oh, they knew all right," Ceola stated, as all the women turned and looked at her with their mouths gaping. "Balfour caught me changing and feeding one night."

"Ceola!" gasped Tildy, looking at Ceola in absolute disbelief.

"I thought he didn't find out until after the Civil War," Lizzie gasped, her hand on her chest.

"I was just so over it," Ceola explained. "I probably had PTSD, not knowing what it was back then, and I wanted Balfour and his family to know what we had the power to do to them if we wanted. Later, Zebulon and I used to have long clandestine talks. He wasn't that bad at heart. He explained that because of the prevailing attitudes of those times, he couldn't free us, so we struck a deal where I told him we would stop sabotaging his experiments if he relaxed our constraints a bit. I had long suspected Idia had betrayed us and even if he could have freed us, we weren't going to return to Benin to confront that heffa. The time wasn't right. What did it hurt us to give a little of our blood if it meant a life of relative comfort?" A stunned silence had settled over the room. Matilda and Elizabeth glared at Ceola, arms crossed, lips poked out.

"Don't be angry guys. He mostly kept his promises over the years. Our relations with Rufus turned acrimonious when he thought we killed his father. Then, things really reached a low point when Cleo was born and I wouldn't allow him to use my child as a lab experiment, which he ended up doing, anyway. He made promise after promise to me and broke them all." Heat radiated off of Ceola, and she folded her arms under her breasts and gazed off into the distance.

Matilda sniffed. "I warned you that man was a snake and that he didn't care about you. When you sleep with dogs, you get up with fleas."

"Whaaat?" Ceola said, confused. "I don't have fleas." Matilda gave her a warning look.

Ceola grinned like the Cheshire cat and shook her head. "He's not who you think he is, Tildy. Anyway...then, he took all of our girls for revenge for his father's death, but we should have expected retaliation. Sorry for that minor interruption. Please continue."

Lizzie took up the narrative. She told them how over the years, the scientific Honeycutts had gotten close to making a serum that would allow them to shapeshift and not age. Pure greed and power were the only things that had prevented the Honeycutts from revealing their secret discovery to the world. Apparently, there was something missing in the current formula, and Rufus was desperate to find the last piece of the puzzle. He had taken the Old-Generation's daughters away, and the daughters became pregnant with Theodora, Celeste, and Naima.

"Your blood came back negative for the strain, and while he gave you to us to raise, in his anger, he continued to imprison and destroy our babies, Cleo, Antoinette, and Zenobia just to spite us for what he perceived as their failure to produce these super shapeshifters." Lizzie tried to continue, but a great swell of sadness overcame her. Tears flowed, and she couldn't get her vocal cords to cooperate. The women gathered around her, holding her tight.

"I need more comfort food," Naima exclaimed. "What else is there to eat?"

"I'll bring some sweet potato pie and peach cobbler out." Leona got up and went into the kitchen. "I'm with you, Naima. To hell with watching our weight. We need something after listening to all of this sadness."

"I'll help you, too, Leona." Teddy rose and followed a grateful Leona into the kitchen. "You're not the housekeeper; let us help you more."

"Where was I?" Lizzie asked, giving the surrounding women a grateful smile as her tears abated in the warmth of their embrace. She remembered and continued. "That's okay because the joke ended up being on him. Just look at y'all now. People give up so quickly. If he had retested you every so often, he would have discovered you all test positive for the strain now."

"I don't understand," Celeste began.

"It's like when some children don't test positive for diabetes until they hit puberty, to simplify it," Ceola explained.

"We were already fed up with Rufus and Idia, but when he took and bred our daughters like they were livestock or guinea pigs, that was the last straw. How dare they take our children? Every time we think we're going to break free of Rufus, he tightens his hold on us. Now, he's using our daughters, the Lost-Generation, to keep us under control. I even hate calling them the Lost-Gen. It's like we're consigning them to be absent from us forever." Tears threatened to fall from Lizzie's eyes again.

"It's taken every ounce of our strength just to survive the harsh realities of our lives day to day. I still can't believe we're in this position. I thought you were safe from Rufus's prying eyes. After you girls went through puberty, Rufus began nosing around again, probing, asking invasive questions, trying to see whether your bodies had undergone any peculiarities."

Ceola chimed in, "We did everything we could to make you appear as normal as possible, but that damn Ozzie betrayed us. He told Rufus all of you had developed the sign on your butt cheeks and Rufus must have told that heffa. Why was Ozzie watching yo' damn butt cheeks anyway? I'm so sick of men like him and the Uncle Bobs. And so, here we are. We've put off your change for as long as we can. We must make our move now before Rufus and Idia try to use you. I've long suspected she didn't tell us the entire prophecy. Now I know it. I just don't know the specifics. There's a reason she's trying to destroy us. She'll succeed over my dead body," Ceola vowed. "We must rise as the Ravenisha and make America ours. But first, we're going to take care of that bitch, Idia."

"Well, I guess the change explains why Teddy has been bitchier than usual," Naima sniped. Teddy looked at her questioningly but said nothing.

Ceola gravely addressed the group. "Now it's imperative we bring forth the change. We all wish we could have trained you a little more, but it's been hard. Even though that arrogant Rufus doesn't have cameras and microphones everywhere, we know he is always surreptitiously watching. That's why we're careful about what we say and do. Now you know why we would only teach and speak to you in our native language in certain places. But all bets are off at this point. Matilda has taught all of you a great deal, but there's so much you still must learn. Still, I have to believe that with all of those martial arts y'all have learned, plus being in the Paranormal Reserves and being proficient with all kinds of weapons, you have what you need to help us defeat Rufus and Idia."

"We all know Teddy is already a killing machine, while Celeste and I are more cerebral," Naima snarked.

Teddy sucked on her teeth. "You know, Naima, I admit I have issues and I may not appear as "cerebral"—Teddy made air quotes—"as you and Celeste think you are. However, I did graduate from a world-renowned college Summa Cum Laude, thank you very much. I bet you didn't know the unearthly blue aura known as Angel's Glow that seemed to shine around wounded Civil War soldiers on the battlefield was caused by a bacteria called *Photohabdus luminescens*. It grew in the soldiers' festering wounds and actually saved their lives. Or did you know that the Lone Ranger may have been based on Bass Reeves, a Black cowboy turned first Black Deputy United States Marshal."

"Okaaay? Who cares about shit like that anyway? You still don't have an advanced degree in anything." Celeste looked at Naima, aghast, wondering where this attack on Teddy was coming from.

Before Teddy could reply, Ceola quickly interjected, "Thank goodness we have ears inside Rufus's lab. You'll meet him and the others later. Also, it's not like we haven't taught you *anything*. Even though Rufus has practically starved us to death to prevent us from changing to rejuvenate and nourish our bodies, that's why we look so damn old, we'll help in any way we can. And you know something else? We're working on a way to get these damn collars off so we can feed and get our strength and bodies back. We have some wrongs to right. Not once has that heffa ever contacted us. Not once. I know God said 'vengeance is mine,' but this time it will be *ours*. Idia and Rufus gon' learn you can't do wrong and get by." Tildy and Lizzie nodded their agreement.

"You're awfully quiet, Teddy. What are you thinking?" asked Leona, who also acted as the resident Iyanla Vanzant as she stood up and removed her ceremonial robe from her carry-all that was sitting by her feet. Lizzie may have been the psychologist, but it was Leona people went to when they wanted to discuss something.

Teddy silently counted to ten in her head before she spoke. She wanted to say she was thinking about beating the shit out of Naima, but since that would accomplish nothing, she instead commented, "I'm just wondering whether Rufus and Idia have thought about the folly of trying to use science to always explain and manipulate the supernatural? Spirit beings inhabit Ravenisha's bodies. Right? How do you replicate a spiritual being in a vial?"

"You're right, Theodora," Ceola agreed. "That's probably why there will always be something missing in their quest to develop a formula to enable humans to shapeshift. Thank you. That gives me something to ponder."

"Okay then, we've got a lot to do and a little less than a week to do it. Let's get to work!" Teddy clapped her hands and jumped up from her chair. She marched over to the walk-in pantry and hit the camouflaged mechanism, causing the back wall slid back, revealing one of the mini armories scattered around the property. Each woman had a to-go duffle fully stocked with her favorite weapons. Teddy picked them up and closed the armory.

"Girl, she didn't just clap her hands at us like we're her pets," Celeste told Naima with false anger as Teddy exited the pantry and threw each girl her duffle bag.

Naima missed hers, and it crashed to the floor. She sheepishly picked it up but not before rolling her eyes at Teddy. "Y'all know I'm not coordinated," she whined, glaring at Teddy, her anger real, unlike Celeste's.

"Look at Miss Thang or I guess I should say our queen. Does she even know where she's going?" Celeste teased while Teddy strode ahead of everyone through the house and out the back door.

"Teddy, wait! We didn't mean we were starting tonight. Don't you girls need to rest? Digest what we just discussed?" Lizzie shouted to Teddy's rapidly retreating back. She was booking it despite wearing clunky heels.

"No, Auntie Lizzie, we're wasting time." Teddy barely broke stride. "We're running out of time, and we can rest after we learn how to change. Come on. Chop. Chop. We've got to get to the top of the mountain and practice changing and then hopefully have time left to get in more tactical training, and we need to coordinate with the Paranormal Division at the army base. We have so much to do."

"But Teddy...," Ceola started. She knew Teddy was like a runaway train once she got fixated on something and it would be difficult to derail her.

"No, Nana, it won't wait. I know how tired you and Aunties Lizzie and Tildy must be after all that talking. Don't worry. If you can just make it through the night, I'll get you some food. Some *proper food*. You won't be able to hunt, but at least the meat will give you energy."

"Excuse me, where do you think we're getting this 'meat,' Teddy?" Naima stopped walking, hands on her ample hips, feet planted. The normally good-natured young woman had reached her limit. She looked at Teddy's back like she wanted to plunge a knife into it.

Teddy must have felt the knife's biting pain between her shoulder blades because she finally stopped walking and slowly turned around.

"Don't be daft, Naima. Obviously, we can't just go to the grocery store and buy it. Don't worry, I'm not asking you to violate your little medical oath. Celeste and I will get the meat ourselves. We all know how you feel about hunting and killing humans. You've made your views perfectly clear," Teddy spat. "Let's go." Upon seeing the elders not moving, Teddy groaned. "What now?"

"Umm, Teddy, dear, we need *fresh* meat to rejuvenate...and preferably for your change, too," responded Ceola.

"Fine," Teddy snapped, "we'll call Ozzie and Caesar." With moues of shock, everyone's mouths dropped open. Teddy plowed on. "Drop the shocked expressions. Y'all been complaining about those men ever since I can remember. Don't act like you'll miss them."

"Dayuhm," breathed Naima. "Even for you, that's kind of ruthless, don't you think? I just don't understand what the rush is. How can you be so cruel?"

"I'm sorry, girls. We should have told you that Rufus demanded we turn you over to him in one week," Ceola said. "This is the endgame. Either we fight or we lie down and die. Once Rufus and Idia have you girls, we will have served our purpose and will be disposed of."

"See? I told you! What would you rather do, Naima, be fucking lab experiments, be tortured and have our bodies thrown away without a trace, or use some old, useless men as protein and maybe, just maybe secure a future for ourselves where we'll come out alive and on top?" Teddy countered in a quiet fury.

"I don't think I can be a part of this." Naima shook her head vigorously. "I'm not a psychopath like you are, Teddy. I'd rather take my chances with Rufus and this Idia." Teddy glared, momentarily at a loss for words, only able to sputter like a stalled car engine.

"Also, who said we were willing to sacrifice our husbands?" Lizzie asked.

The forest fell silent as everyone looked at Teddy and waited for her answer.

Chapter 13

Teddy blew out her breath and struggled to get her emotions under control. When she finally did speak, her voice was low and her words sliced through the air like a blade.

"I. Am. Not going to be anybody's fucking lab experiment, is that clear? What in the hell do you think Rufus will do to us when he's gotten what he wants? Do you think he's going to just let us go? Only morons would believe that. How has staying meek and compliant worked for you all of these years? Plus, y'all need to feed. Desperately. Now, those old men have practically come to the end of their lives. How much longer do you think they really have to live?"

Naima held up her hand and interrupted Teddy. "No matter how long they have to live, it's not our right to take their lives. They raised us like we were theirs. And don't you dare blame them for being in the predicament they're in. Everybody's not violent like you! You could have had a brilliant career with the Atlanta PD, but n-o-o-o, you had to fuck up, what was it? Six years? It's no secret you resigned before you were fired."

"Hold it right there. That's bullshit, Naima. You know damned well I was absolved of every shooting, stabbing, or punch that took a criminal's life. I was a fucking exemplary officer, and my having to resign was political. As for the old men, they tolerated us because they knew

Nana and the Aunties would kick them out if they weren't nice to us. And what's with these little jabs at me, heffa?" Teddy's heavy breathing filled the night air. *That bitch*, she thought, tears forming in her eyes. She would not cry. She would not cry. She knew she could have gone all the way to the top if she'd just gotten her temper under control. Now look at her. How far the mighty had fallen. She was a reserve officer in the Army's "bad news bears" and "mighty ducks" division. Apparently, her reputation had preceded her to her new position at the Paranormal Reserves, a special branch of the Army based in the nearby Cheaha Forest, hence the night before last's fight. *Fuck fucking Naima and everybody else!*

Naima continued as if Teddy hadn't spoken. "We're no better than they are, nor are we above them. We don't get to arbitrarily decide they are meat for our nanas. And there's no way I'd ever consider eating them. Ever!"

"Naima, I ain't got time for this shit!" Teddy shouted, her eyes flashing dangerously as her body coiled tightly. She blew out a breath and continued in a calmer voice. "If you don't want to be a Ravenisha, fine. Leave. Look around. Even the elders have stopped protesting. They know the truth of what I'm saying. You'll be in or out. This isn't about emotion, morality, or ethics; it's about survival. The survival of us. Feeding the beasts within us." Teddy slammed her fist into her hand. "And make no mistake, there will be a war. Idia is going to pay for this shit."

Naima balled her hands into fists and got in Teddy's face, screaming, "Who made you queen over us, Theodora? You need to get your own shit together before you try to boss others. Why in the hell should any of us do what you say? Up here acting like you know every fucking thing with your crazy-ass self! You've never even hunted or eaten a human before. You need to shut your fucking mouth. You're not the queen yet. Bitch!"

Naima towered over Teddy as her spit flew in Teddy's face. Teddy's hand went for her gun seemingly of its own volition.

Everyone's gasps filled the night air as they took a step back. Their hands covered their mouths, and their eyes were wide with fear.

"Oh, so now you're going to shoot me like you resolve all of your problems. No wonder they called you the Black Annie Oakley, Teddy 'Quick Gun' Furie, the Grim Reaper, and Quick Draw McGraw."

"I did everything by the book, heffa, and you know evidence always attested to this." Teddy's voice and body trembled, so great was her fury. "You know or should know that suspects never respected my authority as a woman, especially a Black woman. Villainous guys were always trying me. It wasn't my fault if they didn't think I would really shoot them. Perhaps you're the stupid one if you can't understand this. At least I passed the police department's physical. You couldn't even do that with your fat ass."

Naima, who was what people used to call stout and tall, drove the dagger home. "Well, at least my boyfriend loves my curves. Your stank-ass has never even had a boyfriend with your skunk-striped hair. Who would want you?"

Leona looked faint and began fanning herself with her hands, whispering, "Jesus, Lord. Help us!"

"Girls. Girls. Come on. We don't have time for this. I don't know what has triggered these feelings, but can we discuss them later?" Lizzie implored. She was completely ignored.

Teddy looked up at Naima and gave her the same intense hair-raising gaze the women had seen Ceola give when she meant business.

"You need to back the fuck up off me," she commanded in a voice an octave lower than her normal speaking voice. Menace radiated from her very being. "You obviously have a problem with me that you haven't been woman or adult enough to discuss with me privately. Now, if you think you can take me, give it your best shot, heffa," snarled Teddy quietly, calmly, her weird eyes boring holes into Naima's. "And I don't need any weapon whatsoever to take your weak ass out." Teddy holstered her gun and stood with her right foot planted in front of her left.

The aura emanating from Teddy was so thick and overpowering, Naima and the other women almost couldn't breathe. The air was heavy with the static electricity often felt before a tornado hit. Teddy's eyes were the most disconcerting of all. It was bad enough when she stared at Naima like she was about to kill her. Now, the mismatched eyes were literally shooting lasers. Shocked, the Old-Gen really looked at Teddy and realized for the first time that something more powerful and deadlier than them was in their midst.

Naima slowly looked around at the women gathered silently around them and realized if there was to be a fight, it would be until death, sanctioned by the other Ravenisha. She could tell something had shifted in the air. While it would hurt the women deeply to see the girls fight until one of them was dead, they were like a pride, and she had just challenged the alpha female. And Teddy was definitely the alpha female of their group. She always had been, ever since they were toddlers. Naima felt confident none of the Old-Gen could defeat Teddy in a fight, either, not even the great warrior Matilda. She knew she couldn't best Teddy, with or without weapons.

And oh God, what was going on with those spooky eyes and the laser light emanating from them? She had never seen Teddy's beast before, but if it was halfway as menacing as Teddy the human, she was in trouble. Oh Lord, had she just signed her death warrant? When Teddy went ballistic, sometimes she tore victims' bodies to pieces, especially if she used her shotgun. To say Teddy had problems controlling her rage was an understatement. Naima let out a sob, her body trembling uncontrollably. She had always envisioned a funeral where she would lie in a casket looking beautiful and peaceful, with her body in one piece. She quickly took in a shaky breath, dropped to the ground, and rolled onto her back in a sign of submission.

"I'm sorry, Teddy. You're right. I have been feeling some type of way lately, and it just all came to a head tonight. You have all the talent in the world, and I feel like you're wasting it. Why are you the anointed one and not me or Celeste? With the change coming, my feelings have been everywhere. I know I'm not like you and Celeste, and I feel bad about being so meek. I admit, I'm low-key jealous of you, while at the same time I'm worried to death about your mental health. I'm scared. I'm afraid of what's going to happen to all of us." Naima wailed, "I'm not strong like you." *God, how did we end up in this moment, Naima wondered. I love Teddy, and I know she loves me. Why have I been making jabs at her all night? Could it be my hormones are out of control? I'll make things right with her.*

The night was still as everyone collectively held their breath, waiting for Teddy's response.

"Just go on back to the house, Naima," Teddy told her, relenting, her face in resting bitch mode and the strange sparks of light dimming in her eyes. "I don't want you to do anything that will get your conscience in a twist. It's okay. Everybody isn't warrior material. Celeste and I have this. Go." Teddy waved her hand at Naima, dismissing her.

Naima let out a long exhale and resolutely replied while shakily rising to her feet, "Nah, I'll be okay. I just had a momentary breakdown. I'm coming, heffa. Please don't stop me. I have to do this."

Teddy shrugged her shoulders and looked at Naima with a look that said if you say so. She knew she should hug Naima and offer comfort of some sort, but showing emotion other than rage was just too difficult for her. Plus, she was still mad and Naima owed her another apology.

Naima noticed Teddy's unwavering gaze. While her body was preternaturally still, her spooky eyes were twitching like they were electrified. "What?"

"Aren't you going to apologize for calling me a psychopath?" Even though Teddy asked in a mild, slightly joking way, she was dead serious. Naima had crossed a line tonight. She had deeply hurt Teddy, and Teddy was not the type to forgive and forget. *And she didn't have to talk about my hair*, Teddy bitterly thought. *Naima knows that's one of my sore spots.*

"Hell naw," Naima replied, laughing shakily. "You know you're a tad cray-cray, but I still love you, though."

"Celeste?" Teddy turned to her beseechingly.

Celeste smiled and slapped Teddy playfully on the butt. Even though Teddy smiled with the other young women, the smile didn't quite reach her eyes.

The older women exhaled a sigh of relief. That was a close call. They hadn't really been worried the girls wouldn't resolve their little tiff by themselves. Teddy could be a take charge, take no prisoners, kick butt and ask questions later kind of person, but family was everything to her and she loved the others like sisters. They knew that while Teddy may have given Naima a beat down, she wouldn't have killed her. At least they prayed she wouldn't have killed her. Her emotions had seemed to be all over the place lately.

Tildy's cell phone vibrated. She looked down, exhaled in relief, and replied to the text. The women resumed walking. "I've got food covered, guys. You don't have to worry about securing fresh meat for us. Lieutenant Allensworth and his men will meet us at the rendezvous point and bring our nourishment. I pray we will successfully remove these balls and chains from our necks tonight. We better get a move on. Rufus is probably tracking our movements as I speak. It won't take him long to get here with reinforcements." Tildy increased her stride.

The women continued winding their way further up the mountain until they came to a clearing. Leona, who had continued walking after the argument de-escalated, looked majestic in her white, flowing robe, embellished with purple fleur-de-lis and golden leaves. A fourth-generation Louisianan, Leona had been born with the gift of sight. She had grown up in a prominent voodoo family where she was a high priestess. She smiled reassuringly at each young woman as they walked up to her. "Everything is ready, guys. Let's do this!" She threw off her robes with a flourish, revealing athletic wear underneath. She then astounded the young ladies by leaping onto the nearest rock and scaling the mountainside.

"Lord, don't let these old bones fail me now," whispered Lizzie as she followed Leona. Ceola and Matilda gestured for the girls to follow the others up the mountain. They immediately began complaining that their boots had heels and weren't meant for mountain climbing.

"Climb, now!" Ceola commanded. "Shit, we ain't got all night. I don't trust Rufus as far as I can throw him. If he said we have a week, we definitely don't have a week. And who knows when that she-beast Idia will show up."

Finally, Leona reached a ledge and waited for the others to catch up. While Leona couldn't shapeshift, she was stronger than usual, thanks to Tildy's blood. Huffing and puffing, the women watched as Matilda moved a piece of slate aside and punched a code into the keypad embedded in the rock. The rock slid back, and they began the long descent down into a cavern.

"In answer to your unasked question, yes, there is an easier way to reach our lair, Lizzie said. "That walk in the woods was for Rufus's and his spies' benefit. We perform our Vodun religious rites at the clearing, but it's more for their benefit than ours. This is our true lair."

"Why haven't we been made aware of this place before now?" Celeste asked.

"Because y'all would have unknowingly led Rufus straight here," Matilda replied.

After descending about a mile into the earth, the women came to another door. As Ceola was about to enter the code, the door swung open to reveal a swarm of massive armed and black-clad men.

Chapter 14

The young women filed past the men, checking them out from head to toe. The men looked on in amusement as the women finally closed their mouths and stopped ogling them. Tildy then introduced the women to Lieutenant Augustus (Gus) Alford Allensworth, III and his close friends and brothers in arms, Sergeants Akiro Donté Shaw, Roland Jabari Parks, and Hendrix (Henry) X.A. Vaughn. The girls realized they had seen the men before—had even exchanged greetings in passing—but they'd never been this up close and personal. Or rather, two of the women hadn't. They couldn't stop staring at the tall, heavily muscled young men. The Old-Gen revealed how they had groomed these special men over the years to be their sentinels, as they had Ozzie and Caesar.

Smiling, Ceola said, "We've known them and their people for decades. At one point, we were all on that damn plantation toiling and suffering together. These men volunteered for this assignment, girls, as did their fathers, and they've seen us in our werecat and she-panther forms when we used to have the energy to change and feed. They are all well-trained at that secret army base, Fort Cheaha, near the Cheaha Mountains in the Talladega National Forest. Sometimes, we're inert when we catnap or our energy level is really depleted. We can be especially vulnerable. They'll make excellent mates one day, too," Ceola added with a devilish grin.

The New-Gen gazed at the surrounding space, taking in the high cathedral ceiling. Even though there were no windows, the area was well lit and cool fresh air flowed in cleverly placed vents. The floor was hard, constructed from the mountain's granite, but people sat at their stations most of the time, anyway. Lab equipment sparkled, and there was a cozy air about the place, rather than that of a cold sterile lab.

Leona smiled slyly at the girls. "You know they've been admiring you from afar and have already asked me about your dating status ladies. Teddy, I swear Gus literally licked his lips when he saw you," she teased, unmindful that Teddy and Gus were both embarrassed to death.

"I can't be bothered with no man, right now," Teddy said. She wondered when and how Gus had seen her since she hadn't seen him but quickly flicked the thought aside as she arranged her face in its resting bitch mode. "What?" she asked, looking around at the shocked and disapproving expressions on the women and men's faces.

Ceola patted Gus on the shoulder. "I told you. She can be a little mean, but it's mostly an act. Just be patient; she'll come around. It wouldn't surprise me if she's still a virgin."

"Nana!" Teddy squealed, as a red flush spread up her neck and her cheeks looked like they were on fire. "Oh God, just take me now," she beseeched, averting her eyes from Gus and looking at the wall in front of her.

Naima rolled her eyes. "Whew, somebody pray for this chile."

"It'll take more than prayers," Leona chimed in, shaking her head. "Y'all know she's a little she-devil."

"Well, even she-devils need some good dick now and then. Hell, some good dick may just mellow her out. What?" Lizzie asked when she noticed everyone else looking at each other with *I know she didn't just say that smirks* on their faces. "Uhm, I may be a little long in the tooth, but I'm not dead." Lizzie rolled her eyes right back.

"We'll all be dead if we don't begin," Matilda said.

"Ha, ha, ha, you're all so funny," Teddy pouted, so mortified, her entire face was lobster red. "I'm standing right here, people. What is this? Pile on Teddy day? Can we focus on the task at hand, please?" she pleaded while muttering, "I've never been so embarrassed in my life. Sorry," she told Gus. "I'm just focused and in warrior mode." Now that she was looking at him full-on, she thought while unconsciously smiling, D*ayuhm, he's a cutie. Tall, dark, and handsome.* She liked the way she had to crane her neck to look up at him and how inviting his broad chest looked. And those tattoos were sexy as hell.

When he smiled at her in return and said, "No problem. I understand," in a voice only a Southern-raised Black man could, Teddy's heart did a stuttering beat.

Teddy snapped out of the trance-like state she was in, and when she heard the women giggling and saw them fist-bumping each other out of the corner of her eye, her smile disappeared, replaced by pursed lips and arms folded under her chest. When she realized this just brought attention to her double Ds, she folded her arms across them, instead. She wanted to glare at Gus but instead ogled him again, want and need emanating from her pores. And the best thing of all, Teddy, thought giddily like a cat high on catnip, was that Lieutenant Augustus Alford Allensworth, III was exhibiting the same emotions toward her. Yaaassss, she may not be a virgin for much longer!

"If you two could deign to tear yourselves away from each other, we really need to feed," Ceola called out, beaming.

"Sorry, Miss C. I'm on it, ma'am," Gus rasped, clearing his throat and gesturing for Henry and Roland to follow him. "Akiro, do what you do."

Akiro nodded and sat down at one of the computer stations. He opened his knapsack, removed some electronic equipment, and set about blocking Rufus's access to the women's collars.

"It took me a while to figure out how to turn the collars off, but I think I finally have the correct algorithm. Yeah, baby. I'm in." He stopped typing furiously to give a fist pump. "Sometimes, I wonder if this is too easy. This is like taking candy from a baby."

"You really need to give in to their begging and go work for the NSA already," Leona said.

Akiro smirked. "They think I should work for them for peanuts out of sheer patriotism but patriotism don't pay the bills, baby. Besides, I like walking on the dark side." He shared a knowing look with Naima and gave her an air kiss. Naima grinned and gave him an air kiss in return.

The women quit wandering around when they heard the tapping of brisk footsteps coming their way. The other men returned, carrying body bags, which they unceremoniously threw down. Movement from inside the bags made the bags appear animated, like long black worms inching along the floor.

"Gentlemen, do you mind taking them to the pit?" Ceola asked.

"Sure thing, ma'am," responded Henry, as they picked up the bags and left the room.

"The pit?" questioned Celeste who couldn't decide if she liked Henry or Roland, or maybe both equally. "That sounds ominous."

"Feeding isn't a neat endeavor, girls. There will be blood, guts, and gore everywhere. Because we're in an enclosed space, you want to feed where you can easily hose the room down afterward. Follow us. Akiro, you know where to find us when you're ready," Ceola called over her shoulder as she hurried out of the room. She was ready to eat! Akiro gave a thumbs up while still staring at the screen in front of him and typing furiously.

"Almost done," he muttered. "I just need to secure the perimeter and set up a little feint for Rufus and his men."

Once everyone gathered in the pit, a portentous stillness settled over the air. Whereas the workspace had an air of coziness to it, this stark, circular room felt cold and sterile, like a jail cell. Furnishings and creature comforts were wholly absent; the only things present were a large drain in the middle of the sloping floor and several power hoses. That and manacles spaced around the walls.

The Old-Gen stood quivering, nostrils working overtime. It was as though the enticing scents and sounds emanating from the bags were causing their system to overload. They stared ravenously at the body bags, saliva dripping from their lips, their little muscles quivering in their effort to prevent them from running to the bags and ripping them open.

Akiro came in and said it should be okay to remove the collars. He stood behind Tildy to remove hers, but Ceola surprised them all by saying "Fuck it" and tearing her collar off. Overcome with emotion, Ceola took a shaky breath, flung the collar down, and lifted her foot to destroy the transmitter.

Akiro quickly stopped her. "Whoa there, Miss C. We don't want to damage the transmitter. That will be a dead giveaway to Rufus that you're no longer wearing the collar."

"You're right, Akiro. It's just that I've been wearing that damn collar for such a long time. It feels so good to not have that chain around my neck anymore. When I threw that collar down and was about to stomp it to pieces, I was symbolically crushing Rufus." Ceola pictured Rufus's face in her mind and sighed. "I'll get my chance."

They removed all the collars and disrobed. There was a collective gasp when everyone saw how the bones protruded sharply from their thin skin. You could count their ribs and the vertebra in their backs. Their little legs were just skin and bones, with the femoral heads prominent in all of them. The raised lines on their backs from years of whip lashings that even their otherworldly pantheress rejuvenating blood couldn't fade jumped out from their skin as if in 3-D. Even Tildy's impressive tribal tattoos and piercings seemed diminished. As if on a tidal wave, the pity emotion swelled to anger in the room.

"Oh, Nana," Teddy murmured, rapidly blinking back the tears threatening to flow from her eyes.

"Don't worry." Leona patted her arm. "They're about to take the first step to get their old bodies and strength back." She wiped away tears she'd unsuccessfully prevented from falling.

As the air thickened and prickled with an unseen force, the men, Leona, and the young women stepped away from the older women and stood with their backs against the utilitarian concrete wall. The women began shapeshifting, but because their bodies were in such a weakened state, they could only metamorphose into their werecat forms at first. In this form, while they partially resembled panthers who walked upright, you could still recognize their human faces through the black hair covering them. One by one, they dropped to the floor and morphed into their complete animal forms. No one exploded or cried out in pain. They were simply werecats one moment and panthers the next. The room was silent, except for the soft wet sounds emanating from the women's bodies as they metamorphosed. The young stared bug-eyed at the beautiful creatures before them. Even though the enormous cats were on the bony side, they were still as big as ponies. Gus motioned for his men to follow him as they slowly walked past the growling cats and went over to the body bags. Teddy, always the rash one, rushed toward Ceola and began rubbing the cat all over. Gus was there in a flash, standing near Teddy protectively.

"What a beautiful girl," she cooed, rubbing the big cat's ears and running her hands down its skeletal body. Once it was clear Ceola wouldn't harm Teddy, the other girls rushed over to the other enormous cats and began petting them. As the men finished opening the body bags, the low growling sounds emanating from the cats' throats grew in pitch and volume as they moved away from the girls and eagerly crowded around the men and the body bags.

"Just hold on, guys," said Henry, nervously laughing as one of the werepanthers jostled him. "Dinner's here. Just let me get out of the way first." The men swiftly removed the ties and gags from the unsuspecting prey.

"Where did y'all find the food?" Teddy asked Gus as he quickly jumped out of the way, as well.

"Unfortunately, there are always people society won't miss. Besides, under normal circumstances, they only need to feed once a month," he replied, his eyes constantly moving, scanning the room for danger.

Screams filled the room as some humans jumped out of the body bags and tried to run, while one lay paralyzed by fear at the sight of the huge cats. The humans ran toward the group congregated along the wall and two of the cats swiftly brought them down. The third cat began circling the human still lying in the body bag, batting its enormous paw against the trembling body as if toying with the doomed person. As if in time to an unheard command, the massive cats pounced on and tore chunks of meat from the hapless victims. Razor-sharp claws sliced into the humans' skin like it was butter, ripping away muscles and tendons, which they rapidly devoured. The sounds in the room were deafening. The enormous cats mewled with pleasure while they ate. Between the humans' screams and the sound of flesh tearing and bones being cracked like potato chips, the young men and women unconsciously inched closer to the door. They watched as the werepanthers spared no part of the humans' bodies.

"Oh God, I think I'm going to be sick," Akiro groaned, clutching his stomach. He would have turned green if his skin hadn't been so dark. "And I don't know what's worse, the screams coming from those people, or the sounds Miss Ceola and the others are making. Eww, and what's that smell? When they split open the abdomens, this room started smelling like a sewer! I can't take it. The blood stinks, the room smells like shit. Those intestines look gross. I'm just a computer person, I can't watch this. Are you okay…" Akiro's voice trailed off as he watched Naima's face, then the other women's.

The girls inched closer to the feeding cats. Every young woman now had her eyes glued to the scene in front of her, and instead of fear and loathing, there were looks of longing and rapture.

"Riiight," Akiro said, edging along the wall and opening the door. "I'll see y'all back out front." Roland, Henry, and Gus followed him, but they didn't go far. In fact, they stood just outside the door because they knew it was their duty to protect the metahumans, which now included the New-Gen.

The enormous cats finished every morsel and, with deep purrs of contentment, stretched out on the floor. Roland and Henry hosed the blood and guts-spattered room down and left.

Leona peeked into the room and beckoned for the New-Gen to follow her. "Just a moment," she said as she ran over to the cat she knew to be Matilda and ran her hand over the cat's massive head. With a gentle pat, she left and ushered the girls to another wing of the cavern where they couldn't contain themselves any longer.

"Did you see that!" shouted Celeste, dancing around.

"Yeah, baby, I'm so ready for this!" Teddy was beside herself with glee. "Oh my God, I can't wait!" Grabbing Celeste and shaking her, she screamed "Did you see those humongous canines? They just ripped through bone-like, like..."

"Like humans eating potato chips," chimed in Naima. "They're so beautiful! I wonder if my fur will be more sable-colored like Auntie Tilda's? God, I hope so." She ran over to Teddy and Celeste, and they embraced in a group hug, jumping up and down.

Teddy noticed Gus staring at her as she cavorted with the other girls. *He really is handsome*, she thought again—*especially with that little gap in his front teeth—and there is definitely something between us. He's tall, but not a basketball player tall, and muscular like I like my men, but not a football-player big, and those lips look yummy. I could kiss them all night*, she fantasized.

~ ~ ~

"Well, well, well. Looks like they're ready," Ceola purred behind the girls, her voice gruff, still not yet having returned to normal. The girls whirled around and gawked. Nana and the others wore athletic wear. They were noticeably younger and were now lean, rather than gaunt. The bony protuberances were barely visible. Ceola turned to Teddy. "Girl, tone those pheromones down. Now is not the time to be having those kinds of thoughts."

The New-Gen immediately bombarded the Old-Gen with questions while Gus and his team observed them in a kind of awe. They looked like they were watching a tennis match as their heads swiveled from the New-Gen to the Old-Gen.

Laughing, Lizzie held up her hands. "We can only answer one question at a time, girls. Calm your buttocks," but you could tell she and the Old-Gen were happy the New-Gen was excited to experience the change.

"Watching is one thing. Doing is another," Tildy said, her smile transforming her usually stern features and illuminating her beauty. Turning to the men, she asked them to make sure the facility was still secure, then proceeded to confer with Ceola, Leona, and Lizzie. Akiro walked over to them and murmured something that made the women's joyous expressions become serious.

"Hurry, girls. Time is catching up with us. Intel tells us Idia's plane has just crossed into Brazil. They're making excellent time, damn them."

Lizzie opened another door, and they entered a room that was a cross between a laboratory and a hospital suite.

"Pick a bed and lie down," Lizzie instructed them. "In the past, we metamorphosed into the progeny of La Panthère Noire through ritual and ceremony. You girls are the offspring of our babies, and you can change without the magic."

"I'm ready to do this thing and rule the world," Teddy chortled. Ceola frowned. "What, Nana?"

"Theodora Lulu K'Abella Furie, what have I told you about being humble?" Ceola asked, exasperated. "The world doesn't need another Idia."

"I am humble, Nana, but I also know my worth. Don't worry, I'll never let the power go to my head and be like that Idia heffa. You've taught me well, Nana." With a twinkle in her eyes, Teddy added, "After all, I'm just like you."

"That's what she's afraid of," Tildy joked as Ceola gave Tildy a playful swat.

"Auntie Ceola, I still don't understand how we'll be able to change without using magic," Naima ventured, voice quaking and eyes brimming with tears, her earlier exuberance dampened. "Are...are you sure it's time for us to change? What if you're wrong? What if we can't change?" Naima cried, wringing her hands together. Sweat beaded her forehead, and she began breathing fast and shallow.

"Rufus isn't the only scientist around here. I've been following his experiments over the years. He's just so arrogant that he didn't view me as a threat and thought my dithering about with his samples humorous. He lucked out and isolated the genes from the Lost-Generation that would allow you girls to morph into werepanthers and introduced them to your DNA. Calm down, Naima, everything will be okay. I'm sure you girls will shift without any problems. You're in good hands."

"Okay, let's get going, guys," Lizzie said, keeping them on track and pushing them toward the beds before Naima had a nervous breakdown.

"Girls, your nanas will be right next to you during the process. You will call up your beasts, relax, and follow the instructions we will give you. The first few times, you will only change to the werecat form. That's where you look part human and part pantheress. Then, you're going to will your bodies back into their anthropomorphic forms, relax, and repeat the process. After that, you will change fully into your she-panther, also known as your pantheress, and finally back to human. Expect to be tired as dogs when you're finished. You will need to feed to replenish your energy because it's your first time and your bodies aren't used to doing this," she warned. "Okay, let's begin. Everyone, take off your clothes; you don't want them ripped to shreds every time you change." Turning to the assembled men, she admonished, "Behave yourselves. You've seen naked women before."

~ ~ ~

A good night's rest had not improved Fredi's mood one bit. Rufus slammed his computer on the counter, strode over to Dr. Vasquez, and glared down at her with his hands on his hips. She continued to ignore him by staring at her computer monitor.

"I'm getting real tired of y'all's shit," Rufus quietly sniped.

"What do you propose I do, drag her in here?" Dr. Vasquez finally quit staring at the monitor and turned and glared at Rufus.

"Don't you cut your eyes at me," he snarled before turning and striding out of the room. Dr. Vasquez ran after him and reached Fredi's room first.

By the time Rufus pushed open the door, Dr. Vasquez was still trying to cajole the sullen tween into getting up and getting dressed.

"Come on, buttercup. Let's get up and at 'em," Rufus said with false cheer.

"I don't feel well," Fredi finally mumbled, her ice-blue eyes staring daggers at him.

"Get up. Now. You're young. You'll be fine. There's work to be done. Come on now. Time is money. You need to earn your keep."

"Why?" Fredi shot back. "I didn't ask to be created by you."

Dr. Vasquez tried to intervene. "Rufus, why don't you let her have the day off?" "You shocked her repeatedly yesterday and her body needs to recover from that trauma."

The silence that greeted Dr. Vasquez's suggestion chilled the air. When Rufus did speak, his steely eyes bored into her with an intensity she felt deep in her marrow and she wondered what type of evil she had been working for all of these years.

"Get that child up and in the lab in an hour. And don't ever forget your station and presume to tell me what to do." He turned around and marched out of the room without a backward glance.

If Rufus had bothered to turn around, he would have noticed the slitted eyes and elongated canines of Dr. Vasquez and Fredi as they restrained themselves from tearing him to pieces.

Chapter 15

1546

Yucatan Jungle, the region known today as Guatemala

Dear gods, the world was on fire! Death and destruction rained down on the once-mighty Aztecs like no other maelstrom. Fertile fields of maize, squash, and beans lay in ruins, burned to the ground. There would be no harvesting of the bounty and storing portions away for the winter months. The blood of her people streamed down the great pyramid's steps in rivulets, giving them the appearance of a macabre fountain. The stench was unbearable. Each inhalation of the foul air made her gag, and her eyes burned from the smoke's toxicity. Bodies lay where they had fallen, already beginning to bloat and putrefy in the jungle's oppressive heat and humidity. Blow flies, ever opportunistic, burrowed into the dead's eyes, noses, and mouths to lay their eggs, while high above, vultures circled. The volcano that had never erupted in her people's lifetimes rumbled ominously in the far distance. There would be no more placating sacrifices to the volcano god Xiuhtecuhtli or harvesting turquoise with his blessing.

This day had been foretold by the Jaguar gods eons ago, but the people had forgotten the old legends. Itzpapalotl's family hadn't forgotten, though. They knew this day was coming and when the girl child had been born with hyperpigmented spots forming a tiny paw print tattoo on her left buttock; they knew the Jaguar gods had blessed her, and thus they named her after the goddess Itzpapalotl, or Obsidian Butterfly. Itzpapalotl knew she didn't have much time to find Tezcatlipoca, the Jaguar god of magic, war, and darkness. If only those fools had listened to her, and offered him the sacrifices he requested, and taken the risk she was taking tonight. "If they had just listened," she whispered, balling up her small bloody fists, "many would still be here and those few who were alive wouldn't be at the mercy of those vile Spaniards and their beautiful home wouldn't be destroyed and plundered now." She had to hurry, or they would find her soon. Where was that ceremonial knife? Think, Itzpapalotl. Think! Loud footsteps in the antechamber propelled her into action. She just had time to jump over the body whose heart she had just removed and thrown up the lid on the ceremonial altar and jump in before a cadre of victorious Spaniards came into the chamber to ensure it was empty. She prayed they wouldn't stay long because while she was generally a tough person, her childhood nyctophobia had never fully left her and could crop up at the most inopportune times. Satisfied the chamber was devoid of life, the Spaniards left and continued their mission of clearing the great pyramid and village of every inhabitant—alive or dead. Obsidian Butterfly lay in the cramped, icy darkness long after the footsteps had disappeared. Convinced the Spaniards were gone, Obsidian Butterfly slowly raised the lid, and to her relief, discovered the knife and its scabbard attached to the underside of the altar's lid. She secured the turquoise and jade jeweled encrusted ceremonial knife in the rucksack slung over her shoulder and stayed still until she was certain no one was lurking in the shadows. Tip-toeing her way across the black obsidian floor, Itzpapalotl made sure the coast was clear before she ran like the wind out of the pyramid's various chambers and into the steamy, smoky jungle, which enveloped her without a trace.

High in her hiding place in the mountainous jungle, Obsidian Butterfly watched the sad procession of prisoners being led away by the Spaniards, tears silently streaming down her face. At least they're alive, she thought, muffling her sobs. They could fight another day and ensure the people would continue. She fervently watched the retreating procession for any signs of her family until the last of the forlorn line disappeared from view, but saw no one. Obsidian Butterfly took one last look at the only home she had ever known, turned and made her way deeper into the jungle. Thankfully, the deeper she walked into the jungle, the less smoke from the fires permeated the dense foliage and saturated the air. Spider and howler monkeys kept her company during her trek, jumping from tree to tree, almost as though they were watching out for her. At some point, she took the knife out of the rucksack to admire it and attached it and the scabbard around her waist in case she needed to access a weapon quickly.

She walked for hours through dense vegetation, steadily climbing uphill and stopping only to take water breaks from the gourd she had thought to fashion into a sling and place around her neck. She dug into the bag and removed the last piece of jerky she had placed in her rucksack before her journey. Sweat streamed down her face and her wet clothes dragged her body down like quicksand. Obsidian Butterfly hoped she didn't have much longer to walk as she upended the last of her water into her parched mouth. She finally saw a mountain ahead, but it appeared impenetrable with the jungle's thick, spiny vegetation. She was unconcerned, however, because Tezcatlipoca had already told her to expect this in her dreams. Obsidian Butterfly continued walking until she reached the very base of the mountain.

"Tezcatlipoca! Tezcatlipoca! Tezcatlipoca!" Obsidian Butterfly then waited for him, as agreed.

All around her, the jungle appeared to come alive, teeming with life as the blood-red sun began setting in the sky. Monkeys chattered and jumped from branch to branch, frogs croaked melodiously, and somewhere she heard the distinct snuffling of a jaguar. She inhaled the sweet but damp air and experienced a sense of peace and calm after the day's horrifying events.

The jungle went silent. A sudden wisp of chilly air made her long black hair move in the stultifying stillness of the jungle. Obsidian Butterfly whirled around and simultaneously whipped out the ceremonial knife. She bent her knees, one a little in front of the other to steady her base and assumed the fighting stance her brother, a member of the warrior cuauhocelotl, had taught her. Because he was an Eagle warrior and not a Jaguar, and thus had not approved of her plan for tonight, he had chosen to fight the Spaniards instead of accompanying her on her mission. When she told him of her plans, he laughed and called her a foolish girl. He further threw salt in the wound by adding that she should focus on finding a husband and raising a family instead of believing in stupid old wives' tales. She'd give anything to hear his laughter again, she reflected, even if he did think he knew everything. She could only pray he was still alive, but her heart told her he wasn't. As she wielded the knife in front of her, she heard a soft deep laugh. Obsidian Butterfly exhaled in relief and rolled her eyes. She placed the knife back in the scabbard belted around her waist as her eyes fell on the indistinct figure standing behind her.

"Scare me again, Tezcatlipoca, and you'll be laughing an octave higher," Obsidian Butterfly, who was all of five feet threatened. She squinted up at the nebulous figure towering above her. Why can't I see him clearly? It must be all the smoke from the fires obscuring my vision, she

thought. Besides, who cared what he looked like? She had a job to do—a legacy to fulfill.

"Ah, the lovely Itzpapalotl." She shuddered at the leer in Tezcatlipoca's voice even though she couldn't fully see his features. She knew he was ogling her from the top of her sloping forehead, her long, thick black hair, and beautiful beaked nose, to her shapely hips and short, but muscled legs.

"You know I love fierce women warriors…just before I rip their tongues out and eat them," replied the demigod with a smile that exposed a mouthful of razor-sharp teeth, which she did see. When she stood her ground with her arms crossed and glared at him, Tezcatlipoca sighed and gestured for her to follow him. As Tezcatlipoca walked toward the mountain, the greenery parted before him and closed around them after they passed through. Once they reached the very base of the mountain, the foliage parted again and Tezcatlipoca disappeared into the inky darkness.

Obsidian Butterfly stopped just inside the entryway. Goosebumps rose on her arms, and she began trembling, a sense of foreboding washing over her. Every instinct told her to run, to not enter this unholy place. Her heart thundered in her chest, and she suddenly couldn't breathe. Every inhalation of the damp air felt like she was taking water into her lungs and drowning. Obsidian Butterfly whirled around and scrambled through the thick vegetation to the opening. When icy-stiff fingers grasped hers, she screamed with the little breath she had left. Wheezing, she took in great draughts of air, but the drowning feeling persisted. An explosion of stars clouded her vision, and she felt the jungle swirling around her.

"Woman, calm yourself. Tis only I," Tezcatlipoca said, amused. When Obsidian Butterfly hesitated to step into the blackness or explain her fear, Tezcatlipoca jerked her forward. Again, she hesitated.

"W-w-w-wait, wait, wait, Tezcatlipoca, I think I hear someone calling my name."

Before she could gather her breath to say anything else, Tezcatlipoca threw her over his shoulder and bounded down unseen stairs at an inhuman speed. At the bottom, he gently put Obsidian Butterfly down and lit a torch. Obsidian Butterfly gulped in the cool, slightly fetid air and felt a little better. She turned to get a better look at the demigod. She recoiled and took a step backward. What was this leopard-skin-clad creature staring down at her? Her breath became wheezing once again, and her legs started shaking uncontrollably. She tried to take in deep breaths and release them, but her brain had been bombarded with shock after shock and wouldn't cooperate. Was he some kind of skinwalker? Werecat? She had only heard about such fantastical creatures in stories elders told the young to keep them in line. Obsidian Butterfly stared up at Tezcatlipoca and her eyes bugged, her face scrunched up in shock and revulsion.

Tezcatlipoca let out another low, sinister chuckle. His teeth, sharpened into points, gleamed in the torchlight."What? For once, you have nothing to say? Will wonders never cease? Oh come now, Itzpapalotl. Don't wimp out on me. You know I feed on fear, and if you continue to show me yours, I will kill you for sure, and we wouldn't want that, now would we? You've worked so hard to get here, and you've made so many sacrifices." The demigod sniffed the air. "In fact, is that human heart in your rucksack for me? Come now, get a hold of yourself. Remember your purpose and do it quickly before I lose my patience with you."

"Why is it I can now see and feel you when I couldn't before?" Obsidian Butterfly timidly ventured. Now that the initial shock had worn off, she could feel her heart rate slowing and the fear being replaced by her inquisitive nature.

"Because it takes a lot of energy to go above ground and materialize. I'm in my element now, so my body struggles less to maintain a temporal form," Tezcatlipoca explained.

Obsidian Butterfly stopped taking long, deep breaths. She wrinkled her nose once more, gagging, as a more pungent stench not only assaulted her nostrils, but enveloped her clothes, stung her eyes, invaded her taste buds, and infiltrated her very pores. She'd smelled death before, but this was too much. The odor of sulfur was also overwhelming. She gazed around Tezcatlipoca's chamber of horrors. Oh my god, is that a baby sticking out of that woman's abdomen? Why does he have bodies lying around like this? Shit, look at all of these bones. It's as though these are sacrifices. Oh no, I must be in the actual place where we throw our sacrifices, she realized miserably. I'm going to be sick. Bile, which tasted of jerky, rose perilously close to the back of her throat and burned the tissue. She swallowed it back down and thought, Maybe I can make a run for it.

She somehow blinked back tears that threatened to well up and overflow as she realized with dismay that he'd just run her down in a flash. It'd be just my luck to stumble over that bloated, decomposing body at the foot of the stairs. He's a big bastard but fast, and those sharp teeth could tear me apart in seconds. But—-and this is a big but—-if he was going to kill me, he'd have already done it. Obsidian Butterfly blew out a breath and stood up straight and tall. Her eyes receded back into their sockets and took on a determined stare. He's right, she thought. I have come too far to wimp out now. I have no family anymore. I have no village anymore. Obsidian Butterfly squared her shoulders, looked Tezcatlipoca in his eerie yellowish cat eyes, and said, "I'm ready, Tezcatlipoca."

"Splendid! There is no turning back Itzpapalotl. Once you embrace the beast, you and the beast will become one. Do you understand what I am telling you? You will die eventually, but you will be centuries old before

it happens. You will get weary of life, but you will not cheat death. Do you understand what I am telling you, Itzpapalotl? You cannot die before your time. You will not control the beast, Itzpapalotl. When she is hungry, you WILL feed her, and you WILL feed her human flesh. Humans will fear you, and your existence will be a lonely one at times. You may be forced to eat people you love. If you allow me, I will mentor and teach you all I can. You know what I ask of you in return."

"Yes," Obsidian Butterfly quietly responded, looking down at the floor, unable to meet Tezcatlipoca's eyes. She was still debating if she could make a run for it when Tezcatlipoca picked her up and placed her on his altar. Obsidian Butterfly closed her eyes tightly and took calm, steadying breaths. She felt a shift in the air and heard Tezcatlipoca grunt. Obsidian Butterfly opened her eyes, looked up at the being standing before her, and screamed. When the scream morphed into shrill shrieks of pure terror, a colony of alarmed bats flew out of the cave.

Tezcatlipoca was Tezcatlipoca...but not Tezcatlipoca. A deer's hoof had replaced his right foot, and black and yellow stripes adorned his face. His left foot was a paw with wicked-looking claws instead of toenails. Even his fingernails were clawed. He looked even more like a jaguar now—-hardly human at all. When he opened his mouth, his canines and teeth were massive and sharp. His eyes terrified her the most, though. As she gazed into the narrow slits of the yellow-green orbs, there was no human left in them. It was almost like gazing into the cold reptilian eyes of a snake. In a guttural voice, he ordered Obsidian Butterfly to take off her clothes. Oh God, was that thing now going to rape her? That was not happening, she thought. She would kill herself first. With shaking legs and clattering teeth, she did as he ordered her but not before removing the knife from the scabbard and placing it at her side.

Tezcatlipoca chanted and every so often threw herbs into the fire he had built near the altar. The room exhibited a weird kaleidoscope of colors as Obsidian Butterfly eyed the mirrors strewn around the chamber. He stopped, picked up a chalice, sliced his arm with the ceremonial blade and let the blood flow into the chalice. Then, he picked up Obsidian Butterfly's arm and with no warning, did the same to her. The coppery red, almost black blood began bubbling, and Tezcatlipoca's chanting picked up in fervor and tempo.

Obsidian Butterfly's terror increased. Her arm burned from where the knife sliced into her tender skin. She couldn't seem to stop the violent clattering of her teeth and the shaking of her arms and legs. The room wasn't cold; the fire had created a cozy warmth in the chamber. Obsidian Butterfly's trepidation grew. She wanted to jump up off of the altar and run, but she couldn't move. Oh, her limbs and teeth were moving violently, but she couldn't voluntarily move anything. Well, that wasn't quite true. Her eyes were ping-ponging wildly around in her head, trying to see what was occurring. She tried to call out for Tezcatlipoca to stop. She had made a mistake and wanted to go home. All she could do, however, was gurgle. Foaming spit ran down her chin, and her eyes widened in embarrassment as she felt her bladder release. She tried to hold in the flow of urine that now ran down her legs but couldn't. The air in the room got hazier and heavier.

Tezcatlipoca approached a small stele, upon which an oval object was perched. Dramatically removing the cover, he exposed the skull underneath. Obsidian Butterfly couldn't have screamed even if she wanted to. Her mouth was dry as a cotton ball. Air whistled through her blue lips as she desperately tried to still her heart. Obsidian Butterfly wasn't positive but thought the skull was that of a jaguar. It seemed abnormally large, though. Still chanting, Tezcatlipoca placed the skull on Obsidian

Butterfly's chest and sliced his arm again. This time after he sliced Obsidian Butterfly's arm and allowed her blood to drain into the chalice, he removed the heart from the rucksack and placed it in the skull's mouth. Then, to her horror, he offered the chalice to the skull and poured the blood from the chalice into the skull's mouth. Obsidian Butterfly's bladder contracted and she would have peed on herself again had there been any fluid left to expel from her empty bladder.

Obsidian Butterfly felt like she was suffocating. She would have gotten up and made a run for it if she still hadn't felt so paralyzed. She wanted to cry out to Tezcatlipoca to stop, but it was as though some unseen force had clamped her jaws shut. Why was she experiencing these stabbing pains in her chest? Why was the skull getting heavier and heavier and making it harder for her to breathe? She tried to fight the paralysis and sit up, but she could barely keep her eyes open, much less lift her head. Obsidian Butterfly knew she was completely at Tezcatlipoca's mercy at this point. As she gave in to her fate, a strange peace settled over her. Tezcatlipoca's voice rose in volume, and he stood over her with his head thrown back and his arms stretched wide. Suddenly, he dropped to his knees in supplication, his body pulsating and a purring sound emanating from his throat. When he raised his head, Obsidian Butterfly's calm left, and she screamed again. The face and body before her proved completely animal. Tezcatlipoca had shapeshifted in full. Just when she thought things couldn't get any worse, they did.

Obsidian Butterfly had been so focused on Tezcatlipoca, she didn't notice the skull on her chest becoming animated—-those gigantic canines moving and eating the heart—-until it was too late. By the time she felt the sharp teeth biting into her chest, they had already broken through the cartilage and her ribs, and as a heaviness and terrible pain diffused throughout her body, everything mercifully faded to black.

Chapter 16

"Itzpapalotl, wake up. Wake up!"

Slowly, Itzpapalotl opened her eyes. Was she dreaming? She felt so groggy and discombobulated. No, her nose was again assaulted by the fetid yet sweet smell of death and decay. Looking at Tezcatlipoca, it relieved her to discover he looked human once more. She looked down at her chest and noticed the gaping hole was almost closed, and while she felt some pain, it wasn't too bad.

"I—I'm still human," she cried. It hadn't worked. "Can I leave?" But then Obsidian Butterfly screamed—a guttural sound emanating so deeply in her throat, it sounded inhuman and she felt she had ruptured her larynx. Pain enveloped her entire body everywhere. She couldn't pinpoint one location. Her body spasmed as though she were being electrocuted. Through the haze of her agony, Obsidian Butterfly noticed for the first time the other figures in the cave and the huge shrine of jaguar skulls placed in a pyramidal shape behind the altar. She screamed again, reaching out her hand for someone to please help her. Oh Dios, the pain was unbearable. She felt as though someone had poured acid down her throat and it was eating her insides. She spewed vomit in eruptions so forceful, the spasms jerked her from the altar and onto her hands and knees on the floor. A voice in her head called her name and told her to breathe. Just breathe. Let

the change happen. Stop fighting it. The pain was now at its apex, and Itzpapalotl thought this must be what it felt like to be in the throes of death.

Itzpapalotl relaxed, took a deep shuddering breath, and surrendered to death—and something unexpected happened. Her body continued feeling weird, but the unbearable pain was waning. She could breathe. Even the foul cave air felt pleasant flowing through her nasal passages. Then something happened to her vision. She could see everything in the cave in amazing detail.

She crawled on all fours—on all four paws—to the nearest mirror. Oh, oh... My God, she was beautiful. Her fur was black with brown dots, and her eyes were a beautiful shade of jade. She was massive! Her teeth were as big as the teeth in the skull placed on her chest. Yes, she was magnificent. Her furry round ears were rotating? What were those loud and rhythmical, deliciously throbbing sounds?

Sometime during her transition, one of Tezcatlipoca's minions, who had remained hidden in one of the cave's many recesses, had brought forth the soldiers they had caught and imprisoned just for this occasion. She walked closer to one of the pale humans and sniffed. What was that sound? Then, it came to her. It was the human's heart beating. Was that fear she smelled on the human? She sniffed the sharp, pungent odor again. She liked the way the human's fear made her feel. Yes, she liked it very much. She stuck out her long tongue and licked the human's face. The man screamed as his skin and muscles peeled away. Mmm, delicious, thought Itzpapalotl. It was only when she wondered what the rest of his body tasted like—- which caused her to smile—- that the human stampede inside the chamber of Tezcatlipoca's cave began. Unfortunately, there was nowhere to run and nowhere to hide.

~ ~ ~

The once magnificent city now lay in ruins. Former verdant fields of maize, squash, pumpkins, and beans were barren and charred. The air reeked with a foul stench that permeated one's very being. As the victorious Spaniards led the survivors away from their homes to an unknown future, the survivors prayed to their many gods. No one responded until out of the depths of the jungle, a mighty roar could be heard and the people knew their prayers had been answered.

Itzpapalotl watched the procession, crouched, from her perch on a tree limb. The Spaniards were going to pay dearly for destroying her people. Tezcatlipoca believed she was off fulfilling her end of the bargain. She had more important things to do than exploring dark, musty caves, looking for some magical turquoise amulet he so desperately wanted. She'd come back and search for it later. He'd waited this long; he could wait a little bit longer.

Chapter 17

Teddy hoped everything would turn out all right. For once, she wasn't brimming with confidence. She knew she was different from her two sister-friends.

Ceola, who sensed her unease, placed a hand over hers. "It's going to be okay, Theodora. I know you feel you're different from the rest, but you'll be okay."

Speaking louder so the others could hear, Ceola instructed them to take a deep breath in, hold it, and let it out slowly.

"That's it. Now, close your eyes and clear your minds. Keep breathing. In and out, in and out. While you're breathing, in your head, call your beast. You do that by focusing and thinking Raven, Raven, Raven, fill my spirit. Release my beast. Now! Do you feel a tightness in your chest?" The women nodded. "Good. Breathe with it, and call your beast. Envision your she-panther climbing and clawing her way up from the depths of your soul, filling your molecules, becoming one with your body. It will feel uncomfortable, but stay focused. You want to become one with your spirit animal, not separate from her. Tell your beast to come. Welcome her and when you feel the melding of your bodies, breathe through it and let it happen."

Theodora gave a start. A loud foreign voice said, "I'm coming, Theodora."

Ceola noticed and calmed Theodora with a pat, saying, "It's okay. Your beast is coming. Let her."

A scream erupted from Teddy's mouth, and she jerked so hard on the bed, she fell onto the floor.

Gus just barely stopped himself from rushing over to help her up. He hadn't taken his eyes off of her ever since she undressed. Well, that wasn't quite true. Ever since he met her actually. Damn, she was gorgeous. Those pouty lips and all of that long wavy hair were definitely turning him on. And what was that yummy scent wafting in the air around her? It reminded him of musk, vanilla, and oranges. He could see himself—feel himself—between her muscled legs, pumping in and out of her tight cooch as Teddy's muscles worked his throbbing shaft to the point of pleasure bordering on pain.

"Augustus, control yourself! Damn!" Ceola ordered as she looked down at his obvious erection.

"I can't help it, Miss Ceola. She's so damn fine." Gus groaned.

"No shame." Ceola her attention focused on Teddy. She knew the beast Teddy was letting in was able to seduce the strongest of men. It would be the same with the other young women. One of the reasons the Asoro were required to be single was so there wouldn't be any entanglements. She secretly hoped one of the girl's pheromones would entice Roland and he could finally let go of his past and live his life.

Meanwhile, a white-hot pain enveloped Teddy that made her feel as though her insides were being churned up, but then it was over as she gave in to the pain. The Old-Gen women gasped. While the other girls were writhing on the bed and floor, Teddy had morphed into her werecat being smoothly, quickly, and elegantly. There was none of that skin crackling, visceral bubbling, or bones popping. Instead, Teddy's body had changed in one fluid motion.

"Teddy, I always suspected your heterochromia meant something. Now I'm certain," Ceola exclaimed as she marveled at the smoothness of Teddy's transformation.

Teddy lifted and turned her hairy arms in wonder. She studied her claws and practiced retracting and extending them. The preternatural energy roiling internally made her tremble in excitement, and she grinned.

"Teddy dear, could you open your mouth wide for me?" Ceola studied Teddy's teeth with mounting trepidation. "Oh dear, oh dear, oh dear," Ceola said with a gulp, wanting to take a step back but standing her ground. There was no need to alarm the girl, she thought. "Okay, Lulu, I'm going to go out on a limb here and ask you to think about your beast in its she-panther form. Change, now!" Ceola clapped her hands for emphasis.

Teddy's beast enveloped her, and she metamorphosed, the process smooth as silk. Celeste and Naima were just a little behind Teddy in the changing process. Once they changed into their werecat bodies, they stopped dead in their tracks at the sight of Teddy's she-panther.

The room erupted in pandemonium.

Chapter 18

The fully morphed she-panther growling before them was even more massive than the Old-Gen she-panthers. Everyone stared. Speechless. Once it was apparent Teddy would not harm them, fear turned into exalted awe and appreciation. Teddy's low throaty rumblings were her version of purrs. Teddy's she-panther was gorgeous! And unlike the Old-Gen's bony she-panthers, Teddy's she-panther's sleek muscles rippled. Her glossy fur was jet black, with a white stripe running from her forehead to mid-back. It was the eyes, though, that captured everyone's attention, for one eye was ice-blue and the other eye was jade-green, just like in her werecat and human form. The paws were massive, and when Teddy extended her claws, eyes widened and *damns* echoed around the room as people unconsciously backed up. The teeth proved especially alarming. The massive canines were impressive, but why were they and the rest serrated? Also, were those faint stripes in her skin?

Lizzie whispered, "Ceola, does this mean what I think it does?"

"Maybe. Probably so," Ceola murmured back, stricken. In a louder voice, Ceola asked Akiro, "Did you capture all of this digitally? Good. Teddy, command your beast to rest."

Instead of obeying Ceola's orders, Teddy ran around trying to find a mirror, her colossal body bumping into everything and everyone. She had heard everyone oohing and aahing and wanted to see what the hoopla was about. Dang it, there wasn't a mirror anywhere. She finally ran over to Akiro, who yelped and cowered. Teddy tried to pantomime taking pictures but it was difficult to do while on all four limbs. She resorted to pointing a massive paw at the cell phone and touching her face.

What's wrong with people? she thought. *What happened to the oohing and aahing? Why were there gasps and screams when I smiled? Akiro is acting like I'm going to eat him. What's his problem? I was smiling to show him I meant him no harm. God, what's taking him so long?*

Akiro finally understood and stilled his fumbling fingers. He snapped off a series of shaky photos with his cell phone. He pointed out cameras positioned around the room to let people know everything was on film. Teddy and Akiro even took a selfie. Then, Gus had to take a selfie with her, too. The man had practically run across the room, waving his arms and shouting something Teddy couldn't make out in her excited state. If he was that desperate for a selfie with her, she would happily oblige him, she thought, but really, he needed to calm the fuck down. His heart was racing a mile a minute.

What the fuck? Gus's heartbeat was making Teddy feel all tingly inside. Teddy shook out her fur. This evoked an even stronger reaction from people in the room. She realized she could distinguish them by their heartbeats. Also, she hadn't thought she could understand and think like a human, but once she calmed down, she did and she could. Cool! Uh oh! Teddy detected strong stutter beats coming from the Old-Gen and breathed in an unfamiliar odor. The acridness told her the Old-Gen felt upset and afraid. She didn't know why—just that she detected this in their emotions and she could smell their sweat now. Why was Nana Ceola having a hissy fit and yelling for her to tell her beast to rest?

"Chillax, Nana!" Teddy shouted. Damn, she heard her the first time, Teddy grumbled to herself. Unfortunately, she was unaware that what she thought were words being spoken were instead scary-assed growls that revealed scary-assed serrated teeth that shouldn't have been in her mouth.

Just as she was about to change back to human form, a sense of foreboding came over her. Startled, she jumped two feet in the air as another voice began speaking to her. Naturally, this caused the others to be even more afraid.

"Stay the course, Theodora," hissed, a sinister-sounding alien voice in her head. "When the time is right, I'll call on you and you will answer."

"Who is this?" Teddy demanded.

"Don't ask stupid questions, Theodora. You know who this is," the menacing voice responded.

"But I don't. Who are you? Hello?" Only silence answered her.

As Teddy transformed back into human form, she noticed everybody staring at her—even Naima and Celeste, who were still in their werecat forms. Dumbfounded, she then noticed all the men had their weapons trained on her. All the men except for Gus.

"Whaaat? Why is everybody staring at me? And y'all will want to put those weapons up," she glared at the men. They didn't holster their weapons until Tildy nodded, which infuriated Teddy even more.

"We'll discuss it later," Ceola told her, lips pursed, and nostrils flared. "We need to finish instructing the other girls. I have a theory. Let me just confer with others before I try to explain to you what I think has happened. I know you're upset because weapons were trained on you. Nevertheless…" Ceola shook her finger at Teddy, on the verge of exploding in anger herself. Yup, emotions were running high.

"You damned right about that. You want to explain why these men had guns trained on me?" Teddy got in Ceola's face. Everyone's mouths dropped and people began backing away from them. The standoff continued. Finally, Gus and Matilda began walking toward them. Ceola held up her hand and shook her head. She had things under control.

"I asked you to rest and change back to your human form several times. When you didn't comply, we were afraid." Teddy bent one leg at the knee, put her hands on her hips, and looked incredulous. Ceola expounded. "You obviously have no idea how frighteningly huge and ferocious-looking your pantheress is. We have you on film. You'll see why we were scared shitless when you ignored my orders. Now please get the hell out of *my* personal space."

"Sorry, Nana." Teddy lowered her head. *Damn, I'm in trouble yet again.*

Nana continued to mutter. "Up here scaring people shitless. What the hell has Rufus done, the old fool? Playing Dr. Frankenstein with these young ladies' lives."

As Teddy pouted and seethed, for she knew she better not respond to Nana's mutterings, she caught Gus staring unabashedly at her naked body. Rather than covering up, however, she turned in a pirouette, staring and smiling at him suggestively. Once again, people gaped. This wasn't the Teddy the rest of them knew. The Teddy they knew would have been too shy to parade naked in a room full of virtual strangers. Teddy's hormones kicked in, and she was soon lost in a fantasy of her and Gus intertwined. She didn't realize she was ogling Gus, who was appreciating her ogling him. Gus ran his tongue over his lips.

It was as though it was just the two of them in the room until Ceola's loud "Ahem, Teddy, you may get dressed now! You don't need to get him any more riled up than he already is" cruelly interrupted their love fest.

"Uh, Nana, something happened in my beast form," Teddy whispered while dressing.

Ceola, whose attention was elsewhere—namely on Teddy's anomalies— said, "Could you tell me later?"

"It's really important, Nana." Feelings were still running a little high after her display of disobedience, and she knew Nana wouldn't appreciate being disturbed now, but this couldn't wait.

"Okay girls," Tildy told Naima and Celeste after glowering at Teddy. "Now change back to your human form, and then change to your beast form." The girls did so quickly and easily. "Good!" Tildy murmured. Her attention was still still focused on Ceola and Teddy, a scowl etched on her face. Teddy knew she was in a shitstorm of trouble and there would be hell to pay later from General Matilda Arvelle Arceneaux.

"Gorgeous!" Teddy yelled to Celeste's and Naima's she-panthers, giving them two thumbs up with far more confidence than she was feeling. Why was she always in trouble, dammit? She felt like she was a voodoo child born under a bad sign.

Celeste and Naima's she-panthers were big but not as big as Teddy's. The girls morphed back to their human forms, beaming.

Damn, Auntie Tildy is still staring daggers at me, Teddy thought.

"Auntie Tildy, could you come over here, please? Everyone should hear this." As the women gathered around her, Teddy took a deep breath. "When I was in my she-panther form, I heard a voice that was different from my beast's. She sounded so intimidating when she said, 'When the time is right, I'll call on you and you will answer.' She insisted I knew who she was, but I don't."

"Did she sound like us?" Matilda asked, arms crossed over her chest. She pointedly stared at Teddy and pursed her lips.

"No," Teddy replied without hesitation. The Old-Gen looked at each other, their faces and bodies tense.

"If it wasn't Idia, then it was La Panthère Noire. Right when you think things can't get worse, they do. Ceola, Lizzie, we need to talk. Did anyone else notice…" Matilda began as they both nodded.

Suddenly, alarms sounded throughout the building. Akiro glanced at one of the monitors. "Shit, it's Rufus and his men. We need to evacuate this place, ASAP."

The Asoro quickly mobilized. Hoisting their weapons, they began driving the women deeper into the warren of mazes after they had dressed.

"Wait!" Matilda screamed in a panic. "Where's Leona?"

"I think she went to get her bag." Henry pointed toward the front of the building.

"I'll get her. Just go, go, go," Teddy yelled, pushing the others in front of her. This was the Teddy they knew—the one that took charge. The one that was always altruistic, brave, and there for her family. And rash. Teddy bounded toward the front of the building before they could stop her. She was almost there when she saw Leona running toward her.

"Sorry, I had to grab my bag, and I tried to secure the opening," Leona huffed.

"Okay, I've got this. You catch up with the others and after I secure the front of the building, I'll find you guys."

"No, Teddy," Leona begged. "Forget securing the building. They've already breached it. Let's go."

"No," Teddy replied. "If I secure the front, that'll give you more time to escape. Go. I'll catch up. I promise." Teddy shoved Leona through the passageway and pushed the door closed with her preternatural strength, effectively sealing off the conduit that would have allowed Rufus and his men to reach the others.

Rufus and his fighters had already made their way past the door when Teddy rushed into the antechamber. She threw a rear hand punch at one man, knocking him out cold, and incapacitated another one with a roundhouse kick to the knee followed by a spinning heel kick to the head. Teddy automatically reached for the gun she normally wore at her hip and groaned. Shit, she had left her gear in the other room, as they had to strip when they changed. She should have grabbed the men's guns she knocked out. She inwardly cursed. She continued throwing punches and kicks, but the sheer volume of Rufus's troop soon overpowered her. Plus, Teddy felt like she was struggling through quicksand while wearing combat boots and running on empty. Nana was right. The change had sapped her strength and Rufus's men landed some good hits on her body.

She tried to muster up enough energy to call her beast, but she was just too tired. Doubling over from being kicked in the kidneys and ribs, she felt hands roughly pin her from behind in a bear hug and someone put a gun to the side of her head. Despite her weak struggles, her captor kept a firm grip on her and dragged her over to Rufus. Teddy looked up and immediately knew where she got her ice-blue eye.

The last words she heard were, "We meet at last, Daughter," in a dulcet voice that evoked the old southern aristocracy.

Then, someone tased her into darkness.

Chapter 19

As Teddy slowly regained consciousness, her pupils contracted from the blinding light shining in her eyes. Someone was pulling up her eyelids and beaming that irritating light right in her pupils. Teddy couldn't help but notice a new day was here as the rays from the blazing sun helped pierce holes in her tired eyes. Her head and other places were aching, and she still felt like a limp noodle from exhaustion. Slowly, last night's events returned to her in bits and pieces. She hoped the others made it out of the other lab safely. They warned her not to go rushing off, but she hadn't listened, as usual. If she survived this latest escapade, she promised herself she'd learn to be less rash if it killed her. Her obstinacy was no excuse to continue endangering her life and the lives of others.

She tried to get up from the bed but discovered her captors had strapped her arms and legs to the bed rails and she was really in a lot of pain. Just that movement caused a sharp stabbing pang to radiate from her throbbing sides. It hurt to breathe; she was pretty sure her ribs were bruised, if not broken.

"If you promise to behave, I'll remove the straps," proclaimed that deep voice dripping with honey as Rufus put the penlight he'd been shining into Teddy's eyes away.

Teddy broke the straps as easily as one would break free from plastic handcuffs. Damn, the effort caused a new bout of pain to reverberate through her already aching body. Still, she gave Rufus a sinister smile, while outwardly displaying no sign she was in any discomfort. Rufus curled his lips upward in the semblance of a smile, mirroring Teddy's own smile.

Rufus, trying to ignore the ease with which Teddy had freed herself from her restraints said, "Your eyes are much more beautiful in person than in pictures and on camera. That color green reminds me of someone..." Rufus muttered and brooded, still staring deeply into Teddy's eyes like she was a subject in a lab. Rufus beamed, and the sincerity in his smile transformed his face. "Ah, yes! Dr. Vasquez! That's who also has that shade of jade eyes. But you definitely aren't Mexican, Lulu. So, why would you have one eye the same color as hers?"

"What do you want and why am I here? And who said you could call me Lulu?" Teddy demanded, groaning audibly from the pain that seemed to radiate everywhere now that she was moving around.

Rufus lifted his pale brow. "I gave you that name, you know. Theodora Lulu was my great-grandmother's name. She'd probably roll over in her grave if she knew a Black girl had her name, but there you have it."

Teddy sputtered, "It's your damn fault your great-grandmother would be having a hissy fit. I'm sure none of the Ravenisha wanted you to impregnate them. You motherfucker!"

Ever resolute, Rufus continued as if Teddy hadn't spoken. "I've watched you from afar, longing for this day. You were just a newborn the last time we met. I've always wondered how my experiment turned out. I've kept abreast of your achievements and milestones. Excuse me for a moment, dear." Rufus left the room and returned with a liquid-filled syringe. “It’s morphine, for your pain. I’m afraid the men you knocked out were a little zealous in their retaliation. I apologize for that. I never told them to hurt you, and I have reprimanded them for their actions-”

“Look, Rufus,” Teddy cut in, “I don’t know what you want from me, but it’s too late for us to bond or be friends. As far as I’m concerned, you’re nothing but a sperm donor, mad scientist, and imprisoner. I understand it’s been your money that has allowed the construction of our home, financed my equestrian hobby, paid for my education, and explains my hefty bank account. I don’t give a fuck. You’ve kept my family enslaved and used us as lab rats. It’s just too late to be all kumbaya now. So, I repeat, what do you want?” Theodora asked contemptuously.

Rufus looked like he wanted to say or do something, but he took a deep breath instead. “I want your genes, your power, your lifeforce.” Rufus ignored Teddy’s look of repulsion. “Oh, don’t look so shocked. You know, my great-grandfather figured out what you people are, but science hadn’t evolved then. Do you realize what I could accomplish if I had your genes, dear? How powerful I’d be? It’s just like God to endow the inferior with the best characteristics. What good does it do for you people to live forever when you can’t even get your lives together after centuries? Immortality is wasted on Negroes like youth is wasted on the young.” Rufus’s eyes darkened.

“Home skillet,” Teddy interrupted, mirroring Rufus’s sneer with her own, “just stop, okay?”

If Rufus hadn’t been so enrapt with her eyes, he would have felt the dangerous aura emanating from Teddy.

“You’re beginning to sound like a tired caricature of some old Southern white bigot from olden times. Come on, Rufus. Even Strom Thurmond changed. You know *damn* well Nana is as intelligent as you are, if not more. You don’t even believe that crap you’re spouting. What’s wrong with you? Are you warring with yourself?" Teddy looked Rufus in the eyes and fluttered her eyelashes. "It's okay to admit you like Black people, Rufus—especially Nana Ceola." Suddenly, Teddy glared at Rufus, her lips curled into a sneer. Even though she was in the bed, she somehow made Rufus feel like she was looking down on him. Teddy's sneer turned into a wicked smile. "Also, I know you're dying. I can smell it on you."

Rufus's eyes widened and he stepped back.

"Oops. Yeah, well, anyway if you hadn't been so arrogant, you could have worked alongside Nana in the lab and developed this 'magical elixir' you're so desperate to produce, but oh no, you and people like you would rather cut off your nose to spite your face. Also, cut it with that inferior shit. I'm very intelligent. Hell, according to y'all's damn charts, I'm a fucking genius, so..."

The slap that came out of nowhere was so brutal, the force gave Teddy whiplash to add to her other injuries.

"You will not use foul language in my presence, Theodora Lulu," Rufus raged. "I've ignored your uncouth behavior, but no more."

Teddy stared at Rufus, her mouth opening and closing like a beached fish gasping for air, uncharacteristically speechless. "Wow, I see where I get my cray-cray craziness from." Teddy's eyes watered as she struggled to tamp down her rising rage. "You have a problem with people cursing; yet, you have no compunction about torturing and enslaving people? Now that's some hardcore hypocrisy. I'll give you a free pass on that slap this time, Rufus, but hit me again. I will knock your lights out and then eat you. You feel me?" Teddy snarled, heat rolling off of her and her eyes becoming slits. "I am not my parents or my grandparents. I will take your ass out." Teddy growled as she radiated menace and gave him dead eyes. Taking joy in Rufus's fear of her, she growled even more menacingly.

Rufus took a step back from the bed, wondering how the conversation ended up totally off track and confrontational. This wasn't the way he had planned to finally reunite with his daughter. He had been conflicted about how much of a role he should play in Theodora's life. In the end, he had felt it best not to get too close in case Idia forced him to perform some un-godly experiment on her one day. Now that he was in the same room with her, he realized he would have never been able to hurt his daughters. They were his flesh and blood. Sure, he'd tased Fredericka, but he was disciplining her, not trying to harm her.

"I'm sorry I struck you, Theodora. That was uncalled for, but please, watch your language." Rufus wondered if it was a mistake to be alone and unarmed with this fierce young woman, even if she was his daughter.

"Whatevs. You just better keep yo' hands to yourself." The two studied each other in silence for a moment. Teddy sighed, a flurry of emotions crossing her face as she wondered how best to handle the situation. The old, immature Teddy would have beat the shit out of Rufus, but since she was trying 'to adult,' she recognized a beatdown wouldn't resolve the situation.

"Look, Rufus, I sense something decent deep, deep, deep within you. Perhaps we can have a truce?" Teddy ventured, thinking the man was bat shit crazy, and it was obvious where she got her quick temper.

Surprised at herself, Teddy felt no animosity toward Rufus. She was being facetious earlier about the warring within himself, but she really got the sense that at heart, Rufus Beckett Theodis Honeycutt was not the man he projected himself to be.

"Despite all the people I've killed, I'm actually a live and let live sort of person. I can tolerate you if you can tolerate me. We're really not each other's enemies here. From what Nana has said, you have some okay qualities. That bitch Idia running your lab is making her move. Nana said she's not loyal to anyone, and that includes you, too. Look, we know she's running your operation in Africa."

Rufus held up a hand, frowning. "Idia works for me. What do you mean she's on her way here? That's not what we agreed upon. How positive are you she's on her way?"

Teddy repeated the information Akiro had given them earlier.

"Why would she jeopardize what we're working on to come here?"

Teddy shook her head sadly and gave Rufus a pitying look. "Because this has all been about her destroying the American Ravenisha, the Ravenisha she tricked your ancestors into buying and who have stayed in your family. She must stop the prophecy from coming to fruition or her ass is toast."

Rufus slapped his palm on the bed rail, startling Teddy. "I should have been tracking her movements. I should have known not to trust her, but she's done things over the years to prove her loyalty to me. She's the one who helped me fit the pieces into the puzzle. Oh no, my ancestors and I have been such fools," Rufus cried, barely meeting Teddy's eyes. "Or like y'all like to say, I've been played." After a pregnant pause, Rufus asked, "How have things gone so wrong?"

"Well, if you really want to know," Teddy began, rolling her eyes, and looking down her nose at Rufus.

Rufus held up his hand for silence. "It was a rhetorical question." He frowned, thinking how alike she and Fredericka were; acting as though they were his peers and at times his superiors. He wondered if both girls were a bit mental.

"You know, I think it's time for you to call Ceola and the others and make amends." Rufus raised both eyebrows at Teddy. "It really wasn't a suggestion," Teddy told him in a voice brooking no argument. She looked into his eyes. “I see you, Rufus. I. See. You. I don’t think you will want to battle Idia on your own. You’ll need help. Preternatural being against preternatural being kind of thing. Know what I’m saying? Could you please bring me my phone?” Teddy held out her hand, palm up imperiously.

Rufus wanted to remind the girl who was giving the orders. Instead, he nodded and retrieved Teddy’s phone from her pants pocket.

“Thank you. Umm, also Rufus, I’m starving. Is there any way I could get something to eat around here? Unless you want to be the *ultimate* host, you’ll prioritize finding me some meat. Now!” Teddy commanded. “You know, some *real* meat,” Teddy smiled, baring her canines.

Taken aback, Rufus silently fumed. Now she expected him to get food for her like he was some common servant. *Good God, she is an imperious little cuss*, Rufus thought, grudgingly admiring her moxie before the full implication of her words sank in. He briefly thought about which of his employees he could afford to lose. “To hell with it,” Rufus whispered fiercely. Teddy didn’t know what the hell he was jabbering on about now⊠she just needed to be fed, but she listened politely.

“You know, Theodora, they say a leopard can’t change his spots, but I’m about to prove the naysayers wrong.”

And then Rufus made a decision he never thought he’d make in a million years.

Chapter 20

Fort Cheaha, Alabama

As Ceola's cell phone began ringing during the emergency meeting, Colonel Honeycutt stared at her, a frown marring his features. He impatiently gestured for Ceola to answer the phone.

"Teddy!" she screamed, "Thank God! Thank God!"

"Nana, I don't have much time. Put the phone on speaker so everyone can hear, please."

"Done."

"Shhh." Teddy cut off all the questions she was being bombarded with. "We don't have much time, so listen up, guys. I'm at Rufus's lab. I'm a little banged up, but I've been in worse conditions and situations. I think Rufus and I have come to a truce, which he is willing to extend to y'all." Rufus nodded.

"Hello, Ceola?" Rufus's voice chimed in. "Look, I'm sorry I've been such an ogre to you, Matilda, and Elizabeth. I've been a fool and I'm sorry to say, I'm a product of my time. I am deeply ashamed of things I have said and done. Please forgive me!"

"That's all fine and well, Rufus." She wondered when the other shoe was going to drop. "But you've destroyed an entire generation of our girls. Are we supposed to just forget that?" Ceola raised her eyebrows and rolled her eyes. She didn't believe Rufus for one second. She looked over at Tildy and Lizzie, and her heart almost stopped beating. Tildy's lips were drawn back, revealing her canines. Her hands were opening and closing, revealing clawed nails. If she could have smashed the phone with her gaze, it would be in pieces.

"They're not destroyed," Rufus mumbled so quietly everyone thought they misheard him.

"W-w-w-what?" Lizzie screamed before pandemonium broke out on the other end of the line.

"They're in a state of suspended animation," Rufus said, a little louder. "I'll tell you everything later. Right now, we've got to worry about Idia and her evil army. I greatly underestimated her ambition. Look, could you come to my lab right away? I'll explain everything to you then." Rufus disconnected the call so they couldn't ask him any more questions.

Rufus grimaced and handed Teddy her phone. "Have you met your sister, Fredericka yet?"

"I didn't know I even had a sister until just a day ago!" Teddy squealed, shocked at the news her mother was still alive and she really had a sister. "Wow Rufus, you really know how to keep a secret and spring things on people."

Rufus had the nerve to look contrite. "When you were born, I allowed your grandmother Ceola to take you and raise you when it was apparent you had inherited none of the genes I was looking for. I, er, impregnated your mother again years later, and Fredericka was born. She has, um, I have raised her here in the lab since she was born."

"You have imprisoned her here in the lab since she was born, you mean and used her as a lab rat," Teddy sharply said. "That's what you really mean. Puleeze. Nana told me about your latest skirmish and how you treated your own child. Still, I'd love to meet her, but right now I'm starving, exhausted and in pain. I normally have a high tolerance to pain, but I'll take that morphine, now, please. This is too much. I need to rest a bit and process this."

"Hey, this will be our first trust test." She didn't know why she did what she did next. Something just told her to. Teddy grabbed Rufus's hand, and her piercing, unsettling gaze bored into his eyes. Rufus felt a chill pass through him, and he understood, for the first time, the expression *someone just walked across my grave.*

Satisfied with what she saw in Rufus's soul and that he really was giving her morphine and not poison, Teddy released his hand and nodded. Rufus immediately understood one of Teddy's gifts involved reading minds and sensing people's true intentions. He must have an in-depth discussion with her about this; although, he recollected, his mother's side of the family included a bloodline of witches. How fascinating, he reflected. The girl's special powers were probably endless. He had been a fool to let the grandmothers raise their daughters' babies.

"Thank you for trusting me, Theodora. I won't let you down. I must admit, you and your sister are beautiful," he whispered. "Absolutely beautiful." Rufus injected morphine into Teddy's IV port and sat in a chair beside the bed. "You know," he mused while Teddy's eyes fluttered, "you inherited your love of horses from your great-aunt, Magnolia."

"You must tell me about her." Teddy fell into a restless slumber. Lurking in her subconscious was the acknowledgment that Rufus would have to face a reckoning someday.

Rufus removed his notepad from his coat, opened it, and began writing. Every so often, he stopped, looked at Teddy intensely for a bit, and continued writing. When he finished, he took a picture of the letter with his phone's camera and airdropped the letter to Teddy's cell phone. Then, he folded and placed the hard copy in Teddy's pants' pocket. He hoped he'd be able to make things right but very much doubted it. There was too much water under the bridge and these women just didn't know, they had a plethora of enemies closing in on them from all sides, and it was all his fault. His curiosity was highly piqued. Nevertheless, he knew when to pull up stakes and live to fight another day. He hated to abandon his daughters, but if they were truly the creatures he destined them to be, he knew they could defend themselves. Timing was never in his favor, he thought. Now that he had both of his daughters, he could have actually had a relationship with them in this day and time. There was that little matter of them being the product of rape, but today's insightful therapy sessions could work wonders.

Idia and her no doubt nefarious plan worried him. Had he underestimated her because he saw her as not just a Black woman but an African Black woman and, therefore, felt she'd never be a threat to him in any way? If he could get his girls on his side, he knew without a doubt they could defeat Idia. He had bred them to be superior beings. Things could work out in his favor, after all, and maybe get him back in the good graces of Ceola. That is, if he lived long enough for that to happen.

With these thoughts swirling in his mind, Rufus strode into his lab and went to the wall safe where he removed a bag he kept there just for emergencies. As he took a last look around, an explosion rocked the building and he realized he had to leave now. He was confused, though. There's no way Idia's plane could have gotten here that quickly. What in the world was going on?

Chapter 21

Queen Idia sat in her plane; her first wave should be attacking Rufus's American lab right about now. Smiling, she thought to herself, *Sun Tzu was right. "Great results, can be achieved with small forces."* She also liked his quote "Let your plans be dark and impenetrable as night, and when you move, fall like a thunderbolt." As much as she'd love to have gone to America and confront the ones she used to call her best friends and be free of them for once and for all, she had other more pressing plans. Once she'd secured the turquoise amulet, she wouldn't need to worry about the virus and she could join her army in destroying those bitches. A frown settled on her face and fear flitted across her eyes. Abaku's health was rapidly deteriorating, and she feared she was displaying the onset of the very plague that allowed him to become a werepanther.

Even though she had her scientists working around the clock; they had been unsuccessful so far in developing anything to reverse, stop, or counter the effects. She had been too hasty. The serum just hadn't been ready for human trials yet.

She had been stealing surreptitious glances at Abaku all morning during the flight. The poor man had finally fallen into a fitful sleep. Idia didn't regret many things, but she was truly sorry for destroying this majestic man's body. She stole another glance at him and recoiled in disgust. *Thank goodness he can't see my expression,* she reflected.

Copious bumps covered Abaku's body, dangling like testicles. A doctor had tried cutting them off, but the tumors were embedded too deeply and some were entwined with blood vessels. Abscesses, which constantly leaked a purulent fluid, covered his body where tumors didn't. CT and MRI scans revealed tumors internally, as well. Abaku constantly complained about being in pain and how it felt like his insides were being eaten by acid. He frequently told her he hadn't signed up for this when he endorsed the consent form to be injected with the serum that would turn him into a werepanther.

She understood completely. She, too, had started noticing the beginning signs of the virus taking hold in her. Watching Abaku's decline distressed her. She would have never believed she would get infected in a million years, either, she reflected bitterly. Instead of moaning and groaning like a baby, at least she was taking action and was determined to fight this affliction to the bitter end. If science wasn't the answer, she'd try spiritual means. Idia had been praying to La Panthère Noire around the clock, but so far, the spirit hadn't replied. Idia had many questions for her, such as why was she infected, for starters. She would have thought being La Panthère Noire's acolyte would have protected her from contracting any diseases. Something was afoot in the spiritual realm and she would find out what was going on. Idia was no fool. She was well aware she shouldn't be displaying symptoms from *any* illness. And why had Raven and La Panthère Noire's voices suddenly gone silent on her? Since La Panthère Noire hadn't been helpful, she now needed to seek help elsewhere.

Waiting any longer for an answer would surely mean her death. She needed to find that amulet, and if La Panthère Noire took issue with that, then no matter. She'd take on La Panthère Noire if she had to. Nobody messed with Idia. Nobody!

Chapter 22

Teddy was dreaming she was in an earthquake and someone was calling her name over and over while slapping her several times.

"Ouch!" Teddy winced as she pried her eyes open and did a double-take. Holy hell, who was this kid with the piercing but oh-so-familiar ice-blue eyes and wild, curly, frizzy afro slapping the shit out of her? Even the pouty mouth and strong nose were familiar. While Teddy could barely lift her head without wanting to hurl her insides out, she had to stop this kid. The nerve, slapping her and screaming in her ear.

"Teddy, Teddy, you have to change! Change! Change!"

"I don't know what you mean," Teddy slurred, still struggling to come out from under the throes of her morphine-induced stupor. She grabbed the kid's hand mid-slap.

"Wake the fuck up! Hurry, you *must* change or we're dead." The girl frantically looked around while trying to pull Teddy up and keep her backpack with her at the same time.

"Calm down, kid. It's going to be okay." Teddy sat up, wiped her eyes, and got out of bed. She looked around the room for her clothes, found them, and began getting dressed.

Fredi jerked away from Teddy. "I'm not a kid. My name is Fredericka, and I'm your sister. We've..."

At the sound of footsteps, they went still as a graveyard and scented the air. Fredi relaxed first, as she recognized Dr. Vasquez' scent. A tall, sinewy but ripped, cinnamon-skinned man with long, luscious black hair ran into the room, followed by Dr. Vasquez.

"Daughter!" He rushed forward to embrace Teddy, who was so shocked she allowed him to hug her. He then turned and embraced an equally shocked Fredericka. "And you must be my dear Cleo's other daughter, Fredericka. I am Cochise. Come, girls. Hurry, we need to get out of here. The lab's under attack. Hurry."

"But, b-but, but," Teddy stuttered. "I'm so confused." She wondered who was this fine Native claiming to be her father. How could she have two fathers? Although if she had to choose, she would choose this man hands down. The girls looked at him and Dr. Vasquez quizzically. Teddy laced up her Docs and was ready.

"Hopefully, we'll all be able to talk later, but now, we've got to get out of here, guys," Dr. Vasquez stressed, constantly listening for signs indicating that part of the building had been breached. "I wouldn't put it past Rufus to have booby-trapped this place to blow up if enemies ever violated it. In fact, where is that snake? We'll meet up with the others, somehow, but we have to leave! Now! Follow me. There's a secret way out!"

"Wait, guys," Teddy said, slowing down. "Do I need to change? What's going on?" She still hadn't fed and doubted she could muster enough energy to change.

"No, keep running!" Mariposa Vasquez ordered. "We're under attack by Idia's minions. It's a small army, but we're still outnumbered! Thank God this pod is at the back of the compound."

Dr. Vasquez reached the end of a passage and pressed her index finger on the door's scanner. Once it clicked opened, they rushed through as booms rocked their ears and the building shook and crumbled. Maybe Rufus's over-the-top planning would come in handy.

"Text the other Ravenisha our coordinates," she shouted to Teddy. "Tell them we're exiting the south end of the building."

"On it," Teddy replied, texting while running. "By the way, love your Docs, ladies." Teddy kicked her feet up so they could see hers. "You're one of us, aren't you?"

"Yep!" Mariposa briefly touched Teddy's hand. She continued walking at a brisk pace but gave Teddy a warm smile. "It's so wonderful to meet you, at last, granddaughter. My God, you are powerful. Your aura is blasting me like a freight train."

A light glowed up ahead, and they recognized Rufus's lanky figure. He heard and saw them the same time they saw him, and after the slightest pause, he motioned for them to hurry.

"I have escape vehicles cached here. Oh my God," he whispered, eyes locked onto a wall monitor. "She's sent a platoon. Those werepanthers don't look quite right, though. What has she done? I don't understand. How did they get here so fast? Last I heard, the plane was in Brazil!"

They watched the wall monitor, faces in horror, as it revealed lab workers who weren't able to evacuate the building fast enough to avoid being ripped apart by Queen Idia's minions. Rufus couldn't seem to tear his eyes away from the tableau.

"How on Earth did she accomplish what I couldn't?" he wondered in reverence, eyes still glued to the monitor.

"Go, go, go!" Teddy commanded, pushing people along. "She's obviously outsmarted us." She even shoved Rufus. "Dude, you need to get a move on."

They found themselves in a large bay, which housed the compound's vehicles. Rufus clicked a fob, and an Army-equipped Humvee's engine rumbled to life. After everyone was in, Rufus floored the gas. Tires squealing, the powerful vehicle flew out of the garage and in the opposite direction from Idia's army of beasts.

"Tell me you're about to blow them to Hell, Rufus," Teddy shouted,while looking back at the cavernous gaping maw of the bay's interior.

Rufus smiled as he slowed down to press a button on his phone. "With pleasure." A series of explosions began demolishing the lab.

Ahead, a convoy of soldiers blocked their egress. Rufus slammed on the brakes and the almost four-ton vehicle shuddered as it screeched to a halt. Fort Cheaha's base personnel had mobilized and were neutralizing the threat among them.

"Yes, the cavalry has arrived!" Teddy fist pumped and exited the vehicle along with everyone else.

A brawny middle-aged man left the lead vehicle and stormed toward them. He was tall, but not as tall as Rufus or Cochise. His epaulets clearly marked him as a colonel.

"Goddamnit, Rufus," he thundered, shaking his finger in Rufus's face, "you've really fucked up this time. I told the president not to…"

"Get your finger out of my face, Beauregard," Rufus snarled. "If y'all had listened to me in the first place, we wouldn't be in this situation. Who let those monsters into the country? I told you they were coming. I just didn't know when."

"You just couldn't leave well enough alone," Beau retorted. "While you're off playing Dr. Frankenstein, I always have to rescue your ass and smooth over your messes."

"Why, you pompous..." Rufus raised his fist and was about to hit Beau before being restrained by Lieutenant Allensworth and his crew, who had exited another vehicle.

"Break it up, boys." Teddy looked from one man to the other. "Brothers. Am I right?"

Colonel Honeycutt broke his gaze from Rufus and rolled his eyes; the same ice-blue eyes that Rufus, Fredi, and Teddy had. Turning to Teddy, he offered a quick handshake, introducing himself as Colonel Beau Honeycutt, of the 617.4th Paranormal Division of the Army, including the Reserves. He turned to his adjutant. "Watkins, you and your men secure the site. Neutralize any beast that moves. Coordinate with the other group who entered the site's front and report back to me as soon as things are under control."

"Yes, sir!" Watkins saluted, turned, and immediately began barking orders.

"Follow me back to the base," Beau commanded Rufus and the others, his lips compressed in a thin line. His gaze lingered a little longer than necessary on Teddy and Fredi.

As they turned to walk to their vehicles, snarls filled the air. Two werepanthers had gotten through the debris unscathed and were running straight toward them. Soldiers stared in horror at the creatures barreling their way. They had never seen anything like them in their lives, and their hesitation cost them. They began firing on the beasts, but the creatures pounced on the unlucky personnel closest to them. Heads and entrails went flying, spraying those in the proximity with blood and gore. The soldiers, fully alert now, unleashed a barrage of bullets into the beasts. As the monsters lay on the ground, pools of blood forming around them, they reverted to their human forms. A murmur rose among soldiers as they walked among the fallen mutants that littered the ground. They hesitated, unsure whether to provide medical aid to those still alive. Yes, they were monsters, but now they were human beings. Women.

"Stay on task!" the Colonel barked, correctly reading the situation. Shots rang out as soldiers contained a disturbance in the front. "Remember what they can turn into. Gather every single body and put them in the rig. Now!" He turned to Rufus and placed his hands on his hips. "Okay, Rufus, we outfitted that rig as you specified: steel alloyed with Iconel and arsphogene dioxide. Are you sure that will contain those creatures?"

"Of course, Beauregard," Rufus scoffed. "The Iconel will be impossible to escape, and if they damage it too much, I've engineered it to release the gas I created— arsphogene dioxide, a combination of phosgene and arsine—into the air. I'm just sorry the Iconel bullets laced with arsphogene dioxide aren't ready. Those creatures would be dead instead of incapacitated. The gunsmith promised me a shipment by week's end." Rufus shook his head. "By then, they'll be a day late and a dollar short." His cold eyes took in the carnage around him dispassionately. " Oh, by the way, Theodora, I had some knives specially made for you, too."

"Well, aren't you special?" Teddy commented dryly. Hearing Rufus describe his innovative weapons reminded Teddy how much she missed her gear.

"Er, guys," Teddy asked en route to their vehicle since the army had made quick work of the interlopers. "Is there any possibility of me getting my duffle bag with my weapons or borrowing some of y'alls? I feel kind of naked unarmed."

Colonel Honeycutt stopped and snorted. "I've heard all about you, Quick Draw McGraw. The answer is affirmative but only because we need every able-bodied soldier we can get and I've heard your weapons skills are extraordinary. We should have recruited you for this division anyway instead of the reserves, but I also heard you and your girlfriends have a little attitude problem. Y'all really busted up my demolition men the other night, and for no reason, as I understand it. If, and I mean if, the higher-ups lift your and your friends' suspensions, we're going to have a nice, long talk."

An awkward silence ensued as the colonel waited for Teddy to reply. She just glared at him, or rather through him with those creepy, mismatched eyes. He broke eye contact and ordered everybody to head out.

As others began moving, Beau and Teddy continued looking at each other like they were in a stand-off in a western showdown. Rather, Teddy was giving the colonel the evil eye, and he was trying to return a stank eye as best as he could.

Beau shivered as he wondered whether he could work with Teddy and her girls or if he was even on board with this whole notion of people being able to change into animals. However, the more he thought about it, the reality of the day's events, coupled with Teddy's otherworldliness, left him with no doubt shapeshifters were real and the game had changed. Who woulda thought there would ever be an actual need for a Paranormal Reserves division? As it turned out, there was a need and he was in charge. It had been too long since he had been in the news claiming glory and the spotlight, but that was about to change. *So, take that, Scarbrough, you asshole,* he thought.

Quick as lightning, Teddy reached for his Sig Sauer P320 pistol and fired. His ears instantly began ringing. He was startled and enraged she had disarmed him and the bullet passed so close to his head; he felt his barely-there hair move. He rushed her despite the fact she was armed with his weapon. But before he could even raise his arm, she had brought his own weapon up and had it aimed at his forehead. Goddamn, she was fast.

"You're way out of line, Furie," he snarled.

Gus ran over and held out his hand. "Teddy, give me the weapon."

Teddy glared at the ungrateful colonel. She twirled the gun cowboy style and handed it to Lieutenant Allensworth handle up. Gus lightly tapped Beau's arm.

"Turn around, Colonel."

He did and almost stumbled on a mutant woman inches from him. He realized just how close to death he had been. "Lord a' mercy," he breathed. He turned back around and walked over to Teddy. "I owe you an apology, Furie. Thank you for saving my life. You just scared the shit out of me when you grabbed my weapon like that. Thank God you're one hell of a shot. Thank you again, *Niece*," he whispered conspiratorially as he gave Teddy a brief pat on the back.

"Any time, Colonel."

"Okay, everyone," Colonel Honeycutt bellowed. "Back to the base."

Fredi stood, flanked by Dr. Vasquez and Cochise. Her eyes hadn't moved from Teddy during the entire exchange. They burned with fire, and she stared at Teddy enraptured. Damn, she wanted to be like Teddy when she grew up.

Cochise and Dr. Vasquez had been silent during the exchange, their eyes on Teddy, as well. You could practically see the wheels turning in their heads as they pondered the implications of Teddy's remarkable eye colors. It hadn't been lost on them that one eye resembled Rufus's and the other eye was a dead ringer for Dr. Vasquez's.

Rufus's attention was elsewhere. He examined a fallen woman. Something was puzzling him. He reluctantly got into the vehicle to head back to base but made a mental note to further his examination when they arrived.

Chapter 23

Driving to the base took longer than expected. The distance itself wasn't long, but the convoy had to traverse a winding mountain road and as with most mountainous roads, this one had cliffs on one side and drop-offs on the other. Thankfully, the drop-offs weren't visible because of the trees that grew profusely. Lumber mills' saws had spared them because of their dangerous location. This had allowed trees and bushes to grow freely. Drivers were also extra vigilant to ensure they weren't being followed by any of Idia's army who may have survived. The plan in place was to get to the base and figure out how to hunt down Idia so that they could stop her. Rufus could get his precious serum and the American Ravenisha could be free to live how they chose.

During the scenic ride through the Talladega National Forest, Cochise and Dr. Vasquez sat in front of Teddy and Fredi. Cochise introduced himself as Cochise Ramiero Nezahualocelotl Martinez and Dr. Vasquez as his mother, Itzpapalotl, which meant Obsidian Butterfly.

"Your mother!" exclaimed Fredi, who had been looking back and forth between the parties. "But that's Dr. Vas…ohhh. I get it now. Is that why you call me Citlalli, Dr. Vasquez?" Fredi's face screwed up in confusion.

"Yes, Citlalli, I gave you an Aztecan name since you're an honorary member of our tribe now." She gave Fredi a motherly smile. "And just call me Mariposa."

"What does Citlalli mean?" Fredi asked.

"It means star or star goddess. You are so brilliant and your aura is so bright. You remind me of a star."

Cochise's obsidian-colored eyes watched Teddy intensely during the entire trip, taking in her being as if memorizing every cell and molecule, while Teddy did the same to him.

Once they arrived at the cleverly hidden base near Cheaha Mountain, they all assembled in a conference room. Matilda, being Matilda, couldn't help but note that it was interesting how settlers used Creek Indian names for cities, edifices, etc. after driving the original residents out. Cheaha, really *chaha*, meant high place and Talladega, a town between the Creeks and Natchez.

"Umph. I'm surprised y'all kept the Native's names. Why y'all always taking people's land, then claiming Native ancestry when it benefits you? Nevermind. Don't bother responding." Rufus and Beauregard just stood, arms folded across their chests.

"I'd like to hear your reply, myself," Cochise added.

"Look Cochise, you are a conquered people. This land is ours now. You can't change history. I feel bad for you, Matilda," Rufus said with a smirk. "You must live a tortured and unhappy existence to always be so confrontational and mean."

Matilda's mouth dropped open, and she stood toe to toe with Rufus, who was quite tall himself. "Gee, I wonder why that's been the case."

Heading off the impending argument, Colonel Honeycutt told Rufus he could conduct his examinations on the mutants if he'd like since they were all gathered up and thrown into the back of the big rig.

Matilda rolled her eyes at both men. Beau noticed and couldn't help himself. "Matilda, one would think you'd be nicer considering you tried to push me off of a cliff and kill me when I was a child."

"Oh my God!" Matilda exploded. "For the thousandth time, you fell into that ditch because of your own stupid ass. I threw the ball, but I certainly didn't think you'd be stupid enough to jump into that ditch after it. Dumbass. Like I would ever voluntarily play with you in the first place."

"What did you expect, you acolyte of Satan? I was six-years-old. I broke my leg," Beau began, red-faced.

"That's old enough to have enough sense not to jump into a deep ditch full of rocks thinking you're going to catch a ball, ignoramus."

"You devil's concubine. You knew that gully was dangerous."

Matilda snarled, but a commotion behind her made her turn around to see what the fuss was about. She and Beau glared at each other and found seats as far away from each other as possible.

Screaming with joy, Ceola ran toward Cochise and enveloped him in an enormous hug. She cupped his face in her hands and hugged him again. "It's so good to see you, Cochise. You were this close to being my son-in-law." Ceola smiled as she put her thumb and forefinger together.

"It's good to see you and the others, too." He kissed Ceola on the cheek. "I sure do miss your *biscones*." He turned and drew Mariposa to his side. "I heard you already met my mother, Obsidian Butterfly, or rather Dr. Mariposa Vasquez." The two women smiled warmly at each other as they embraced.

"I knew your scent was familiar," Ceola told Mariposa.

Fredi eagerly absorbed all the information she was hearing. Normally, Teddy would have been all ears, as well, but she was strangely removed, looking around for a place to sit. The other women in the room warmly greeted Cochise and Mariposa.

Teddy ignored them all and gladly sat down and laid her head on the table. She was still starving and even more exhausted. The little adrenaline burst she had experienced back at Rufus's lab was gone. A warm hand rubbed her back in gentle circular motions.

"Hang in there, baby girl," Ceola murmured. "I know you're starving and fatigued. We'll get you some food soon."

"Okay, let's get started," Colonel Honeycutt said from the front of the room, bringing people to order. "Should she be in here?" he asked, directing his gaze to Fredi. He gave his version of a smile, which made him look like he had gas. "Sweetie, why don't you go and play with your dolls in the lounge?" Fredi fixed Colonel Honeycutt with an icy stare and growled.

Taken aback, he recovered and tried to laugh. "Okay. Okay. Calm down. I see I misspoke. Perhaps you'd be happier playing video games, instead."

Fredi rolled her eyes. "Yes, I should be here," she growled. "I may be small, but I'm just as deadly as Teddy. I'm not a child. I'm twelve-years-old—almost thirteen. That's practically grown. Besides, I know everything about everybody anyways, and Rufus would have *never* come up with that compound for the Iconel, the gas, or the serum if I hadn't helped him. I'm a genius, and you need my input. Therefore, I'm staying. Just try and make me leave." She crossed her arms across her chest and fixed Colonel Honeycutt with a defiant glare.

"I suppose this is one of yours, too, Rufus." The colonel rolled his eyes.

"Whatevs," Fredi said.

Rufus looked at Beau and shook his head in warning. "Beauregard, have you ever tried arguing with a pre-teen? Save your energy. It's not worth it. You've gotta learn when to pick your battles."

A chorus of *Amens* filled the room, as Ceola, Elizabeth and Matilda nodded their heads in agreement. Even Celeste and Naima nodded.

Beau looked down his nose at Rufus. "You can give in to some little child all you want, but I'll be damned if she's going to run my life and my meeting, even if she is my niece and a genius." He turned to Fredi, who had removed her laptop from her backpack and was furiously typing, her fingers flying across the keys. "Now, don't make me have to tell you again, you little cuss. Go to the lounge. Now. This is grown folks' business." Beau fixed her with a stare that would have curled the toes of many soldiers under his command.

Fredi stopped typing. When she looked up, her eyes were slits, and a growl came from her mouth, where elongated canines made it difficult for her to talk. Rufus's eyes widened and his mouth dropped open.

"I said I'm staying," she hissed. "Why don't you worry about why they assigned you to this division. Your records indicate you were an exemplary soldier until 1982. Hmm, it says here a Colonel Scarbrough took disciplinary action in February 1982 and things just went downhill after that. November 1984, May 1992, blah, blah, blah, March 2001 disciplined for behavior not becoming of an officer. Well, well, well, Mister Beauregard you must have really pissed this Scarbrough person off," Fredi gleefully began as Beau, his face mottled red, rushed her.

"How did you breach those files? That information is classified you little cuss! Aaaargh!"

Gus exploded from his seat to restrain the sizable man from attacking Fredi, but Matilda held him back with a shake of her head, an amused smile on her face. They could all feel the otherworldliness radiating off of Fredi. As Beau rushed forward, Fredi leaped from her chair, her features panther-like. While her body was primarily human, her claws were already lightly making their way down Beau's shirt, ripping it into shreds and drawing blood.

"Get off of me, get off of me!" His shrill screams filled the room as he batted Fredi ineffectually.

Wearily, Rufus croaked, "Fredericka, please, stop. He's your uncle…and an adult. You've made your point." Rufus looked at Fredericka and then Dr. Vasquez. Those two had some 'splainin' to do.

Fredi jumped down and sat back in her seat, laughing maniacally as her features morphed back to normal. "Your face…" She doubled over in laughter. "You should have seen your face. What happened to the big, bad soldier? I didn't even hurt you that much, either." Fredi's laugh was infectious. It was high-pitched and almost like the squawk of a parrot.

Unable to stop herself, Teddy joined in, and soon, the entire room was laughing.

Ceola and the other Ravenisha looked at each other. It wasn't necessary for them to speak. They had all seen Fredi's teeth. They looked just like Teddy's. Rufus definitely had some explaining to do.

"I tried to warn you," Rufus said, snickering, as Beau stormed out and slammed the door, furiously yelling into his cell phone—something about classified information being breached.

Fredi stopped laughing. She gave Rufus a scowl so frigid a polar bear would have shivered had one been in the room. Glacial-blue eyes met glacial-blue eyes.

"You think this is funny? I have an uncle? Who else are you keeping from me? I'm not some lab rat. I'm a human being. I have feelings. Well, I may not be completely human, but still. You kept me imprisoned in a lab for all of my life. You deprived me of any semblance of a normal childhood. You deprived me of the love of my mother, sister, Nana, and uncle. And, and, and, you bastard, you showed me no love at all. You tased me, treated me like shit. When you did acknowledge my presence, it was only because I provided a service to you. I hate you!" she shouted, dangerously close to a breakdown. "How could you? You monster! When we leave this base, I'm living with Teddy and Nana and the rest of my people, and don't you dare try to stop me!" Fredi's voice had risen to a strident pitch and her little chest fluttered like a hummingbird's.

"Calm down," Rufus replied, a red flush creeping up his neck. He tried to put his arm around Fredi, but she angrily slapped it away and growled at him. Rufus looked at Fredi for a long moment and then looked away—into the flashing eyes of his brother's.

Beau stood quietly in the doorway. From the constant widening of his eyes, head shakes and mouth drops, it was apparent Rufus had kept him in the dark as well. He angrily waved away the medic trying to bandage the long red stripes, which still leaked slight amounts of blood. "My God, I didn't know. That's why you kept me at military school all of my life."

An IT tech, a hipster-looking man who projected an air of supreme confidence, followed the medic. No computer nerd here. The tech looked at Fredi through his stylish glasses. His head was shaved low on the sides, and he sported a man bun and goatee. He was clearly a civilian, even if his skinny jeans, ankle boots, T-shirt, and many finger, ear, nose, and brow rings hadn't given him away. His eyes raked Fredi up and down, his expression clearly stating his disbelief that a tween could break into the government's system. He beckoned for Fredi to follow him, telling her she was in deep trouble. The already upset girl merely rolled her neck, crossed her arms, and stared at him. She looked him up and down like she was examining a slab of beef before she turned her head away and stared at the wall ahead of her.

Rufus and Matilda chimed in together. The IT tech would take Fredi nowhere. She was a minor. If he had questions, he could ask them then and there.

The IT tech looked like he was about to argue, but one fierce glare from Matilda disabused him of that notion.

"What algorithm did you use to hack into the army's computer system?" When Fredi told him, he said, "Shit." He looked at her in disbelief and turned to leave the room, his lips puckered tighter than a cat's butthole. He paused at the door and said if she was that advanced, there was nothing he could do to stop her. He left muttering about damn kids these days and how they spent too much time on computers, the little freaks.

Rufus looked more closely at Fredi. Aggrieved, he gave a tremendous sigh. "Fredericka, where is your collar, and since when can you change? How come no one bothered to tell me this?" Rufus looked at Dr. Vasquez, who held his gaze. "I'm surprised at you, Dr. Vasquez." She merely studied her short black-painted fingernails in response. "If I had known, I…"

"You would have what? Treated me even more abysmally?" Fredi said, sneering. "Mr. Akiro is part of my hacker's group and once he and I figured out I had on the same collar as the Ravenisha, he walked me through the steps to remove the deathtrap. I took it off this morning and disabled your little remote, too. You better not hurt me ever again. And Rufus, I won't be little always. Tase me again, and see what happens."

Rufus shook his head in grim capitulation. "I'm sorry for tasing you. I felt that was the best way to control you since my other methods were impotent. But how many times have I told you not to address me by my first name, Fredericka? It's either Mister Rufus, Dr. Honeycutt, or dare I say, Papa?" Rufus thought regretfully he hadn't realized the full extent of Fredericka's genius. If he had known, he would have worked the girl harder.

Fredi looked at Rufus like he had lost his mind. "Wow, you are something else. Are you really this tone-deaf? I'm not talking to you. I. am. Mad. At. You. God!" She punctuated each word with a hand clap.

A thump alarmed everyone as Teddy slid from her chair and onto the floor.

"She really needs to feed," Ceola said, worry in the lines around her eyes and mouth. She looked up and nodded for Lieutenant Allensworth and his crew to come forward. "This conversation will keep. We've got to feed Theodora right now." Ceola turned to Henry and Roland and whispered some instructions to them.

"Yes, ma'am, on it," Roland said, and the two men jogged off.

Meanwhile, Gus picked Teddy up and held her in his arms.

"Colonel, where's a room where she can feed?" Tildy asked. "The room needs to be easily cleaned."

Leona interrupted whatever the Colonel was about to say. "No, this can't wait, and yes, Teddy needs to be here to take part in the discussion."

"Follow me, then," the Colonel said, resignedly, now realizing it was futile to argue with these women. This one even seemed to know what he was thinking before he even spoke. "This better be a quick process. My men tell me Idia's plane is making excellent progress."

"It won't take long at all." Ceola smiled sweetly at him.

Celeste and Naima sat quietly through the drama, at a loss for words. Numbly, they got up and followed the others.

The group walked down the hall, and Colonel Honeycutt gestured them into a stark room with a concrete floor just off of the garage where vehicles were hangar'd. Rapid footsteps made them all jump and reach for weapons.

"Colonel," huffed a private first class, "the Special Forces men took a prisoner off of the truck. We tried to stop them, but one of them turned his semi-automatic on us."

A commotion ensued from the hallway as Henry pushed his way in, dragging one of Idia's minions. She weakly tried to fight, but the special metal in the truck had sapped all of her strength and Henry's grip was firm.

"Stand down, soldiers," Colonel Honeycutt ordered his men.

Gus gently placed Teddy in a chair. He wrapped a blanket around her and discretely removed her clothes.

"There are too many people in here," he barked. "Stand back, y'all. Let the woman breathe. Let's have only essential personnel here."

As the room cleared out, Fredi pushed her way to the front. She turned to the Old-Generation. "I got this. You may leave."

Matilda fixed her with a steely gaze for a moment, but then she only grunted "Umph" and she and the others left. The only ones remaining now with Teddy were Colonel Honeycutt, Gus, Fredi, and the soon-to-be nourishment for Teddy. Everyone else went next door and watched the proceedings on a monitor.

"Okay, Teddy." Fredi knelt in front of Teddy, looking up into her face. "You've got to feed. Come on, you've gotta change."

Teddy weakly lifted her head, unable to even focus her eyes on the girl in front of her. Fredi bit down on her wrist and drew blood.

"What is that chile doing? We're not vampires." Lizzie squinted, putting her face closer to the monitor.

"She's going by instinct," Dr. Vasquez murmured in wonder, speaking up for the first time and also peering intently at the screen. "Her mind is really like a little computer."

"Come on Teddy, drink." Fredi placed her bloody wrist on Teddy's mouth. Teddy took a few laps of blood and then drank more. She perked up as her synapses began firing—energized by Fredi's blood.

Several things began happening at once. A low growl rolled throughout the room, reverberating off of the walls. Teddy's eyes became slits, and she dropped to the floor on all fours. At the same time, the minion who had reverted back to her human form began stirring.

"Heads up!" Gus shouted, raising his weapon, as the prisoner, becoming more aware of her dire predicament, began changing. Fredi held out her arm, motioning for Gus to stand down.

Colonel Honeycutt, who hadn't watched this process in person before, having spent most of his life at military boarding schools, slowly backed up to the door, his eyes as big as saucers, a hand over his mouth as Teddy's she-panther fully formed. The room suddenly felt too small. Teddy's massive black pantheress bounded over to the prisoner's smaller cat and immediately brought her down with one powerful swipe of her big claw. She then bit into her skull with those massive canines. Brain matter and fluid flew everywhere.

"Oh shit, oh shit, oh shit." Colonel Honeycutt trembled, unable to tear his eyes away from the spectacle before him.

As Teddy's she-panther cracked open the skull and consumed the brains, people assembled around various monitors throughout the base began searching for something to vomit in. However, it was when Teddy crunched on the skull bones that turned the stomachs for many, and they rushed off, trying to stem the flow of liquid flowing out of their mouths.

Meanwhile, Rufus watched enrapt, his eyes like stars. "My God," he breathed, "she is absolutely beautiful. What a magnificent creature!"

Teddy made quick work of the prisoner-turned-prey. There was a gasp as a smaller pantheress slowly crawled over to Teddy on her belly. This one was striped and blonde with piercing blue eyes. No one had noticed Fredi changing, save for a few people.

"Lord, I'll be," Rufus breathed. "Dr. Vasquez, were you aware Fredi could fully change? I suspected she would be able to one day, hence the collar. I just didn't know how to induce the change."

Dr. Vasquez nodded, her eyes never leaving the two she-panthers.

Ceola's eyes widened. "Wait a minute, y'all. They're very faint, but Teddy's fur is striped like Fredi's. I thought my eyes were deceiving me earlier."

"That's what I wanted to bring to your attention back at the lab," Matilda said. "Not only did I notice the stripes, but the skull looks like that of a tiger, doesn't it? And the teeth are serrated. Fredi has the same anomalies."

Fredi's pantheress mewled in front of Teddy's, still on her stomach. Teddy made a snuffling sound and Fredi crawled closer. She bit off a leg and consumed it. Teddy flipped the dead minion on her back, disemboweled her with her razor-sharp claws, and then she and Fredi consumed the guts. They began working on the chest cavity next. The room was silent, save for the sounds of the prey being consumed. Teddy even shared some of the most nutritious organs, such as the liver, with her sibling, who gobbled everything down like she hadn't eaten in days.

Beau stared, unblinking, his mouth open, his mind going a mile a minute. Things were making sense. The stories he had heard growing up, Rufus's little hints and taunts over the years that he knew a secret that Beau didn't, Rufus constantly threatening to feed him to the monsters if he didn't do what Rufus wanted, daddy's secret lab, the women's otherworldliness and place in the family. It all made sense now.

Celeste and Naima's stomachs rumbled loud enough for everyone to hear. Low growls emanated from them as they stared longingly at Teddy and Fredi eating.

When there was nothing left, the pantheresses began grooming each other, contented. Abruptly they stopped, ears pricked toward the door. Growls burst from their throats, their hackles rose and their tails grew fluffy. They loped toward the door, eagerly jostling each other. A great commotion erupted outside the room, and alarms began sounding.

"What now?" Colonel Honeycutt grumbled while he drew his weapon and made for the door. As soon as he flung it open, he was almost knocked down as Teddy and Fredi's she-panthers flew by him. Fortunately, the door's jamb saved him from tumbling.

As he, Lieutenant Allensworth, and his troops sprinted down the hall, they were knocked off of their feet by six massive black she-panthers dashing by them to join Teddy and Fredi. As they reached the area that housed the big rig, pandemonium greeted them. Fur, blood, and bodies were flying everywhere, as the Old-Gen and New-Gen pantheresses, along with Fredi and Mariposa demolished the awakened prisoners.

As Rufus counted the she-panthers, he realized what was confusing him. He moaned, "Dr. Vasquez is a shapeshifter, too? How did I not know this?"

"The big ones are ours!" Gus shouted to the other soldiers, firing as he entered the fray. Between the soldiers and she-panthers, the surviving members of Idia's army were soon dead or dying while the Ravenisha, Mariposa, and Fredi feasted on the defeated, smaller she-panthers.

Preternaturally, the she-panthers' attention was suddenly drawn to the big rig, and they encircled it, growling. There was movement in the very back. Without warning, out flew another mutant, jaws snapping, claws indiscriminately slashing as it leaped over the Ravenisha and ran out of the bay. Everyone was so stunned by the thing that had just emerged from the rig, their inactivity allowed the monstrously misshapen panther to escape into the surrounding forest.

Chapter 24

As the Ravenisha, Fredi and Mariposa reverted to their human forms, their open mouths, wide eyes, and scrunched-up features revealed their revulsion and shock.

"What the hell?" Teddy asked. "Did y'all see that thing? Ugh, I don't look like that when I'm in my she-panther form, do I? That was a big buttload of ugly."

"It looks like Idia's been experimenting and the results aren't pretty," Mariposa commented, concern etched on her face. "That was *not* a normal werepanther, and it didn't look like the other mutants..." Everyone turned and glared at Rufus.

"You don't seem very surprised by the appearance of that thing, Rufus. What have you done now? I want to know everything, and don't you dare bullshit me," Colonel Honeycutt snapped. "You!" He pointed his finger at Mariposa. "Vasquez, Butterfly, whatever the hell you're calling yourself. You work alongside Dr. Frankenstein here. What in the hell was that?"

Dr. Vasquez shrugged in response, her gaze fixed on Rufus. She turned to Colonel Honeycutt, jade eyes narrowed. "I suggest you change your attitude and learn how to address women if you want my cooperation. You may refer to me as *Dr.* Vasquez."

Beau turned to his soldiers and ordered, "Escort Rufus and Vasquez, I mean *Dr.* Vasquez, back to the conference room while I make sure the facility and perimeter are secure. Guard the door and make sure they don't leave. Johnson," he barked at a soldier, "notify local law enforcement agencies to be on the lookout for that creature...and set up a press conference for later today."

"Yes sir." Private First Class Johnson saluted.

"Where are the medics?" bellowed Colonel Honeycutt.

"Colonel, I'm a trained nurse. I'll help," Naima volunteered.

"Thank you, ma'am." The Colonel tipped his head toward Naima. "And somebody, get these women some clothes!"

"Colonel," Akiro shouted, waving for people to follow him, "I have images of that ugly werepanther available."

"We'll be right there, Sergeant. Let's make sure that thing is truly gone, soldiers. Report back to me immediately."

A chorus of *Yessir* echoed throughout the cavernous bay.

Once in the conference room, Beau took control. "Rufus, Doc, are the creatures' bites contagious? Do I have to worry about my men changing into a monster if one of those creatures bites or scratches on them? No offense, ladies," he said after seeing the expressions of disgust on the women's faces.

Fredi walked over to Rufus and with her hands on her hips and crowed, "I told you so."

"Don't start, Fredericka Zola Honeycutt," Rufus responded, his mouth tight and his eyes glittering as bright as diamonds.

"I told you so, but you wouldn't listen to me." She wagged her finger in Rufus's face.

Rufus fixed her with an icy stare. “This is where I would shock you with a taser if I could.”

Fredi gave him the finger, stuck her tongue out, and ran over to the Ravenisha. “And this is where I would kill and eat you if I could.”

Beau watched the interaction in disbelief, hands on his hips. How had he lost control of this meeting?

Rufus turned to Dr. Vasquez. “My head is spinning. Mariposa, how could you stab me in the heart like this? You’ve had the ability to shapeshift all along as well? Yet, you aren’t one of them,” he said, nodding his head toward the Ravenisha, making it a statement and not a question.

“You’re joking if you think I would tell you anything, Rufus,” Mariposa replied contemptuously. “Why would I have done that? So you could put a collar on me and experiment on me, too? I don’t think so.” She laughed humorlessly and pointedly turned her head away from Rufus.

Rufus turned to Cochise. “So, do you shapeshift, as well?”

“Nope,” Cochise replied. “I’m just a plain ol’ human male.”

“Er, Beauregard,” Rufus began.

Beau shook his head, “And this is where the other shoe drops. I don’t want to hear this Rufus. I really don’t. Do you have control over anything in your life? Anything at all?”

Rufus hemmed and hawed. “I have about as much control over my life as you have over this meeting. I need to go back to what’s left of my lab and er…make sure they didn’t take something.”

“I knew it!” Beau crowed triumphantly. “I suppose this ‘something’—he made air quotes—is what this Idia is after, huh? Did this “something” turn some poor person into those mutants?” He saw the affirmation on Rufus's face. "Goddamnit! Harley," he yelled and turned to a soldier. "I want you and Private First Class Johnson to escort Rufus back to his lab. Shoot him if he tries to escape."

Private First Class Johnson guffawed, "Brothers!"

"I mean it, Johnson," Beau deadpanned. "If the motherfucker tries to escape, shoot him."

Fredi opened her mouth to say something but closed it. Everyone was looking at Rufus like they could kill him.

"Er, excuse me," Fredi said in a small voice, moving so close to Teddy, she was practically nestled into her side. "You don't have to go back to the lab."

Rufus threw his hands up in the air. "Fredericka, you are incorrigible," Rufus told her, shaking his head.

"I learned from the best," Fredi retorted.

"Okay, where are the vials and disks?"

"I'm not sure if I should tell anyone," Fredi replied.

"Sir," a soldier tapped on the door and poked his hand in. "We have secured the perimeter. It looks like that thing and some stragglers made it back to their plane, and the plane has taken off despite all attempts to stop it."

"Thank you, soldier," Colonel Honeycutt replied, dismissing him.

"Sir," said Akiro, catching the colonel's attention, "the president is on the phone. She wants to speak with you immediately."

"I'm sure she does," responded Beau dejectedly. "Any way we can set up a video conference?"

"Consider it done," Akiro responded.

Once they were all seated at the conference table and waiting to be connected to the video system, Ceola turned to Fredi and asked, "Fredi, dear, how did you know to give Teddy some of your blood?"

Fredi looked earnestly at her Nana. "Dr. Vasquez said Teddy and I were special because of Rufus's gene-splicing experiments, Nana. Every time she took my blood and analyzed it, she would say, 'Remarkable.' " Fredi imitated Mariposa's accented voice. "Then, she'd sigh and say how she wished she could study Teddy's blood because Teddy's a chimera and how even Rufus didn't know and how Teddy was a beast because she had *two* strains of werepanther in her."

"Fredi, thank you. That's enough," Mariposa cut her off, laughing. "I meant beast in a good way," she added, smiling at Teddy.

"How did I not know any of this!" Rufus angrily shouted as everyone at the table turned and looked at Teddy, who visibly squirmed under their gazes.

"Don't y'all look at me. I'm not being anyone's lab experiment. I don't know how many times I have to tell y'all that."

Rufus gazed at Teddy joyfully, hope in his eyes. "Don't you realize what this means, Theodora? Don't you know how special you are? My God, this could not only help me but advance humans so much."

"Nope to the nope, and hell to the naw." Teddy's eyes shot daggers at Rufus and Cochise.

"Why are you giving me the stank eye, Daughter?" asked Cochise. "I really loved your mother. I'm not a scientist, and I'm just—"

"We know," voices chimed. "You're just a plain ol' human man."

"Mr. Cochise, that's a lie and you know it," Fredi said. "If your mother is Dr. Vasquez, then you are not a plain ol' human man. You have a little somethin' somethin' in you."

Murmurs started around the table. Cochise made a zipping sign across his mouth as he looked at Fredi.

“Excuse me,” a voice interrupted them, and a pregnant moment of silence descended on the room. “I need someone to tell me what the hell is going on and start at the beginning,” the president ordered.

Since no one said a word, Fredi spoke up, explaining to the president everything that had happened today and revealing how Rufus had been experimenting on her to create his serum in a clear and succinct manner.

When she finished, the president responded, “Thank you, Miss…?”

“I prefer to be called Fredi, not Fredericka,” Fredi stated, glaring pointedly at Rufus.

“I'm not going to even ask how you know everybody's business,” remarked Matilda. “You're too much for me.”

“I'm probably too much for everyone. According to Dr. Vasquez, I'm too precocious for my own good,” Fredi said so seriously, people at the table couldn't help but laugh. “It's a wonder I'm not crazy like Teddy, though, from all of that inbreeding,” Fredi added, crinkling her nose up.

“Excuuuse you?” Teddy's eyebrows rose almost to her hairline.

“Sorry, Sis, but Rufus fathered Cleo, and he fathered you,” Fredi declared in a superior tone. “Downright nasty.”

“Home skillet, he also fathered you, so theoretically, you're just as inbred as I am.”

“Which is why I'm surprised I'm not crazy like you.”

“Now girls, that's the history for many African Americans,” the president said. “So, the only goal was to develop a serum that would turn humans into these werecats or shapeshifter beings. Not to cure cancer, eradicate diseases, or just to benefit humanity, despite what Dr. Honeycutt would have us believe." She shook her head, eyes sad. "Will men ever learn? Well, I think it's obvious we must destroy this serum."

"That's kind of harsh to blame everything wrong with the world on men, Madam President," Colonel Honeycutt interjected.

Fredi gave him a scathing look before saying, "She means humankind when she refers to man. I don't think she literally means males only." The women in the room quietly chuckled. Fredi patted the colonel on the hand. "It's okay, Mr. Beauregard. Rufus is always saying that while you were born with brawn, he was born with brains."

"Thank you, Fredericka," Rufus hissed. "Now, please, just…"

"I know, I know," Fredi intoned. "Be quiet. Children should be seen and not heard."

"Fredi, gurrl, you a mess, although you're going to have to learn to exercise discretion if you want to hang with me. I can't be sharing secrets with you if you're going to tell the whole world." Teddy winked, and Fredi responded with a wide grin.

"Hey, wait a minute. I'm a mess? At least I'm not a crazy killer. Between those people sacrificing Aztecs, those bloodthirsty, ruthless Chiricahua Apache, Rufus, and Nana Ceola, it's a wonder you're not a serial killer," Fredi goaded.

"Fredi, just let it go! I don't know why you all up in people's business, anyway. Is nothing private, anymore? I know I wasn't this annoying when I was twelve," huffed Teddy. When no one responded, Teddy took in a deep breath and exhaled noisily.

"Wow, thanks a lot for backing me up y'all. Guys, I just thought of something," Teddy drawled. "Why would Idia's minions flee so quickly? They came here for a reason. You're not telling me Idia brought an army all the way from Africa just to what? Intimidate us? She wanted something from that lab. Fredi, I know you said you surreptitiously took Rufus's vials and disks. If that's the case, why didn't Idia's people fight us harder to get those vials and disks? There must have been something else she was looking for. And do we know the planes' destination? Also, do we have to worry about consuming those mutant panthers? Rufus, I noticed you examining that woman back there. Are all of them showing signs of abnormalities?" Everyone in the room turned and looked at Rufus.

"Damn," Rufus said again. "Initially, she only had the serum, but she couldn't reproduce it. She needed my formula. And now she has it. We're in a world of trouble. She has all the tools she needs to reproduce the formula to make more mutant panthers. No matter. She won't be able to make a Theodora or Fredericka without the Lost-Generation, and I'm not even sure she'll be able to duplicate what I've done even if she had the Lost-Generation. Also, thank the Lord she doesn't have my formula for the Iconel and gas."

"You mean *our* formula," said Fredi, crossing her arms.

Rufus took a deep breath, gazed around the table and stood. "Fine. This is my mess. I'll clean it up. I've studied you women all of my life. My initial goal in meeting with Idia was to spread my empire. Idia assured me her people would be cheaper and that Benin's government would push things through that the US government would take years and many studies to approve. Yes, the end goal was to duplicate your shapeshifting abilities. I thought the US government could create an army of superhuman soldiers. However, I soon learned other governments had the same ideas using other creatures, which is why I continued developing and marketing the incomplete serum to governments who wanted to create their own werepanther armies. I was limited in how far

I could go because of America's strict human research rules, and Idia has actually achieved what I was prohibited from doing. Then, when I got sick, my goal changed. It became more important for me to harness the Ravenisha's lifeforce. I figured your blood could eradicate my diseased blood and allow me to live for as long as you do. Fredericka repeatedly warned me not to trust Idia because she would use the serum to build her own werepanther army, but I didn't want to listen to a child. Idia doesn't have all the ingredients, hence the mutations." There was a stony silence as Rufus paused. "And now, some of my loans and promises are coming due and entities will want the Ravenisha as payment. I'm truly sorry. I'll rectify this erratum in any way I can. I take full responsibility."

"I'll go with him," Teddy immediately volunteered. "It's better for one of the Ravenisha to go with you, in case they missed a minion or two earlier."

"Excellent idea, Teddy," Lieutenant Allensworth said. "I'll accompany you in case you need more firepower or just someone to watch your back."

"Be safe out there, guys," the Colonel told them. "We've got everything under control here and we'll have a video feed on you at all times. Teddy, the Lieutenant will show you where you can pick up some weapons. And Rufus, thanks for coming clean. You didn't create this mess entirely by yourself. We're all in this together. We'll somehow make things right."

Teddy nodded her thanks, and she, Rufus, and the lieutenant left for Rufus's destroyed lab.

Once they were out of the way, Colonel Honeycutt turned to Mariposa. "Maybe now you could tell me what in the hell a chimera is."

The president chimed in. "Me, too."

Dr. Vasquez cleared her throat. "Remember this is all speculation until we can test Teddy. Generally, a chimera is formed at the embryonic level when an organism has a mixture of cells that come from two distinct species, or an individual cell has been mixed with two or more zygotes. People can also get chimerism by organ transplantation, grafting, or mutation. Teddy's case is probably a lot more complicated and due more to mutation. I suspect my son, Cochise impregnated Cleo, and in a short amount of time, Rufus's sperm also penetrated and fertilized the same ova, leading Theodora to have genetics from both men. Again, I can only speculate here."

"I interfered where I shouldn't have, I'm afraid," Ceola interjected, looking at Cochise. "I saw Cochise was crazy about Cleo and knew Rufus was planning to impregnate the Lost-Generation. I begged Cochise to impregnate Cleo before Rufus could. Who would have ever guessed Rufus would seize the Lost-Generation so soon after Cochise and Cleo got together?"

"Cochise can't shapeshift, but because he is my son, that ability was passed on to Theodora from my side. She has Cleo's genes, and heaven forbid if you add Rufus's genes to the mix. Theodora probably has yet another set of panther genes because Rufus has been injecting himself with all of your Ravenisha blood over the years."

"So, Theodora is a hybrid, essentially," the president stated.

Here, Mariposa paused. "Honestly, I don't know. Chimeras are not hybrids, but Theodora's case is so remarkable and outside the norm, I wouldn't correct someone if they called her a hybrid. So far, we only know that physically, one eye is blue like Rufus's and the other eye is jade green like mine. I was told she changed quicker than the others and she's bigger. Yet, would I call her a different species? No. I really need to get her in a lab to answer some of these questions. And Fredi is remarkable, also. Look at her superior mind and how quickly she changed into her beast. I bet both girls have abilities no one knows about—not even them."

"Dr. Vasquez is right," Ceola added. "I suspected as much myself. The heterochromia, her reflexes, climbing, and jumping abilities have always been stellar. And let's not mention her skill with weapons."

Rufus's voice filled the room. "Plus, I suspect she has some kind of ESP that allows her to detect whether people are telling her the truth."

Ceola sighed. "You're right, Mariposa, we need to get her in a lab. She is an unknown entity at this moment. I guess it's a blessing she hasn't mutated like that thing we saw today. I'd like to know if Rufus's serum and bullets would affect her, too. I'm sorry, Teddy, but we do need to find out what makes you and your sister different from Celeste and Naima. I know the history of experimentation on us. You know I'd never mistreat you or allow anyone else to."

Teddy was quiet as she took all of this in as she listened to the conversation with her earbud. She wondered if that explained her mental instability.

"Okay, well, here's what I would like for the moment," the president stated into the silence. "Colonel, if it's determined this Idia did, indeed, secure a set of Rufus's research and is misusing it, I want it back in our hands. I don't care if you have to hunt her down to the ends of the Earth. Use the Ravenisha."

"Yes, ma'am," Beau replied.

"Dr. Vasquez, I want you and Rufus to get back in the lab, along with Ceola, and work on the science part of things. Try to figure out why Idia's werepanthers have mutated so much and make sure a bite from one of her sycophants won't infect other people. If people are somehow infected, I want an antidote ready."

She turned to the rest of the Old-Gen Ravenisha and New-Gen Ravenisha. "And I want you guys, the Old-Gen, to help in the lab in any way you can. Matilda, you are to work with Colonel Honeycutt. And so there won't be any ambiguity in what I'm asking, I will put everything in writing, as well. I've heard about Teddy's prowess as a hunter and killer; therefore, I'm going to take a tremendous risk and assign the New-Gen the job of helping Colonel Honeycutt and his men track down Idia and her warriors. I'll let Lieutenant Allensworth and his men know they're also assigned to tracking down this Idia and neutralizing her and her army. I'll talk to them separately after this video call even though I know they're listening in, as well."

Matilda crossed her arms and looked like she was through. She was a damned general and more seasoned than Teddy, Fredi, and Beau put together. How dare the president dismiss her experience. Consult with Beau, her ass. Hell, *she* should have been commanding *him*.

"What am I assigned to do?" Fredi asked in a small voice.

"You're to stay with the older women and not get in anyone's way," the president replied, smiling.

Fredi bristled. "That's just insulting. I might as well be a scientist. I practically grew up in the lab. I can also fight. I know karate, judo, Krav Maga, and Muay Thai from watching YouTube and, and… the only thing I haven't done is shoot a gun," she pouted, folding her arms across her chest. "Besides, I'm the one who helped nourish Teddy back to health."

"And we're thankful to you for that," Ceola assured Fredi. "You can help me in the lab. I've done my own research, but it's not the same as Rufus's since I haven't been trying to find some magical elixir. Since you helped him, I'd appreciate any help you could give me. Also, I'd like to verify that it's safe to consume those mutant panthers' flesh ASAP. Does that sound okay?" Fredi nodded her head, yes, temporarily mollified.

"Okay then. I'll let you guys get to it. Keep me updated." The president faded from view.

"Colonel," Ceola proclaimed, "I think everyone should use my lab since Rufus's site has pretty much been razed."

"Agreed. Cochise, since you're a civilian, I'm going to have you stay here with the women."

"Absolutely not," Cochise protested. "I know my way around guns and tactical maneuvering as much as anybody else. I've only been a sheriff's deputy for twenty-five years."

"Fine, then you can guard the women in the lab. Look,"—the colonel held up his hand,—"I know what you're going to say. These ladies have government clearance. You don't. Does that answer your question?"

"I suppose so," Cochise mumbled, unhappy with being ordered to stay behind.

As a unit, the Old-Gen and Leona pulled out and brandished their weapons. "Do we look like we need a bodyguard, Colonel?" questioned Ceola.

"No ma'am, you don't," replied the Colonel looking down the barrel of her gun. "Will you just humor me then? And are y'all licensed to carry those weapons?"

"Of course, Colonel," Lizzie replied, while they holstered their guns.

"How do you have weapons and Teddy doesn't?"

"We grabbed the duffle bags before we evacuated the lab earlier." Celeste, who had been quiet, responded.

~ ~ ~

Teddy, Lieutenant Allensworth, and Rufus arrived back at the base an hour later.

"The other safe was indeed empty," Rufus informed them unhappily.

They discussed the prior conversation in more detail and then people split up and went off to perform the task assigned to them.

As the New-Gen Ravenisha prepared to track down Idia and her evil army, Lizzie came into the small conference room they were in. "Y'all stay together now. Remember, there's strength in numbers, Miss Teddy." She pointedly looked at Teddy. "Don't put yourselves in a perilous position trying to be heroes."

"I gotcha, Auntie Lizzie." They hugged.

Teddy turned to Naima, her face softening. "Look, it's okay if you want to stay here at the base and nurse the hurt soldiers. I won't hold it against you. I bet Akiro would be happy for your company."

"Thank you, Teddy, but I belong with my sister-friends. I'm a Ravenisha. If you fight. I fight." They embraced.

"Okay, Akiro, where's Idia's plane?" Teddy changed from soft to all business in a flash.

"You're not going to believe this," Akiro responded, eyes glued to his monitor. "The planes, yes, planes plural, apparently landed somewhere in the Central American jungle. Guatemala, to be exact." He glanced away from the monitor and gestured for Naima to come to him. When she did, he gave her a long kiss. The others looked at each other with *did you know about this?* expressions.

"What!" exclaimed Obsidian Butterfly. "*¡Esa bruja!* I bet I know what she's doing. How she ever found out, I'd give anything to know, though. Hmm, why isn't she using whatever spirit made her? Hold up," she called to Teddy and the rest. " I'm coming with you. You'll never find what she's looking for without me."

"Then, I'm coming with you, Mother."

Dr. Vasquez turned to Ceola. "I've kept meticulous notes on every experiment I've done. I'll give you access to them before I leave."

"Thank you." Ceola hugged a surprised Dr. Vasquez. "You be careful in that jungle, Sistah. Know the Ravenisha have your back."

Mariposa looked at Ceola, her eyes moist, and gave her a big hug back. "And you and the rest of the Ravenisha can always count on me to have your backs. I didn't know Cleo, but I looked forward to meeting her. While our planes are being prepared, I think now is the perfect time to tell you my story and what that bitch is up to."

Chapter 25

Fort Cheaha was bustling with activity. There was a heady mix of excitement and anticipation in the air. Base personnel had cleaned up almost all traces of the earlier conflict. You could barely detect the sweet stench of offal under the ever-present aroma of diesel fumes. Lieutenant Allensworth glanced at his phone and whooped.

"Listen up, guys. The ammunition manufacturer is on his way with our new and improved bullets, knives, and explosives. Yeah, baby!"

Beau was having a one-sided conversation with the Ravenisha and Mariposa about the world's knowledge of the existence of other fantastical creatures and how no one batted an eye these days whenever vampires, witches, werewolves, etc., were sighted. He confessed he had initially thought the Paranormal Reserves Department's creation was at the insistence of loony UFO conspiracists, but he was a genuine believer now. Yetis were being reported in the Himalayas, and Mounties were sure they'd seen sasquatches while patrolling the Rocky Mountains. The world was going to hell in a handbasket. He had been one of the last holdouts, but he could no longer ridicule others and keep his head stuck in the sand after witnessing the creatures he had recently seen with his own eyes. And damn that Rufus for keeping him in the dark. Just think, preternatural beings were right under his nose while he was growing up and he hadn't known.

"So far, those of your ilk have kept to themselves, but I just know the day is coming when y'all try to wipe out the human race. Bases like this one will be ready, too, to blow your asses to kingdom come. No offense."

"Beau, if I were you, I'd just shut up now," Matilda growled. "I could school you on how no damn human will be blowing our asses to kingdom come, but I'm trying to be cordial here. I'm really trying. In fact, just listening to you is making me realize we need to police ourselves and raise our own armies. I'll be damned if I'm going to be policed by *creatures* lesser than me. Never again!" The others nodded in agreement. "And need I remind you I was a general before I came here. You can dismiss my experience and expertise at your own peril."

By the time they were finally ready to board the plane, the ammunition had arrived and everyone had loaded their guns and grabbed extra boxes and magazines of bullets. Teddy was especially happy with her knives, as they seemed to have been constructed specifically for her. She and the other Ravenisha found seats together on the plane. As the plane taxied down the base's runway, Teddy blasted "Bad Girls" by M.I.A. over the plane's sound system. Back at base, people laughed as they could also hear the music over the base's sound system.

Colonel Honeycutt shook his head. "Those girls definitely bring a unique flavor into the mix."

Meanwhile, the Old-Gen Ravenisha and Rufus had arrived at Ceola's lab, while Leona had returned to the house with two of Colonel Honeycutt's soldiers as guards. Fortunately, the lab had only sustained minor damage when Rufus and his men broke in earlier. They called men to repair the door, and the Ravenisha and Rufus set about deciding on the division of labor.

Matilda suddenly stopped what she was doing and looked around the lab. "Y'all, wait a minute. Where's that little girl? How did she get out of our sight? I'll go look around the building for her, although I didn't pay attention whether she got in one of the vehicles at the army base."

Ceola held up her forefinger, signaling for Tildy to wait. She whipped out her cell phone and called Colonel Honeycutt, who confirmed she wasn't on the base. Ceola blew out her breath and scowled. "I bet I know where that little she-devil is. Colonel, contact the pilot and have them search the plane."

A quick search of the aircraft by a few soldiers found Fredi hiding in one of the duffle bags. The Ravenisha motioned for her to sit next to them and a soldier escorted her over, keeping a firm hold on her arm. Fredi yanked her arm from his grip, rolled her eyes, and plopped down in the seat, pouting.

Teddy walked to the front of the aircraft and approached the pilot. "Please let the Colonel know we found her. It's too late to turn around. I guess I'll be responsible for *the little she-devil.*"

She turned around, walked back down the aisle, and sat across from Fredi. She folded her arms across her chest, imitating Fredi, and stared at her. An uncomfortable silence ensued, and Fredi broke eye contact first. Teddy finally spoke.

"Fredericka, while I am disappointed in you, I can't say I'm really surprised. What were you thinking, hiding away on this plane? Now, I have to worry about your safety, as well. Why are you so disobedient?"

"Does she remind you of someone?" Celeste asked.

"Yep, two peas in a pod," added Naima with just the hint of a smile.

"I wanted to come with you, Teddy. I really can fight. I won't be a burden, I promise."

"I hope that's true," Teddy assented resignedly.

Teddy noticed Cochise staring at her. It had been disconcerting the way he and Rufus had stared at her lately. While she had always been keen to know who her father was, to now suddenly learn she had two fathers was a bit much to process. Why did Rufus have to be one of them? He seemed like a vile man, even if he appeared to be regretting his actions now. She wondered what Cochise's story was. At least Cleo had excellent taste in men, she mused. While Rufus looked okay, it's not like Cleo chose him; he raped her. However, Cleo had chosen Cochise, and he was fine. His dark, intense eyes; strong nose; and full lips reminded her of that cute Native warrior from *Dances with Wolves*. What was his name? Wind In His Hair. That's it.

"So, why have you been an absentee father?" Teddy asked point-blank without preamble.

"Ouch." There was a pregnant silence. "I'd like very much to have a relationship with you, Teddy, if you would allow me. If I had known of your existence, nothing or nobody would have stopped me from having a relationship with my daughter." Cochise's eyes flashed.

"Yeah, you and Rufus want to have a relationship with me now that I'm grown and don't need you." Teddy couldn't believe the nerve of these men. But maybe that was her anger talking. And she didn't want her anger to scare off family when she was already without a mother. "I guess I'm open to it," Teddy groused. "Just don't expect me to call you dad. Tell me what my mom was like. I mean, how did y'all even meet? Hey, at least now I know what people mean when they say I've got that Indian hair. Although I'm jealous because mine isn't straight and luxurious like yours. And how come I didn't get your or Rufus's height?"

Cochise laughed as he came over and motioned for Celeste to swap seats with him. "I'll do better than that. I've been compiling a montage of the pictures and videos Cleo and I took throughout the brief time we were together. Give me your cell number, and I'll send them to you. In the meantime, I'll give you a running commentary while we watch them together." He looked up at Fredi. "And you're welcome to watch and listen since Cleo is your mother, as well."

"Thank you, Mr. Cochise."

They spent the rest of the plane ride with Cochise regaling the girls with tales of his and Cleo's adventures. Teddy learned they met at the town's filling station, of all places, when Cleo backed into his truck while he was pumping gas.

"Apparently, my mother was already scoping out Rufus and the town. She had heard about the strange women who were similar to her and their relationship with Rufus. She went to school and studied science, with the plan to get hired by Rufus. She was in the area for a job interview at his lab and I had tagged along because I had never been out of New Mexico. When I saw your mother at the gas station, I knew she was the one despite her bad driving skills. We were pretty much inseparable that summer. I was going to marry your mother even before we found out Rufus had impregnated her, but I was practically run out of town by that bastard. He told me he'd make me disappear and my body would never be found if I so much as stepped foot in the state of Alabama again. He said he had the protection of the government and he'd do what he said, too. I went back to New Mexico. No one ever told me a thing. I understand now that your mother has been missing for all of your life, and that explains why I never heard from her. In fact, I would have never known if Mom hadn't gone to work for Rufus and seen video feeds of you and put two and two together. You're so much like your mother, you know, but I also see a bit of myself in you." He bent down and pulled a knife from his ankle sheath. "I've been told you're quite handy with a knife." He wiggled his eyebrows and handed the weapon to Teddy.

She hefted it, turning it over and over. "It's beautiful, Cochise. I've never seen a knife like this before. Whoa! I've never felt anything like this when I've held a knife before either. It's like the knife is vibrating in my hand. Why is that?"

"That's because I made it and it's claimed you," he proudly proclaimed.

"May I hold the knife, Teddy?"

"Sure." Teddy handed the knife to Fredi and showed her some moves, much to Fredi's delight.

"What is this blade made of?" Teddy queried, looking at her reflection in the shiny black blade.

"Black obsidian." Teddy moved to hand the knife back to Cochise, but he shook his head and insisted, "No, you keep it, Daughter. The knife has a purpose, and you have clearly been chosen to carry out that purpose. I'll make you one, too, little one," he told Fredi, who did a little happy dance. Then, he removed the knife's ankle sheath and handed that to Teddy, as well.

"Thank you so much. It's beautiful," Teddy gushed, moved by the gesture. "I especially love the turquoise on the handle." Teddy looked at the knife closer. "Ooh, is this also jade? Real jade?" Cochise nodded. "Hey, it's arranged in the pattern of a paw. Are you sure you don't shapeshift?"

Cochise shook his head. "No, I wasn't blessed with that ability, and that design just came to me. Maybe I saw mom's paw print at some point and subconsciously included it in the knife's design. Mom wears a lot of turquoise and jade. I don't think that gene is passed on to males." He hesitated before he added, "But I know mom's genes affect me in some way. Fredi is right about that. How old do you think I am?" The girls studied him.

Fredi said, "Well, you look like you're in your early thirties."

Cochise laughed. "I'm almost fifty, but thank you. I also may be a little stronger and faster than your average human, and people have noted that my senses are extraordinarily developed. Many people mistake mom and me for brother and sister, instead of mother and son. Oh, I almost forgot. I have presents for you and Fredi. I made them as soon as I found out I would get the chance to meet you."

As he talked, Cochise reached into his carry-on bag and removed two small pouches. He handed one to each girl. Teddy and Fredi opened their pouches and pulled out a beautiful necklace. They were miniature replicas of the knife Cochise just gave Teddy, made from real turquoise, jade, and black obsidian.

"I made these knives from a special material, and they have magical powers. Never take them off except to use their magic, okay?...I risked my life to get the material to make them. Guard them with your lives."

"Thank you, Mr. Cochise. It's beautiful." Fredi put her necklace on with help from Naima.

"Thanks, Dad," Teddy blurted, surprise etched in her voice at the slip of the word dad. *Where did that come from? I must be losing my edge. I don't know this man from Jack in the Box and I'm calling him dad. Get a grip, girl!*

Cochise broke into an enormous grin. "Dad," he said, nodding. "Now that has a nice ring to it."

Teddy smiled back, laughing, "Yeah, it does, doesn't it? The word just kind of slipped out of my mouth." She also put her necklace on.

"Uh, Cochise, just how did you know you would meet us?" Teddy asked.

"My raven, Clyde, showed me in a vision."

"Say that again," Fredi exclaimed, her mouth dropping open, along with Teddy's.

"Clyde, my raven, told me. I'm a shaman, ladies. Fredi, do you know what that is? The raven is my totem animal."

Fredi nodded. "Well, why didn't the spirits tell you about Teddy?"

Cochise chuckled. "I don't know. You'll have to ask them. It's kind of like why psychics don't win the lottery."

"Yeah, okay," Fredi replied, not convinced.

"Also, Mom called me. She's been keeping me abreast of the happenings at the lab and monitoring the situation."

Noticing Cochise still staring intently at her and frowning, Teddy raised her eyebrows.

"I sense something isn't right, Daughter. I must admit I'm worried about you and the little one." Cochise's dark eyes bored into Teddy's and his brow furrowed.

Teddy looked down and then grabbed his hand. She searched his eyes and Zzzzap! They both jumped. Teddy was practically slammed back into her seat. And did her vision just become filled with ravens? What type of fuckery was this?

"This has never happened to me when I've grabbed someone's hand before. What's going on?" Teddy bent over, put her head between her legs, and took several deep breaths.

"Talk to me, Daughter. Tell me what has happened," Cochise demanded, a note of urgency in his voice.

"Well, before the change, I could touch someone's hand, and know whether they were a good person, you know? After the change, I could read people much more deeply. For example, I grabbed Rufus's hand instinctively, and I knew if I could trust him or if he was lying. I actually probed his thoughts. But even when I held Rufus's hand, there was none of the electricity I just felt with you. Instead of reading or feeling your thoughts, all I saw were ravens. Everything has felt sort of weird since I heard this strange voice in my head—which wasn't the voice of my beast—during the change rasping, 'Stay the course, Theodora. When the time is right, I will call on you and you will answer.' I asked her who she was, but she wouldn't tell me. She said I knew, but I don't. I told Nana, and the others, but then the alarms sounded and we had to quickly flee. Do you know who—"

"Sonofabitch!" Cochise interrupted Teddy. "This is so bad. I don't know her name, but I sense she's an evil spirit. Clyde's been trying to warn me. I should be at home in New Mexico, working with my Navajo friends. You'll probably both need an Enemy Way and or a Night Way ceremony done—plus my ceremonies," he mumbled, voice trailing off as he jumped up to talk to Obsidian Butterfly.

Teddy made a mental note to corner Cochise or Obsidian Butterfly later and ask what they suspected was going on. Cochise said it was bad. What did he mean? There was bad, and then there was really bad. When she asked Fredi if she had heard a voice in her head besides her beast's, Fredi had shaken her head no, but was Fredi being truthful? Cochise said *she*. Oh no, could it be La Panthère Noire?

Why would La Panthère Noire contact her instead of one of the Old Ravenisha? This couldn't be good, Teddy thought, worry lines etched across her forehead. She put a finger in her mouth and chewed on the skin.

Chapter 26

They landed at the Guatemalan air force base in La Aurora, the closest base to the ruins Mariposa believed Queen Idia was trying to find. After deplaning, the soldiers went to their assigned barracks and unloaded their things. They met again in the common room and took a seat anywhere they could find a chair. Dr. Vasquez stood and addressed the room.

"Hello, for those of you who haven't met me, my real name isn't Mariposa Vasquez. My true name is Itzpapalotl, which means Obsidian Butterfly in the Aztecan language. I was born in this area many centuries ago. I am a shapeshifter. When I was younger, I made a deal with one of the Jaguar gods of death, Tezcatlipoca. In exchange for the shapeshifting gift, I promised to help Tezcatlipoca solidify his power base by finding a mountain which only those with superhuman strength supposedly can breach and bring back for him a magical amulet that's hidden there." Cochise looked away from everyone, his face unreadable. "I'm sorry to say I ran away, instead, hell-bent on revenge on the Spaniards for destroying my people and way of life. Some say that over the centuries, Tezcatlipoca has tried to contact other shapeshifters to do this work for him. But I fear Queen Idia is seeking Tezcatlipoca herself in order to steal the amulet. It's my hope I can summon Tezcatlipoca first and convince him that Idia will betray him. Are there any questions?"

"I never knew any of this," Rufus complained, watching Dr. Vasquez on video back at the base.

Fredi raised her hand. "Yes, Fredi?"

"I'm just wondering, if this Tezcatlipoca person is a demon, bullets can't kill him, right?"

"You are correct. I should have mentioned this before. Don't waste bullets on him, soldiers. He's a spirit, so they'll just pass through him. My son, Cochise, who is half-Chiricahua Apache, is also a shaman. If things go sideways, he'll deal with Tezcatlipoca. Any more questions?" When no one answered, Dr. Vasquez told them to get some nourishment, rest, and sleep as they would head out into the jungle at dusk. She left them with the words of Sun Tzu. "Be extremely subtle even to the point of formlessness. Be extremely mysterious even to the point of soundlessness. Thereby you can be the director of the opponent's fate."

Teddy and her crew commandeered a room and stretched out, relaxing. As Teddy dug in her pants pocket for her cell phone, her fingers brushed across a folded piece of paper. Confused, she withdrew the note from her pocket, studied it, and then unfolded it. She started reading.

> My Dearest Theodora,
>
> As I sit here watching over you while you sleep, a wave of regret washes over me. You remind me so much of your beautiful mother. I wish things could have been different, and I am truly sorry for the way I have treated your family. If you were to ask me why I did or said some things I did, I would be at a loss to explain it myself. It does not suffice to use that old trope that I'm a product of my time. I was an ogre, even though I truly loved

Ceola and your mother. I can't change the past, but I can influence the future. I fear I will not live through this battle. If I am not outright killed, then the tumor in my brain that has been steadily increasing will. I have deeded all of my holdings to you and your sister, Fredericka. I know money can't bring you happiness, or change the past, but it can sure make your lives comfortable. I have generously provided for Ceola and the others, as well. Also, I have been keeping an enormous secret. Your mother and the others are alive, or rather they are in a state of suspended animation. I admit I experimented on their bodies, and my last experiment accidentally resulted in their current state. You can find them here: 34°58′35.83′N85°48′51.31′W. I have also provided Ceola and the rest with the coordinates. I don't mean to be deliberately mysterious, but others are searching for the Lost-Generation, too, and we must not allow their location to be discovered.

Perhaps, one day, we can be as father and daughter. I extend my olive branch to you, my daughter. Take care of your sister. She's been so excited to meet you.

Your Father,

Rufus Beckett Theodis Honeycutt

"Wow, the bastard has a heart after all," Fredi said looking over her shoulder. Teddy jumped and stifled a scream. *Where did she come from?* Teddy wondered before silently handing the letter to Celeste so she and Naima could read it.

When she finished, Celeste looked up. "Why now? His change of heart is great and all, but I'd be wary, Teddy."

"Yeah," added Naima, handing the letter back to Teddy. "A leopard doesn't change its spots."

Lost in her own thoughts, each girl lay down and eventually fell into a restless sleep.

~ ~ ~

Deep in the bowels of the Earth, Tezcatlipoca finished his conversation with his unwelcome guest. "I have told you all I know. Now leave me. The others will be here soon."

Chapter 27

Southern United States, Ravenswood, Ceola's lab

Akiro, who had stayed behind to man the monitors and direct the troop remotely, announced, "They landed without incident and are resting. They will head out at dusk."

As Rufus walked around Ceola's lab, his eyes took in how different it was from his own. Whereas his lab was more traditional, as mentioned earlier, Ceola's lab was cozier. Even though it was in a cave, it was well lit and decorated. African art and masks adorned the walls, and they had constructed lab stations from the mountain's granite. Functional rubber mats were in front of workstations to cushion people's feet from standing for interminable periods of time on the granite floors and cool air constantly circulated. Rufus noted the high-tech video equipment, along with the lab equipment. "I'm impressed, Ceola. This is a really well-done lab setup. If only…" His voice trailed off.

Lizzie piped up. "If only you hadn't been a damned fool and treated us like your equals, instead of your inferiors. Is that what you were going to say?"

Rufus stopped walking. "Look, I've already apologized for the way I've treated you in the past, despite y'all murdering my father in cold blood."

"How many times do we have to tell you we didn't murder your father?" Matilda shouted.

"Go on and confess, for God's sake! Y'all put my family and me in a pickle several times over the years. Who do you think had to make up a story for the sheriff every time an overseer mysteriously disappeared? Who do you think kept you and your *Asoro* together? Cut me a little slack here, okay? I even wrote Theodora a letter of apology. I've deeded most of my holdings to both Theodora and Fredericka upon my death. I've left y'all taken care of financially, as well. I know I have a lot of atoning to do. If you haven't guessed by now, I'm terminally ill. Brain cancer—Grade IV glioblastoma." Rufus blew out a breath. "Even Beauregard doesn't know."

"God don't like ugly. Then, it's even more time you told us where our daughters are," Ceola stated, unmoved.

"Yes, you're right." Rufus sighed and gave them the coordinates where their daughters could be found. "I beg of you, though, please wait until after this mission is over before you make the rescue. Others are after them, as well. Promise me you'll wait," Rufus begged. "They've kept this long. What's a little longer?"

"A cave!" Matilda exclaimed when Rufus told them what the coordinates stood for. "What's so special about a cave? I thought you had hidden them in a bunker somewhere, or a private, uncharted island, or a private unknown lab. A cave? You've got to be kidding me."

"Yes, but this isn't just any cave system," Rufus replied. "This is one of the biggest caves in Alabama. There are hundreds of chambers, with most of them never being explored. Just having the cave's coordinates isn't enough."

"Well, if that's the case, for once, I agree with you. They're actually safer where they are at the moment." The other women agreed.

"Although, what's so special about them that other people would be after them, Rufus?" Ceola asked, trying to get Rufus to admit to all of the genetic manipulations he'd done.

"Erm, nothing much." Rufus hemmed and hawed, paced, and averted eye contact with Ceola, Matilda, and Elizabeth.

Tildy stepped in front of him, cutting off his pacing.

"Oh, all right. Think about it, ladies. Notice how your daughters could breed a Theodora, a Fredericka, and to a lesser extent a Celeste and a Naima?" At the women's still confused looks, he continued.

"Yes, y'all had children able to change into she-panthers, but you still heavily relied on the magic part to help them change. This New-Generation needed no magic at all. The Lost-Generation was impregnated around the same time by men chosen and er, enhanced by me. I only impregnated Cleo. I don't know how Cochise snuck in, but even that was fortuitous. Who would have ever guessed his mother would be a shapeshifter, as well? It's as though God predestined this project. We carefully monitored everything, and we gave the women daily injections of a serum I had invented. Let's call it Magic Potion Number One. You see how smart Fredericka is. I know Theodora is just as intelligent. We haven't even tapped into their hidden abilities. You could say these are designer shapeshifter babies, in a way. They should also be extremely healthy," Rufus said smugly. "I'm not too worried about them eating those pathetic mutant panthers Idia has created. Anyway, I was working on self-regeneration and cryogenics before my partners began trying to kidnap the Lost-Generation, so I did the only thing I could do. Spirit them away for as long as I had to. Plus, Idia had started pressuring me to hand over all of the progenies. That wasn't part of any bargain I struck. I also knew if I was patient, the babies would grow up and they could rescue and guard their mothers."

"I have no words." Tildy shook her head. "Do people mean anything to you, Rufus? Or do you just view everybody as vessels? Potential lab experiments?"

"Girl, I think even I'm speechless," Ceola said. Lizzie only looked at Rufus and frowned.

Ceola clapped her hands together. "Okay, no need to dwell on that which we can't change. There's a lot of testing we need to perform. We'll access the data Rufus has already compiled from our blood. For now, we need to test the blood of those soldiers bitten by the mutants and are still alive. We don't need any more mongrels running around. Rufus, I know you're dying to test Teddy's blood."

"Yes, and I already have a sample." At Lizzie's inquisitive look, he said, "I took it while she was in my lab. Her healing ability is remarkable. She was beaten pretty badly by my men, I'm sorry to report. Even though she had recovered some when she arrived at the base, you'll notice that after she fed, there were no signs she had ever been beaten."

"Right, we must analyze Teddy's and Fredi's blood," Lizzie said, typing furiously.

"Good, it looks like we have plenty to keep us busy for a couple of days. Let's get started. Oh, and Rufus, I'm assuming your cancer was caused by the serum you've been injecting in your body over the years and not Magic Potion Number One?" Ceola made air quotes around Magic Potion Number One.

"That's my hypothesis. I'm exhibiting pathologies I've noticed in the mutants, although to a much lesser extent. That's why I examined their bodies so carefully."

"Hmm," Ceola said. "Now, I'm really starting to question if it's safe to consume those mutant werepanthers, no matter what you believe. Until we learn more, let's advise the Ravenisha not to consume any mutant werepanther flesh."

"I'll let everyone know," Lizzie replied.

"Akiro?" Rufus called. "Is there any way you could hack into my lab in Benin and access their files? It would help us tremendously if we could look at the changes they've made to the serum. Idia has locked me out of my own files."

"On it. If I can't hack the system by myself, do I have your permission to involve my community of hackers?"

After a moment of hesitation, Rufus nodded his head. "Yes, yes you do."

Rufus walked over to Ceola and took her hand in his. "Don't fret, Ceola. The girls haven't been injected with the serum that causes these mutations, and I'm almost positive their immune systems won't be affected by whatever virus is causing the mutations."

"I hope you're right, Rufus. I'd still like to work on an antidote as a precaution. Just in case." Ceola extracted her hand from Rufus's and wiped it on her lab coat.

"As you wish," Rufus replied, with a nod of his head.

"Is that it Rufus?" Matilda asked. "Are you sure you don't have something else to tell us? Look at me. At us. We swear on your mother's grave we didn't kill your father. Think back to that day. Are you sure no one else was on the property?"

"That's it. I've told you everything I can. Wait a minute. My God! Something's bothered me about the scene all of these years. It was too clean! Forgive me, but y'all are kind of messy eaters. The bathroom was too clean for my father to have been killed there."

"Now, we're getting somewhere," Ceola added. "The pieces are coming together."

"That bitch!" Matilda growled. "I bet you anything Idia snuck onto the property, killed your father, and had a lackey plant his body parts." Tildy stopped pacing and placed her hands on her hips."Yes, that makes perfect sense. I don't know if records of international travelers coming to Alabama in the fifties are still on file, but it's worth checking. Maybe she had to apply for a visa." Matilda's eyes began changing as emotion filled her. She threw her head back, yelled and punched the nearest wall. Ceola and Elizabeth's hair stood on edge, and they began growling, rage emanating off of them in waves.

Rufus stood frozen in place, stricken, his pale face even whiter, lips trembling. "Oh no. If this is true, I've unfairly persecuted you women for years. I'm so sorry."

The Ravenisha tried to calm down and focus on the task at hand, but Matilda summed up things perfectly. "We will find that bitch and make her pay. There will be no place she can run to or hide. As Walter Scott once said, '*Revenge, the sweetest morsel to the mouth that ever was cooked in hell.*' "

The women gave the Ravenisha war cry, their ululations and roars reverberating off of the cave's walls and filling the room over and over.

"Er, looks like there's activity, guys," Akiro called out in a shaky voice. All eyes turned to his monitor.

Chapter 28

Central American jungle, Guatemala

The assembled soldiers hoisted their backpacks onto their backs and moved out to the waiting convoy of vehicles that would take them as far into the jungle as possible. Idia's planes hadn't been detected since radar showed them having landed nearby over twenty-four hours ago.

Lieutenant Allensworth, his men, the New-Gen Ravenisha, and some Paranormal soldiers split off with Dr. Vasquez and Cochise. A small group of Colonel Honeycutt's men separated to continue searching for the hidden planes. Dr. Vasquez led the way to the area that had once been her home.

The trek through the dense underbrush was brutal. Foliage with sharp spines tore at their clothes. They had to be on the lookout constantly for poisonous snakes, not only cleverly concealed on the ground, but camouflaged on tree limbs. Spiders and ants were rampant, and the mosquitoes were relentless. Mercifully, the underbrush soon gave way to areas of undergrowth and the troop could walk without becoming entangled in vines, bushes, and small trees. The heat, humidity, and bugs were still unrelenting, though, even as dusk gave way to darkness.

"I'm glad I didn't wear my good Stetson," Cochise grumbled while tying his long hair back in one braid. "This humidity is something else. There's a reason I choose to live in New Mexico."

"Are we almost there, yet?" Fredi asked for what felt like the hundredth time.

"No!" everyone shouted back.

"I have to pee!" Teddy called out as everyone groaned. "I don't know why y'all groaning," she harrumphed. "I'm the one who can't seem to master the art of squatting and ends up peeing all over myself instead."

"I guess we should take a pee break," Mariposa smiled. "Men, just turn your backs. I don't want the women wandering off and accidentally squatting on a pit viper or a coral snake or some other dangerous critter in this rain forest, especially since it's dark—the time when dangerous creatures are most active."

"Could somebody not named Teddy show me how to squat?" Fredi giggled.

"I'll do it," Naima volunteered.

"Goddamnit!" cursed Teddy rejoining the group. "I'm wearing adult diapers next time. It doesn't matter if I pull my panties to the front or to the back, they still get wet."

"Teddy, baby, you know we love you," Roland said, "but that's just too much information. I mean, Gus here, who would love to be your man, would agree that's too much information even for him. We don't want to hear that shit. And it's not sexy."

"Augustus." Teddy turned to Gus for support.

"I'm afraid I can't help you there," Gus laughed. "Roland's right. Men don't want to hear stuff like that. Sorry."

"Fine," Teddy huffed. "And y'all remember women don't want to hear about y'all's aching balls, either, or see you scratching them. That's definitely not sexy."

"Oh, come on," said Henry, joining the conversation. "Why did you have to take it there? Why do you always have to go for the jugular?"

Teddy responded in her Oprah imitation of Sofia from *The Color Purple*. "All my life, I've had to fight," but stopped in mid-sentence at the sight ahead of them.

After hours of hacking through nothing but greenery, arising in front of them as far as the eye could see was stone. Lots of stone. While the jungle had finished what the Spaniards had started, even the jungle's attempt at reclamation hadn't totally obscured the fallen world's magnificence. Even though soldiers had destroyed the fields centuries ago, they hadn't been able to destroy the edifices and the buildings had withstood the sands of time.

Upon approaching the old ruins that were once her home, Mariposa fell to her knees. After a moment, she swiped the snot away from her nose and stood; then, she turned to the others and waved her hand toward the ruins. "This was my ancestral home. Let's not waste time determining whether Idia and her army came by here. I smell their foul scent, as I'm sure the Ravenisha and Fredi do as well. It does not matter if they have a day's head start on us, because I can get us to the mountain where I met Tezcatlipoca eons ago in a couple of hours. It will take us far less time than it took me then. And I doubt they found this location as quickly as we did."

She turned and continued into the jungle, as sure of her way as if she had a GPS in her head. The others followed wordlessly. The only sounds they heard came from the jungle's denizens, such as the squirrel monkeys and lemurs that accompanied Obsidian Butterfly many eons ago.

"Guys," Mariposa cautioned after walking a little ways and nodding down at the frog inches from her boots, "don't pick up any frogs, no matter how pretty they are. Frogs, such as the blueberry poison arrow, the red poison dart, and the yellow-banded poison frog are beautiful, but I'm assuming you noted the word *poison* in their names. Do not touch," she warned, giving Fredi an extra look. They gave the frog a wide berth and walked on.

An hour in, Cochise held up his hand for the others to halt. Walking forward, he peered intently at the ground in front of him and then studied the surrounding brush. "How strange," he muttered.

"What is it? What's the matter?" questioned Lieutenant Allensworth and Teddy, simultaneously reaching for and switching the safety off of their weapons.

"I see footprints here, and here, and broken off branches show someone was here recently. But the footprints just stop, and the foliage appears intact."

"Shit," Teddy hissed. "Everyone, screw on your suppressors. Make sure your weapons are locked and loaded." She removed a pair of night-vision goggles from her pack and began scanning the treetops. She didn't really need them, but they'd back up her excellent vision in dim environments, like this jungle. In the distance, thermal imaging shapes appeared before her, camouflaged in the trees. "Smart," she mumbled, "but not smart enough. Okay, troop, I have a bead on the mutants." Teddy directed the others to look where she was looking. "Apparently, they can't see us now because of the foliage, and we're downwind to them, but we'll be obvious if we continue. They're just sitting in the trees up ahead waiting for us to pass underneath them."

"Listen up," Lieutenant Allensworth softly commanded. "We'll flank them and take them out as silently as possible. Let's divide up and encircle those motherfuckers. Make sure you attach your suppressors. We don't want to alert the major group of our presence. Go, go, go," he drove each group forward.

As he turned around, he noticed the Ravenisha had already disappeared into the canopy. *Where did they go*, he wondered unhappily? *Did they even hear his orders? If they heard his orders, were they following them?* As he walked stealthily on, he hissed for Mariposa, Fredi, and Cochise to stay with him. The jungle went quiet. Suddenly, the popping sounds of suppressed gunfire came in rapid bursts and bodies thudded as they hit the ground. *Well, that answers my questions,* Gus thought, growing angrier by the second. As Lieutenant Allensworth's group caught up to the others, they came upon some soldiers being sick. The Ravenisha dropped from the trees, startling everybody.

"Panthers are excellent tree climbers," Teddy crowed while holstering her gun.

Gus, barely controlling his temper, gave Teddy a steely look. "Private Furie, I gave orders, which you expressly ignored. That can't happen again."

"Oh, for crying out loud, Gus," Teddy responded, hands on her hips.

"Lieutenant Allensworth," he corrected her.

"What?" Teddy asked, her tone registering her disbelief this conversation was even occurring and that he was pulling rank on her like this in front of everyone.

"In the field, you will refer to me as Lieutenant Allensworth and my men as sergeants."

"What is this, a pissing contest? We followed your orders, *Lieutenant* Allensworth. We heard you loud and clear. Remember, big cats have acute hearing—along with excellent night vision. What? Are you mad because we climbed the trees and killed the mutants before your men could even get to the base of the trees? Well, fuck you, *sir*. That's your problem. We're not going to slow down or dumb down our skills to make y'all feel better." Teddy stalked off and abruptly stopped in her tracks. She drew in a sharp breath.

"Ohhh," breathed Naima, coming to a stop beside a frozen Teddy.

Teddy whirled around. "Don't let Fredi see this." However, the girl evaded several hands reaching for her and pushed her way over to Teddy. Fredi screeched and buried her head in the nook between Teddy's neck and shoulder. Teddy spoke into her headset's mic."Do you guys see this? It certainly looks like Rufus's bullets work."

Colonel Honeycutt stopped what he was doing at the base and in Ceola's lab, eyes were glued to the monitor to the vista Akiro had targeted for them. A dozen of Idia's army lay strewn on the ground. Dead. They were still in their animal form, faces frozen in a rictus of pain. Areas penetrated by bullets were still putrefying, a rancid, fetid smell emanating from the ragged wounds. A soldier kicked a carcass over so people could see the exit wounds.

"Fuck me," breathed Cochise through his mouth, turning his head away.

The exit wounds were huge ragged holes. In some werepanthers, fur and bone had dissolved to expose ravaged organs. Entrails jumped, appearing alive as the poisonous gas continued eating its way through the animals. The bodies looked like desiccated husks after the gas finally stopped touching their otherworldly skin.

"Hold up," Celeste said, shaken. "Rufus, will those bullets affect us that way, too?"

After an interminable pause, Rufus's voice came over their mics. "It's my hypothesis that the substance in the bullets could hurt true Ravenisha, but they would heal as long as vital organs weren't too badly damaged."

"Your hypothesis?" Naima angrily said.

Before she could light into Rufus, he replied, "Well, it's not like I could test the effects of the gas and steel on any of you. It was just your nanas' and Fredericka's blood. Theodora and Fredericka are probably able to withstand the poison better than you and Celeste. But don't worry, I'm sure you'd heal from my special weapons, long as they don't penetrate a vital organ and damage it too badly."

"Ain't this a motherfucker?" Celeste mumbled bitterly.

"Try not to get hurt, guys," Ceola interjected. "We'll work on designing body armor for you right after we find a vaccine. Meanwhile, carry on."

Teddy gave a baleful look at the soldiers assembled around her. "Y'all better not shoot us. I mean it. There better NOT be any accidental shootings, friendly fire, knifings, or any of that shit."

"Let's keep going," Mariposa said. "We're almost there, but we have an uphill climb." She and Fredi frowned at each other and unsaid words passed between them. They had helped Rufus with the formula, after all.

Teddy gave Lieutenant Allensworth a hateful look. She waved her hand dismissively, indicating for him to proceed in front of her.

The group continued pushing its way into the vegetation, moving more cautiously now. The earlier joviality and conviviality were gone, replaced by a sullen silence. They finally reached the mountain's base without further incident. There were signs of recent activity, but since surveillance showed no one was in the vicinity now, Lieutenant Allensworth nodded, indicating it was okay for Mariposa to proceed.

She made her way to the clearing where she had walked many eons ago. She closed her eyes, cleared her mind, and whispered Tezcatlipoca's name three times. Then, she waited. And waited. And waited. Obsidian Butterfly sighed. "Tezcatlipoca, come on. I know you're here. Let us in, please. I know I owe you. I'll still honor my promise to you." The sounds of vegetation parting broke the stillness. They turned several flashlights on, and the group made their way cautiously down the damp, moss-covered stairs.

After finally reaching the bottom, Obsidian Butterfly gasped; not at the appearance of Tezcatlipoca sitting on his altar with his arms crossed but at the inner chamber's appearance. "Wow. No bodies and a tolerable aroma. Well, how have you been, Tezcatlipoca?" she asked with a fake smile. The demon god just stared at her, his eyes full of malevolence. "Look Tez," Obsidian Butterfly blithely continued, "I'm sorry, okay? I'll make it up to you. I promise. You know I would have never come back to this place unless it was important. Has a Queen Idia and her army been here, by any chance?" Still, Tezcatlipoca said nothing. He did, however, shift his body slightly.

Teddy stepped forward. "Look, if she has, she will betray you. Guaranteed, just like she betrayed my nana and my sister-friends' nanas. I understand she's after some amulet. You want the same amulet, right? I'll personally bring it to you if you help us."

"I sense you speak from your heart," he snarled, speaking at last. "At least your tongue isn't forked, like this one's." He gestured at Mariposa, yellowish eyes flashing in a face otherwise set like stone. "And your words feel true."

Tezcatlipoca finally got up and walked over to Teddy, where he placed a dirty finger on her chest. Recoiling, he skittled back, howling and holding his finger.

"Excuse you!" Teddy walked toward Tezcatlipoca to get in his face for touching her.

"No, don't come any closer," he commanded, looming over her. Shaking, he held up the finger he used to touch Teddy. Everyone watched as it shriveled up, and only bone was left. Sniffing, he looked around and spied Fredericka. "How? It cannot be. Keep those two away from me," he ordered Mariposa.

Trembling, he turned to Teddy and Fredi. He looked over their heads as he talked to them as if the very act of looking at them hurt his eyes. "Beware demon sisters. Yes, you have impressive power, but I sense you are unaware you have this power. This tells me your destiny is not in your hands, but those of another. I don't know who resurrected this angry spirit, but I wish to God they hadn't. Ominous times are coming." Tezcatlipoca hesitated. "And demon sisters, you must ensure the evil in you never wins. I don't mean La Pantera Negra, either." He held up his hand to stop the inevitable questions tumbling from the girls' lips. "I've already said too much. You'll figure it out."

He turned to the rest of the group and continued. "Yes, another one was here with her army. If you hurry, you may catch her. She was desperate for the amulet. She thinks its powers can cure whatever she has in her that has changed her and some other creature into their current forms. What's the word humans use? Mudate?"

"Mutate," someone corrected him.

"Yes, that's it. Follow me, I'll show you a shortcut."

“That was easier than expected. Thank you for trusting me, Tez,” Mariposa said.

Turning, he gruffly replied, “It’s not you I trust, she-devil. It’s her I trust, the pantheress warrior queen.” He nodded in Teddy’s direction. “And don’t you worry, Itzpapalotl. You will settle your debt with me. Don’t you worry.” Cochise stepped forward menacingly, but Obsidian Butterfly held out a restraining arm. Taking a last look at the group filling his den, Tez sighed and turned. “Follow me.”

After walking up and down and taking what felt like switchbacks for what seemed like hours underground, Tezcatlipoca finally stopped and pointed into the darkness.

“Keep walking and you will find yourselves nearly at the mountaintop. Once you have reached the top, you’ll see an opening to another cave. In that cave, you will find the amulet everyone is searching for.”

“Why haven’t you simply done this and gotten the amulet yourself?” Teddy asked, puzzled because the mountains were so close to each other.

“Because I am largely confined to this cave, Queen. While I can leave, it takes a lot of energy for me to exist in the outside world.”

“That’s why he wants the amulet,” Mariposa added. “It’s believed that when a demon wears it, their body solidifies and they can walk the earth as a man. Trust me, Tez, you think you want to walk among men, but you really don’t. The Earth is so messed up, even aliens avoid this planet. You’ll see. One week. I bet you after one week of interacting with humans, you’ll be ready to come right back to your cave. You’ll see, especially when you discover they don’t revere you, aren’t afraid of you, won’t listen to you, will try to study or kill you and laugh at you…to your face,” Mariposa said, knowingly.

"You ain't never lied." Teddy snorted in agreement as she led the group out of the cave and into the dawn of another day.

Tezcatlipoca stood rooted to the same spot, long after the group had departed from his sight. *Of course, they're just trying to deter me from using the amulet. Humans can't be that bad,* he opined. Then, his thoughts became darker. What fool resurrected that she-demoness La Pantera Negra? Ye gods, the young pantheress queen had a lot of maturing to do before she could defeat such a powerful she-demoness. Maybe his cave was the safest place for him for the time being. Interesting times were ahead, indeed.

As the group continued making their way up the mountain, they came to a sudden stop. Unbelievably, Queen Idia and her army were waiting for them on the path. Queen Idia, who was once beautiful, wasn't looking well. Great bumps that looked like testicles covered her face and probably her entire body. Some bumps leaked a pustulant fluid.

Back at the lab, Ceola, Matilda, and Elizabeth gasped. They stared at the monitor, transfixed.

"My God, she used to be so beautiful," Elizabeth exclaimed.

"God don't like ugly," Matilda said, a devious smile on her face.

Ceola only glared at Idia's image. A low rumble began in her throat, and she snarled, "Fuck that bitch!"

Idia examined Teddy from her head to her toes, a look of disdain on her face. Looking behind Teddy and spotting Celeste, Naima, and Fredi, she snorted. "Half-breeds. You don't deserve to be called Ravenisha."

"Fugly ugly-assed fuckasaur," Fredi retorted.

Idia looked down at Fredi, venom radiating from her pores. "I'm going to enjoy watching the light go out of your pale eyes, young one."

“Take a number,” Fredi taunted before Teddy pulled her back.

“What do you want, heffa?” Teddy said, striding forward until she was inches from Idia’s face. Idia involuntarily took a step back, yielding, assessing this dangerous being in front of her. Sniffing, she noted Teddy and the young one had a scent on them that overwhelmed even the scent of La Panthère Noire. She didn’t know what it was, but she didn’t like it. Her instincts were screaming she’s facing predators even more dangerous than she was. She also sensed the one standing in front of her had a whiff of the same scent as the one known as Obsidian Butterfly.

“Ugh, what happened to your face,” Teddy sneered, looking at the misshapen bumps protruding from Idia’s face and body, with distaste. “And Idia, if you hurt one hair on my sister’s head, I will kill you. That’s a promise, not a threat.”

“Y-y-y-you’re wasting your time b-bitch,” Idia stammered, looking into Teddy's mismatched eyes and trying to save face. “The amulet isn’t here. Someone already beat us to it.”

At those words, there was a mighty roar, and the ground shook. Teddy and the others—even Queen Idia—immediately whipped out their weapons, ready to fire. Somehow, Tezcatlipoca had materialized before them, and he was furious. Every time he breathed, a hot gust of foul air blew over the assembled enemies. As Fredi’s shirt billowed away from her, Tezcatlipoca’s eyes zoomed in on her necklace. Then, he noticed the same chain around Teddy’s neck, and his eyes widened in disbelief.

“Nooo! Who did this blasphemy?” He roared again and stomped his foot. He reached out a trembling hand but still couldn’t force himself to touch either female. Teddy lifted the necklace out of her shirt for all to view.

"I don't understand," she uttered, truly confused. "What's the problem? These were gifts."

Idia joined in with Tezcatlipoca howling. "They ruined the amulet!" she cried, hatred in her eyes. When Fredi did a not so covert job of looking at Cochise and giving him a thumb's up, the gesture wasn't lost on Tezcatlipoca and Idia.

"Why you..." Tezcatlipoca started. He began fading in front of their eyes, his power used up completely, but not before his anger revived the long-dormant volcano. Idia snarled and lunged for Cochise. As she leaped, Idia saw Teddy's gun aimed at her forehead. She pushed one of her minions in front of her as Teddy fired, killing the minion in her stead. Idia whirled, changed, and bounded down the mountainside.

"Everyone, haul ass!" Lieutenant Allensworth shouted, also heading down the mountain. Everyone turned and ran in a panic as the ground continued to shake.

The volcano continued making ominous sounds and the ground's shaking intensified. Just as a toxic plume of smoke and ash spewed from the volcano, substantial chunks of rocks began raining down on the fleeing bodies. Soldiers fired on some of Idia's minions, killing them, but everyone's primary concern was to get off of that mountain, alive and as soon as possible.

Day became night as volcanic ash eclipsed the rising sun and immediately negatively impacted people's vision. Soldiers coughed and gagged as they struggled to strap on their night vision goggles while running. Fredi's eyes stung, but she ran on, determined to get off of the mountain with the rest. An eerie tableau greeted them as their vision was peppered not just with green blobs of fleeing people around them, but also of red-orange blobs from the chunks of molten lava falling down on them. Despite the steaminess of the jungle, minor fires started here and there. Steam developed from the jungle's moisture and the volcano's fire. They had to get off of that mountain before it scalded them to death.

Because Idia and her army were in their pantheress forms, they made it down the mountain faster than Teddy and the others. Therefore, Idia and her people had disappeared into another part of the jungle to their vehicles, which would take them to their planes before the Americans had even reached the mountain's bottom. The Americans continued running hard, and to their relief, finally saw their convoy up ahead, waiting for them. Everyone piled into the idling vehicles, which zoomed down the perilous mountain road back to the base. Along the way, they saw Idia's planes taking off but were impotent to stop them.

"We'll get her," Teddy promised while also vowing to talk to Mariposa and Cochise about this entity she and Fredi needed to avoid like the plague.

Back at the base, it was soon apparent that not only was Cochise missing but also Fredi and Mariposa. Everyone agreed that they had seen Cochise on the mountain standing near Fredi. After that, things got hazy as no one could remember when they last saw him. No one had seen Fredi and Mariposa disappear either. There was too much smoke in the air. At one point, they were even fleeing the mountain alongside Idia's mutants. As much as they wanted to go back and search for the missing parties, they had to immediately evacuate the area before it became unsafe for planes to fly. Reluctantly, they boarded the plane, taxied down the runway, and lifted off. It was hoped that Fredi would be safe with Mariposa and they'd make their way back home.

Lieutenant Allensworth called Akiro and asked him if he saw anything on the video feed.

"Give me a sec." Akiro could be heard typing furiously. "What the hell?" he mumbled. "I see something, guys, but the images are cloudy."

"Let's see," commanded Gus. The airplane's monitors came to life, and Akiro enabled the system so everyone could view the monitors. There they were at the impasse near the mountaintop. They could clearly see Teddy, Fredi, and Idia. A shadowy image of a man-like being appeared, then disappeared. They could see Cochise at the edge of the screen, close to the mouth of a crevice. He suddenly whipped his head around and looked like he was about to take off running. He was gone in the blink of an eye.

"Could you slow it down even more and replay it, Akiro?" Teddy asked, staring intently at the screen. "I thought I saw something." The images crawled across the screens in slow motion. "There!" Teddy cried, and Akiro froze the frame.

Something appeared behind Cochise and enveloped him. No matter how many times they replayed and slowed the clip, no one could discern what the indistinct blob was. They finally agreed that it looked like something was wrapped around his feet. Maybe.

Lieutenant Allensworth spoke into his headset. "Did you get all of that, Colonel?"

"Unfortunately, I did. Damn, the dreadful news just doesn't stop, either. Rufus and the others have made an inauspicious discovery at the lab. I'll tell you more when you land."

Chapter 29

It was somber at the lab where the Old-Gen and Rufus stopped working to stare mutely at the lab's video monitor. This news added another damper to their day. Earlier, they discovered that some of their own soldiers bitten by Idia's evil army had displayed signs of infection. They were being quarantined in one of the dorms on the base where they could be safely monitored without contaminating the local population. So far, the men bitten had tested negative for signs of the strain. The scientists had concluded that women with certain genetics were more susceptible to mutating once the gene invaded their bodies than women who didn't possess the X-factor gene or genes. What that gene was, however, was still unknown. They inspected the women's bodies for "the sign" visible on the Ravenisha's buttocks, but none of the infected women exhibited any such sign.

After discussions with the president and the colonel, the parties determined they would have to euthanize the infected women humanely if they found no antidote. It was just too dangerous to have them out in the general population where they could infect others and create more mutant werepanthers. Lizzie had tried to argue for them to be kept captive, but they overruled her. Keeping them alive but in captivity wasn't a viable option, as they didn't have the facilities nor could they build the facilities to properly contain and feed them. What if the women infected their family members when they visited, purposely or not? No, the risks were too great. They had already prepared syringes filled with lethal doses of the arsphogene dioxide and the liquid form of Iconel as a precaution. It would be mass-produced and distributed to law enforcement, emergency centers, and personnel throughout the United States immediately.

"There has to be something all the infected women have in common," Ceola mulled, as she sat down at a workstation, preparing to go through all the paperwork again. "Akiro, I need their medical reports downloaded."

"On it, Miss C."

Hours later, there was a whoop from Ceola. "I think I found the connection. So far, besides exhibiting higher levels of estrogen and progesterone, all the women infected have an abnormality in their chromosomal sequence at the same place."

Rufus tapped his chin. "My serum also has high levels of estrogen and progesterone. The serum's properties must find it easy to bond with these women's hormones. How that could be counteracted, though, I have no idea."

"Right," considered Lizzie, "because these changes are happening at the cellular level, it's not going to be easy to offset their effects."

"Yeah," Ceola agreed. "We need scientists versed in molecular biology and genetics. Who knows some good ones? What about you, Rufus?"

He sat down heavily in a chair, head in his hands. "Just give me a moment," he mumbled in a barely audible voice. "These headaches are becoming more frequent, and the pain is getting worse." He groaned.

"I'm sorry you're suffering, Rufus." Ceola walked over and massaged his temples. He smiled at her gratefully, closed his eyes, and leaned back into her hands. Ceola's face was unreadable, but turbulence lurked in her eyes.

"Thank you, Ceola. The spell seems to be letting up some now. Unfortunately, I brought this all on myself. Okay, molecular biologists and geneticists," Rufus pondered, index finger on his chin.

Chapter 30

The cadre needed to make a quick pit stop in Ravenswood to pack more supplies, strategize, and pick up the Old-Gen. There was also the question of whether this would be an official government mission or a private one. They were approaching downtown, and since Rufus had built everything to cater to his lab's employees, it was well done, indeed. There was the ubiquitous town square, the trees now mature. It was big enough to house a small lake and provided a tree-lined three-mile walking circuit. There wasn't a big box store in sight. Those stores had been consigned to the mall on the outskirts of town.

The mixture of restaurants, cafes, and stores had managed to stay in business since they opened and were still going strong. They even had a French bakery, Boulangerie Ravenswood, which also housed a pâtisserie. Go figure. A French bakery in a small town in Alabama. And next to the French bakery was the charcuterie store, The Hog's Head. The butcher was an up-and-coming young man who was making a name for himself. The store also had a fine selection of wines and cheeses. The women liked the stores so much, Thursdays had been dubbed French Day, with breakfast, lunch, and dinner being French-themed.

While Rufus lived in one of the area's historical antebellum mansions, the town's library was housed in the other big antebellum mansion. You couldn't have everything, Teddy sighed. And she supposed there were far worse uses for the mansions. She knew they had converted some of them into mental institutions that had long been closed. She supposed many of the antebellum homes had either been torn down or passed into private hands.

She also had to give Rufus props for not building cookie-cutter houses in a development-like setting. Houses downtown and on the outskirts had been built in an updated version of the late Victorian styles reminiscent of colonial and classical revivals, Queen Anne, and Craftsmen. There was one elementary, middle, and high school—and one hospital. At least there were two banks. Well, a bank and a credit union. With a start, Teddy realized how much she liked Ravenswood as they passed through it on their way home. It was a clean place but not at all sterile. Yes, there were CCTVs everywhere. But when was the last time a crime had been committed in Ravenswood? she thought.

At some point during the drive, Gus turned to Teddy. "You know we need to discuss what happened yesterday. I never thought we would interact with each other like that. I felt we had this connection. We were on the same page, you know?"

"I agree," Teddy responded, still chafing. "Look, just say what you need to say. Stop beating around the fucking bush."

"Calm down. Jesus. So, I'm assuming you won't emasculate me in the bedroom like you did in the jungle yesterday, and that you'll allow me to be the man?" Gus asked, a hard edge to his voice.

"F-f-first of all," Teddy sputtered incredulously, "I did not emasculate you earlier. Second of all, what makes you think we will be sleeping with each other at all, much less regularly? That's rather presumptuous of you."

Gus stared ahead, his eyes on the road, gathering his thoughts before he spoke. “When we’re in the field, we need to keep things professional, and you need to address me by my rank. You know you were wrong, Theodora.”

Teddy blew out a breath. “Fine. You’re right. I was out of line. It was disrespectful of me to ignore your rank and call you by not even your given name but a shortened version of it. I’m sorry. But you were also wrong to tear us down like you did.”

“Fine, I can be the bigger person and admit you Ravenisha are faster and stronger than us mere mortals but come on, Teddy. Don’t act like you’re obtuse. I know there’s a spark between us. You know there’s a spark between us. Need I mention the sex between us will be hotter than hell? I’m going to predict here and now we’re going to be husband and wife. I don’t play games. I’m honorable and a man of my word.”

Teddy was silent for a full minute. “Leona told you that, didn’t she?” Teddy pouted.

“Maybe,” Gus conceded, grinning, “but I can make up my own mind, woman. I know what I want and I choose you, but you’ve gotta let me be a man.”

“I’m not just going to *let* you be the man, home skillet,” Teddy laughed. “Believe you me, I don’t want someone I can run roughshod over, either. You’ve gotta *be* a man if you want to be with me.”

“Oh, it’s like that, is it?” Gus chuckled.

“It’s like that, and that’s the way it is. Oh, and Gus, you better be good. I’m not just giving it up for any ol’ body. I watch Red Tube and Porn Hub, so don’t think I’m going to be some little sexual innocent.” Teddy batted her eyelashes. She leaned over and whispered, “In fact, I want to go down on you right now sooo bad.”

Gus started to smile and reply, but all too soon, the house came into view. Gus pulled to a stop, wondering why Sheriff Tucker's patrol car was parked in front. He and Teddy exited the vehicle and went inside where they found everyone assembled around the big round table.

"You're just in time," Sheriff Tucker called out. "I was explaining the call I got from these two detectives from Benin while y'all were gone." Amos consulted his notes. "Detective Inspectors Patience Nguma and Felice Touissant of the Police Républicaine du Bénin called and explained they've been watching Idia Adechi for many years now, and are close to making an arrest. People been noting strange going-ons at the lab in Cotonou and local people been disappearing ever since Idia came on the scene. There've been whisperings of witchcraft and Vodun; however, they're sure an actual person, namely Idia Adechi, is behind the disappearances." Sheriff Tucker licked his finger and flicked to the next page. "Them gals wanted to know why Idia was so interested in this part of the United States and Central America. They also wanted to know whether Rufus Honeycutt was a complicit partner in these disappearances with Adechi." Sheriff Tucker scowled at Rufus. "And guess what else? One of them said her full name was Felice Legba Touissant and that she hasn't heard from her brother, Abaku Legba, who works for Idia, in months. This Abaku is also an undercover Benin state policeman. He agreed to infiltrate Idia's company, but Felice is afraid something's happened to him."

Colonel Honeycutt got up and made some phone calls in private. Upon returning to the room, he motioned for Akiro to set up the video equipment and held up a finger to get everyone's attention.

"Apparently, there have been unconfirmed sightings of monsters wiping out entire villages in Guatemala, and it looks like Idia and her army of monsters aren't through with us. We believe they're making their way to the American border and into the United States. It's time for everyone in this room to cut the bullshit." Colonel Honeycutt looked pointedly at Rufus. "We need to know what we're dealing with, whether we're in danger of being infected, and how to neutralize the danger. Those shapeshifters look sick, unlike our shapeshifters."

Everyone noted the "*our* shapeshifters," and most let the comment pass.

Matilda crossed her arms as she muttered darkly. "Oh, now it's *our* shapeshifters, is it? You fickle motherfuckers."

Ceola stomped her foot, exasperation on her face. "Tildy! Shhh!"

The colonel pulled up Google Earth footage found by Akiro and zoomed in. The picture showed some Guatemalan villagers running in all directions and unfortunate ones being savaged by two creatures. "Akiro, could you zoom in on those monsters?"

"Yessir, Colonel." As he magnified the images, gasps sounded in the room, along with a collective "What the hell?"

Rufus gazed at the screen, unable to hide the revulsion on his face. "The mutations look to be even more severe a day later." After Rufus brought everyone up to speed, he confessed, "I have been in the dark as much as y'all have been. I've been injecting myself like I said. Yet, I've never shapeshifted. I do believe I'm stronger and I feel the aging process has been significantly retarded. However, things took an unexpected adverse turn. My genes began mutating, and cancerous lumps began forming in my body. I stopped the injections once I discovered the cancer, but apparently, it was too late. It looks like Idia is mutating, as well. Some component of the serum is affecting people's DNA differently. What is clear, however, is we must eradicate the mutants before we have a plague on our hands. What's also clear is the fact that we have so many versions of the serum out there, I'm afraid we can never rein them all back in. Somehow, the serum has taken on a life on its own."

"Ugh, I can't believe you didn't see this coming since you're so superior to the rest of us. Anyways, Colonel, we must equip law enforcement with those special bullets as soon as possible."

"I agree, Teddy." Colonel Honeycutt scowled at Rufus before saying, "Sheriff Tucker, I'll notify the president and ask her to call a state of emergency right now."

Sheriff Tucker stood, put his hat on, and said, "I'm going to gather up my men and some others. Get that ammunition to us as soon as you can. When those fuckers come this way, we'll be ready to blow their asses to kingdom come. This is so fucked up." The Sheriff glared at Rufus. "Instead of one version of the monster out there, it sounds like there could be potentially hundreds. What kind of labs have you been running, Honeycutt?" Sheriff Tucker shook his head in disgust.

The rest of the day passed quickly. The plane was refueled and extra ammunition was packed. Liaisons reported no sightings of Idia or Abaku, so it was assumed they were heading back to Benin. There was still no sign of Fredi and Mariposa. It was deduced that Idia had kidnapped them. The Old-Gen, meanwhile, had their own plans. Standing on the porch, Matilda turned to Ceola and Elizabeth.

"See you two in the morning," she said with a wave, then skipped down the steps.

Ceola and Elizabeth walked to the edge of the property where three cottages had been erected. Their surprised spouses let them in, and they made love to their estranged husbands. Sated, all parties fell into a deep sleep afterward. After catnaps, the women quietly changed and woke the men. After explaining why they must die, they quickly bit off their estranged husbands' heads with their massive jaws. They first consumed the skull and brains and continued feeding until not a trace of the men remained.

The Old-Gen had engaged in a lively discussion earlier and the verdict for the men not to suffer hadn't been unanimous. Ceola had voted for the men to have to suffer long, violent deaths. Surprisingly, Matilda, who was somewhere feeding on a stranger, had voted for a merciful death. They had agreed on one thing, though, and that was the men must die. Their betrayal had been too great, the price too high.

~ ~ ~

As the Old-Gen walked out onto the porch early the next morning, all eyes were drawn to them. Conversations stopped midstream. Who were these confident, beautiful women? Ceola, Matilda, and Elizabeth looked as though someone had dipped them into the fountain of youth. While they were portraying themselves as middle-aged in human years, they could have passed for late thirties or early forties. They were no longer lean - they had meat on their bones in all the right places. The grey hair was gone. The wrinkles? Gone! The bent postures? Gone! They were now dressed similarly to their granddaughters in skinny jeans, tight black shirts, and black combat boots…and they were looking good. The shoulder holsters made them look even sexier. The New-Gen walked behind them.

"Wow," breathed Gus and his men, eyes wide.

"I expect your private plane to be ready at 1100 hours, Rufus," Ceola said in a voice that brooked no argument.

"I never thought I'd see the day when Black women would tell me what to do," Rufus huffed. He widened his stance and put his hands on his hips. "What's wrong with catching a ride on the army's plane?"

Ceola stalked up to him like a boss-ass bitch, eyes fierce. "Would you rather Black women give you orders, or eat you? And we're going in the private plane because it's more comfortable. Any more questions?"

"Dayuhm. Shots fired," added Henry unnecessarily.

"You, you, y-you she-devils," Rufus stuttered, resignedly with no heat in his voice.

"Whatever. Just make sure that plane is ready and you're giving your all to working on that cure. Colonel," said Ceola, turning to Beau.

"Yes ma'am," he saluted.

"Smart man," she purred. "Thank you for your men's services and the ammunition. I think Sheriff Tucker here can handle guarding the lab and the town while we're fighting Idia on her own turf. We'll literally be traveling to the valley of the shadow of evil and death. "Back to where it all began."

A Blackbird cawed ominously in the big tree that graced the front yard. Gus shivered as he protectively put his arms around Teddy, inadvertently telegraphing his possessiveness of her, which of course, everyone noticed.

Chapter 31

Laboratoires des Honeycutt, Cotonou, Benin

It will be over soon," Idia cooed, cradling Abaku in her arms. He had been moaning in pain ever since coming down from his latest murderous rage. During his indiscriminate ravaging of the innocent villagers, he had killed children this time.

I have to put him down soon, she thought. *Put him down like the rabid dog he's become. Oh, Raven, what have I done to this once magnificent man? No, what has Rufus done to my bae?* she fumed. Now, the tumors were suppurating, and the virus' mutation was making it harder and harder for him to change back into a human man. Idia didn't know for sure but believed his internal body was also full of those hideous lumps. Abaku constantly coughed up that repugnant liquid that continuously seeped from the external bumps. Also, Abaku's mental faculties had long deteriorated. *And the worse thing of all,* Idia thought, *was that he infected me because we had unprotected sex.* Not being infected with human diseases was supposed to be one of the perks of being a shapeshifter, though. *This was some fuckery,* Idia bitterly steamed. If they didn't find a cure, she would take out as many people as she could before she killed herself. She only hoped she could kill herself, she bitterly fretted, remembering the curse's decree that the Ravenisha wouldn't die until their time.

Why hasn't La Panthère Noire answered her prayers? She hasn't been as faithful as she should be, but still, La Panthère Noire should treat her followers better. You couldn't expect people to believe in and follow you when you did nothing in return for them, she raged inwardly. Idia thought about her life and the choices she had made. She knew she wasn't an angel, but she wasn't totally evil, either. She just always believed women were men's equals, and in her struggle to prove her point, she had made some rather unfortunate decisions.

She didn't regret forming an army of women, though. It had been a joy teaching the women how to fight and watching them become more and more confident as their skills progressed. She felt that while women weren't as strong as men physically; they were better warriors because they weren't as rash and used their heads more. If only those brothers hadn't overtaken her village, forcing them to flee into the mountains, which put her on the path she was on today. If she was being honest with herself, she didn't regret the unholy alliance she had made with La Panthère Noire. In the final analysis, what was the difference between killing because you were warring with a people and killing those people for food? She and her army could have brought the continent to its knees at any time over the years, but she was only just now contemplating that step. She couldn't be that bad of a person. The only reason it had gotten to this point was those foolish men had refused to even consider her for president of the Republic of Benin and La Panthère Noire had ignored all of her prayers. Was it even possible La Panthère Noire was trying to get rid of her for new blood? Revealing her true self to those self-important men had been a mistake because it was only a matter of time before they tried to eradicate her and her army. But what else could she have done, she pondered, to show them her might? How much more superior she was than them? Damn them! Looking down at Abaku, she thought, here's another example of one of her objective failures.

Like she didn't know Abaku had come to her initially as a spy. Hah! It had been a fun challenge converting him over to her side. She knew that between the sex, money, and power, Abaku was hers as soon as they fucked. That's exactly why men shouldn't be in power, Idia seethed. *They're too weak at heart.* Although, she guessed she was, too, because she truly loved Abaku. She hadn't meant to fall for him, but it was harder for women to fuck men and not feel anything for them. Women were in the more vulnerable position since they were the ones being penetrated. It was easier for men to fuck someone and for it not to mean a damn thing. Her mother had told her this when she was growing up, but she hadn't listened. She wondered if Abaku truly loved her, as she did him. She concluded a bit sadly, probably not. After all, he was a man. She couldn't remember the last time she had felt so sorry for herself.

"Enough!" she said aloud. It was time to go to the lab and light a fire under that little mongrel girl and Indian woman's asses. She needed a cure for this terrible affliction yesterday.

~ ~ ~

"Hello, bitches," Idia greeted Dr. Vasquez and Fredi, striding into the lab where they were being held at gunpoint by Felice Touissant. Idia inclined her head toward Felice. "You may see your brother now. He's finally sleeping. Try not to disturb him." Felice smiled gratefully and left the room, practically running.

Idia then turned to Fredi and Mariposa. "I'm sure you're wondering why you're here."

"Actually, it's not that difficult to figure out." Fredi's tone was laced with boredom, and she studied her fingernails. Idia inclined her head for her to continue. "From the looks of you and the other one, something has gone terribly wrong. You obviously think Dr. Vasquez and I can concoct some magical elixir to cure you so your bodies will miraculously return to normal."

"Wow, I'm impressed, mongrel." Idia smiled, even though the smile didn't reach her eyes.

"Let's stop it with the mongrel, shit, Idia." Fredi's eyes raked over Idia and her lips curled. "You know the politics of what you're doing is wrong. First of all, I'm Black. Even though Rufus is my father, the mere fact my mother is Black means I am considered Black. You know this. Don't act stupid. Are you low-key jealous because my features, which I had no control over, are considered 'exotic?' " Fredi made air quotes to underscore her point. "Anyways, you are no Blacker or purer than anyone else; we're all mongrels. We're all Africans. At least I haven't hurt my people the way you have. What happened to sisterhood, Idia? Obsidian Butterfly is also our sister. As an indigenous woman of color, she definitely belongs to the club. I've never taken a single women's studies class or African American studies class, and I know this."

"Blah, blah, blah." Idia walked over to Dr. Vasquez with a syringe in her hand. "Actually, you're absolutely right, Fredi. I wish things had been different. But I fear my relationship with Ceola and the others has clouded your opinion, whether or not you believe that to be true. This is just a little incentive to keep you on task," she said, holding the syringe up while gesturing for armed guards in the room to come closer. While the guards held weapons to Fredi and Dr. Vasquez's heads, Idia grabbed Dr. Vasquez's arm and injected the syringe's contents.

"This is a quicker-acting version of the formula Abaku and I have in our systems, so it would behoove you two to work quickly to find a cure. We have almost a day before the Americans get here. I must say I never expected Rufus to come up with a formula to change a human into such a perfect werepanther, though." Idia gave Mariposa an admiring look. Neither Mariposa nor Fredi corrected Idia's mistaken assumption.

Fredi walked over to a monitor and began typing. Stopping, she looked up and asked, "Password?"

One of the lab techs typed in the password, and Fredi resumed typing. Rufus's face appeared on the monitor, with Colonel Honeycutt hovering in the background. Fredi explained what had happened and asked Rufus if he had worked on the formula since she last worked with him. He replied he had just resumed today and agreed it was imperative that he, Fredi, and Dr. Vasquez put their heads together to find a solution. Rufus informed them that he had contacted some scientists who should arrive in a couple of hours to help them. Fredi made it a point to let Rufus know of Idia's admiration for his work in transforming Dr. Vasquez into a shapeshifter. Rufus nodded his understanding of what Fredi was conveying to him.

Fredi looked up from the keyboard, full of ennui and defiance. "Oh, and Idia, just so you know, my big sister is going to kill you. That s a promise, not a threat."

"Yes, yes, I know. I'm so afraid, I'm practically shaking in my boots," Idia responded.

"You should be afraid. Very afraid," Fredi quietly intoned, almost sadly, and turned her attention back to the computer monitor.

Even as an icy dread settled in Idia's heart, she believed she would beat death. She hadn't lived for centuries without being formidable in her own right. Teddy was just a girl. She wasn't a queen…yet.

Chapter 32

Meanwhile, on the plane carrying the Ravenisha and male fighters to Benin to battle Idia and her army, Gus and his bros stared in disbelief at the women seated around them. Rather than trying to get some rest and sleep, they had kicked off their shoes and were dancing to music with wild abandon. Beyonce's "7/11" was blasting on the plane's loudspeakers, bass thumping. Before that, it had been "Diva" from Beyonce's Homecoming Live, then G-Eazy's "1942." The song ended and there was merciful silence.

"Whew!" Matilda caught her breath, fanning herself. "I haven't danced like that since I don't know when." Just then, Aretha Franklin's "Respect" came over the loudspeakers. "Yaaassss!" Matilda shouted, jumping up and dancing again.

"What are they on?" Roland whispered as Teddy danced over to them, shouting the letters during the R-E-S-P-E-C-T part.

"I don't know, but I hope they don't tire themselves out." Gus frowned. When Lizzo's "Truth Hurts" began, the men had had enough. Gus removed his computer and slammed the tray back into place. "I'm going to turn off the music. If I don't return in five minutes, come rescue me." He walked a few steps, then turned around. "I'm serious, guys. Come rescue me if I'm not back in five minutes."

Gus must have found the sound system because the plane suddenly went silent. Immediately, the women began grumbling and looking around for the source of their fun being dampened.

"Gee, what a spoilsport," Celeste told him when he returned to the main cabin. Jeers and boos accompanied him as he walked down the aisle.

"I think we need to play Jazmine Sullivan's "Bust Your Windows" someone yelled as something cold hit him in the head.

Shocked, Gus turned around and saw that Teddy was right behind him, her arm back, another piece of ice in her hand.

"Did you just hit me with a piece of ice?" he asked incredulously. "Are you an eight year-old?"

"Oh, don't be such a grumpy old man," she said before hitting him with the second piece of ice.

"Grumpy old man, huh? I'll show you grumpy." Gus picked Teddy up and threw her over his shoulder. He took her into the restroom and slammed the door behind him.

When they emerged fifteen minutes later, Teddy's hair was a mess, and her lips were swollen. Gus was grinning sheepishly, his eyes only on Teddy. They didn't even care the entire plane was staring at them. Celeste and Naima turned and glared at their men, arms folded across their chests.

The rest of the flight was spent quietly. Teddy and Gus slept, reliving the passionate kissing they had engaged in in the cramped bathroom in their dreams. The Old-Generation members slept on and off, strategizing while they were awake. When they were about two hours out from Benin's Cotonou Cadjehoun's Airport, Gus awakened everyone to discuss the task at hand. Recent surveillance showed Idia and her coterie were still at the lab in Cotonou.

Teddy suggested that Colonel Honeycutt's men neutralize the lab, and by neutralizing, she stressed the importance of killing every single mutant werepanther they encountered. They acknowledged that a contingency of Idia's evil army would probably meet them at the airport, no doubt a diversionary tactic to give Idia and her closest followers time to escape with the prisoners into the mountains. Killing the mutants at the airport would set them back time-wise. However, the strain was so contagious; it was important to ensure the mutants couldn't pass it on.

Henry noted he had spoken to the Benin government army's attaché and had received assurances they wanted to stop Queen Idia and her evil forces before she destroyed their country as much as the Americans. They had been suitably horrified when she had demonstrated her she-panther form, threatening them to make her head of the republic. It was unfortunate that the special ammunition was in such short supply. However, they would share what they could with the Benin army and factories back home, which were working around the clock to manufacture more bullets, grenades, knives, etc. It wasn't easy, though, because of the difficulty of assembling the Iconel and gas. What they really needed was a vaccine they could inject the populace with—a vaccine that would prevent them from reacting to bites and scratches from the mutants.

As they prepared to land, Benin's military informed Gus that Idia and her entourage had just hurriedly fled the laboratory. Gus advised Benin's version of special forces to stand down since they didn't have the special ammunition and they wanted to avoid contamination at all costs. As expected, once they deplaned, a small cadre of mutant werepanthers met them. They quickly disposed of them and Benin's army witnessed the bullets and grenades' efficacy. They eagerly loaded their weapons with spare bullets that the Americans brought with them. Before the groups separated, an envoy reported that the Ravenisha might want to make a trip to the Laboratoires des Honeycutt, after all.

Everything was so unfamiliar, thought Ceola, Elizabeth, and Matilda, staring out of the windows of the armed vehicle in which they were riding. Even the language! They had tried to converse in their native tongue with people at the airport and their people had looked at them like they were speaking gibberish! They weren't rude. In fact, they had run off and excitedly returned with elders who they thought could converse with these women who were speaking in what was to them an ancient dialect of their language. The Ravenisha, engulfed like celebrities, had finally given up and reverted to French and English. Videos taken of them went viral, and professors—from anthropologists to linguists, ethnologists to scientists—began clambering to learn the identity of these women speaking a dialect that hadn't been heard in modern times and was thought to be lost. Realizing the Pandora's Box they had opened, the women wisely ran for the armored vehicles awaiting them.

Even though they had read books and seen pictures of present-day Africa, they were still unprepared for the emotions that roiled through them as they gazed out of the armored vehicles' windows at high-rise buildings, modern luxury hotels, highways full of automobiles, and roundabouts modeled off of Paris' street circles. They finally arrived at Rufus's futuristic flying saucer-shaped building. Exiting the vehicles with their weapons, they noted the vast parking lot was largely empty, except for armored vehicles like theirs. The place was eerily quiet and devoid of any significant presence. The lone guard on duty let them in with no resistance. They gathered the few remaining scientists who had opted to stay in the building's lobby. Some were on their cell phones while others stood chatting with each other like this was any other day at the office. The Ravenisha pushed onward. Their acute hearing picked up the sound of someone keening in one room. Lieutenant Allensworth and his men were right behind them.

Teddy was the first one to find the source of the wailing. Cautiously opening the door, even though her senses told her this wing of the building was otherwise empty except for this person, she nonetheless cleared the room before signaling to the others it was okay for them to enter. Blood was everywhere. It was as though someone had filled buckets with blood and helter-skelter splattered the liquid around the room. Even the ceiling hadn't been spared.

Felice Legba Touissant sat on the floor in a pool of putrid-smelling blood, cradling what was left of the head of her dead brother, Abaku, in her arms. She showed no signs of noticing or acknowledging the visitors until Ceola tried to shift Abaku's ravaged body so they could get a better glimpse of it.

"Nooo!" Felice screamed, tightening her grip around her brother's corpse.

Lizzie walked over to the grieving woman and gently pried the dead man from her arms. She then held Felice, assuring her they only wanted to take a quick look at Abaku.

"This man has suffered." Teddy eyed Abaku, cataloging the numerous wounds covering his devastated body. Great suppurating sores had burst open, revealing mushy tissue and organs. It looked like Abaku had been eaten from the inside out—as if the werepanther inside of him had tried to eat and claw its way out. For all the many holes that must have caused him untold pain, it was obvious what had finally killed him had been a bullet to the head.

"What happened?" Teddy asked, searching Felice's face intently.

"S-she, s-she, k-killed him." Felice finally got the words out, tears running down her face. "She was supposed to find a cure for him, but she said she didn't have time and it was too late, anyway."

"Idia killed him?" Ceola asked, puzzled.

"No," Felice shook her head. "It was the young one. Fredi killed him. She said he was suffering and would die, anyway. She took my gun from me in the blink of an eye and she put it against his head and pulled the trigger before anyone could do anything. Fredi tried to shoot Idia, but she swatted the gun away. Then...Idia made her pay." Felice trembled, remembering images only she could see. "The girl was right, though. I see that now. I just wasn't ready to let him go," she whimpered. She looked up at them for the first time. "It will be a miracle if that child lives. Idia beat the shit out of her. They had to carry her out of here. I wish I was dead. I have *nothing* to live for now. Nothing! Abaku was all I had."

"You must be Felice Toussaint. I'm so sorry for your loss. Sheriff Tucker told us you called. We'd planned to contact you when we landed. Did Idia say where she was going?" Ceola asked.

"Yes, she left a message for you," Felice responded in a dead voice. "She's returning to the homeland. Come after her if you dare."

"Okay, we're leaving now." Ceola turned to leave but then stopped and looked down at Felice. "You can stay here and feel sorry for yourself, or you can come with us and help us fight the bitch who ruined your brother. The choice is up to you. Let's go," she commanded the rest in the old language.

When they reached the front of the building, they noticed that Felice had joined them. "Good choice. Welcome, Sistah."

Matilda turned to one of Benin's army members, and said, "Make sure you completely incinerate the body in that room."

A countdown began over the loudspeakers. Dix, neuf, huit, sept, six, cinq, quatre, trois, deux, un, zéro.

"What the hell?" Gus muttered, his body tensing and instantly alert. Gus nodded his head toward the door and motioned for everyone to vacate the building.

Unfortunately, the discussion about the disposal of Abaku's body delayed them and before they could exit the building, the front doors' locks clicked. People began looking around, concerned, especially as the building's lights dimmed. Startled, they assumed firing stances, weapons at the ready as they suddenly heard the sound of someone running toward them. The footsteps grew closer and closer until a dapper man, clad in a suit, rushed into the room from one of the building's many corridors. Though his features were now ravaged by the affliction that had affected Idia and Abaku, it was apparent this individual's androgynous face had once been beautiful. The man came to a dead stop and put his hands in the air.

"I give up. This is what they say on American TV, no?" His Benin French-accented English was erudite. "I'm just going to sit on this counter, okay?" He lithely hopped onto the receptionist's counter and crossed his legs, enjoying the attention. Behind him, a large picture of Idia dominated the wall.

Since Gus and the others had their guns trained on the interloper, Teddy walked over to the front doors and inspected them. She lifted her gun, shot the locking mechanism, and with a well-placed strike, kicked the doors open with so much force, they exploded, glass shards falling everywhere.

"You go, girl!" the man clapped. "So much for security doors, eh?"

Teddy turned her attention to the man and made a motion for him to continue.

"Why don't you tell us who you are and why we shouldn't kill you for starters."

"Just a moment. I absolutely must take my medicine before I go mad."

As they watched, the man removed a syringe from his pocket and injected himself through a port embedded in his skin. He noticeably calmed down as the serum's fluid flowed through his veins.

"Whew, I feel better," he said, fanning himself. He checked the clock on the wall. "It will be a while before those stupid beasts break free," he muttered. "I've got time."

Ever astute, Gus spoke into his headset and told the army gathered outside to search the building. Destroy any mutants on sight. He told them to use explosives, when possible, to take out large numbers of them. All eyes turned back to the unknown male.

"My name? Easy. Jules Baptiste. The second part isn't so easy. I most definitely should be killed, but I'll give you a reason I think I should live, nevertheless. The scientists here didn't know my werepanther would manifest differently from the other male and female werepanthers. They injected the same serum into me they injected in Abaku, and of course, I had a different reaction. To tell the truth, I'm a hot mess," Jules acknowledged ruefully. "But on the positive side, my werepanther form is the closest one to the ideal of what they're looking for so far. There's one little problem, though—the deformities." Jules pointed to his face.

"How intriguing." Ceola walked over and turned Jules' face from side to side. Her razor-sharp eyes took in every bump and protuberance.

"I would love to get you into my lab. You have the same lumps Abaku and Idia have, but you don't appear to be sick. What are your plans, Jules?"

"Well, if you haven't figured it out by now, security at this lab wasn't the best. Idia was so concerned with building her army, she didn't really notice who was being injected with what or when. That's the problem when you hire people with no moral compass. That serum is all over the world, honey." Scanning the look of dismay on their faces, Jules was incredulous. "You can't be serious! *Mon Dieu!* You are serious! You really thought the serum was locked up tight here? Silly Americans."

"Rufus," a grim-faced Gus said into his headset, "are you getting all of this?"

"I could weep. We knew this, but to have it confirmed is still hard to take."

Loud explosions made them all jump into action.

"So, what are your plans, Jules?" asked Teddy, always on the task at hand.

"I have a score to settle," Jules said, smiling enigmatically. He thought to himself, *Idia will pay for kidnapping me and injecting me against my will.*

"You need to come back with us, Jules," Matilda said, stepping up and unsheathing one of her knives. "Ceola is an excellent scientist. Let her work on fixing those deformities."

Just as Jules looked like he was about to relent and come with them, another loud explosion ripped through the building—this one strong enough to make the floors shake. Realizing everyone was off-balance, Jules changed into the misshapen creature they remembered jumping from the rig at the army base and, leaping over them once again, he escaped through the gaping maw where the doors once stood. Matilda quickly took off after him, aiming and throwing her knife. The blade buried itself in Jules' werepanther's back leg. Howling, Jules pulled up, twisted his werepanther's head around, and yanked out the knife. Flinging it to the ground, he continued running and disappeared into Cotonou's many warrens and mazes. Matilda and Teddy reached the knife and stopped. They knew it was useless chasing Jules, so they gathered up the knife and as much of the blood as they could and headed back to the lab.

Frustrated, the Americans and Felice piled into the vehicles and headed back to the airport where they would board the plane that would take them as close to the Mont Sokbaro Twin Falls as possible.

Ceola stared out of the window, oblivious to the sights as they raced along the streets. As usual, Idia had a huge lead over them, but this time, they would be the ones following Sun Tzu's words in the *Art of War:* "Let your plans be dark and impenetrable as night, and when you move, fall like a thunderbolt." Ceola unconsciously clenched and unclenched her fist. *Idia doesn't know the shitstorm she's about to face. I've been plotting this day ever since they stuffed me on that slave boat like a sardine. Every time a whiplash fell across my back. Every time someone took me sexually against my will. What the hell was Idia thinking? Did she think we would never come for her? That we would stay in America, accept our lot in life and allow her to live in peace? She must be out of her fucking mind.* Ceola growled.

As if sensing what she was thinking, Elizabeth said, "I've been dreaming about this day for centuries, too."

Matilda nodded and growled, "Me, too. I've dreamt of tearing that bitch to pieces in so many ways." The New-Gen Ravenisha looked at each other, eyes wide, never having seen their grannies like this before.

"Well, y'all can't have all of her," Teddy said. "I've got to get a piece of her ass for what she's done to Fredi." The women nodded and fist-bumped.

"And save a little piece for me for what she's done to Abaku," Felice added.

"Her ass done got so big, it looks like there'll be enough for everybody," Lizzie added cattily.

"Oooh, look at Auntie Lizzie throwing shade," Celeste laughed.

They had left the plane by now and were standing on the tarmac waiting for their vehicles to be unloaded. A loud report sounded, followed by sputtering bangs. Everyone drew their weapons and aimed them in the direction of what sounded like gunshots.

"What on Earth?" Matilda asked as a little rust bucket drew to a shuddering stop on the airstrip. The three suitcases that had been strapped to the top and had miraculously stayed secure until this point began sliding down. Black exhaust coughed from the tailpipe.

Jules stepped out, looked around, and spotted an army member. "My luggage goes on that plane." He imperiously walked over to the Ravenisha and Asoro. He didn't even turn around to see if the baffled army personnel followed his order. He looked between Gus and Teddy and then stopped in front of Lieutenant Allensworth. "I've changed my mind. My knowledge of demonology will prove useful to you." At their raised eyebrows, he added, "I omitted to tell you I am Professor Jules Baptiste, expert on all things demonic."

~ ~ ~

Dr. Vasquez gazed between the slats of the cage that imprisoned her and Fredi. Little forethought had gone into their prison. Maybe in Idia's world, there was no need to imprison people or they hadn't had time to build the proper quarters. She and Fredi were in a steel cage that had a dirt floor. They had only been provided with a bucket of water, a bucket to use as a toilet, and fire-making material. They had already endured a night of rain with no cover. Dr. Vasquez had protected Fredi as best as she could. Idia's personal guard had secretly brought umbrellas, and the plants and herbs she asked for so Mariposa could tend to Fredi's wounds. Mariposa fumed. Idia didn't have to treat them like this. She was positive Idia could have imprisoned them inside. She was just being a bitch—cruel to be cruel. Well, Mariposa could be cruel, too. Idia better watch out. She had painted her face with soot from the fire used to warm their cell. She came from a great warring lineage and she would find a way to free her and Fredi.

Dr. Vasquez crouched down to check on Fredi. She was slowly fading, barely conscious, breathing shallow. As tears fell from her eyes, she tore what was left of her clothes into strips and re-bandaged Fredi's wounds, which she had tended as best she could. The rest was up to the girl. Mariposa rocked her in her arms, chanting an old Mayan healing song, the tenderness in her voice at odds with her fierce face markings. She prayed the Ravenisha would find them in time, but even if they didn't, Idia was a dead woman. Dr. Vasquez prayed the serum Idia injected into her didn't kill her first.

~ ~ ~

The joviality was gone, replaced by looks that meant business. Everyone linked hands—even those who were atheists—and Roland said a prayer for the group's victory and safe return.

"Am I the only one who feels funny praying to God and Jesus to bless me in battle?" Teddy questioned, knowing she was stirring up trouble. "You know, we're basically asking the sky people to help us be victorious in killing our enemies before they kill us."

"Don't try to understand it, Teddy. You'll drive yourself crazy." Matilda warned. "It's like asking Black people how they can embrace the same religion their masters worshipped. It's best not to think about it if you want to stay sane. Let's just free Fredi and Mariposa, kill that traitorous bitch, and get the hell outta here. Besides, you have to believe in something greater than yourself to make it in this world."

A chorus of *Amens* greeted Matilda's statement.

After studying a topographical map, and getting a feel for their surroundings, the troops left the makeshift airstrip on the aptly named Honda Africa Twin off-road motorcycles that had been shipped over via the plane. The plan was to stop twenty miles from the Twin Falls and make camp for the night. They were undecided whether they should ride the bikes as close as they could to the old homestead. Noise from the bikes wasn't the issue, for they knew Idia was expecting them, but they didn't want to trumpet their arrival.

The Old-Gen marveled at how the further they rode away from civilization, the more the landscape was the same they remembered. Paved roads gave way to dirt roads so badly pockmarked with holes as big as craters, it did a disservice to the word *road* to identify them as such. These "roads" gave way to trails, and as the canopy thickened, Matilda warned the group to slow down and be extra diligent.

Scores of mutant werepanthers exploded from the jungle's canopy. "Shit! So much for that warning!" someone yelled, opening fire. They had rushed headlong into the dark and dense foliage, and now they were trapped on all sides by mutants. The things had even managed to knock all of them off of their motorcycles and were going for kill bites. The Ravenisha and Asoro quickly got into fight mode, but the mutants kept coming. Felice crawled away from the overturned motorcycle she was on, found a tree base and curled up in a ball. Celeste saw her and ran over.

"Felice, you have to fight. You're a police officer, for crying out loud. Here, take this gun and kill some mutants!" A mutant chose that moment to jump on Celeste and Felice. Celeste blew the mutant's head off and left the beast on Felice. As liquids and organs boiled and ran out onto Felice, something inside of her snapped. She pushed the mutant off of her, grabbed the gun, and joined the others. The battle was fierce, but Jules surprised everyone by stepping up. He changed into his beast and took down mutant after mutant. The Ravenisha and Asoro were outnumbered and often double-teamed, but they prevailed. Silence finally descended over the jungle.

"Well, damn, that was a clusterfuck," Matilda noted, breathing heavily. "We should have expected an ambush, though." She looked around and noted that everyone else was breathing heavily, as well. Mutant bodies were piled everywhere, still sizzling. She and the others were covered in blood and gore. After assessing the damage, they decided to ride on and tend to the injuries away from the battle site.

While helping to set up camp that night, the Ravenisha realized the hunger that was gnawing in their bellies was becoming all-consuming. Once they had resumed feeding again, it seemed the more they ate, the more they needed to eat. Normally, they would only need to feed monthly, but years of being unable to hunt had left them ravenous. They had fed before boarding the plane to Africa, knowing they would be hungry and aggressive about now. While this had been a deliberate maneuver, the reality of the situation was hitting them in the gut hard. They also realized too late that feeding on mutants they killed earlier wasn't an option once they were tainted with Rufus's chemicals.

With all cylinders firing, their senses sharpened, and in full hunter mode, they undressed. With their clothes and weapons stowed in backpacks secured to their backs, they changed into their pantheress forms. The Ravenisha eagerly raced up the mountain to hunt for any lookout guards Idia might have posted who could be their dinner for the night. They weren't worried about the guards being deliberately poisoned to incapacitate them, as they reasoned they would smell the poison, and if someone poisoned the werepanthers, they wouldn't be able to stand guard. Also, as much as the thought hurt them, they realized if fellow Ravenisha were on guard tonight, they must consider them prey, as well.

Midway up the mountaintop, the Old-Gen she-panthers motioned for the New-Gen to follow them. Keeping to the shadows, always staying down wind and making nary a sound, they ran up the mountainside and cut across the mountain's top until they were looking down from a promontory. They could just make out the werepanther forms of Idia's army members, scattered across a one-mile radius, patrolling the patch of land they had been assigned. After watching, waiting, and determining no one else was around, each Ravenisha chose an evil army werepanther. She stalked her werepanther with stealth and quickly pounced and bit into the skull or throat and killed the werepanther before it could sound the alarm.

The Ravenisha radioed the "all clear" to the base camp. The men would drive the motorcycles further up the mountain and once they were within hearing distance, they would walk the rest of the way. The Twin Falls would help dampen the loud motorcycles considerably. They were happy they didn't have to kill any fellow Ravenisha, but they knew they had only been given a short reprieve.

"My God, they're magnificent," Idia whispered in awe as she watched the New-Gen make mincemeat out of her mutant warriors through binoculars she held to her eyes. Ignoring the Old-Gen, she rued if only the circumstances had been different. If she had those young women on her side, she'd rule the world.

After a brief rest, the American Ravenisha forged their way deeper into the mountains. Jules stayed behind with the Asoro. They followed the trail feet and paws had etched for many centuries, knowing they were on a collision course with their one-time friend whose betrayal centuries ago had finally led to this showdown. It was apparent Idia and her followers had been this way recently, as branches were freshly broken and no one had tried to cover their footprints. The sun set, and night fell. Still, the women hadn't found Idia's new location.

The tired cadre continued making their way on the path the next morning until they came to a note pinned to the ground with a knife. Ceola removed the note, read it, and rolled her eyes. She showed it to the others. The note said, "Welcome, bitches. Turn around while you can."

"Fuck her," Matilda growled. "We will continue on. If I remember the map correctly, we can't get the drop on her in any way."

"Yeah," Teddy noted, "I don't like being on this path in the open like this. We're basically sitting ducks."

"How right you are," purred a voice behind them.

The American Ravenisha whirled around. Idia stood in her werecat form behind them, holding Dr. Vasquez in a firm grasp, a claw point digging into her neck. Her guards flanked her as other warriors emerged from the brush.

"Drop your weapons on the path," she commanded, "and continue walking forward."

In case the American Ravenisha were thinking they would open fire, the African Ravenisha raised their weapons and aimed them. The American Ravenisha immediately noticed the weapons were state-of-the-art, the latest technology in the art of warfare and killing. They were outnumbered and outgunned. They did the only thing they could do and prayed that Lieutenant Allensworth and his men would find them in time.

Chapter 33

The American Ravenisha did as ordered and continued walking as Idia's warriors picked up the dropped weapons and surrounded them. As they walked, the old friends greeted each other, for the animosity wasn't between them. It was clearly between Idia and the women who were once her closest friends. It was a full day's hike until they came to Idia's new homestead. While the other path was visible from years of feet and paws trekking back and forth on it, this path was much fainter. Even looking at it with their keen eyesight in daylight, it was barely visible at all.

Towering trees and dense foliage enveloped them. Exotic flowers abounded, emitting a tantalizingly sweet musky scent. The forest was alive with the chatter of monkeys and birds, and thunder from the great waterfall could be heard even as they ventured deeper into the jungle. Under other circumstances, the women would have taken it all in and commented on the area's beauty. They now trudged on, barely paying any attention to where they were walking, preoccupied with thoughts ranging from how did they let Idia get the drop on them to how would they get out of this mess?

Ceola and the other Old-Gen wondered how many times Idia had snuck away from the old camp searching for a new home base until she found this place. She obviously never meant for them to live here with her, they realized. Up ahead, they could see a granite mountain before them. However, as they approached the edifice, they realized the structure rising before them was a palace. Women warriors, who stood on each side of the entrance, knelt as Idia approached. An indistinct murmur built as many of the Old-Gen Ravenisha who had stayed in Africa recognized their friends Cheola, Zamandla, and Eklezabela.

"You were always a power-hungry heffa," Ceola mumbled upon witnessing the genuflecting the poor warriors had to do in Idia's presence and the gaudy opulence on display.

"And you were never ambitious enough, Cheola. That's why one of us ended up a slave and one of us is a queen with her own kingdom."

Seemingly unbidden, more guards appeared. Two took Mariposa from Idia, and the rest flanked the new prisoners. The New-Gen Ravenisha glowered at Idia, attitude emanating from their pores.

"No, this heffa doesn't have a gold and diamond throne," Celeste scoffed as Idia sashayed to the front and sat on her throne.

"How ghetto," said Naima, crossing her arms. "I bet those are blood diamonds, too."

"I'm almost going to hate killing you bitches. I actually admire your little attitudes. But I know you'd never be loyal to me."

"You got that right," Teddy sneered, violence pouring off of her.

"Ah, yes, the fruit of Ceola's spawn," Idia drawled with bravado. "And I believe the little mutt's sister? Speaking of mutts, I must respect her resilience. Somehow, she's hanging on by the slimmest of threads."

Teddy willed herself to remain silent. It was hard, oh so hard, not to rip Idia's fucking head off. But now was not the moment. So, she stood there, trying her hardest to look nonchalant while inside, her heart broke for the pain Fredi must be enduring.

“What, no threats? I’m shocked, I tell you. Shocked.” Idia crossed her long legs, swung them back and forth, and grinned.

“Why would I need to threaten you? I’ve already told you I’m going to kill you, bitch—and then eat you.” Teddy immediately cursed herself for giving Idia the pleasure of a response. If only she could learn to shut her damn mouth.

Idia bared her canines. “I do so admire your optimism. Look around you. Even if you broke free, you’re vastly outnumbered.”

Upon the arrival of others, Idia ordered her right-hand guard, “Manacle them and then bring the old ones forward.”

“Yes, my queen,” replied the guard, a formidable woman in her own right. She and the others quickly bound the newcomers’ wrists and ankles.

They bound the Old-Gen in a strong vine that grew in the area. The women were immediately suspicious because they knew once they were no longer under the guards’ constraints, they could break free from the vines. At the New-Gen’s questioning looks, they could only shake their heads and shrug their shoulders. Perhaps Idia was that confident in the numbers on her side ensuring her victory should a battle occur. Meanwhile, they bound the New-Gen in chains, on whom the irony wasn’t lost.

“You’re just as bad as any slave catcher or slave master,” Naima snarled.

“Tell it to someone who cares,” Idia spat back.

Rising, she walked down the steps and beckoned for the guards to follow her. “Take them to the pit.”

“Well, that’s never a good place to be taken,” Lizzie quipped as they were pushed and pulled along by guards after Idia.

Meanwhile, Teddy quietly took in her surroundings, plotting their escape. She also opened her nostrils wide, frantically trying to scent Fredi.

Chapter 34

The women traversed many corridors and warrens before they finally emerged outside. Their destination was an enclosed garden with a pond in the middle of what looked like a crater in the ground. Tiki lights lent an eerie glow to the black water. Strangely, an assortment of warriors gathered around the perimeter in gleeful anticipation while others reluctantly shuffled over and stood as far away from the perimeter as possible. Now and then, the breaching body of something dark broke the pond's surface. Teddy knew it wasn't a tire. Her heart sank, and she realized it was probably an anaconda. Soon, the pond was undulating with multiple large ripples, indicating the presence of several giant anacondas.

Teddy made a mental note of all of this as her eyes constantly roved her surroundings. It was important to know who she was going to spare and who was deader than dead when she broke the chains encircling her. She was trying to be patient and let Idia make her move, but the suspense was killing her. *Idia better act soon,* she thought.

"Wow, Idia. No chit-chat? Last dinner? Catching up?" Lizzie couldn't keep the hatred from her eyes as she glared at Idia. "This seems so anti-climatic. We haven't even been here for an hour. What if we have questions for you?" Idia ignored Lizzie and the rest of the American Ravenisha.

Once everyone was assembled, Idia relished the moment, taking in the tableau around her. This was obviously the mountain's plateau, and you could see for miles in all directions in good light. With a start, the American Ravenisha realized the African Ravenisha had known of their presence the moment they arrived. It had been nothing for Idia to use mutants as sacrificial lambs, and they had been played all along. Idia had herded them to this location for a reason and they had played right into her hands. Several things began happening at once.

"Throw them in the pond," Idia commanded without preamble. There were gasps and cries of dismay from the Ravenisha who knew and liked Cheola, Zamandla, and Eklezabela before their ill-fated trip to America. However, before the rising outcry could gather full steam, the guards loyal to Idia shoved the Old-Gen over the crater's edge, where they rolled down the incline to the water's border.

When Idia gave her command, Teddy yelled "Now!" She practically willed them to free themselves and change before they hit the water.

The Old-Gen women strained to rip off the vines while they were rolling. The more they tore at the spiny vines, the deeper they dug into their skin. Finally, the vines broke as they morphed into their she-panthers. Before they could even take a breath in relief, the massive anacondas leaped out of the water with a speed that belied their size and had them locked in their jaws. The giant snakes quickly dove underwater, simultaneously coiling their thick muscled bodies around and around their prey. Now and then, a snake breached the roiling water, rolling, and the stricken New-Gen espied a glimpse of black fur. In the beginning, the water turned red, as the werepanthers' claws dug deep furrows into the snakes' skin and muscles. However, with every breath the she-panthers took, the giant boas squeezed a bit of life out of them. The she-panthers fought as hard as they could, but the boas had instinctively wrapped their bodies around the she-panthers' necks first.

Idia turned to the New-Gen and said with a smirk. "Poor babies. That can't be a pleasant way to go, can it? I scoured South American rain forests, swamps, and basins for years until I found these beautiful females. You know, female anacondas are bigger than males. Girl power, right? You're next, bitches," she taunted. "We can't die by our own hands but we can be killed and eaten."

Without warning, Teddy bent down and grabbed the knife out of her ankle sheath. Despite still being manacled, she took a running leap into the pond. Celeste and Naima followed suit. As they changed into their werecat forms, their great claws tore the manacles off.

Whirling around furiously, Idia rounded on her chief guard screaming, "How did they break those pure silver chains? Put down those guns, you fools. You'll hurt the snakes."

"My queen," the guard replied, trying to steer Idia away from the area, "the point is not how did they break those chains right now. That they could break them effortlessly and they're bigger than we are means we've got to get you out of here. Now! I can have the helicopter ready in minutes."

Idia pulled up, anger radiating off of her. "I will not run from those curs, Aasira," she hissed. "I am queen here. This is *my* kingdom."

"But my queen," Aasira began.

"I said I'm not running, and that's final. Assemble my warriors. I have a final ace to play." Idia whirled around and stalked off, robes billowing behind her.

Aasira watched her leave, hatred in her eyes before saying mockingly, "Yes, my queen bitch." With that, she turned and ran to the edge of the pond where the New-Gen was emerging, leading a visibly weak and hurt Old-Gen. Seeing Aasira, Teddy snarled, ready to attack, knife gripped in her hand.

"Hurry," Aasira whispered, helping the women up the steep bank.

"Aasira, my God, is that you?" Ceola wheezed, holding her ribs while great welts crisscrossed her skin where the anaconda's muscles had tightly coiled around her body.

"Yes, ma'am. I was Nahwi's great-granddaughter. Hurry, I'll show you where we keep our feeding supply so you can rejuvenate your bodies." Aasira then turned to Teddy. "Idia is assembling her warriors, and she will probably kill the young one. You must hurry."

Teddy suddenly grabbed Aasira's hand and looked up into her eyes. Aasira gasped for breath, and a chill seized her. Then, the moment was over as Teddy abruptly let her hand go.

That was uncomfortable, Aasira thought. *It felt like someone just stole my thoughts or walked over my grave.*

"Which way?" Teddy asked her. Not trusting her voice, Aasira pointed in the direction that would lead the New-Gen to Idia and beckoned for the Old-Gen to follow her.

As the girls made their way back to the throne room, it hit them how close to death their nanas had been. When a sob escaped from Celeste, they stopped jogging and embraced each other for a moment, each girl overwhelmed with the emotion of seeing the person who had raised her so close to death.

"I thought they were dead," Teddy bawled.

"Girl…" Tears poured from Naima's eyes, and she couldn't even speak.

When they finally composed themselves, Celeste said, "You get her ass, Teddy. We've got your back."

Naima added with a vehemence no one thought her capable, "And if she has hurt our little sister, you make her ass wish she had never been born."

"Roger that!" Teddy and her posse fist-bumped.

The girls continued following Idia's scent, and it led them straight to her.

They filed into the throne room and stood before Idia, arms crossed, silent. Idia noticed Teddy was staring at some point on the wall in front of her and it was really disconcerting with those mismatched eyes. She had expected the woman to fly at her in a rage. It was actually more intimidating that she hadn't lost her temper. Something told her she would need to kill this one quickly. Finally, Teddy stirred.

Teddy stared at Idia, her eyes dangerously still and focused. "What do you think is about to happen here, Idia?" Her eyes bored daggers into Idia's. "If I were you, now would be the time to pray." Teddy started slowly walking toward her. "If you think you can defeat me, you are sadly mistaken," Teddy growled, her eyes emanating an eerie blue light. "Why don't you scurry off of your pathetic-ass little throne and escape while you still can?" Teddy roared before changing into her beast and leaping into the air and colliding into Idia with a great crash.

While Idia hadn't been expecting such a bold and brazen attack, she quickly changed into her beast while flying off of her throne and smashing into Teddy.

All around Teddy and Idia, women started changing into were-panthers and claws came out and fur began flying. The Old-Gen ran in and joined the fray. They were immediately double-and triple-teamed as they tried to fight their way to that traitorous bitch, Idia. Aasira stood hidden in an alcove for a long moment outside the palace's walls. With a resolute nod of her head, she picked up her sword and joined the Old-Gen Ravenisha's flank.

Celeste and Naima had Teddy's back, their she-panthers almost as lethal as Teddy's, which was ferocious and powerful. Swift and economical. Teddy killed several of Idia's warriors while fighting Idia. Already, Idia's pantheress had sustained deep wounds, and Teddy was just toying with her. Idia soon realized she didn't stand a chance against Teddy's she-panther, and she fled the room, Teddy snapping at her heels. Matilda and Ceola saw them leave. They howled in frustration as they continued to be double-teamed by the African Ravenisha and mutants. Ceola and Matilda made a great team. It was apparent they had fought together for many years. Even though they were a bit rusty after not fighting and changing a lot over the years, they soon found their rhythm. Watching them feint, leap, twirl, and go in for the kill was like watching a couple dancing the tango. Bodies began piling up.

Once outside, Idia's beast whirled around, unsure where to run. She knew Teddy's beast would kill her, and rather than let that occur, she resolved to die on her own terms. There was only one option left, and she ran up to the very top of the mountain. Laboring and losing vast quantities of blood, Idia looked back and saw Teddy's beast calmly stalking her, for she knew she had her prey cornered. Once Idia's beast reached the top, with a cry of despair, she flung herself from the mountain to the rocks below. She landed with a sickening thud, her bones exploding on impact and brains seeping from her cracked skull onto the ground beneath her.

Teddy looked at Idia's carcass, puzzled. *Why did that heffa do that? Won't her body just regenerate itself?* Teddy shook off her thoughts and bounded down the mountain. Still in pantheress form, she dragged Idia's broken body back to the throne room by her massive teeth. Teddy changed to her werecat form and sat on Idia's throne with her legs and arms crossed, a look of ennui on her face. Word of what had occurred had spread, and the few warriors who were still fighting quit once they saw Teddy dragging their incapacitated queen.

Silence descended over the palace, and stunned shapeshifters began changing back to their human forms. The mutants had been slaughtered, and only Ravenisha survived. Silently, the shocked warriors came into the palace to watch what they all suspected was about to happen. An energy force seemed to settle over the room, and Idia's body began knitting itself back together, reanimating. The legend was true. Those with the blood of La Panthère Noire couldn't kill themselves. A rumble built.

Matilda started to say something to Teddy, but Ceola sadly shook her head and put her hand on Matilda's arm. "She has to learn on her own."

With a start, the newly healed and resurrected Idia opened her eyes and jumped up. She looked at Teddy incredulously. "You had your chance to eat me. You can rest assured, I will show you no such mercy." Idia hobbled away from the stunned onlookers. As she gathered her strength, she barreled past people and objects in her way.

Teddy cursed herself for her cockiness as she pursued Idia. What was she thinking? She should have just eaten Idia and destroyed her once and for all. She could see that the Old-Gen were furious as they, too, powered their way after Idia. She rued her intention of trying to let everyone have a bite of their nemesis.

As soon as Teddy smelled Fredi's scent, she knew what Idia would do before it happened. Desperately, she picked up speed, but Idia had too much of a head start. Teddy flew into the room, only to see an inert and half-dead Fredi in the grasp of Idia's massive jaws. Teddy circled Idia, hissing impotently. Idia bit deeper into the helpless girl's neck each time Teddy lunged toward her. Turning, Idia ran back into the room with her throne, Fredi still in her mouth, Teddy following.

The scene that greeted Idia wasn't encouraging. Many of her warriors lay dead, their hearts, livers, and brains consumed. The ones who weren't dead lay on their backs in positions of submission to the rejuvenated Old-Gen Ravenisha, the New-Gen and Obsidian Butterfly's she-panthers. In a rage, Idia slammed Fredi's body on the floor and bit down on the girl's chest cavity, crushing it in her massive jaws. The child gasped once and died. Before she could bite the girl's skull off or eat her brains and heart, the Old and New-Gen Ravenisha surrounded her. She just knew Teddy was going to kill her right then and there, but she didn't. Idia noticed everyone's focus was riveted on the tween, not her. She whirled around and bounded from the room. No one followed.

An eerie wailing began, raspy and deep-pitched, as if the being had the mother of all colds. The laments culminated in a tremendous howl that filled the palace, and deep in Idia's subconscious, she knew she had just signed her death warrant.

Chapter 35

Teddy was inconsolable. Tears poured down her face as she threw her head back and keened while Fredi lay still in her arms. Queen Idia couldn't believe her luck as she watched from behind a pillar. Even the Old-Gen warriors' attention was focused on the still form. Her own warriors weren't even looking for her. As the Ravenisha gathered around Fredi, Idia saw her chance to escape and quietly made her way out of her palace and into the jungle, chuckling at the impudent girl's continuous bad choices.

Obsidian Butterfly took Fredi's death just as hard as Teddy. She had raised the child in the lab from birth. While stroking the girl's face, her hand brushed across the blood-slicked chain around her torn neck. Mariposa frowned. Something was niggling at her. Something she remembered about the amulet's power. *What is it?* she thought. Tezcatlipoca wanted the amulet because its powers would have enabled him to have a human form. Idia wanted the amulet because of its healing powers. The amulet was also known for something else. If only Obsidian Butterfly could remember. *Think, think, think.* Suddenly, it came to her.

"Teddy, Teddy!" Mariposa screamed, grabbing a catatonic Teddy by the arm. Teddy snarled and wrapped her arm back protectively around Fredi. Mariposa shook her. "You can bring her back," she babbled. "You can bring Fredi back."

Slowly, a light of hope and awareness grew in Teddy's eyes. "Wait. What? I can bring her back? Please, God, I'll never let anything hurt her again. I promise. I'll do anything, Dr. Vasquez. Anything! Just tell me what to do."

There was a murmur as Teddy and the other Ravenisha gathered around Mariposa. She excitedly told them the items she needed and the warrior women ran off to gather them. Hearing booted footsteps coming up the path, Mariposa sighed in relief when she saw Felice among Lieutenant Allensworth and his men since she was sure she'd need a human sacrifice. As she explained the night's events to them, Matilda pried the girl's body from Teddy's arms. She walked outside and laid Fredi on the altar. To everyone's surprise, the surviving warriors followed them and formed a circle around the body.

Teddy narrowed her eyes as she looked around the group. No one else had given a thought as to Queen Idia's absence, but not Teddy. Sometimes, it paid to be anal. She beckoned Gus over and explained the danger Idia still posed. Gus promised he and his men would make sure Idia didn't get within an inch of them. They were on the watch.

There was a low mumble as the crowd parted and anticipation built. The Old-Gen Ravenisha walked to the altar and stood beside Teddy. They weren't alone. Aasira stood to one side of Cheola and Raven stood on the other side. Idia had kept Raven chained because she knew Raven deeply loved Cheola, but Aasira had freed the big cat and kept her nearby.

Obsidian Butterfly took a deep breath, closed her eyes, and began chanting in her old language. She paused and removed the turquoise-and jade-handled knife from the scabbard around her waist. She sliced her arm deep enough for blood to flow into the chalice brought to her. She resumed chanting and then sliced Teddy's arm. Obsidian Butterfly then walked over and motioned for Raven to step up and sit beside the tween's body. Nodding, she indicated that it was time to bring Felice over to the altar. Felice gave no signs she was aware of her impending death. She had lapsed back into a catatonic state, mourning her brother. Gus brought the non-resisting woman over and incapacitated her with a chokehold. He placed her limp body on the altar, and Obsidian Butterfly raised and brought the ceremonial knife down, slicing through skin, cartilage, ribs, and the pericardium with the efficiency of a butcher. She quickly removed the beating heart and placed it in Raven's mouth. She then poured the blood from the chalice into Raven's mouth. She looked at Teddy and said, "Okay, girl, you have to take it from here. Listen to the voice in your head. Call the spirit's name three times."

Jules watched all of this apprehensively from a little distance away. Just because he was a demonologist didn't mean he wanted to be in close proximity to them. A coldness spreading throughout his body warned him that a portal had been opened and something was about to make an appearance.

Teddy stepped forward and called La Panthère Noire's name three times. As Teddy's pupils dilated and began glowing, a blue aura emanated from them. As soon as the voice sounded in her head, Teddy recognized she was listening to the being that spoke to her the first time she changed. Teddy knew, with a sinking heart, she had to follow this being's orders, for she would do anything to bring Fredi back to life. She just hoped the consequences wouldn't be too great. She listened to the voice and followed its directions. She removed her necklace and plunged the miniature dagger into her palm. She then plunged the dagger into Fredi's ravaged heart and repeated the words the entity and Raven instructed her to say. Teddy made sure blood from her wound dripped onto Fredi's heart. Raven rested her massive head on Fredi's leg. Teddy then tilted Fredi's head back and let some of her blood run into Fredi's mouth. Fredi's heart lay still in her destroyed chest. Teddy gazed down at her dead sister and stroked her cheek. Teddy then tilted Fredi's head back, opened her jaws, and gave her the sacred breath of life.

Teddy felt the energy transfer when it happened. It was as if a bolt of lightning had struck her and everything she touched. She screamed into the star-studded sky, her hands grabbing Raven's fur as her body arched and her eyes shot that weird laser light into Fredi's chest. Simultaneously, Fredi's inert body arched above the altar and began trembling. Her wounded chest and neck began knitting together, and she began gasped for breath. During this auspicious moment, the warriors' ululations reached a deafening volume.

As Fredi's pale-blue eyes fluttered open, Teddy breathed a sigh of relief and hugged the girl tightly. Stroking the tween's unruly curls from her face, she cried, "I've never been so happy to see those ice-blue eyes. I thought I had lost you forever, my brave little sister."

Fredi weakly squealed as a humongous black head filled her vision and a long red tongue gently swiped her face.

"Raven, get down," Ceola laughed. "Give the poor child some breathing room."

Fredi looked around her, dazed, her arms around Raven's neck. Raven had her head bowed, but her eyes, which looked glazed, pierced Teddy's.

"See what a brilliant team we are, Theodora? Continue to follow my orders and the world will be ours," purred the foreign voice.

"Did you hear that?" Teddy mouthed to Fredi. The girl nodded her head, frightened. They didn't have time to discuss this, though, for all around them, the Ravenisha had linked arms and were singing. They all understood the significance of what had occurred. This little girl, who had been born in a lab, had been reborn from the spirits of Theodora, Raven, and La Panthère Noire, and was now one of them—a Ravenisha.

"I tried to be brave like you when Idia was hitting me. I told her you were going to kill her ass. You saved me, Big Sister, just like I knew you would. I've always had faith in you. I love you, Theodora Lulu. I will always love you and be your greatest cheerleader."

"And I promise from this day forward, I will always love, cherish and protect you even if you can be a pain in the ass sometimes Fredericka Zola. You know, you now have six mamas, don't you? I'm not perfect, and you absolutely have my permission to call me out when I'm being a bitch to you. K? I told Idia I was going to kill her ass, too, for hurting my baby sister, and you best believe I am." Teddy growled as the girls fist-bumped and hugged.

"I'll never let anything hurt you again," Teddy told the tween in a voice that came from so deep within her soul, the air darkened and prickled as that dis-quietening light emanating from her mismatched eyes slowly dimmed. "I love you so much."

"And I love both of you girls," Raven said, purring, her eyes back to plain emerald-green panther eyes. The girls looked at each other, for they knew this was now Raven speaking and not the evil one. What on earth was going on?

Surveying the surrounding scene, Teddy decided to ignore Raven until she could get further guidance on what to do about the spirit that seemed to have made itself at home in her and Fredi's bodies. Something was off, though. When she looked into Raven's eyes now, she saw nothing but kindness and compassion. Was it possible that Raven was possessed, too?

Teddy turned to hug and thank Obsidian Butterfly again for thinking of the amulet to save Fredi. Tears coursed down Obsidian Butterfly's cheeks, mixing with the soot she had spread across her face. She tried to smile through her sadness.

"Don't worry, we need to clean up Idia's mess, but then, we'll make sure we find Cochise. You can count on us," Teddy said as she hugged Obsidian Butterfly.

"We'll get him back. You have my word," Matilda said.

"And mine," added Ceola.

"And mine," added Elizabeth.

"Don't forget me," chimed Fredi.

Obsidian Butterfly smiled a genuine smile for the first time in days. "Thank you, guys. I am so lucky to have your love and support." She wiped her eyes with her hand, further smearing black sludge all over her face.

Teddy turned back to Fredi. "We're all going to have to do and be better going forward, LittleSis. We definitely can't go back to our old lives after tonight. I'm thinking we can work something out where the Ravenisha can benefit society and still take care of our needs. Are you in?"

"You know it!" Fredi squealed, giving Teddy an enormous hug.

"Good, because, girl, that hair. You know we're going to have to look fly if we're representing the Ravenisha to the world. Whew, I've been dying to comb and braid this hair. And I'm not the only one, either. Leona can't wait to get her fingers in this bird's nest."

"You'll have to catch me first," Fredi laughed, morphing into her she-panther and running away.

"No problem, home skillet." Teddy changed into her she-panther and ran after Fredi, along with Raven. Celeste and Naima, who had watched the scene unfold with tears in their eyes, morphed into their she-panthers and joined the chase. They didn't go far, however. After briefly cavorting, Teddy brought the pride back to the altar. Fredi looked at her in confusion. She wanted to play some more.

"I have some unfinished business."

Ceola nodded to show she understood what Teddy meant.

Teddy turned to Fredi and took her in her arms. "I'm going after Idia. She's a dead woman walking. I want you to promise me you'll stay here. I mean it, Fredi. I can't go after Idia if I'm worried about you tailing me. Understand?"

"I understand, Teddy. I want you to get her ass! Just save a chunk for me, okay?"

"Sorry, home skillet. I'm not taking any chances this time. I'm going to devour her ass from the jump" Teddy turned and nodded to the others. She shifted and set off after Idia.

"Teddy, wait!" Matilda screamed. "Where are your weapons? Why did you shift? Don't you know you have to conserve your energy? You really need to let us accompany you. We all have a beef with that bitch."

"No, I got this," Teddy called over her shoulder and she jogged off into the canopy. At least she heeded Matilda's advice and shifted back to human form.

Jules blew out a breath of air when he felt the dark spirit leave. He hadn't come across the name La Panthère Noire during his studies, but he had sensed her evilness. Did these women not realize the danger they were unleashing? They were creating a breach between the demon and human worlds with impunity and had apparently been doing it for a while.

Matilda couldn't keep the concern from her face as she watched Teddy depart. Fredi watched the exchange silently, her arms crossed, lips pursed.

"She isn't ready, Ceola. She's already made two bad decisions. I'm also afraid she's used up too much energy already tonight. Idia is going to kill her," Matilda fretted.

"I know," Ceola cried, "and there isn't a damn thing we can do about it."

Elizabeth put her fist to her mouth to keep from crying out. Celeste and Naima exchanged looks and worry etched their features, as well.

Chapter 36

Teddy resolutely tracked Idia's path into the jungle: she had to redeem herself. She noted that Idia hadn't gone far before she sharply veered left and began climbing. Despite Teddy knowing she would have to be on the alert because Idia now had the advantage of the cliff's height over her—plus, she was familiar with the terrain—Teddy approached the cliff's edge throwing caution to the wind. However, a sense of déjà vu and wariness slowed her down as she continued tracking Idia's scent. A ledge came into view, and as much as she wanted to rush to leap on the ledge, Auntie Matilda's maxim of never rushing to jump up on something without having a sense of what awaited you made her hesitate. Trees grew plentiful here, and their branches swayed in the wind. Was Idia hiding on the ledge, waiting to ambush her?

As Teddy continued looking up, trying to decide whether to jump, she realized her mistake as a rush of air from below hit her as Idia leaped up and attacked. Idia's claws dug deeply into Teddy's shoulder. Teddy felt drops of saliva, then Idia's fetid breath engulfed her. It was because Teddy's reflexes were so quick she was able to move her neck away from Idia's bared canines. Idia's fangs sank into the meaty skin of Teddy's shoulder as easily as a pair of daggers being plunged into a ripe peach. The pain didn't start until Idia's jaws locked shut and she began shaking her head and flinging Teddy from side to side like she was a Raggedy Ann doll. Idia, who had flown at Teddy from one of the tree branches *below* her, now pulled her down through the jungle's canopy.

Teddy bellowed like an enraged bull, and snarling, the two werepanthers scratched and clawed as they tumbled and crashed through the trees. Teddy freed herself from Idia's clutches at a great price as a sizable flap of skin and muscles were torn. The werepanthers landed and circled each other warily. Blood streamed from Teddy's shoulder wound.

Idia had thought to grab a weapon on her way out of the palace and she had placed it on the ground before she leaped upon Teddy. Idia brandished her spear at Teddy now, advancing and retreating. Teddy desperately looked around for a weapon, but she didn't even see a fallen tree branch. Idia suddenly lunged. Teddy quickly deflected the spear from its targeted femoral artery, but Idia was still able to slice open a gash in her thigh. Idia twirled around and attempted to stab Teddy again, but this time, Teddy was ready for her. She grabbed the spear's shaft, reached down, and removed her knife from its sheath. In one fluid motion, she thrust the knife up! Damnit! Her knife thrust was blocked by Idia, who grabbed her wrist. Locked in battle like sumo wrestlers, the werecats were literally hand-tied.

With a great scream, Teddy wrested her wrist from Idia's grasp, and with both of her hands on Idia's hand holding the spear, she flipped the queen werecat over onto her back. She tried to rip the spear from Idia's hand, but Idia held firm. Teddy grabbed her knife and quickly jumped up. Idia jerked into a standing position in one fluid motion. The warriors faced each other. Teddy did the only thing she knew. She threw her knife, aiming for Idia's heart just as Idia threw her spear. Both women tried to twist their bodies out of the way at the last minute.

Teddy and Idia looked down at their chests, shock spreading across their faces. Teddy grasped the spear,'s shaft. The tip was embedded in her chest. She gave a mighty yank and pulled. Idia yanked and pulled, but she couldn't remove the knife from her sternum. It was as if the knife refused to come out. *What type of fuckery is this,* she thought? She noticed Teddy was breathing heavily and not moving and saw her chance.

Teddy knew she had to move, but it hurt so much to breathe. She felt so heavy, like someone was stabbing her in the chest every time she took a breath. *What happened to my energy?* she sluggishly wondered as blood spurted from the wound.

~ ~ ~

Back at the palace, the Old-Gen continued to fret over Teddy's chances of winning a battle against Idia. They were deciding if they were going to break the cardinal rule of not interfering in battles for power when Matilda stopped talking and looked around the room.

"Y'all, where is that little girl?" The women stopped talking and frantically searched the area. Fredi's blonde curls were nowhere to be seen.

"Damn her little hide!" Matilda fumed as she began gathering weapons and leaving the palace. The others followed suit and they set off on the trail.

~ ~ ~

The Old-Gen morphed into werecat mode to quickly get to the scene, and along with Raven, they found Teddy and Idia locked in battle. They stayed back once they saw Teddy was holding her own. Maybe the girl had learned something after all. Matilda immediately found Fredi hiding behind a tree and yanked her out with such force, the tween was actually afraid for a nano-second.

Around them, a crowd silently gathered. To the surprise of many, the current leader of Benin was there with a small platoon. Gus and his men had encountered the leader and learned he was the descendant of the king Idia killed centuries ago. He had a score to settle and had thought he would sneak up on the unsuspecting queen and take her out. Unfortunately, Gus told him he had to take a number and get in line. Gus made it very clear that if he or any of his men accidentally hit Teddy, they were dead. Thus, the leader watched impotently from the sidelines with the others as the two warriors battled it out. Already, he was making plans to use the Ravenisha. They would be put to work for their nation, and their nation only.

Idia shifted into her full beast pantheress, going for the kill. Teddy, anticipating this, transformed into her pantheress, drawing on pure adrenaline, and aggressive as ever, flew at Idia, massive canines bared. The two she-panthers collided, claws and teeth slicing through whatever flesh they could reach. Idia flung Teddy down and was on her in a flash, burying her gigantic head into the side of Teddy's neck, missing major vessels by mere centimeters. Teddy howled and scraped her claws across Idia's face, hooking an eyeball with one claw and tearing it free. Idia reared back in pain. Teddy seized the opening and kicked Idia off of her.

Teddy used her massive size to dominate Idia. She clawed Idia's skin to ribbons and tore out chunks of flesh. It was difficult to do great damage, as Idia was also big, nimble, and versed in martial arts. Teddy expended a lot of energy being the aggressor and inflicting many non-fatal wounds. Teddy and Idia circled each other, haunches and necks low to the ground. Idia rushed Teddy, and they crashed into a tree, breaking off branches along the way. *Now, there are branches I could have used as weapons*, Teddy thought.

Once again, Idia buried her head in the wound she had previously made. She shook her head back and forth, massive teeth gnashing, destroying muscles and vessels in Teddy's left shoulder. Blood gushed, and Teddy screamed in pain. Idia, sensing she had the upper hand, began slicing into Teddy's chest, drawing more blood and gore. Teddy could only go on the defensive, and it was apparent she was getting weaker and weaker.

Fredi watched her sister being ravaged by the woman who had killed her, and she wailed. Beside her, Raven paced back and force, hissing.

"No, Teddy! Get up. Fight! Fight! Please," Fredi cried, seeking solace and burying her head in Matilda's arms.

Teddy felt her lifeforce leaving as her vision dimmed. Inhaling was hell: she felt like she was drowning. How had this happened? She had beaten Idia so easily the first time. The advantage should have been hers, she thought. She was bigger, stronger, younger. There was a lesson in here somewhere, but she was just too tired to think about it at the moment, and she couldn't breathe. She needed to lie down and rest a little bit.

A white streak passed before her fading eyes and jumped onto Idia's back. Goddamnit, she told that girl to stay at the palace. Now here she was, trying to save her. She just vowed she would never let anything hurt Fredi ever again. What was she thinking? Fredi was even smaller than she was, Teddy cried to herself and stole a look at Tildy. The warrior's eyes were blazing daggers into her. Her arms were crossed tightly across her chest, her mouth in a grim line. Teddy had seen this look many times. It was the *I'm so disappointed in you, Theodora look.* Teddy gathered her wheezing breath. Her front was streaked with blood.

Idia whirled around, Fredi still clinging to her, her claws slashing and her canines tearing out great chunks of Idia's flesh. Teddy rolled onto her side, panting. She tried to stand, but fell back against the rock, still unable to get up. She willed herself to heal. To get a burst of energy. An infusion of strength. Teddy watched helplessly as Idia did a backflip. She was now on top of Fredi, her canines poised to rip Fredi's neck out once and for all. Then, she would bite into her sister's skull, eat her brains, and then her heart.

Nooo! Teddy screamed to herself. *Get up! Get up! Somebody, please help me.*

Idia felt certain the others would intervene at that point, breaking the tradition of not interfering with battles of power struggles.

However, Idia, Warrior Queen, had decided to go out in a blaze of glory, and she would at least take this little mutt with her. She opened her mouth wide and went in for the killing bite.

Chapter 37

Massive jaws tore into Idia's side like a freight train. The force blew her off of Fredi and into the rocky mountainside. A loud thunk split the air as her body made impact with the rock. Her ears were ringing. *That wasn't so bad,* she thought, as she slammed into the rock's face so savagely, she dented the cliff's face and chips of rock rained down on her. Teddy's serrated shark-like teeth, in conjunction with her massive canines, made quick work of Idia's side. Idia turned her pantheress head weakly and noticed her whole left shoulder and side were gone. There was just nothing there. No left side at all, save for some intestines dangling and jagged ends of bone protruding. Everyone could see her heart beating unsteadily through exposed broken ribs. The pain was unbearable and all-consuming when it came.

She tried to say to this impudent girl, "I am Idia, Warrior Queen," but all that came from her mouth were mewls and blood. She watched in disbelief as her arm and other body parts disappeared into Teddy's mouth. And damned if that little mutt wasn't jostling Teddy for a piece of her. Watching beings devour parts of her body while she was alive was surreal. Idia was so shocked, she involuntarily morphed back to her human form. She could do nothing when Teddy, who morphed back into her werecat form, stood over her triumphantly, her obsidian knife in her right hand and murder in her eyes. Idia's blood dripped from Teddy's massive canines, and her left arm hung uselessly at her side.

Idia noted with satisfaction that Teddy hadn't been able to completely heal the wounds she had earlier inflicted. However, she couldn't celebrate because she knew that while blood still ran from Teddy's neck and shoulder, the wounds would heal with one feeding. And oh, the irony. Her newly tumor-free flesh had already helped Teddy heal. How the girl had managed to heal herself enough to change into her pantheress was a mystery.

Teddy lunged toward Idia with a growl. She had stupidly allowed the woman to live twice and wasn't about to make that mistake again. It was time to finish this.

"If you think I will beg you for my life, you're sadly mistaken," Idia somehow rasped defiantly, staring up at Teddy, who was now being held back by her bitch friends. As Idia forced herself to look into those cold mismatched eyes emitting that eerie light, she suddenly understood that no amount of begging would have saved her life, anyway.

Teddy morphed into her human form and turned to her family. "It's okay. I'm not going to gobble her down in one fell swoop. We'll all eat her." She reached down, grabbed Idia's remaining arm with her good arm, and pulled Idia roughly along. Teddy stopped, made sure Fredi was okay, and beckoned for the tween to walk with her.

The battle had been gory, long, and hard-fought, but nothing had prepared the defeated warriors for the sight of Teddy dragging their beloved Queen Idia, bleeding and missing an arm, practically a side of her body, along the ground as if she weighed nothing and was nothing. As Teddy strode among the fighters like the true warrior queen she was, the women parted, too shocked to do anything but gape. Teddy stopped before the prime minister and briefly nodded. He returned her nod and smiled.

Idia could barely take in the people around her, especially with only one eye. She suddenly drew a sharp breath. "You! What are you doing here?" she hissed.

"Getting my revenge like everybody else," Jules gloated.

Idia tried to remove herself from Teddy's grasp and lunge at Jules, but she weakly fell back on the ground as Jules cackled. Teddy dragged Idia through her palace and ascended the altar's steps. She roughly threw Idia at the feet of her nana, Ceola. Idia tried to rise, but Teddy placed her foot on the woman's neck, keeping her down.

"Theodora, don't be disrespectful," Ceola chided. The rage emanating off of her betrayed her seemingly kindness. "Let her up."

"Cheola, how could you stab me in the back like this?" Idia cried, staggering pitifully to her feet, seeing her last chance to live. "I thought we were friends. I—"

"Quiet!!!" Ceola roared as she backhanded Idia. "You caused all of this. You and your vanity. Your greed. Your jealousy. Besides, I can stab you in the back like this the same way you repeatedly stabbed your supposed best friends in the back."

"I'm not the cause of these abominations you call New-Gen Ravenisha," Idia screamed before Teddy punched her so hard, the stone split when she fell.

"Hit me all you want, bitch," Idia weakly laughed, choking on the blood filling her mouth. "You'll *never* be a Ravenisha." Idia cowered as Teddy bared her sharp, blood-stained canines, growling. Her remaining eye sat precariously in its torn eye socket.

"Refer to my granddaughters again as abominations, Idia, and I'll kill your ass myself. As I was saying, this is all your fault. Inviting the beast into us. We didn't mind that. We were willing participants. But you lied to us, Idia. You flat out lied about the vision you saw. I hope the king's dick and the jewels he gave you were worth the loss of our friendship. It was his idea to send us to America as slaves, wasn't it? And you were too dumb to realize he was breaking up the power base we had, all because of the threat we were to him and others. You're so low-down you even betrayed and killed the king, didn't you? You betrayed us. Sold us into bondage. Scarred us mentally and physically." Ceola began slowly clapping. "You missed your calling. You would have been a great actress. You had me totally fooled. Well, the joke's on you now, isn't it? Not only did we survive, we thrived, and we've made the Ravenisha even stronger, and our "mutt" granddaughters have powers you could only dream of, heffa. I may not be the tallest, or the most charismatic or the most beautiful, but I was always the smartest one." Ceola sneered. "Oh, and the irony of the king's descendent being here to witness your downfall."

Idia gazed at Cheola, Zamandla, and Eklezabela, her nose and lips curled.

"You can look at us with disdain all you want," Matilda told Idia with joy, "but there's no cavalry coming to your rescue. The police have arrested the one person on your team in the Benin government. Your reign has ended, Boo Boo. And you remember Nahwi, don't you? The old woman you cast from the tribe?"

"Nahwi was my great-grandmother." Aasira growled and punched Idia.

"Now, how is that for justice?" Matilda cackled.

Idia still said nothing, staring off into the distance, eyes fading, body swaying. Elizabeth walked over and looked into her dying eyes. She helped Idia sit on the stone steps before she fell over.

Ceola removed her top. Matilda and Elizabeth followed suit and turned around so Idia could witness the brutality inflicted upon them with her own eyes.

"Look at what they did to us, Idia. We endured it because of the prophecy. We trusted you," Matilda snarled.

Idia recoiled and hung her head. Then, she lifted her head defiantly and glared at the women.

"Why did you betray us, Idia? Did you ever love us the way we loved you? At least answer that question," Elizabeth cajoled.

After a pause, Idia began crying. "You were all my best friends, truly, up until that day I found Raven and had that awful vision. That old woman, Nahwi was right; I did lie to you about what I saw. Everything was foretold. Even this ending. If you three had stayed in Africa, I would have been deposed—cast off like trash. The Africa Ravenisha would have had no queen; there would have been a council of elders, instead. If I wanted to remain queen, I *had* to sell you to America. The consequences would be great, though. A new generation of Ravenisha would be even more powerful, and one day destroy me. I chose to remain queen and do everything I could to ensure there would be no new generation of Ravenisha who could shapeshift without magic and be more powerful than me. It would have worked, too, if that stupid Rufus hadn't inadvertently ruined my plans by making more Ravenisha and then hiding them from me. What would you have done in my place?" she cried.

"I wouldn't have broken up our sisterhood, Idia," Ceola said, while the others agreed.

"Oh, you were always so noble," Idia sneered. "Bitches! Raven is not who you think. They have betrayed us all. I and I alone know how to fight Raven and La Panthère Noire. You need me alive. You need me as your queen. Save me." Raven hissed, and Idia visibly cowered. The light dulled even more in her eyes, and she quieted.

Turning, Ceola addressed the tired women gathered around them in the old language. "After tonight, you will have no dictatorial queen. Only a symbolic one." Ceola gave Teddy a meaningful look.

"Sistahs, we don't need anybody ruling over us, for we are all queens in our own right. I propose we have a council, instead, of wise or elder ones as prophesied. You need not fear the granddaughters. Welcome them into the fold. Teach them. They will probably spend their time in the outside world, anyway. You know how the young are these days. Let this be their place of refuge when they want to recharge their batteries. Their home base, so to speak. Are we in agreement?"

Every single woman replied, "Yes" in the old language.

"Anyone opposes?" Seeing that no one was in opposition, Ceola nodded her head. "Good. Let us now rest, mourn, bury the dead, and celebrate new beginnings in the morning. There are many things we must update you on. There are weapons now that can hurt even us, as powerful as we are. Some of you have already seen the effects on the mutants."

Theodora strode forward, her body having healed even more. "I need everyone to change for the ritual feeding. Quickly, quickly now." As understanding dawned on everyone's faces, Idia began snarling, spittle flying everywhere.

"How dare you? Raven, save me! You fools! Can't you see that Theodora and Fredi aren't even like you? They're abominations and no matter what Cheola just said, Theodora will be your queen." When she saw Teddy wasn't playing and was changing, she pitifully staggered lopsidedly down the steps, using the last of her energy to change along the way. Teddy let her get about a hundred yards away before she took off in pursuit, her beautifully muscled body eating up the yards as if they were inches. When she leaped and dug her claws into Idia's back, the other she-panthers raced toward them. With a mighty roar, Teddy bit through Idia's skull, killing the great warrior queen once and for all. As Idia's brains streamed out of her skull, Teddy waited until the elders had eaten their share before she and Fredi ate part of the brains and then devoured the heart. As the rest of the she-panthers converged on Idia's body, the sounds of growling, ripping flesh, and crunching bones permeated the still night.

The prime minister recoiled in horror, quickly ran off, and threw up in some brush. He motioned for his guards to follow him, and they quickly fled down the mountain.

As the sun rose the next day, there was no sign that Idia had ever existed. Through all of this, Raven and La Panthère Noire were silent.

Chapter 38

Sentinels assigned guard duty awakened the tribe the next morning before dawn. They delivered alarming news.

"What now?" groaned a tired and aching Teddy.

"An army of about two hundred men is an hour away," reported a warrior. "They look like mercenaries."

"What?" Gus cried in disbelief. Roland got on his radio. After a moment, he came back with a puzzled look on his face.

"No one knows anything about them—or rather, no one is claiming to know anything about them," he amended.

Matilda beamed. "Come, Aasira, let's inspect the weapons."

"We have an armory," Aasira proudly said. "It's my job to make sure we're up to date on the latest weaponry and armed warfare. If necessary, we can take down a nation. I have always admired you, General Zamandla," she added, smiling shyly.

"Wait a sec, Auntie, Aasira, Lieutenant. I think we need to engage in guerilla warfare. These women know these mountains and jungles better than the mercenaries. What do you think?"

"I agree," Gus replied, while also listening to his radio. "Akiro just flew a drone over them. He said we should be able to take them out with the Ravenisha's help." He and Aasira high-fived each other. Gus gathered his men and yelled, "Okay, suit up and lock and load. Meet back here in ten."

Digging through the duffles, the Old-Gen and New-Gen found clothes and weapons and met back in the clearing, where they discovered Gus giving Fredi a quick tutorial on how to fire a semi-automatic. Ceola winced as she walked up to them.

"I know, I know. Not only does she have to learn how to defend herself but go on the offensive." He handed the gun to Fredi. "Okay, repeat what I just showed you."

Fredi removed the magazine, put it back in, clicked the safety off, sighted an imaginary target, aimed, simulated pulling the trigger, and pointed the gun down at the ground, her finger still on the trigger guard.

"Good." Gus nodded approvingly. "I should have known you'd be a natural." Fredi beamed.

"Oh, Lord!" Celeste exclaimed. People's eyes widened as the warriors returned dressed for battle. The old Ravenisha were carrying modern weapons, but their outfits hadn't been updated since the 1800s.

"Wow." Teddy unsuccessfully tried to contain her laughter.

"Those outfits belong in a museum," Celeste added while trying to suppress her own laughter.

Teddy and Matilda gave Fredi a look of don't you dare laugh.

The women were wearing skirts made of traditional African cloth that stopped below their knees with bodices beaded from cowrie shells. It was noted with relief that at least they were wearing tennis shoes or hiking boots.

"We really like those outfits they wore in *Black Panther*," one warrior said, "but that damn Idia was too cheap to have something similar made for us. She had no problem decking herself out in all sorts of finery, though."

"Once this is over, we'll have something like those outfits made as our new uniforms if everyone agrees." Lizzie shook her head and tried to keep quell the smile threatening to grace her face. "How is the cloth even still holding together on those old things? Talk about a blast from the past."

Ceola frowned, her forehead scrunched up. "I wonder what happened to our uniforms. I was so nervous the night before we were to leave for America, I didn't even think about mundane things like storing my personal belongings."

Teddy, Celeste, Fredi, and Naima were still trying to contain their laughter.

"Now, now. That's enough about their uniforms." Naima noted that some women were getting angry. "The beadwork is beautiful," she said with a smile, talking out of the corners of her mouth. "Y'all better hush talking about their outfits before they turn on our butts."

The women finally settled down and focused on the enemy at hand. After looking through binoculars, Aasira went over to the old warriors and began dispensing instructions. Once done, she ran back over to Gus and the American Ravenisha. "I know this land and these warriors' strengths and weaknesses. I have assigned them spots that will afford them the greatest advantage. I trust you will do the same with your men?"

Gus nodded.

"We will fight wherever you need us," Ceola assured Aasira. They turned their heads as they saw Raven walking toward them.

"Where do you think you're going, ma'am?" Teddy asked, looking into Raven's jewel green eyes once she reached her.

Raven lifted a humongous paw, and Teddy held it in her hand. Looking into Raven's eyes, Teddy opened her mind, and she and Raven communicated with each other. This was something new she'd learned the other night. When they were done, Teddy turned to the group and recounted what she had been told.

"These are men Idia was brokering a deal with. Once they heard we had raided the lab, and that Idia had fled, they began heading here."

A shot far off in the distance interrupted Teddy.

"Here we go!" someone yelled.

"They desperately want to capture a Ravenisha to be their lab rat."

Aasira digested what she had just heard. "I will let the warriors know to avoid capture, by any means necessary. I assume these strangers are unaware we cannot kill ourselves, so if necessary, we can always commit 'suicide' to avoid capture."

Teddy turned to Raven and ordered, "You, my friend, need to skedaddle. We'll be okay." Grinning, she held up a chunk of explosives. "This will take out most of them right here." Raven head butted her. "Oh, all right." Teddy removed the detonator from the pack and then held out the explosives so Raven could pick up the strap with her teeth. "Get in front of the biggest column and place them where they can't be seen. And don't let those guys see you. I just have to be in the proximity so I can see when they come up on the explosives to detonate them. K, let's roll."

Teddy, Raven, and of course, Fredi took off at a jog. Gus, Henry, and some Ravenisha warriors followed them. Sure enough, they discovered the mercenaries had split up so that a few had gone ahead, while the primary group stayed in the middle and a group trailed behind. Raven quickly scaled the rocks and hid the explosives. She stopped for a last hug and pats of "good girl" from Teddy and Fredi before she disappeared into the mountainous jungle.

"We're going to save her," Teddy told Fredi as they watched Raven vanish.

"Why do we have to be so far away?" Fredi whined after they had taken their lookout positions. "I can't see the action without binoculars."

"Really, Fredi?" Gus asked, exasperated. "When we get back stateside, we're going to have some nice long talks, read some books and watch some movies about war. This isn't a video game. People will lose their lives today."

"Whatevs." Fredi sucked her teeth.

"Steady, steady, Quick Draw McGraw," Gus cautioned Teddy as her finger hovered over the button. The men were drawing close but not close enough for the explosives to inflict maximum damage. As about half of them walked past the explosives, Gus said, "Now," and Teddy pressed the button.

Gus kept them back until after the dissipation of the blast wave, shock waves, heat, and the blast wind had all passed. A subdued Fredi uttered, "Oh," afterward as she wiped off some gore that the force of the explosion had splattered on her with. She was learning it was one thing to consume a human body in a metahuman form, but it was quite something else to have human body parts smacking you in the face and inundating your body when you were a fellow human. Teddy and Gus looked at each other and smiled. When Gus asked if anyone wanted to inspect the blast site, Fredi quickly replied, "Naw, I'm good." Teddy debated whether she should make her witness the horrors of war up close and personal, but thought it might be a bit much for the twelve-year-old to "digest."

“Gus, are you there?” Henry’s voice urgently called over the radio.

“I read you loud and clear, Henry.”

“It’s Roland. He’s badly hurt, Gus. In fact, he’s…” Henry began crying.

Chapter 39

On my way. Over and out. Roland's hurt bad," Gus called over his shoulder as he sprinted away.

The Ravenisha warrior closest to them said, "Go. We've got the last group covered." Pointing to her headset, she added, "Sounds like help is on the way. You go. We've got this."

Something nudged Gus from behind. Turning, he exhaled with relief as he noted it was Teddy and Fredi in their she-panther forms. He smiled when he saw they had even thought to put their backpacks around their necks this time. Teddy was gesturing for him to do something.

"I don't understand." Gus held out his hands and shrugged his shoulders. He was so preoccupied with worry over Roland's fate, it was difficult to concentrate. Fredi jumped onto Teddy's back, then jumped off. Understanding dawned on Gus's face. "I don't know about this. You've got to be kidding me. It would be faster, though…"

Teddy stretched out on all fours and Gus gingerly climbed onto the she-panther's back. As Teddy got to her feet, Gus almost slid off. "So, this is where I'm going to wish I had learned to ride bareback. Damn, at least horses have manes," he griped while trying to grab ahold of Teddy's white streak.

As Teddy picked up speed, the only thing Gus could do was wrap his long legs around her body and his arms around her neck, and hanging on for dear life—especially when she and Fredi began scaling the mountain's face. The she-panthers ascended the mountain, leaping agilely from boulder to boulder without a care as to the drops beneath them. Gus closed his eyes, prayed, and held on. He eventually got used to the crouching motion Teddy made before she leaped onto a rock or ledge: relaxing and letting his body go with her motion. Before he knew it, the she-panthers stopped.

Dread and trepidation filled Gus's heart. He slowly opened his eyes and slid down Teddy's she-panther's body so he was facing her fur. Gus knew from the surrounding silence, save for Henry's sobs, the news was bad. He inhaled, exhaled, and relaxed his shoulders. Then, he slowly turned around and made a sound like all of the air had been knocked out of him. Gus dropped into a crouch and cradled his head in his hands. "No, no, no. Not Roland. Please God, not Roland."

Roland lay on his back, eyes and mouth closed. He could have been asleep or in a coffin. His face was unmarked, not a drop of blood to be found. Below the neck was a different story. Roland's chest and abdomen were bathed in blood. He could have been shot in the legs, or the blood could have been from his chest and abdomen.

Gus fell to his knees and cradled Roland's head in his arms, sobbing. "Take me instead, God. Why would you let a piece of shit like me live and kill Roland?" He felt arms envelop him, and when he looked up, he saw it was Teddy.

"T-Teddy," he cried, barely able to get her name out. "Y-you have to save him. You have to. You don't understand. This man deserves to live much more than I ever will. Please help him."

"Shh," Teddy whispered, gently stroking Gus's face. She nodded at Gus and Henry. "Help me take Roland to the altar. I don't know if my power works on men, but let's find out, shall we?"

Once again, they found themselves at the altar. Teddy called Raven, and she came, although the role they expected her to play in this resurrection was unknown. Teddy quietened her mind and called her beast. She breathed a sigh of relief when she realized her beast was coming to her and not that sinister-sounding spirit that filled her with dread. When she reached for the knife on her necklace, her beast stopped her.

"No, use the knife at your ankle. And Teddy," her beast cautioned, "you can't save everyone. For some people, it's just their time."

Teddy indicated her understanding and slashed her arm as instructed. She slashed Raven's leg and mixed the blood from the two wounds. Then, she poured some into the chalice that was still there from the last resurrection. As the blood flowed, she quickly plunged her knife into Roland's still heart and tilted his head back. She opened his mouth and poured blood from the chalice down his throat. She held her arm out for Raven to lick closed the wound. Then, she fit her lips over Roland's and gave him the sacred breath of life. She envisioned a vein of her lifeforce flowing into Roland's heart, filling it and spreading throughout his body via his blood. A great rhythmic sound thundered through her and Roland's body arched off of the altar as if a bolt of lightning was coursing through it. His eyes flew open, and he gulped in deep draughts of air. His eyes roved wildly until they found and stopped on Gus, and he held out his hand.

Gus, crying tears of joy, ran over and embraced Teddy and Roland together, almost pulling Roland off of the altar. Roland slowly sat up and just stayed still for a moment. His body trembled, and he focused on steadying his breathing.

"Thank you, Teddy. You truly have been blessed with a wonderful gift. I…I…don't laugh. I saw the Other Side. People are right. There is no need to fear death."

He turned to Gus and shook his head. "Brutha," he lamented, "when are you going to stop blaming yourself for what happened when we were kids?"

Gus shook his head, refusing to meet Roland's eyes.

"Ain't nobody here would blame you for what you did, Augustus. Forgive yourself, man. I'm grateful to you."

"Me, too." Henry laid his hand on Gus's shoulder as he flanked his other side.

Roland stood and faced the crowd. "We grew up on the same plantation as the Ravenisha. Actually, I guess I should say we grew up in a company town. Rufus hadn't built the town of Ravenswood yet for his lab employees. This wasn't one of those nice social experiment company towns. Instead, it was one of those shanty towns that kept African Americans in deplorable living conditions and dependent on their employer. The tar paper shacks often had no electricity or water. Roads were unpaved and constantly a muddy mess. The Honeycutts had moved into pharmacology, and our fathers worked in Rufus's warehouse packing and shipping supplies. When we were kids, maybe eight, nine years old, Gus's, Henry's, Akiro's and my parents would leave us alone with this man everybody called Uncle Bob. He was somebody's second or third cousin, and because he didn't have a job, his job was to babysit us. I think you all can guess what happened whenever 'Uncle Bob' would babysit. We tried to tell our parents what he was doing, but they didn't believe us. And when Bob found out, he beat the shit out of us. I don't know how no grown-ass man could beat up some little boys, but he did. We just told our parents we got into a fight with each other." Roland paused for a long time at this juncture of the story, tears pouring from his eyes.

"Finally, when we got older, about eleven, twelve, oral sex wasn't good enough anymore. He wanted to penetrate us anally. We were in a state by then because every time we'd see him, he'd threaten us with how he was going to tear our booties up. No matter how we tried to not be alone with him, somehow, he got Gus by himself one day. I remember hearing this tremendous racket and running into the room and finding him beating up Gus. Apparently, Gus had told him no." Gus nodded to confirm.

"This must have set him off in a rage. Gus still has a scar on his eyebrow to this day. So, I volunteered to take Gus's place."

"Why did you do that, Roland?" Gus cried, barely getting the words out. "You've been fucked up ever since."

"I know, but it was my choice. You can't carry guilt around for something that was my choice, brother."

"Dude, you were just twelve yourself," Gus protested.

"Let me finish. I have to finish telling the story, okay? So, Bob stopped beating Gus, and he grabbed me. He slurred something about how I'd do for then. Man, I still remember how his breath reeked of alcohol. He made me take my pants and briefs off and bend over the bed." Tears freely ran down the men's faces. "With no lubricant except for spit, he forced his dick in my ass. I didn't even notice Gus leave the room. I was too focused on the agony I was feeling. Any time I'd cry out, he'd just thrust harder and tell me to shut up and take it like a man. The next thing

I knew, there was a deafening boom, and he was mercifully out of me. I collapsed on the bed, crying. At one point, Gus must have left and come back into the room with Henry. And that's when you ran in, Miss Ceola."

"I remember. The other Ravenisha and I had been keeping an eye out for you boys as best we could, given our circumstances. Rufus prohibited us from visiting your mothers in the beginning, but we eventually badgered him into letting us visit. That's why we rarely went inside those little company cabins. Rufus warned us he was always watching. I cleaned Roland up and put him to bed. I took the gun from Gus and put it in a safe place. I told you boys not to worry about Bob's body or the room—that I would take care of it...and I did. I changed and ate him. I only wish you boys had said something to me or any of us sooner. You can trust we would have believed you. I'm sorry you have suffered all these years. You should have been in therapy. We've got to stop preying on our children. *Uncle Bobs* have ruined so many girls' and boys' lives."

"Shiit, if it were up to me, we'd be enacting mob justice like they do in India and Mexico." Matilda's voice was laced with fury.

"Yeah, but I can see the wrong men being castrated sometimes, Matilda." Lizzie shook her head. "That's not the answer." Matilda harrumphed.

The women enveloped and embraced the men in a group hug for a long time. Someone struck up a song in the Fon language, and the women rocked, sang, and cradled the men. Everyone also made sure Fredi was okay.

Ceola, Elizabeth, and Matilda spent the rest of the night conversing with the surviving warriors in the old language. To their pleasant surprise, they re-discovered familial connections, and most of the warriors actually thanked them for killing Idia. The warriors regaled the

New-Gen and Asoro with stories from the past while passing around a jug of homemade liquor. No one slept a wink and everyone drank too much. Raven and Teddy had a lengthy conversation, the contents of which said conversation, which frightened Teddy to death. But that's another story. The next morning, there were hugs and kisses with promises to visit each other. The Ravenisha gave the New-Gen, including Fredi, beautiful weapons carved by the old-timers, along with their blessings. One warrior even gave Lizzie an authentic battle outfit. Lizzie knew exactly where she would hang it, along with the old weapons they had been given once the items had been preserved and encased in appropriate display containers.

Their acceptance into the fold by even the staunchest of Idia's supporters was aided tremendously because of Raven's gamboling and frolicking with the girls. Raven's copious licks kept the poor girls' faces constantly drenched. They agreed Raven would need to travel to the United States, and it pleased everyone when Aasira volunteered to bring her as soon as she could.

Ceola turned to Jules. "I'd really like you to return to the States with us. We'll find a cure for those tumors."

"Oh, all right," he relented. "I'll come later. Please take the luggage I had put on the plane. I have some business to take care of first. I would prefer to be in Paris sitting at a cafe on the Cour du Commerce Saint André having a nice cafe au lait, but…where do you live?"

"Ravenswood, Alabama."

"Yes, well, even Ravenswood has to be better than this place. It will be nice to be amongst civilized people in a metropolis." It wasn't lost on Jules that Ceola, Matilda, and Elizabeth all turned their heads to conceal their smiles. He had a niggling feeling that the army base hadn't been in Huntsville as Idia had led her minions to believe.

Fredi started to say something, but Teddy's glare and head shake stopped her just in time.

Fredi, riding on the motorcycle behind Teddy, whooped and hollered the entire way back to the plane, making everyone's headaches worse. The men knew they were in for a loud trip back to the States.

The Prime Minister was at the airport to see them off. "Cheola, General Zamandla and Eklezabela. A quick word if I may?"

"Of course, Prime Minister," Matilda responded.

"I just wanted to thank you again for avenging my ancestor and ending that cruel woman's reign of terror on our people. There is a bright future for you here. It's time you returned to your homeland. We could use such powerful women as yourselves."

"Thank you, Prime Minister. We'll discuss your invitation and get back to you," Ceola said. She, Matilda, and Elizabeth pasted on fake smiles. They had no intention of being under the thumbs of men ever again.

Much to everyone's surprise, the women catnapped the entire way back. Apparently, even strong, young warrior women who could shapeshift into fearsome she-panthers weren't immune to the effects of alcohol. Even Fredi settled down once they were in the air. Chuckling, Gus thought back to all of them doing the Wobble, followed by two Prince songs, "FunknRoll" and "The Ride," but that was it. Once "FunknRoll" ended, they went to their seats, reclined them, and threw blankets over their weary bodies. They were out as soon as "The Ride" finished. Gus had the pilot dim the cabin lights.

Even though he, Henry, and Roland were exhausted and hungover, they had a conversation they should have had years ago. They called Akiro, and he joined via FaceTime. They actually talked about their feelings and how the events of their childhood had impacted their lives. Each man noted that after last night's experience, it felt as though a burden had been lifted. They all vowed they would go to therapy, not only for themselves but for their future partners and families. Roland even shyly admitted that after he was well mentally, he would be open to having a special lady in his life, too. The bruthas gave him fist daps and, unable to help themselves, embraced him in enormous bear hugs. They heard sniffling coming from the monitor and turned toward Akiro.

"Don't start, man." Roland's lips curved up in a bittersweet smile. "I'm all cried out. You know we all love you like a brother, but we've shed buckets of tears recently."

"I know," Akiro replied, still sniffling. "I saw everything on the cameras. I just want to thank y'all for keeping me safe. I know y'all sacrificed so much to protect me, too, and I just wanna thank you." He broke down.

"Akiro, stop it, man," Gus moaned. "I refuse to cry. I refuse to cry."

"Bruh, we're disconnecting. See you soon," Henry said, crying.

"This is pathetic," Gus grumbled, clearing his throat repeatedly. "We've got to get ourselves together. Those damn women are making us soft."

The women, who had also been silently crying, just smiled, thinking the men had a lot to learn about felines. They were awoken from their catnaps as soon as the men started talking.

The plane fell into silence again, and Gus had a good nap before he woke up and began working on his report to Colonel Honeycutt. It looked like they had arrived in just the nick of time. Idia had been prepared to inject far more people than they had initially thought. It was clear she had intended to build an army—one that could take over a vast swath of the African continent. Gus shuddered at the thought of those mutant panthers being set loose on people. *What was Idia thinking?* he wondered. *Did she really believe she could control those creatures?* Gus thought about all the accidents he had read about involving circus big cats turning on their trainers and shuddered again. Even though he and Teddy were growing closer and closer, he knew he could never completely let his guard down.

While his men and Benin's army had killed every beast they saw, he hoped none had slipped through the cracks. *That's all the world needed,* he thought. *For some people to be injected with that virus for nefarious purposes.* Deep down, he knew they weren't out of the woods, though. It was obvious some vials were missing and unaccounted for. Either the scientists truly didn't know where they had gone, or they weren't telling, and he absolutely believed Jules when he said the vials were probably all over the world by now. Gus was a cautious and suspicious man. He would suggest to the powers that be to just assume the vials were taken for nefarious purposes and to be prepared for the coming battle with mutant panthers and other preternatural beings. Gus signed the report electronically, hit send, and went back to sleep.

Chapter 40

When the plane finally landed at the base's little airstrip, everyone filed off. Their feet dragged and they didn't even seem to have enough energy to talk. They wondered where everyone was. The base, which normally bustled with activity, was oddly silent. As they rounded the corner, sheepish smiles broke out on their faces when they discovered their peers lined up on two sides to welcome them back. Colonel Honeycutt stood at the front, along with someone from the top brass, who was introduced as Brigadier General Jedediah Nash Scarbrough.

When it was Gus's turn to salute and shake the Brigadier General's hand, the brigadier general said, smiling warmly, "Welcome back, *Captain* Augustus Alford Allensworth. Thank you for your exemplary service. I fully expect you to make general one day."

He turned to face the women, a fake smile plastered on his face. "And you must be the Ravens. Thank you for your help. We look forward to establishing a relationship with you gals and working together in partnership."

The women glared at him. Matilda grounded out, "we'll see." They stalked off, leaving the Brigadier General holding out his hand, smile frozen on his face.

"Did they just dismiss me? Was it something I said?" he asked the men around him. Not used to being treated this way and certainly not by women, he strode after them.

"Should somebody stop him?" Roland asked.

"Naw, he'll learn soon enough," Beau replied, a wicked smile on his face.

"Ladies, ladies!" Brigadier General Scarbrough called. They stopped walking, turned around, and glared. "I sense a hostility from you that is quite unwarranted."

"So?" Teddy asked.

Taken aback, Scarbrough still bravely plowed on. "Did I do something? Say something?"

Celeste glowered. "We're in the Reserves. No reinstatement or special promotion for us? We're not some little ladies who just 'helped' the menfolk." She made air quotes around helped. "We fought just as hard as they did and killed just as many mutants, if not more. And it's Ravenisha, not Ravens."

"Oh, I get it. You're feminists." Scarbrough's gaze raked over the women, his face screwed up in a rictus of pain.

"Don't say anything else, Brigadier General!" Gus shouted, running up to him. "Why don't we all unpack our things and take a few moments to gather ourselves?" He smiled placatingly.

"Why don't you go fuck yourself, *Captain*?" Teddy retorted.

"Really, Teddy? Don't escalate the situation. You know I'm Team Ravenisha. I'll handle this."

As the women turned and stalked away, Brigadier General Scarbrough looked at Gus. “Do you mind telling me what in tarnation is going on here? I’m this close to writing them up for insubordination.”

“Are you married, Brigadier General?”

“Yes, but what does that has to do with anything or why that’s anybody’s business is beyond me. She’s *nothing* like those women, thank God.” Brigadier General Scarbrough snorted, still clueless.

“Are you this obtuse with your wife?” Gus held up his hand. “Don’t answer. Something tells me you are.”

Brigadier General Scarbrough put his hands on his hips and glowered at Gus. “It must be something in the water down here.” He then turned to Colonel Honeycutt, “Are they always this insubordinate?”

Beau wisely ignored the question and gestured for the men to follow him, but not before giving Gus a warning look, which Gus ignored.

As the men walked down the hall, Gus explained how the women felt slighted, devalued, and under-appreciated. His promotion didn’t help matters. Scarbrough tried to explain he had promoted Gus because he had men under his command, he followed orders, was an exemplary soldier, and his promotion was a reward for a job well done.

“You’re elite Special Forces soldiers, for crying out loud!” he said in exasperation. “Those gals are Reserves, and I have suspended them from that. What am I supposed to do?” he cried, looking around at Colonel Honeycutt, who shrugged his shoulders.

“You’re going to have to think of some special title to award them,” Gus opined. “Suspension or no suspension, or they’ll make *all* of our lives hell. And no, flowers and candy will not work on them. They’re bossy, and they like power. And to be fair, they kicked ass better than us out in the field. Technically, their kill ratio *was* higher. And Brigadier General, please don't call them gals."

The Brigadier General looked at Gus quizzically for a moment, and Gus's heart sank. He had gone too far. A smile slowly spread across the Brigadier General's face, and Gus thought, *Uh oh, this can't be good, either.*

"Well, since you seem to know so much about them, when you figure that something out, let me know. You have until the end of the day, Allensworth. I have better things to do with my time than deal with pain-in-the-ass women. They need to stay at home where they belong. What was the government thinking allowing women and gays in?" Beside him, Beau pursed his lips and stiffened, secretly praying their mics were still on and that Akiro was capturing every word of this conversation.

"Come on, Brigadier General, you can't be serious." Gus protested the assignment and the ass-backward attitude.

"With a higher title and pay grade come greater responsibilities." Brigadier General Scarbrough said with a smirk. "By the way, I voted for Obama, so no one can say I'm not progressive." Gus and Beau's mouths dropped open. "Now, if you'll excuse us, Colonel Honeycutt and I have some matters to discuss. Again, good job," he told Gus before breaking off with an unhappy Beau to go into his office.

Gus started to enlighten the Brigadier General on how his attitude would get him in hot water one day but decided to let the man learn the lesson the hard way. Sighing he caught up with his boys and the Ravenisha to return to Ravenswood Farm.

~ ~ ~

Fredi awoke, feeling refreshed. Up front, Teddy and Gus were in a heated discussion about what had transpired at the Army base. Teddy sighed as she fretted how her neurosis was going to drive Gus away before he could really get to know her good qualities.

Fredi marveled at the pine and oak trees lining both sides of the little country road they were on. It was like they were driving through an enchanted forest. Fredi's ears popped as they climbed higher and higher. She noted that up here, some trees' leaves were already turning colors. Fredi could now see a fence bordering the road; yet, they still drove on a ways. Finally, the big SUV they were in slowed, and Gus signaled they were turning, even though no one else was around. Fredi read the Ravenswood Farm sign as they drove through the open gates. Unlike the back way in, the front road was paved and wended for two miles. Gus stopped at the massive house in front of them, and Fredi saw an equestrian center off to the side of it.

"We're home, little she-devil," Teddy said while exiting the vehicle. "In case you were wondering, Obsidian Butterfly stopped by the lab first. She'll be here later. Cochise's kidnapping, along with the Jaguar god's words regarding our powers really got to her. She wanted to talk to Nana and the rest about all of this."

Feeling shy, Fredi was a little behind Gus and Teddy as they made their way up the stone front steps to the wrap-around porch. Her head continuously swiveled as she tried to take in the sights around her. Engraved with a panther's head, the beautiful wooden front door, was flung open, and she was enveloped in everyone's arms. Overwhelmed, Fredi just stood in the foyer, taking in everything, from the big tinted floor-to-ceiling glass windows to the light oak floors.

Teddy took her hand. "Here, I'll show you to your room upstairs. You're in my wing. I hope you like it. Leona and the others helped me buy clothes and decorate your room." After some twists and turns, Teddy opened a door and walked into the room.

"Oh my God, this room is huge! It dwarfs my little cell at Rufus's lab." Fredi twirled around slowly, greedily taking in everything. The same light wood floors as downstairs were upstairs. Fredi noted her large canopied bed was so high, there was a step stool beside it, and in one corner, sat a proper desk and chair.

Teddy, for once uncharacteristically unsure of herself, said, "I hope you like the bed. I've always loved high beds, and I have to use a step stool to climb on my bed, too. Oh, and the quilt was made by Nana and the rest of the Old-Gen. They're teaching us to quilt and we get together for our quilting bee every Wednesday night. Just so you know, you're about to learn how to quilt, whether that was something you always wanted to learn how to do or not." Teddy finally stopped to take a breath of air.

"I love the bed, Teddy! I love everything. It's my dream come true!" Fredi exclaimed, as her eyes continued roving around her new living quarters. They took in the cute chandelier and its matching floor lamps scattered throughout the room. Papasan chairs were placed around a space to form a sitting area, and shag throw rugs dotted the floor. Impulsively, she ran and leaped onto the bed, eschewing the stool entirely. She lay on her back and made imaginary snow angels.

"Here's your closet," Teddy said, her voice muffled. She exited Fredi's spacious walk-in closet which already had clothes hanging from the rack and shoes neatly lining the shoe organizers. "Annnd, this is your bathroom."

Behind her, Fredi gasped as her eyes took in the claw-footed bathtub and its jets, the huge shower with the rainforest shower head, the double-sink vanity. She thought the light-colored floor tiles and vanity were marble but wasn't sure. Whatever it was, it was beautiful. The blue accents in the tile and around the bathroom were also pleasing to her.

"Everything's beautiful, Teddy." Overwhelmed with emotion, she barely got the words out. "Thank you, Big Sis. I'm so grateful for everything." Teddy gave her a tight hug.

"I'll help you unpack, and then I'll take you on a tour and show you where everything is." Teddy noticed Fredi's attention was on the equestrian center as she knelt on the window seat and gazed out of her window. Teddy smiled, let herself out of the room and quietly closed the door.

Chapter 41

It felt good to be home, Teddy thought, stretching in her large, high bed as the sun's warm rays shone through the room, enfolding her in a rainbow of welcoming caresses of warmth. What a difference the passage of time made. She remembered how dejected she had been the last time she woke up and the sun was streaming through the window. Today was truly another day.

Thirty minutes later, Teddy was at the stable, her mount for today saddled and ready. She had called the barn manager, Christian's sister, Gaby, before she got in the shower and begged her to ask one of the working students to saddle Pandora. Panda was a Dutch chestnut mare with a blaze, white socks, and a strawberry gold mane and tail. Teddy knew she had to be on her A-game today. Some people believed chestnut mares were she-devils. Not only because of their sex, but the fact that their chestnut colors often invoked images of fiery redheads. Unfortunately, Panda fit all the stereotypes. She wasn't dangerous or anything like that, but she was definitely the boss mare, and you'd better ask her to do movements correctly, or she was quick to let you know if you didn't and made you pay. But when Panda wasn't ill-tempered and Teddy was riding her correctly, she was wonderful, and Teddy knew if they were both trained correctly, they would be a force to be reckoned with in the show arena, one day. She thought of the old horse saying you tell a gelding, ask a stallion, and discuss it with a mare. It was so true. She also knew when the stars aligned, on a good day, a mare was unbeatable, no matter what the discipline was—dressage, jumping, or eventing. Riding Panda could be a pain sometimes, but what was life without a little excitement?

"Hi Panda girl! How are you today?" Panda whinnied softly in reply, her adorably floppy ears already pricked forward, taking in every sight and sound around her. A lot of riders didn't like mares, but Teddy had always had an affinity for them, and they seemed to like her touch, too. Teddy thought some of it was because she felt she was misunderstood the same way mares were often misunderstood.

"I see you're riding Panda today," Callie, one of her boarders, noted with glee. "Hey guys!" she called to everyone within hearing distance, "Teddy's riding Panda today. Whoot! Whoot!" Callie's brown eyes twinkled mischievously.

Li Ming, another boarder, came running into the arena breathlessly. "Oh good," she chortled, "the lesson hasn't started yet." She ran back out of the arena, shouting, "Hey guys! Teddy's riding Panda today."

"Y'all wrong for telling everyone I'm riding Pandora. You better be happy I'm such an affable person, or I'd throw your butts out of the arena." When she got to the entrance and yelled "Door!" like she was supposed to, Pandora almost knocked her down because the noise spooked her. Getting the horse to stand still at the mounting block was a production. *Oh Lord,* she thought as she finally mounted Panda, the horse barely standing still long enough for her to get on. *Maybe I should just scrap this lesson and go back to bed. Panda seems lit already.*

Christian noted the concern on Teddy's face. "Why don't you warm her up in the canter first, Teddy? That way, you can get some of her excess energy out. While you're cantering, work on bringing her back to you for a few steps and then let her stretch out again. Don't worry about getting her round. Just canter on a loose rein and try to relax. She doesn't look like she's breathing fire today." Christian patted Panda on the side of her neck. "You'll be fine. Off you go."

"Uh, don't you see she's jigging at the walk, Christian? M-maybe I should lunge her first." She wondered if she and Christian were looking at the same horse. How could he not see that Panda was breathing fire?

"That's because you're tense and she can feel it," Christian responded, unperturbed by Teddy's impending breakdown. "Sit up and in the saddle, not perched on it. *Ja. Ja.* Take a deep breath in and let it out slowly. *Ja.* Like so. See how when you did that, she relaxed, too, and blew out her breath?"

"Yes," Teddy responded, feeling better and more confident now that Panda wasn't jigging at the walk. Teddy willed herself to relax and take deep breaths as she walked Panda around on a long rein. Gradually, her shoulders dropped from around her ears to a normal position. Teddy gathered the reins slightly and bent Panda a little around her inside leg. She put her outside leg back and asked for the canter. "Good girl!" she exclaimed as Panda began cantering around the arena, acting like a perfect lady. A wide smile broke out on Teddy's face, and she giggled with glee at the rocking horse canter she was riding.

A commotion outside of the arena wiped the smile off of Teddy's face, causing her to tense up immediately. Fredi ran into the arena, her eyes as big as saucers, followed by Thor and Lily, who were being chased by the Great Danes. She ran right in front of Teddy and Panda. Panda shied and Teddy almost fell off.

"Goddamnit, Fredi!" she exploded. "Don't you know not to run in front of horses like that? And get those animals out of here!" Teddy fumed, trying to get Panda back under control. The girl's face was crestfallen as she burst into tears.

"Trot, Teddy," Christian commanded as he took hold of Fredi, "and then pick up the canter again. If you don't make a big deal out of this, Panda won't." Turning to the railbirds, Christian warned them to be quiet or they wouldn't be allowed to continue watching the lesson. Teddy did as she was told, and Panda soon settled down, even blowing out her breath as they cantered. The exhalations were a good sign. They meant Panda was relaxed. When Panda cocked one floppy ear back and one forward, Teddy relaxed as she thought *Yes, there is a God.*

"What's your name, little one?" Christian asked, guiding Fredi and the boisterous animals to the sideline.

"Fredericka, but you can call me Fredi."

"Okay, Fredi, you must learn about arena etiquette. *Ja*? You never, ever run into an arena like that."

"Okay," Fredi replied in a small voice.

Christian continued. "Because this is an indoor arena, you approach the door cautiously. You never know when a rider may come barreling out, or heaven forbid, just a horse may come barreling out. As you approach the door, you loudly say, 'door' so people and animals know you are coming in. Then, you walk in, not run. *Ja*?"

"*Ja*," Fredi responded. "May I ride?" she shyly asked. "I've never been on a horse before, but I've always dreamed I would learn to ride one day."

"Of course." Christian raised his eyebrows at Teddy, who nodded her head affirmatively. "I'm going to have one of the working students show you how to get the horse ready and I'll be right with you after Teddy's lesson. Okay?" Fredi nodded her head and smiled.

Fredi turned to Teddy and asked, "Are you going to watch me ride, Teddy?"

"You bet! I wouldn't miss your lesson for the world. I'm just going to cool Miss Panda down after my lesson and I'll be right back. We'll go to the tack store after your lesson. You're going to absolutely love going to the tack store," she told Fredi excitedly. "There's nothing like the smell of all of that leather, horse cleaning products, the various horse supplements and treats. And later, I'm going to have you ride one of the Walkers. Their gaits are totally different. Many older people love them because they're so smooth and not as hard on the back as these big moving warmbloods. You'll have fun going through all of their gaits." Teddy finally stopped to catch her breath. "Welcome to the club!"

Ceola, who had run out of the house after Fredi and had watched the entire proceedings from the sideline stepped forward. "You're going to have to let me comb that hair, young lady, before you get on any horse." She briskly cut off Fredi's protestations. "How do you think a helmet is going to fit over that wild afro? Come over here and stop giving me grief." Fredi pouted and stomped after Ceola back up to the house. Ceola glanced down at Fredi's tennis shoe-clad feet as well. "You need the appropriate riding shoes, anyway. Someone should have some paddock boots around here that will fit you." Ceola and Fredi took the pets back with them.

Christian clapped his hands together. "Okay now. Panda looks nice and warmed up and relaxed. Let's get to work." Since he still had an audience, Christian taught not only Teddy but the railbirds. Panda was an obedient girl, mostly, and Teddy was beaming at the end of the lesson, effusively giving Panda neck pats.

"I'm going to cool her down on the trail around the property."

"Do you want company?" Linda Shigio, a boarder asked.

"Sure," Teddy replied. "The more the merrier."

"K, just give me a sec." Teddy was still smiling as she and Linda exited the arena.

While Teddy was cooling down Panda, she saw Molly, one of the working students instructing Fredi about something and Fredi listening raptly. Teddy smiled, thinking, *Yes, another fellow rider.* Winston Churchill may have quoted, "There is nothing better for the inside of a man than the outside of a horse," but many a mother has said that with their daughters, there was nothing better for instilling discipline, patience, courage, focus, teamwork, getting their schoolwork done, and keeping their minds off of boys than a horse. Teddy and Linda were done walking the horses just as Molly was showing Fredi how to safely lead the lesson horse into the cross ties to tack up for her lesson. Teddy quickly untacked and curried Panda. She cleaned the tack, put Panda out in a paddock, and headed to the arena to watch Fredi's lesson, as promised.

Fredi entered the arena, leading her mount, Indiana Jones (barn name Indy), under the watchful eye of the working student. Teddy nodded approvingly. "We'll go shopping for some clothes and boots for you when you're done, missy, *if* after your lesson you decide you'd like to continue. Maybe I'll even schedule a hunter/jumper lesson for you tomorrow if you're okay with today.

"Yes, please. Molly told me I'm learning dressage today."

"Okay, Fredi, let's mount Indy and have fun, shall we?" Christian beamed as he led Indy by the lunge line into the center of the arena. Fredi's stirrups were adjusted, and Christian schooled her on the basic riding position. After walking a bit and getting a feel for the movement at the walk, Christian taught Fredi how to post the trot on the German Riding Pony.

As Indy began trotting, Fredi squealed, “Ooh, the trot is so bouncy.”

“That’s why you’re learning how to post.” After trotting in both directions and working on posting on the correct diagonal, Christian told Fredi, “Splendid job. Let Indy cool down on a long rein at the walk, and I’ll see you later.”

Fredi frowned. “But I want to rock like Teddy was doing.”

“It’s called cantering. Okay, I’ll let you see what it feels like, but you have a long way to go before you’re ready for that movement, young lady. Remember, sit up like you’re a princess. Once Indy goes into the canter, I want you to ride the motion like you’re riding a swing, *Ja*?”

“But Mr. Christian, I’ve never ridden a swing before.”

Teddy walked over and demonstrated how Fredi should scoop her seat bones. “Got it?” Fredi nodded her head.

“Ready?” Christian asked. Fredi nodded again. “Okay, let’s get Indy going on a circle. “Caannter!”

As Indy rocked back on his hind legs and began cantering, Teddy shouted, “scoop, scoop, scoop.” As they went around in a circle, a strange sound came from Fredi as she cantered and her eyes were tightly shut. Christian trilled his tongue for Indy to stop cantering and he came down to a walk.

“Are you okay, Fredi?’ Christian asked, frowning.

Fredi opened her eyes and revealed that she was crying. “Why did we stop?”

“I thought you were frightened.”

“Oh no,” Fredi replied. “That was the best feeling I’ve ever had in my entire life! I want to canter forever!” Teddy and Christian beamed at her like proud parents.

"I'm glad to hear that. It sounds like I have another student on my roster. We're done today, though, young lady. Give Indy a pat and let's dismount." Noting Fredi's pout, he explained, "Indy isn't a young horse, Fredi. You had a great lesson on him today, and you even got to canter a little. You sat the canter beautifully, by the way. Pat him, thank him for being a wonderful boy, and let him relax in his paddock and munch on a little grass. We don't run horses into the ground here. I love your enthusiasm, and I look forward to teaching you. Tomorrow," he added, smiling.

After showing Fredi how to dismount, Teddy told Molly that she would show Fredi how to untack the horse and groom him before letting him munch some grass before they put him back in his stall and attached paddock.

Once dismounted, Fredi dropped the reins, and ran over to a startled Christian, and gave him an enormous hug. She then ran over to Teddy and gave her an enormous hug, as well. Then, she ran over and hugged Molly. She saved the biggest hug for Indy. Around the arena, some women couldn't help but shed a tear or two at the scene.

Teddy grimaced, her lips turned down in a frown. "Fredi girl, you've got a lot to learn. You don't ever just drop your horse's reins like that and leave him unattended. He could have run off and tripped over the reins. What you just did is a no-no. Thank goodness Indy is a chill pony and just stood here or else you'd have been chasing him all over this property."

"Yes, ma'am. Sorry-o. I was just so excited, though." Fredi took the reins from Teddy, taking special care to hold them correctly and not wind them around her fingers. Teddy smiled and hugged her again.

Christian clapped his hands and shouted, "Next!"

Spying Gus at the rail beaming with the now calm Great Danes, Zeke and Sugar Bear, Teddy motioned for him to come with her, Fredi and Indy. Gus came over, and while he gave Indy a wide berth, the Great Danes cavorted right at poor Indy's feet.

Teddy shook her head. "Well, it's obvious you haven't been around horses, soldier. That's going to change, though." She grinned at him. Gus and Teddy gazed at each other, all eyes on them.

"Hey Teddy, you want to tell us who this fine specimen is?" someone called out. "Y'all stay out of my business," she yelled back, as another voice said, "Mm, mm, mm, I bet horses ain't all she's riding."

As they walked away, Teddy put a little extra sway in her walk.

"Shake it but don't break it," someone else shouted.

Gus let out a full-throated laugh as someone catcalled him. "I think I could get used to this."

"I bet you could," Teddy side-eyed Gus.

"I have a lot to learn, guys.Besides everything else, Nana is teaching me how to cook.She said she taught you.She showed me how to make blueberry scones this morning. I mean biscones." Fredi finally took a breath and giggled.

"I know it seems like a lot now," Teddy responded, "but you'll get it down in no time. Nana is a wonderful teacher, and so are Miss Lizzie and Leona."

"You are, too. And Christian is going to teach me German and Miss Tildy is going to teach me how to fight."

Many people congratulated Fredi on having an excellent lesson as they walked to the cross ties.

Smiling from ear to ear, Fredi stage-whispered, "Everyone is so nice here. I never want to leave."

Teddy laughed. "We'll see if you still feel that way after you've scooped horse poop and cleaned tack and stalls."

After untacking Indy, and giving him, Gus, and the Great Danes baths, they put Indy in his paddock. The merry trio then made their way back to the house. When Fredi saw the Old-Gen rocking on the porch, she ran up to them and excitedly described her lesson. She ended with "and Christian said he would be happy to teach Indy and I."

"Uh oh," Teddy whispered to Gus while motioning for him to follow her inside.

Lizzie stared at Fredi. "And I? And I? Who taught you English? Do you say Christian said he would be happy to teach me, or Christian said he would be happy to teach I? Which is correct? The lesson was a wonderful experience for I? Or the lesson was a wonderful experience for me? I thought you were a genius." She looked pointedly at Fredi.

"Christian said he would be happy to teach Indy and me."

"Thank you, young lady. I'm so tired of people misusing "I". They probably think they sound proper, but they just sound uneducated."

Teddy peeked around the door and crooked her finger at Fredi. "Come on, grasshopper. You can help us cook dinner."

"Thanks for rescuing me. I've never cooked before today," Fredi replied excitedly, following Teddy into the house.

"You might want to take a quick shower and change clothes. We'll be in the kitchen when you're ready."

"Be right back," Fredi called, zooming up the stairs.

Chapter 42

Later, after a scrumptious dinner of fried chicken smothered in gravy, dirty rice, fresh creamed corn, collard greens, hot water cornbread, and biscuits, followed by a million-dollar pound cake and ice cream, the girls piled onto the humongous swinging Papasan bed on the porch and read. Fredi quickly grabbed a book from the library and hopped onto the bed with them. The girls read for hours, only getting up to go to the bathroom. The house cats, Thor and Lily Belle, cuddled next to them, purring contentedly.

Darkness fell, and someone turned on the porch lights. The girls read on. They noticed Fredi giving them puzzled looks now and then, wondering when they would stop reading and do something—like return to the tack store or go riding. However, all they did was continue to read, until one by one, they fell into a deep and peaceful sleep, the silence penetrated only by the singing of cicadas and the deep croak of frogs.

Fredi couldn't fight the sleepiness no longer. Putting her book aside, she yawned and sat up, startled. She hadn't even noticed the armed men sitting in the rockers, keeping watch over them and the Great Danes lying calmly at their feet. Gus smiled and put a finger to his lips. "Go to sleep, little one," he whispered. "You're safe under my watch."

Fredi yawned again, snuggled up against Teddy, and immediately fell into a deep and dreamless sleep.

The next day at breakfast, the women were still fuming from the Brigadier General's perceived slight.

"I don't know why we even bother," Teddy scowled. "We do all the work, and they get all the credit and glory. Same old shit every time."

"At least y'all were acknowledged. They just ignored us," Lizzie noted as the rest of the Old-Gen nodded, along with Fredi and Obsidian Butterfly.

"They didn't even have the decency to lift our suspension," Celeste groused.

"I'm done with the Reserves," Naima announced. "And if y'all have any self-esteem, you'll quit, too."

"You know, Naima, you're absolutely right," Teddy agreed. They looked to the Old-Gen for their opinion.

"Good. Now, you can devote your time to finding your mamas. Yes, you're included, too, missy," Ceola told Fredi before she could ask if she was part of the group. "You're a Ravenisha now. One of us. But even if you weren't, we would have allowed you to go on the hunt because Cleo is your mama, too."

"Y'all want me to call those motherfuckers and let them know we quit?" Teddy whipped out her cell phone. "Shit," snapped Teddy punching in the numbers. "I'll happily tell them where they can stuff those piddlin'-ass jobs, the punk-ass motherfuckers."

Lizzie snatched Teddy's phone from her hand. "That's okay, pumpkin. I'll take care of it. Why don't you go and take a nice relaxing bath?" Lizzie smiled and hit the "End" button.

"Why?" Teddy asked belligerently.

Everyone started replying at once. “Because tact isn’t your strong suit.” “We don’t want to burn bridges.” “Girl, you are not diplomatic at all.”

“Yeah, you aren’t exactly known for your tact, Teddy baby,” Leona said gently. “I love you.”

“Y’all remember the time when Teddy told the Mayor he looked like he was expecting?” winced Tildy. “Just walked up to him and blurted out, ‘Damn Mayor, you look like you six months pregnant’. It would have been funny, too if the Mayor’s abdomen hadn’t been swollen from ascites from the cancer that ultimately killed him.”

“How was I supposed to know he had cancer? Heffas!” Teddy sulked while stomping up the stairs to her room.

Fredi, close behind, teased, “Tactless Teddy. It has a certain cache, wouldn’t you say? Tactless Teddy?”

“Oh, hell naw. Somebody come and get this little girl.” Teddy whirled around and screamed. “What the hell? Where is she? Where did she go? Oh my God!”

Below, the women abruptly stopped laughing and talking and stared agog up at the stairs where just a moment ago two people had been standing.

“Fredi! Fredi!” Teddy screamed in a panic.

Suddenly she heard a laugh, and Fredi materialized from the carpeted runner on the stairs she was lying on. She danced around Teddy, singing, “You can’t camouflage. You can’t camouflage.”

Rufus ran in, and Ceola explained what had just happened.

They could hear Lizzie telling whoever she was on the phone with, “It’s okay. She just materialized. I can’t believe I just said those words.

No, there's no need for y'all to come over here. Everything is under control. We're fine. Hello? Hello?"

Teddy bounded down the stairs and made a beeline straight to Rufus. "How come she can camouflage and I can't?"

"I wasn't aware." Rufus was totally flummoxed.

"Don't bullshit me, Rufus," Teddy responded in high dudgeon. "This smacks of fucking favoritism. Yes, I said fucking because I'm fucking mad as fucking hell. I'm going to ask you one more fucking time. Why is it she can fucking camouflage and I fucking can't?" Teddy's eyes became slits, and her canines elongated.

"Calm your buttocks, Theodora Lulu K'Abella. Right now!" Ceola ordered.

Fredi stomped down the stairs, crying, "Her hair is longer than mine and it's not frizzy and, and, and, she can bring people back from the dead and I can't. Plus, she has some kind of spooky way of knowing if people are telling the truth or not. She's just jealous!"

Rufus took a deep breath, closing and opening his eyes. "Theodora, you don't have that ability because I didn't have the expertise back then. By the time Fredericka came along, I had learned how to manipulate genes better to introduce camouflaging to the allele."

"Rufus, please tell me that ability wasn't added to the formula Idia stole." Worry laced Ceola's voice.

"I wasn't that stupid, Thank God."

"Hush up right now!" Tildy ordered, glaring at Teddy and Fredi, who immediately stopped crying mid cry. "Making all of that damn noise, acting like damn children. Act like you have some damn sense. I can barely hear my phone ringing," Tildy thundered as Fredi looked like she wanted to cry again.

Now that the girls were quiet, others could hear their phones' non-stop trilling.

"That was Maybelle." Lizzie eyed her phone suspiciously. "Some mean-looking foreigners were at the convenience store asking for directions to the farm. You know how we deliberately misled the GPS so people won't have our correct address?"

"Yeah," Tildy replied, putting her phone away, "I just got a call from Ophelia. She and Calvin noticed a caravan of strange vehicles headed our way. Thank goodness their nosy asses sit on their porch all day. Comes in handy sometimes."

"The sheriff's on his way," Ceola said, pressing the "End Call" button on her phone.

Teddy ran into the armory, Fredi on her heels. Naima and Celeste soon joined them, followed by the Old-Gen Ravenisha. They grabbed their weapons and were soon armed. Footsteps thundered on the porch as Gus and his men ran in, followed by Colonel Honeycutt and Brigadier General Scarbrough.

"We heard about your visitors," they panted. "Sheriff's on the way with reinforcements."

As the women emerged from the armory, Brigadier General Scarbrough told them to go to a safe room, if they had one.

Teddy racked her pump shotgun. "You've got to be fucking kidding me. Every woman in this room is a warrior, born, bred, and trained. We are Ravenisha. You want to protect someone, protect yourself. We got this." She walked over to the other women, and they gathered around each other. "I'd like to ambush them before they reach the house, guys, because I don't want any of the horses shot." The women nodded in agreement and ran out the door, Tildy shouting additional instructions.

The men looked at each other, and while running behind the women, planned how they would support them. Colonel Honeycutt shouted into his phone for the sheriff and his men to form a blockade on the major road, impeding the foreigners' egress should they try to escape. The men found the women ensconced at the top of the hill behind trees and boulders, waiting for the foreigners to arrive. They soon saw the caravan making its way up the mountain at a furious pace.

"What the hell do they think they're doing?" Teddy voiced what everyone else was thinking. "Maybe, they're just here to visit and look mean. Surely they must know we'll fight back." She motioned for her friends to follow her. Matilda nodded to let her know the Old-Gen had their backs. Teddy and the New-Gen walked out onto the road, guns raised. As the cars came into view, they slowly stopped.

The front door opened in the lead car, and a man stepped out, a machine gun in his hand. He called out in an Eastern European voice, "The gun is pointed down, okay? I'm going to walk slowly toward you."

Teddy nodded, but before she could meet him halfway, a Humvee screeched to a stop, and out stepped Rufus. Teddy couldn't help groaning in dismay. What was Rufus doing?

"Ah, just the man I came to see," the Eastern European man said.

"I warned you not to come here, Stefan," Rufus intoned in a flat voice. "I told you I would gladly send the money you lent me plus interest."

"Pfft, you silly old man. And I told you I didn't want the money. I want the serum or I'll gladly take these beautiful women. They are products of the serum, no?"

"And if I say no? I don't know about them being products of any serum," Rufus lied, "but two of them are my daughters and hell will freeze over before I allow you to put your filthy hands on them. Besides, you obviously haven't done your due diligence. If you think these women will allow you to take them, you're sadly mistaken. They can all kick your asses from one side of town to the other."

"It would be very unfortunate of them to try. Andres," Stefan called. "Show Rufus what happens to people—especially women—who displease us."

A burly man with a wrestler's physique stepped out of the car. He walked to the back, and the car's driver popped the trunk's lid. The man reached in and effortlessly lifted a blob from the trunk and flung it to the ground as if it were a bag of kibble. He bent down and began dragging the object around the car. At this point, The Ravenisha had watched the show with ennui, but when Andres brought the object to the front and kicked it for good measure, he finally had their full attention.

The woman's duster dress had ridden up, revealing a compression knee-high, the elastic at the top held in place by a knot. The other knee-high was missing. Her jet black wig was askew, revealing short woolly grey hair underneath. It was only when he turned the limp body over the women gasped and there were cries of "no" as they recognized the body of Maybelle. The fiends had strangled her with the other compression knee-high.

"She was a little too lippy for me," Stefan sneered. "I had decided to let her get away with it, but on further thought, I changed my mind, so we went back and took care of her."

As Teddy walked closer, Stefan lifted his gun.

"Home skillet, you do know this isn't going to end well for you? What did you think would happen today?" Teddy asked as Fredi materialized behind Andres and shot him in the back of the head. Teddy then shot Stefan, but not before he reflexively pressed the trigger on the machine gun and a bullet hit Rufus squarely in the chest. Upon hearing the gunfire, Sheriff Tucker and his men joined the battle and killed the foreigners, assisting the Ravenisha and Gus and his men.

While the fight was ongoing, Ceola and Naima rushed over to Rufus, picked him up, and drove him the scant distance to Ceola's lab. Rufus had a pulse, but it was weak and thready. He didn't have much time. Colonel Honeycutt called the base's medic and ordered him to the lab stat.

"Whew, boy!" Sheriff Tucker exalted after the skirmish. He and his deputies exchanged high-fives. "I haven't had so much fun since that boar hunt last year. It's going to be a mother getting rid of these damn bodies, though." He looked around, hitched up his pants, and spit.

"Not really, Sheriff Tucker. We're always hungry. Alive is the best, but recently dead works, too. We'll have a feast tonight," Matilda leered as the Sheriff's face turned green and his smile disappeared. "If your men could just stack them in the old ice shed, that would be great." Matilda actually smiled at the men before she disappeared into the forest.

Brigadier General Scarbrough, who overheard the conversation, looked at Gus long and hard. "Did I just hear that? We can't sanction this. Sheriff, Colonel. I thought I understood these Ravenisha, but obviously, I don't. We can't sanction these women consuming the flesh of these dead men. Why..." His voice trailed off as he noticed the other men looking everywhere but at him.

"The president is aware of this, Brigadier General. It's a done deal." Colonel Honeycutt looked Scarbrough in the eyes, winked, and grinned. He was enjoying letting Scarbrough know he was on speaking terms with the president of the United States of America. "Right now, the Ravenisha are the cats' meow, no pun intended. In fact, where did they go?" Colonel Honeycutt looked around at the almost empty road.

"You know where they are." Henry cradled his weapon and nodded his head toward a grove of trees. He then hurried over to the grove and disappeared.

"I don't think you want to walk over there." Sheriff Tucker, Brigadier General Scarbrough, and Colonel Honeycutt ignored Akiro and went over to the grove, anyway. Along the way, it wasn't lost on them that there were far fewer bodies littering the ground now than earlier. They heard the sounds before they reached the trees.

Colonel Honeycutt stopped short of the tree line. "You know, I've seen this before. I'll just wait for y'all right here. Walk in real slow-like. You don't want to threaten or startle them." The other two men continued walking, taking Honeycutt's advice. A few seconds later when they rushed past him, throwing up, he asked, "Enjoy the show?"

It was a while before the men could speak. Brigadier General Scarbrough removed a handkerchief from a pocket and wiped his mouth with a shaking hand. "You're not telling me those creatures back there are those R-raven? R-ravenisa? Ravenisha women. Damn, why can't I remember that ghetto name? I refuse to believe it. Those are the biggest goddamn panthers I've ever seen in my life. The video feeds I've seen don't do them justice. Those things are unreal. Why aren't we killing *them*?"

"Come on, follow me," Colonel Honeycutt beckoned for the two men to follow him back into the grove.

"You must be crazy, Beau," Sheriff Tucker protested. "I'm not going back in there." He unholstered his gun with a shaking hand.

"Stop being pussies. You'll be okay," Colonel Honeycutt chided. The two men reluctantly followed him, making sure the Colonel stayed in front of them.

"Ladies, I know you like to stay in your she-panther forms for a bit after you feed," Colonel Honeycutt said, "but these gentlemen are nonbelievers and they need to see you change back to your human forms." The two men noticed Gus and his company standing guard for the first time.

"Y-you were with them all along?" stammered Brigadier General Scarbrough?

"Yessir, Brigadier General Scarbrough," Gus responded. "We're the Asoro, their watchers. We will protect them with our lives if need be."

"I see… Whoa!" the Brigadier General exclaimed as Teddy and Fredi quickly changed form first. Fredi hid behind Teddy, uncomfortable with her body being exposed to these men's prying eyes. Henry quickly threw her clothes over, and she put them on. The others changed back into their human forms. Before they dressed, everyone just stood looking at each other in a cringe-worthy silence. Matilda was openly defiant, her tattoos and glyphs decorating her magnificent body, which was in itself a piece of artwork. The men could only gape in awe.

"Seen enough?" Teddy finally broke the silence, her different colored eyes daring them to say something.

"Yes, thank you," Brigadier General Scarbrough replied in a subdued voice.

"Gotdaayuum," the Sheriff exclaimed, drawing the word out. "Y'all some bad mama jamas. Whew, I wouldn't want to come up on y'all in the woods at night." The women laughed. "What?" the Sheriff asked, puzzled.

"Sheriff," Celeste replied. "No one says mama jama anymore. Whew, we're going to have to update you on the latest slang."

Akiro began singing, "*You're a bad mama jama, just as fine as you can be.*"

Mercifully, the trill of his cell phone interrupted him. "We're on our way. Ceola needs you at the lab ASAP. It's Rufus. He's dying."

Chapter 43

It only took them a couple of minutes to zoom up the mountain and rush into the lab where they found Rufus in a hospital bed, hooked up to various machines. He was as still as a cadaver and looked ready to do the danse macabre at any moment. His skin was so white, it looked like paper. His wheezing breath was labored, and suppurating sores had broken out all over his body—like the ones on Abaku in his last moments. It was a miracle he was hanging on considering one of the errant bullets from Stefan's gun had hit him squarely in the chest. When he opened his eyes upon the arrival of the Ravenisha, they were a shockingly electric, almost neon blue against his paper-white skin. He tried to speak but was too weak. Teddy and Fredi walked forward.

"Mariposa, do I do the same thing I did to Fredi?" Teddy asked, her expression one of moue.

"I don't think so, Teddy, because he's not dead yet."

"Oh," Teddy whispered.

"I would start by calling my beast," counseled Mariposa.

Teddy quietened her mind and called her beast. When her beast responded, Teddy revealed Rufus to the beast and asked her how to heal him. The beast told her. Teddy turned to Fredi. "Okay, home skillet, I want to use your necklace this time. We're not going to suck up all of my necklace's power."

She reached for Fredi's necklace, but Fredi slapped her hand and moved away. "No, Mr. Cochise said, I'm not supposed to take my necklace off."

"You twit." Teddy rolled her eyes, "I took my necklace off to save you."

Mariposa turned to Fredi. "Citlalli, let her have the necklace. She'll give it right back." Fredi reluctantly removed the necklace and handed it to Teddy but not before giving her the stank eye.

Teddy closed her eyes and listened some more to her beast. "Oh, hell naw," she blurted out. "Why me, Lord?"

Naima checked Rufus's vitals. "Girl, hurry up. This man is dying!"

Teddy slowly removed her clothes and morphed into her werecat form. Even though the medic had been shown videos, he was still shocked, at witnessing a human morphing into a werecat in person. Teddy walked over to Rufus and slashed her arm. As blood welled, she plunged the knife into the wound to open it a little more. She held her arm over the wound, thus ensuring some of her blood would touch his heart. She then walked to the front of the bed and lifted Rufus's head and bent it back. She put her arm to his mouth, letting her blood drip down his throat. A warm breeze blew over the room, and the ever-present static electricity made Fredi's hair even frizzier. Rufus took in a deep breath and exhaled a death rattle.

"Welp, I didn't see that coming," Elizabeth quipped.

"Me, neither," Ceola said.

Tildy gleefully rushed over to cover Rufus's body with a sheet, but Obsidian Butterfly put her hand out.

"Be patient, Tildy. His time will come but unfortunately, it's not today."

Teddy put her mouth to his lips and blew some of her lifeforce into him, re-animating his lifeless eyes. Rufus labored to take in a breath of air. He was strong-willed and determined to live. He breathed in and exhaled shakily, repeating the process twice. Soon, Teddy's breath, plus her red blood cells, infused his broken, sick body with her fresh, healthy vitality and Rufus's breaths were no longer shaky. Once it was apparent Rufus was on his way to recovering, Teddy morphed back into her human self. Muttering "Why me, Lord?" she handed Fredi her necklace and put her clothes back on.

As Rufus lay on the bed, still taking big gulps of air, the sores on his body faded and the wound on his chest knitted closed. He would see his oncologist as soon as possible, but all of the symptoms he'd been suffering were gone. Tears poured from his eyes. He tried to get up, but Ceola, and Beau gently pushed him back down. People averted their eyes and let him cry in peace. Finally, he accepted a tissue that someone handed him.

The disappointment was palpable in the room as it became apparent Rufus was going to live.

"Theodora," he called in his stentorian voice. "Fredericka, come here, please." The girls reluctantly walked over.

Rufus looked at both of them lovingly, and tears began falling again. When neither girl got any closer and just stood looking at him, he asked, "Was I really that bad?"

"Yes," they replied simultaneously. Their arms were crossed, and they could barely suppress rolling their eyes. Disappointment rained off of them in waves.

"And stop looking at us like that. You look hella creepy," Teddy groused. "I don't know why I bothered to save you."

"Since actions speak louder than words, will you let me show you how sorry and sincere I am? Don't worry, I told you exactly where your daughters are. I just hope no one else has found them." Rufus addressed everyone but especially the Old-Gen.

"Okay, Rufus," Ceola said. "We expect transparency from here on forward. And you understand this. You will have no power over us. None. Nicht. Nada. You understand me? We are free!"

"I understand, Ceola," Rufus sighed. "I understand exactly what you mean."

"Good," she purred, patting him on the cheek. "I'll say, Rufus. You must have had an after-death experience. Anything you want to share with us?" Ceola raised her eyebrows.

Rufus shook his head. "I know y'all still want to kill me for taking your girls away from you."

"You think?" Lizzie replied.

Rufus stared at the floor and finally raised his head. "If you'll just give me a chance, I swear I'll make it up to you. Here, Teddy can take my hand and feel my sincerity."

"Yeah, you good. I've touched you enough for one day." Teddy's eyes began fluttering, and she began swaying on her feet. Gus noticed and swept her up into his arms.

"Don't worry, Augustus. She just needs a little catnap. Healing Rufus took a lot out of her. She'll probably be re-energized by the time you get her home and into bed. Oh, and Augustus, my grandbaby's milk isn't free," Ceola warned. "Also, don't think you'll be shacking up with her or that she'll be shacking up with you. And if you haven't proposed to her within three years, you need to get a move on. Three years is plenty of time for a couple to learn everything there is to know about each other. I'll be damned if you're going to suck up five, ten, fifteen years of my baby's life and then decide to leave her for someone younger. Do you understand me, young man?"

"Don't worry, ma'am, I'm already looking at rings."

"Well, all right, all right, all right, all right," Matilda said. Ceola laughed and nodded her head in approval.

After Gus left, she turned to Fredi, who was sleepy, too. "Come here, baby. You're about to fall down. Let's all take a catnap and then work on that dang serum."

Ceola turned to Colonel Honeycutt, Brigadier General Scarbrough, and Sheriff Tucker. "I'm sure you gentlemen have work to do. Go on, get out of here. The show's over."

"Yes, ma'am!"

"Thank you for your help today," Ceola called.

"Our pleasure," they called back.

"You go on and get your naps," Henry told her. "We got the lab covered."

"Thank you, Henry," Matilda replied. "Y'all better get a move on with Celeste and Naima. You know they mad as hell at y'all now."

"I know," Akiro groaned. "How can we ever live up to Gus?"

"I don't know, but you better try," Lizzie added, smiling. "Oh, and you better believe the same rules apply to you two."

"Roger that," Henry smiled, looking at Celeste.

"Naima already has her ring picked out," Akiro added. "I bet y'all didn't know she was so bossy." He smiled as Naima playfully swatted him.

Matilda looked at them. "You jokers. Why didn't you say something just now? Letting us run on and on."

"In all fairness, ma'dear," Celeste smiled, taking Tildy by the arm, "we did tell them to just agree with everything y'all said."

~ ~ ~

After the naps, Ceola, Mariposa, and Fredi assembled in the lab's principal room and continued working on an antidote for the serum. Rufus insisted on helping, but the women weren't having it. They finally reached a compromise and allowed him to stay on one condition. He couldn't stand and had to sit in the wheelchair provided for him. He'd argued in vain he wasn't an invalid, but the women had shot him down, reminding him he was on his deathbed only hours ago. They tested Mariposa's blood and discovered that despite being injected with the infected serum, her body displayed no reaction whatsoever to it. Fredi was able to isolate the properties in her blood that had allowed this to occur and they were almost positive they were close to finding the magical elixir, which would work on the other werecats and normal humans.

Since she had vials of the Old and New-Gen Ravenisha's blood, she tested theirs first against the preventative vaccine she made for those who carried La Panthère Noire's strain. Fredi let out a joyous whoop every time she peered under the microscope and saw her serum's cells consume the infected serum's cells. Ceola called Teddy and told her to bring everyone back to the lab to be vaccinated. The vaccine was even effective on Fredi.

Rufus, Gus, and the rest of the Asoro were the next groups vaccinated. Unfortunately, not all the human women who initially tested positive for the strain reacted favorably to the inoculation. Additionally, scientists discovered that the vaccine had a four-day optimal injection window to positively affect an infected human. They deduced they only needed to remove one component from the antidote to inoculate humans safely with the serum. Base medics humanely euthanized and cremated those unfortunate women contaminated over four days ago who proved to be non-responsive to the vaccine.

After congratulatory hugs and kisses, Rufus noted, "I think we should test our blood again tomorrow before we have the vaccination mass-produced, yes? There is that little matter of the vaccine being approved by the FDA, but hopefully they'll fast track it like they did for COVID-19."

"I concur. We'll probably have to continue testing our blood for up to a year to ensure everything is okay. I'm positive it is, but scientists don't rely on positive feelings," said Dr. Vasquez, smiling.

As it turned out, Teddy really didn't need any more than a little catnap to rejuvenate her body. By the time Gus carried her from the lab back to her bed, all of Teddy had awakened, including certain erogenous body parts.

Gus slowly opened his eyes and grinned sleepily at her. "I should have known you'd be a tiger in bed." Teddy decided she wanted to listen to that sexy rumble for the rest of her life.

"You mean pantheress?" Teddy grinned, giving him a lingering and leisurely kiss, her nubby tongue caressing his in that cat-like way he loved. "Augustus Alford Allensworth, III, I'd love to stay in this bed with you forever." Teddy peppered Gus's' face with kisses.

Rolling her over onto her back, Gus told her, "I thought you did enough riding last night."

"Oh, I can never ride enough," Teddy moaned as Gus entered her. Gazing into each other's eyes, while moving in tandem, waves of pleasure rode over them and it was as though they had been together forever. "Shit, you know we're not using a condom this time," Teddy mumbled against Gus's lips.

"I just got tested and I'm negative. And I want you to have my babies." The heat from Gus's gaze seared Teddy's soul.

"So, so, tempting." Teddy kissed Gus as she reached over and retrieved a condom from the nightstand. "But Nana didn't raise no fool. Also, handsome, as much as I'd love to have your babies one day, I'd have to be in heat for that to happen."

Teddy and Gus awoke from a nice long nap, refreshed and re-energized. Gus hadn't meant to fall asleep with Teddy; he must have been more exhausted than he thought he was, and Teddy's bed had looked so inviting. Once he had gently laid Teddy down, he told himself he was just going to lie down next to her for a little bit and rest his eyes. Hours later, he awoke to find his arms wrapped around Teddy and her arms wrapped around him. He could have stayed in that position forever, except Miss Teddy had him out in the garage now, inspecting her restored 1970 convertible Chevrolet Chevelle SS 454. The car was a work of art: black with white stripes with a red leather interior. Teddy was telling Gus how she loved going for early morning or dusk drives, but when she noticed how lovingly Gus was running his hand over the car, she walked around to the passenger side and got in.

"Let's go for a ride."

"Seriously? I can drive this baby?"

"You *can* drive a 4-speed manual, can't you?" Teddy questioned, a smirk on her face.

"Woman, is the sky blue?"

"Not always. Well then, let's roll."

After adjusting the seat and mirrors, Gus drove slowly out of the long, winding drive, getting a feel for the car, and enjoying the throaty rumble of the motor. At the end of the drive, Gus made a left, and seeing no other vehicles on the road, he aired the cobwebs out of the carburetor, as they say. The powerful car quickly accelerated and deftly handled the single-lane country road's many twists and turns.

After driving for a bit, Gus pulled off to the side at the lake and he and Teddy just sat in the car, listening to the engine growl as the sun slipped down the horizon, painting the sky the deep reds, oranges, and purples only an Alabama sunset could produce on a late fall evening. Sighing in contentment, Teddy slid across the seat, straddled Gus, and twisted her body to turn off the engine. As Teddy pulled her skirt up and underwear down, Gus unbuckled and unzipped his pants, his shaft already thick and throbbing. Grinning lazily, he quickly rolled on the condom Teddy handed him. As Teddy slowly lowered herself down on him, Gus murmured, "Beautiful," as a tear trickled out of the corner of his eye.

"What's beautiful, babe? Is anything wrong?" Teddy asked as she licked the tear away.

"No, nothing's wrong," Gus said, meeting Teddy's thrusts with his own in unison.

"You're beautiful and I'm just so grateful to God for letting me experience a moment like this in my life. I love you, Theodora Lulu K'Abella Furie."

"I didn't think I could love you more Augustus Alford Allensworth, III, but I do," Teddy cried, riding him until a star wasn't the only thing exploding at that moment.

Chapter 44

The next day, the household was awakened by the aroma of percolating coffee, sausage, bacon, pancakes, and the ever ubiquitous grits. Boisterous voices raised a clamor from the kitchen. Rufus, Teddy, and Fredi were wearing riding attire, having come from an early morning ride. Gus was wearing his usual uniform of camo pants, boots, and a T-shirt, and Leona was at the stove, flipping pancakes on a griddle. They were all howling at some awful joke Fredi had just told.

"Oh Lord, I've never laughed so hard," a red-faced Rufus howled. "My daughter, the comedian. Fredericka, where did you learn that awful joke?"

"From you, of course. You told it to Dr. Mariposa, and I just embellished a few things." Fredi smiled the smile tweens do when they're really laughing at someone instead of with them.

"I've never…you're right," Rufus marveled. "Whatever am I going to do with you?" The others began slowly trickling in.

Teddy had slipped the larger knife Cochise had given her out of its sheath and was turning it over and examining it more closely. Frowning, she noticed when she held it up to the chandelier's light what she had initially thought was a design carved on the blade was a language, instead.

"Mariposa, could you come to the kitchen, please?" Teddy called. Fredi gestured for Teddy to hand her the knife.

"I can read Aztec glyphs a little. Fredi squinted at the hieroglyphs. I think this roughly translates to Volcano of the Obsidian Serpent."

"Let me see it, Citlalli." Mariposa reached for the knife. "Hmm, I think you're right, as usual."

"Okay, you have gone from being a smarty-party to just plain spooky." Teddy stuck out her tongue at Fredi.

"Now girls," Mariposa laughed. "The problem is, I've never heard of a volcano with this name." She looked around the room at the gathered Ravenisha. "You know, I think Cochise is trapped somewhere on or near that mountain."

"If he is, we'll find him," Teddy told Mariposa. "Sooo, Rufus, now would be a wonderful time for you to tell us who all is out there trying to use and abuse us."

Teddy sat down with plates of food for her and Gus. Fredi plopped down next to her and began eating off of Teddy's plate. Teddy looked at her, sighed loudly, and turned back to Rufus.

Rufus at least looked bashful as he addressed Teddy. "Well, there's the Russians."

"Naturally." Naima rolled her eyes.

"The Chinese, and—"

"Oh Lord, don't say it," begged Celeste. "Please don't say the North Koreans."

"The North Koreans," Rufus finished.

"Where did they get money to pay for anything?" Teddy asked, puzzled.

"People have money for what they want," Matilda said. "It's always been that way."

Rufus continued. "The Chinese allowed me to repay them with interest. The other two want the serum or the women."

"Of course. Don't tell me. They really want the serum now that they, along with the rest of the world, have seen images of us in action." Rufus looked at Teddy, surprise etched in his features. "I'm not psychic; it's just a logical leap."

Fredi shot a quick look at Rufus, lips pursed. "Don't make me pull out my laptop, Rufus." He gave her a warning glare. Fredi sighed and sneered. "What doofus Rufus meant to say is there's only one government after us. That's North Korea. The rest are billionaires from China, Russia, etc. It's a free-for-all, basically. Anyone with money could be after us."

"I wouldn't expect a child to understand," Rufus finally said dismissively.

"Understand what? That your ass is beyond greedy?"

"So much for a truce and forgiveness," someone muttered.

"How much money is enough? You already have so much, you'll never be able to spend even a fraction of it in your lifetime. I could understand if you were using the money for good, but your kind never does. And to pimp your own daughters out is indefensible. I may be a child, but I understand my so-called father loves money and power more than he loves me and my sister. You didn't even need to borrow money to finance the experiments in the first place," Fredi cried.

Rufus got up and crouched down in front of Fredi. "Look, Fredericka, and you too, Theodora. It is absolutely true that at one time, I did value money and power over my daughters. And yes, because I didn't value you, I was going to pimp you out, as you say. But now, I wouldn't trade you and Theodora for anything in the world. Laughing at your God-awful joke just now made me realize all the years we could have been sharing such awful jokes and laughter with each other. And seeing how much you girls love riding makes me want to weep. We have a strong equestrian tradition in this family, and I could have been fostering your interest instead of being a hypocritical bigot. Again, I'm sorry, Fredericka. I'm sorry Theodora. I promise I'll be a better father. I'll spoil you rotten," Rufus said, smiling gingerly. "There's one thing you have to understand. I'm not a saint."

"You can say that again," Matilda muttered.

"Yes, I am a bad person. I'm ruthless, mean as a rattlesnake, and a sonofabitch. But the people I love, I dearly love, and I'll do anything for them. I bred you to be the same way."

Fredi looked at Teddy for guidance, and an unspoken conversation passed between them. Finally, they blurted, "You can't force us to love you, you know. Our love and respect will have to be earned."

"Fair enough," Rufus smiled.

"Nana…" Teddy turned to Ceola, who unsuccessfully tried to wipe the tears from her eyes before others saw them. "I really need to discuss something with the family."

"Of course, Teddy." Ceola gave Teddy her full attention. "What's wrong, baby?"

Teddy opened her mouth to respond, but the doorbell chimed, and Fredi jumped up to get it. She returned to the kitchen, Colonel Honeycutt and Brigadier General Scarbrough on her heels. Nana gave her a questioning look, but Teddy shook her head and put on a brave front for the newcomers.

"Sorry for interrupting you folks' breakfast." Colonel Honeycutt looked longingly at the food, a little drop of drool appearing at the corner of his mouth.

"Sit down, Beau, Jed," Leona motioned to two empty chairs. "It'll just take me a moment to make plates for you."

"That's okay, Miss Leona," Brigadier General Scarbrough said. Colonel Honeycutt looked like he wanted to protest.

"I said sit down," Leona commanded.

"Yes ma'am!" Both men found empty chairs and sat down. Leona fixed them plates, which she put in front of them.

"Coffee?" They nodded their heads gratefully. "Sugar and cream are on the sideboard in front of you." She poured their coffee from the percolator. The men noticed the chill directed at the Brigadier General but wisely ignored it.

"Ahem." Brigadier General Scarbrough cleared his throat and tapped a spoon against his water glass. "I'd like to make a quick announcement, if I may." All eyes turned toward him, the Ravenisha's still hostile. "First, I just want to say you women are remarkable. I've never seen anything like you in my life. I've reviewed footage of you in Central America and in Africa. Without your skills and service, this world could face a pandemic, the likes of which it has never known if more mutants are made." Still not mollified, the Ravenisha only gave Brigadier General Scarbrough tight smiles. "Damn, y'all some tough gals to please."

Fredi raised her hand. "Brigadier General, I thought you said this was a quick announcement."

"Fredi!" Ceola reprimanded sharply.

Brigadier General Scarbrough smiled his fake smile. "It's okay. I've got my own tween at home. Where was I? Right. We have reinstated you in the Special Reserves, and all of you will have the title of captain for your service. Here's the proclamation from the president.

I, Juliana du Boise, President of the United States of America, along with General Robert Abraham Shelby of the United States Armed Forces, hereby commend Ceola Lulabelle Eudora Furie, Matilda Arvelle Arcenaux, Elizabeth Sarah Gadsden, Theodora Lulu K'Abella Furie, Fredericka Zola Honeycutt, Celeste Layla Arcenaux, Naima Lee Gasden, and Itzpapalotl (Obsidian Butterfly) AKA Dr. Mariposa Vasquez, collectively known as the Ravenisha, for your exemplary bravery and service to the United States of America. You are hereby all commissioned to the rank of captain and will be afforded all the privileges that come with that rank. Because of your special skills, I am also granting you permission to use deadly force when prurient in protecting the citizens of the United States of America and the country itself. the Ravenisha will be stationed at the Fort Cheaha base, along with their Asoro.

Welcome Ladies and thank you for a job well done!

Juliana du Boise

President of the United States of America

General Robert Abraham Shelby

The United States Armed Forces

"Now, that's what I'm talking about, baby," Celeste exalted.

"Finally, somebody who understands our worth and value," Teddy yelled. "God bless the president of the United States of America. And my bae, Gus."

The women stood, raised their fists in the air, and shouted, "We are Ravenisha!"

Brigadier General Scarbrough jumped in his seat when they gave their war cry, and the coffee cup in his hand trembled.

"Erm, you do realize my mother has a rank of general among her people, don't you?" Celeste gave Brigadier General Scarbrough a hard stare.

An insistent knocking at the front door interrupted their jubilation and any reply the Brigadier General was about to make.

Chapter 45

"Whoever that is obviously hasn't heard of a doorbell," Celeste grumbled as she went to answer the door. When she opened it and discovered a lean, well-muscled, freckled, curly-haired white woman on the other side with shades on, she frowned. "Are you sure you have the right address, Miss?"

The woman replied in French-accented English, "This is Ravenswood Farm, *oui*?"

"Yeeessss," Celeste replied, drawing out the word slowly.

The woman smiled. "Then this is the right address. May I come in?"

"Of course, where are my manners?" Celeste found herself addressing the woman's back, as she had already stepped across the threshold and made her way into the kitchen area where people were finishing breakfast.

"I'm so sorry to interrupt your breakfast. Oh my," she exclaimed. "Is this one of those famous southern breakfasts I've read so much about with grits?" The woman pronounced grits greets.

Leona, ever the gracious hostess, told her to have a seat and she'd bring her a plate.

Sitting, the woman removed her shades and looked at them with the green eyes they knew so well. No one said a thing.

The young woman cleared her throat, then briefly made eye contact with everyone."Good morning, my name is Jenay Katzenberg. I was one of the scientists working at Laboratoires des Honeycutt in the Republic de Benin. I'm here to join the Ravenisha."

"Well, um, you don't just up and join the Ravenisha, boo," Leona said sweetly. "You're either born a Ravenisha or made one by La Panthère Noire and Raven. These gracious women might allow you to join the sisterhood, though."

"Girl, I know you ain't in here with your freckled face telling us you can shapeshift," Celeste challenged.

"Celeste, you're a fine one to talk with *your* freckled face," Teddy interjected.

Rufus held up a hand for silence. "Miss Katzenberg, are you telling us you can change into a pantheress worthy enough to be a Ravenisha and not one of those mutant things that was part of Idia's evil army?"

"Oui, I mean yes, Mr. Honeycutt, that's exactly what I'm saying. Besides studying genetics at the Hebrew University of Jerusalem, I also studied anthropology in Paris. You're not the only one interested in shapeshifting, you know?"

"Well, why don't you go join those groups?" Matilda asked. "Man, Black people can't have nothing. Y'all talk about everything we embody and create as being inferior and yet you always want to claim it for yourselves."

"That wasn't my intention." Jenay looked down at her plate. "By the way, Miss Leona, this is delicious."

Unmoved, Teddy chimed in. "You say this shit now, but the next thing we know, you'll have appropriated our culture and be married to one of our men."

"And how will that be my fault if they prefer me?" Jenay challenged, her eyes flashing for the first time.

Teddy began to rise from her seat, but Ceola put out a restraining arm. "She's right, that's on our men." The Black men in the room wisely remained quiet as the temperature in the room plummeted.

Ceola turned to Jenay, who had stopped eating. "Please, finish your meal. As you may or may not know, the Ravenisha are first and foremost warriors. Have you completed your service in the Israeli Army?"

"Yes, I have. I, how do they say it, kicked ass at everything. Look, if you don't want me, I'll go," Jenay rasped, on the verge of tears.

"Oh spare us the melodrama, you little vixen," Matilda snapped. "If you've done your research as I suspect you have since you know who everyone is, then you know we'll let you into the sisterhood. That's the Black folks' way, after all. We always welcome people into our club. It's the reversal that's not true. However, the Ravenisha is a different story. What Leona told you is true."

"Thank you. I'm honored. But…that's not the only reason I'm here. Before their plane landed in Guatemala, Monsieur Cochise sent a group text. My father, Gabriel Katzenberg, who's a rabbi, was one recipient. Madam Obsidian Butterfly, Madame Theodora, have you told the others about La Panthère Noire's plan to take over Theodora's body and soul? She aims to use your powers—and Fredi's—in her quest to rule the world and topple Lord Talonius. A huge battle has been foretold where either Theodora or La Panthère Noire will survive, but not both," Jenay, blurted, looking directly at Teddy. "Jules Baptist and I have had many discussions about this."

As a stunned silence grew in the room, Fredi crowed, "Oh, dayuhm. The shit's about to hit the fan now."

"I just want to say I didn't feel it was my news to tell." Obsidian Butterfly looked around the table, silently pleading for people to understand.

Gus looked at Teddy, his lips in a line. "Couples don't keep things like this from each other Theodora," he ground out, a muscle in his jaw working.

"If I were you, I'd start crying. It might elicit a little sympathy," Fredi told Teddy as she took a sip of her coffee. Teddy began to say something, then noticed Fredi's beverage.

"Hold up. Wait a damn minute. Y'all didn't let me drink coffee until I was well into high school."

Ceola held up her hand. "Don't try to deflect, missy. And, it's mostly milk anyways."

Teddy looked around the table at the angry people glaring at her. When her eyes rested on Matilda's and she saw her fierce stare shadowed by hurt, that was it. She couldn't hold it together any longer. She burst into tears and started bawling.

"Girl, I could whup your damn ass." Matilda got up, went over to Teddy, and enfolded her in a hug. "Shhh, now, it's go be okay. Ain't nobody gonna hurt my baby. You know I love you like I love my own. Even if you hadn't saved Celeste's life, I'd still love you to death, my fierce one. You my godbaby. Shhh."

Fredi cried, "Raven is evil. I don't want to be evil!"

Teddy looked at her and nodded, "I don't want to be evil, either."

"Hush now girls," Ceola sighed. "It's not Raven who is the evil one here. I firmly believe Raven is under the throes of La Panthère Noire, as well. We had a lengthy discussion on the plane on the way back and determined Idia kept us in the dark about many things. We're going to find out everything we need to know to get our lives in balance with the universe though. You can count on it."

Rufus stood and called for order. "Calm down, y'all. Just calm down. This room is full of wondrous people with amazing minds. We have all the bases covered—science, law, medicine, mysticism, military, and theology, if I understand correctly, Roland?" Roland nodded in assent.

"Okay, let's get the story from the beginning. Theodora, I believe the creature has spoken to you. You begin. Miss Jenay, we'll allow you to finish your story, for I believe it interweaves somehow into these women's?"

Jenay nodded in affirmation.

"Theodora, the floor is yours." As Teddy began standing, Rufus smiled. "You don't really have to stand. It's up to you."

Teddy sat back down. "It all started when Nana was instructing me on how to change. First, I heard my beast's voice telling me she was coming. Then, what frightened me was that I heard another voice telling me to stay the course and when the time came, she'd call on me and I would answer. I asked her who she was, and she told me I knew who she was and not to be stupid."

"I remember now, Teddy. I'm sorry. I was so distracted at the time. We meant to talk to you later, but things kept happening. It's almost as if the universe was in cahoots with La Panthère Noire to prevent you from telling us."

"Then, on the plane to Guatemala, Dad, Cochise I mean, could feel La Panthère Noire's presence in me and to a lesser extent, Fredi."

"That's when he told me he sensed a malevolent presence in Teddy that was so great, he immediately had to contact his circle of fellow shamans, near and far, from all religions."

"He was livid, Teddy," Mariposa added. "He said he hadn't found his daughter just to lose her to some evil spirit. I had to listen to every heinous wound he would inflict on that spirit when he caught her. I'm afraid Fredi was right about the Aztecs sacrificing people and the Apache being bloodthirsty. Back in the old days, you didn't want to be captured alive by the Apache if you were their enemy." Mariposa grimaced.

As Fredi gloated, Teddy continued. "The next time I heard La Panthère Noire's voice was when I brought Fredi back from the dead." Teddy looked at Fredi pointedly.

"This time, I heard the voice, too. She said, 'See what a great team we are, Theodora? Continue to follow my orders and the world will be ours.' "

The room digested this last bit before Rufus, astute as ever, asked, "And is that all, Theodora?"

Teddy avoided eye contact with everyone instead of replying.

Rufus turned to Fredi. "I didn't hear anything else they said. They shut me out."

"I can't say anything," Teddy cried in anguish. "La Panthère Noire and I talked in the early morning hours of our last night in the mountains. Or rather, La Panthère Noire talked and I listened. It was horrible. I want to tell you, but I can't. Please don't ask," Teddy pleaded. "La Panthère Noire threatened to kill all of us if I ever spoke of the contents of that conversation. Oh God, she said she would take total control of my body and soul and that I would cease to exist." Teddy buried her face in her hands and sobbed.

"Not on my watch," Gus growled.

"Oh no, you mustn't do anything, Gus. She said she'll kill you and everyone else I hold dear if I don't obey her."

"That damn Idia," Ceola growled. "I could kill her all over again. Old Nahwi was right. And we're all to blame. I thought La Panthère Noire was on our side. That she would protect us. She just wants to use us like everybody else. Damn if we didn't bring that creature back to life. If we're being honest, we were after power and riches, as well."

Ceola leaned over and looked intently into Teddy's eyes. "La Panthère Noire, I know you're in there. Listen to me, and listen to me good, you demoness. You're not omnipotent, and you of all beings should know you don't mess with a she-panther's cubs. You better run," Ceola hummed.

Pressure built as the room became saturated with a sewage-like odor and the musky scent of panther. Teddy's hair stood on end, her eyes dilated, and a snarl along with a gaseous sulfur-like odor erupted from her mouth. La Panthère Noire tried to force her to change into her werepanther form, under the assumption that she could control Teddy's beast, but Teddy resisted with all her might. The women around the table joined in with Ceola, and their voices soared in harmony until La Panthère Noire was driven back deep within Teddy. As the room quieted again, people were shocked as they realized that as the beast overtook Teddy, Jenay had grabbed Teddy's hand and had begun praying in Hebrew. As she finished her prayer and looked up, it was into the grateful eyes of people around the table.

Teddy suddenly leaned over and vomited a viscous, foul-smelling black substance. Gus and Fredi immediately gagged and covered their noses. Gus rose to clean up the mess, but Leona held her hand up.

"I'll take care of it, Gus. You sit back down. If I need more help, I'll let you know."

This time, Jenay asked for Teddy's permission. "May I touch you?" Teddy nodded her assent. Jenay gently rubbed circles on Teddy's back and the tension and stiffness left her body. "Good. Theodora, get as much of that evil essence out of you as you can. That demoness has a powerful spirit, but I'm a strong believer. We can and will defeat her, especially with my father's help. I also feel your strength and power. Teddy, you mustn't allow her to control your beast. You must fight her with all of your might and keep total control of your own beast. You did a good job just now. You instinctively erected shields around your beast and prevented La Panthère Noire from controlling her. You must learn to do that at will. I'll teach you."

"And this is where I believe you come into this tale, Miss Jenay. The floor is yours," Rufus said, inclining his head.

"Lord a' mercy," Colonel Honeycutt said. "I don't know about y'all, but I need a drink."

"I could use something, too." Brigadier General Scarbrough wiped his sweaty face with a handkerchief he pulled from a pocket.

Leona walked back into the room, having put away the cleaning equipment she just used. "I think we all could. It's 5 o'clock somewhere. Why don't you gentlemen come help me stock and bring the mobile bar in here?"

After they had served everyone—they gave Fredi a virgin Cosmopolitan, much to her displeasure—Jenay began.

"As I noted earlier, while working at Rufus's lab in Cotonou, I experimented with the serum's formula on the side until I found the combination that enabled me to change from a human into a pantheress. Why it finally worked, I don't know."

"Jenay, we're not sure either, but apparently some humans, primarily females, have a certain gene that when spliced with some of the serum's genomes, enables the change to occur at the molecular level."

"Thank you. Is it Dr. Furie?"

"Yes, it is Dr. Furie, but please, call me Ceola or Nana."

"I admit I was made aware of the existence of you remarkable women by unethical means—as was everyone at the lab. I guess Idia still lived in a time where she expected her word to be law. We were told to simply concern ourselves with our part of the research, but once we figured out we could access everybody else's areas, of course we did."

Jenay stopped at Rufus's shocked look and shook her head in amazement. "Rufus, you left your Benin lab completely in Idia's hands. That was a grave mistake. Anyway, the saying 'It's a small world' is so true. You know cameras are everywhere, and the American scientists communicate with the Benin scientists via computers. So when I saw Dr. Vasquez, I immediately recognized her as Cochise's mother. I have Dr.Vasquez, or rather should I say Obsidian Butterfly, to thank for my love of anthropology." Jenay beamed at Obsidian Butterfly. "And here I thought Mariposa was a beautiful name."

"Her actual Aztec name is Itzpapalotl, which translates to Obsidian Butterfly. She named me Citlalli, which means star goddess," Fredi gloated.

Teddy gave a shaky smile. "I love the name Citlalli. You are truly a star." She smiled at the girl.

"So," continued Jenay, "once Dr. Vasquez and I started talking, I discovered her son, Cochise, was a shaman, I said oh, what a coincidence; my father was the Jewish equivalent. He's taught me so much, including metaphysics and mysticism. Father and Cochise began emailing and are now like this." Jenay held up two fingers crossed to show the closeness of the men's relationship. "So, when Father received a text from Cochise, apparently he dropped everything, ran from the synagogue in a panic…and no one has seen or heard from him since. Calls to his cell phone go straight to voicemail, which is now full. I'm worried about him. He's not a spring chicken in great health, and stupid decisions I made earlier in life made his health even worse."

No one said anything. They needed a moment to ponder Jenay's news.

"Please," Jenay began in a quavering voice. "I need your help. My father is all I have left, and I'm not coming to the table empty-handed. I'm not a saint, but your silver is safe, and I'm not going to slit your throats while you sleep. I much prefer peace over violence."

"Well, none of us here are perfect," Teddy grudgingly admitted. "That's all fine and well, Miss Katzenberg, but…"

"Please, call me Jenay."

"Why are you just now showing up? Why didn't you try to help sooner?" Teddy directed her unsettling and unwavering gaze at Jenay.

"I came as soon as I could." Jenay couldn't keep her eyes off of Teddy's face. Teddy's eyes were beautiful.

Teddy's raised eyebrows, side-eyes, and pursed lips said otherwise.

"Teddy, be grateful she's here now and offering her help," Roland cajoled, as Gus nudged Teddy.

"Wow, how can I be mean to Jenay when you two are ganging up on me?" Teddy asked, smiling. "Okay Jenay, welcome and if you can help us, I'd be ever so grateful."

"Now that wasn't so hard, was it?" Gus asked, kissing Teddy on her cheek. "And see, your face didn't break when you smiled."

Teddy gazed into Gus's eyes and kissed him lightly on the lips. As the kiss deepened, Fredi's mouth dropped open in disgust.

"It's too early in the morning to be assaulted with this shit!" She stomped out of the room.

"Fredericka, what have I told you about using that kind of language! Although, in this case, I have to agree with you." Rufus stood and left the room, too.

One by one, people got up and left as Teddy was sitting in Gus's lap now. Ceola, Obsidian Butterfly, and Lizzie took Jenay to the "catio" and sunroom to chat with her some more.

"Thank you Jenay, for helping me earlier!" Teddy shouted when Jenay left the room.

"You're quite welcome, Theodora," Jenay replied before she left the kitchen, a weight lifted off of her shoulders.

Leona pulled up a chair and sat next to Matilda. In a radio announcer's voice, she said, "And here is an example of the rutting session of the Homo sapiens sapiens with a Homo sapiens ravenisha species. Let's see if they do it upright or on all fours."

"I'm voting for all fours," Matilda panted.

That finally got Gus and Teddy's attention. "Come on, babe. Looks like we've got an audience. Besides, you need to brush your teeth."

As Gus slung Teddy over his shoulder, she said, "We're going to do it upright and on all fours," as Gus bounded up the stairs.

Matilda purred. "Well, all right, all right, all right, all right.

~ The End ~

Epilogue

Fredi looked at the results printed on the lab paper with shaking hands. Auntie Tildy was right. She screamed and ran out of the lab. Dr. Vasquez silently watched the meltdown.

She picked up her phone as soon as Fredi left and only said, "The shit is about to hit the fan," and then ran out of the lab after the teen.

Ceola gathered everyone around the great table at the main house. She would only say, "We're all about to find out," in response to their questions about what was going on. When Rufus sauntered into the room, she glared at him with her arms folded across her chest.

Rufus sighed melodramatically. "What have I done now?"

The front door slammed so hard, the house shook.

"Rufus!" Fredi screeched. "You motherfucker!" Fredi tore into the room, Dr. Vasquez hopelessly trying to contain her. Teddy quickly jumped up and helped Dr. Vasquez restrain the enraged teen. Fredi broke free and was on Rufus, her bared canines scraping into his throat, just missing the jugular and carotids. The shock in the room was palpable. It took Dr. Vasquez, Teddy, Tildy, and the Asoro to get her off of Rufus. Only once she was enfolded in Teddy and Tildy's arms did she calm down in mind and body.

"What's wrong, Fredi?" Teddy asked, rubbing her sister's back.

Hiccupping, Fredi looked at Teddy. Her eyes pooled with tears, and her shoulders sagged as she told Teddy sadly, "You're going to be just as angry when I tell you what I discovered." Fredi slumped in one of the chairs, the weight of the world—her existence, what she was—heavy on her young shoulders.

"I ran Teddy's and my blood again after people noticed Teddy's subtle stripes and my not-so-subtle stripes and how our skulls look slightly different. This time, I used the sample from Rufus's secret stash he had labeled Unknown. The sample wasn't unknown at all. He knew exactly what it was," she cried. "We're not just werepanthers. It's not right. We're not lab experiments or animals bred for the purpose of introducing not only foreign DNA but extinct DNA."

As she told the others what she discovered, there were gasps and looks of disbelief. Rufus had crossed a line. That lowdown snake. Where did he even get that extinct DNA anyway? Teddy was uncharacteristically quiet and calm as she listened to Fredi. She'd almost pulled it off until her eyes began to shoot the blue fire laser sparks.

Rufus held his hands up. "I can explain everything. Before you kill me, please. Just hear me out."

After the victorious defeat of Queen Idia, the successful vaccination rollout, and everybody's promotions, life at Ravenswood Farm wasn't all rosy. To no one's surprise, Gus proposed to Teddy and she accepted. Teddy had always wanted a fall wedding, so a date was set for some time in October. Celeste and Naima were happy for their sister-friend but in disbelief that she was going to beat them to the altar. So as not to be outdone by Gus, the other Asoro proposed to their women as well. A triple fall wedding was planned, instead. Teddy asked a giddy Fredi to be her maid of honor. Even though the Nanas were pleased, they did think the couples were moving too fast.

Also, something was going on with Teddy, and Gus and Ceola were worried. Teddy was having nightmares and had fallen several times during her riding lessons. La Panthère Noire's presence in her body definitely rattled Teddy, and the other Ravenisha knew that time was running out. They had to step up their efforts to find Cochise and Rabbi Katzenberg and drive La Panthère Noire out of Raven, Teddy, and Fredi before the evil spirit totally consumed them.

Fredi's behavior was worrisome as well. The teen was having nightmares, spending long hours lying on tree limbs, and moodily staring off into the distance. Sometimes, they saw her talking to a Blackbird. They tried to attribute the change to her turning thirteen, but deep down, they knew that the ordeal the teen had undergone had changed her in unknown ways, and they suspected that during her resurrection, La Panthère Noire had managed to infiltrate her body, as well. After all, the poor pumpkin had been beaten, killed, and brought back to life. That was a lot for an adult to handle, much less a tween, they reasoned. They vowed to help her get through whatever she was battling, no matter what. If their prayers, love, and therapy weren't enough, they would do whatever had to be done to make Fredi whole again.

The Old-Gen was eager to bring the Lost-Generation home. While they knew the cave's location from the coordinates, the cave was vast, boasting over a hundred chambers. They just hoped and prayed that no one else had beaten them to the Lost-Generation and spirited their bodies away. They were positive they were going to bring the Lost-Generation home soon, but first, they had to kill the entity that was trying to find them. La Panthère Noire was determined to make her move and possess those remarkable creatures, Teddy and Fredi. She would be unstoppable with their help. Damn, Rufus, why couldn't that man have done right? Well, whatever deal he'd made with this entity wasn't their problem. It did throw a wrinkle in their plans, though, but they knew they could always call on their sisters back home for help.

Jules reluctantly packed his remaining belongings and bought his plane ticket. Those stupid Americans were going to need his expertise in demonology to find Cochise and Rabbi Katzenberg to save Teddy, Fredi, and Raven. Jenay's call had been disturbing on so many levels. Also, he'd make his contribution to science if they could really make those unsightly bumps disappear.

Brigadier General Scarbrough was ordered to undergo sensitivity training after the audio of the crass remarks he had made had somehow been leaked. The training did no good whatsoever.

Mariposa remained hopeful that Cochise was out there in the ether, along with Jenay's father. Leona, who had been communicating with the spirits, had reached him several times before losing contact because the spirit world connection was so tenuous. Mariposa was positive she was going to bring her son home. She had to be, for his shamanistic abilities were integral to freeing Teddy, Fredi, and Raven from La Panthère Noire's evil sway. La Panthère Noire was about to learn though. You don't come between mothers and their cubs. A battle was coming, and Mariposa would likely have to enlist the aid of her frenemy, Tezcatlipoca. Even though Mariposa would rather walk across hot coals barefoot, she'd do anything to free her son.

Cleo awoke, teeth chattering, skin blue, fingers numb. She looked around the unfamiliar room, assessing her situation. Slowly, as consciousness returned, she realized where she was. Did it really matter she was in yet another lab? The goal remained the same. Freedom and reunification with her children. She had scores to settle—with Anatoly being at the top of her list…and then she was going to find Rufus.

When those threats were removed, she would find her mother and her daughters. She hoped they were alive and well. Once she was reunited with her babies, no one was going to separate them ever again. But first, she had to find Antoinette and Zenobia. She prayed they were still alive, as well.

Family Tree

Old-Generation Ravenisha

Ceola Lulabelle Eudora Furie—African warrior known as Cheola. One of the Old-Generation shapeshifting Ravenisha. Married to Oziegbe Furie. Parent of Cleodora.

Matilda Arvelle Arceneaux—African warrior known as Zamandla. One of the Old-Generation shapeshifting Ravenisha. Married to Leona Delphine Glapion-Arceneaux. Parent of Antoinette.

Elizabeth Sarah Gadsden—African warrior known as Eklezabela. One of the Old-Generation shapeshifting Ravenisha. Married to Caesar Amadi Gadsden. Parent of Zenobia.

Queen Idia—African warrior whose name means "Warrior Queen." Queen of the Ravenisha, the shapeshifting African warrior women. Also known as Idia Adechi.

Lost-Generation Ravenisha

Cleodora Furie—Ceola's daughter. Mother of Theodora and Fredericka.

Antoinette Arceneaux—Matilda's daughter. Mother of Celeste.

Zenobia Gadsden—Elizabeth's daughter. Mother of Naima.

New-Generation Ravenisha

Theodora Lulu K'Abella Furie—Daughter of Cleodora. Raised by Ceola and the other Old-Generation Ravenisha.

Celeste Layla Arceneaux—Daughter of Antoinette. Raised by Matilda and the other Old-Generation Ravenisha.

Naima Lee Gadsden—Daughter of Zenobia. Raised by Elizabeth and the other Old-Generation Ravenisha.

Fredericka Zola Honeycutt—Daughter of Cleodora and Rufus. Raised in a lab in isolation by Rufus.

The Asoro—A special group of warrior men tasked to watch and protect the Ravenisha during their weak moments over the centuries.

Lieutenant Augustus Alford Allensworth, III

Sergeant Akiro Donté Shaw

Sergeant Roland Jabari Parks

Sergeant Hendrix X.A. Vaughn

Itzpapalotl—Aztec shapeshifter. Name means "Obsidian Butterfly" in the Aztec language. Also known as Dr. Mariposa Vasquez. Mother of Cochise Ramiero Nezahualocelotl Martinez.

Cochise Ramiero Nezahualocelotl Martinez—Half-Chiricahua Apache son of Obsidian Butterfly. Theodora's father. Shaman.

Tezcatlipoca—Jaguar God of the Dead in Aztec mythology.

Rufus Beckett Theodis Honeycutt—Father of Cleodora, Theodora, and Fredericka.

Colonel Beauregard Tennyson Honeycutt—Rufus's brother. Head of the Paranormal Reserves Division at Fort Cheaha.

Acknowledgements

There are so many to thank for their help over the course of transforming my hot mess into something readable. I would like to thank early editors Rebecca Brewer and Samantha Zaboski. A special thanks go to Gianna Martella, who read the very first draft. That draft was truly awful and Gianna bravely slogged through it and suggested revisions. Thank you Xavier Comas for you awesome cover. Thank you Maxwell for your superb copy editing. Thanks go to Walt for your formatting skills. I'd also like to thank Mari Naten of Pacific Equestrian Center for reading the dressage sections and being one of my great instructors. Thank you to the Young Rider volunteering with me at the 2019 California Dressage Society championship show, who agreed to read the dressage sections. Thanks also go to the Black Writers Collective (Sharon Browning, Julisa Marcel-Clarke, Tommye Johnson, Alexandria Lynch, Terri Marks, Shaundale Rénā, and Tia Ross. Kyra Barr, thank you for your words of encouragement.) Special thanks go to Tommye and Sharon. Thank you, Ravenswood Collective beta readers. (Amanda Powers, Ann Tran, Tamala Warnsby and Michael Pfirrman. Thank you for everything, Michael.) Thank you, readers Paula Esmo and Tracey McKinney. Thank you, Travis Gibson and Niall Stahl, for answering my weapons questions. Thank you, Rekesha Pittman, Get Write Publishing.

Thank you, Amara Lawson-Chavanu, Kobe Lawson-Chavanu, for all of the help you provided. Your millennial views taught me a lot. Callie Lawson Freeman, thank you for working on my Instagram account. James Freeman, IV, thank you for your support—you always knew it would happen. Thank you, Bakari Chavanu for your technical support. Thank you, Jacqui Glanville for all of your support, and for telling me you had a dream I was going be a writer during the reunion in the Poconos. This was before Jacqui knew I had even started writing. Special thanks go to Darin Latimore, MD for reading the full manuscript, offering suggestions, providing your home as a writer's retreat, and offering me support every step of the way. Thank you for letting me ride Oreo and spend time with your Great Danes, Tiny and Minnie. I can't wait to meet Gracie and Olympia.

Thank you, Ifetayo Lawson Freeman, for your all of your support. I couldn't have a better youngest sister. Special, special thanks go to my sister, Candace Lawson, MD. You have championed my writing from the beginning and this book would not have been possible without you. And last, but not least, thank you readers for sharing in my journey into the world of the Ravenisha.

Ravenswood is a fictional town near Huntsville, Alabama. Any mistakes are all mine.

Made in United States
North Haven, CT
02 December 2021